PASSION'S CAPTIVE

Amelia was astounded. . . . A man she couldn't see, couldn't identify, was actually whispering endearments to her!

Carefully, James Henry released her wrists. Resigned, she moved her arms to her side. Taking her hand, he raised it to his lips, kissing it gently. "I want to make love to you," he murmured, as his lips began to trail over her fingers.

Amelia could feel a strange sensation stimulating her senses. She couldn't quite understand what was happening, but she knew that the warm lips gently touching her fingers had the power to send exciting chills through her entire being.

Releasing her hand, he placed his face next to hers. Tenderly, he whispered, "Let me show you the ecstasy that can be found in a kiss."

Then his mouth was on hers, demanding her response. Amelia's conscience screamed at her to remain coldly passive, but for the first time in her life, her passion was being awakened. Against her own volition, she returned his kiss. . . .

HISTORICAL ROMANCE AT ITS BEST!

by KATHLEEN DRYMON

TEXAS BLOSSOM (1305, $3.75)
When Sorrel's luscious curves silhouetted the firelight, Mathew felt lust and desire like he never felt before. Soon, he was enmeshed in her silvery web of love—their passion flowering like a wild TEXAS BLOSSOM!

WILD DESIRES (1103, $3.50)
The tempestuous saga of three generations of women, set in the back streets of London, glamorous New Orleans and the sultry tropics—where each finds passion in a stranger's arms!

TENDER PASSIONS (1032, $3.50)
While countless men professed their adoration for Katherine, she tossed her head in rejection. But when she's pirated away by a man whose object is lust, she finds herself willing!

by CAROL FINCH

RAPTURE'S DREAM (1037, $3.50)
By day Gabrielle is the insufferable waif who tests Dane Hampton's patience; by night she is the phantom lover who brings him to the heights of ecstasy!

ENDLESS PASSION (1155, $3.50)
Brianna was a sensuous temptress who longed for the fires of everlasting love. But Seth Donovan's heart was as cold as ice . . . until her lips burned his with the flames of desire!

DAWN'S DESIRE (1340, $3.50)
Kathryn never dreamed that the tall handsome stranger was wise to her trickery and would steal her innocence—and her heart. And when he captured her lips in one long, luscious kiss, he knew he'd make her his forever . . . in the light of DAWN'S DESIRE.

Available wherever paperbacks are sold, or order direct from the Publisher. Send cover price plus 50¢ per copy for mailing and handling to Zebra Books, 475 Park Avenue South, New York, N.Y. 10016. DO NOT SEND CASH.

Surrender To Ecstasy

BY ROCHELLE WAYNE

ZEBRA BOOKS
KENSINGTON PUBLISHING CORP.

ZEBRA BOOKS

are published by

KENSINGTON PUBLISHING CORP.
475 Park Avenue South
New York, N.Y. 10016

First printing: January, 1984

Printed in the United States of America

For Mike, because he never stopped believing in me

PROLOGUE

In the autumn of 1854, settlers from New England migrated to Kansas Territory, naming their new home Lawrence, in honor of their leader, Amos Lawrence. The continuous arrival of emigrants from the North resulted in rapid population growth. Crude cabins were quickly replaced by buildings of brick and frame and stone.

The town's growing success aroused the envy of the pro-slavery elements in the Territory. The town of Lawrence was attacked by those abettors of slavery, in what was called the Wakarusa War. But the citizens of Lawrence defended their town and supported the Union, and the war ended in December of 1855.

In the spring of 1856, Alabama, Florida, and South Carolina sent several irregular troops to Lawrence to win the Kansas Territory for slavery. Lawrence was burned and looted. The two newspapers, *Herald of Freedom* and the *Kansas Free-State* were destroyed. The plundering and destruction went on for hours, but, ironically, no one was killed, even though those impetuous men representing pro-slavery sentiments were wild with drink and hungry for plunder.

Following the attack on Lawrence, the men of the town organized roving bands, known as Jayhawkers. Considering Missouri a hotbed of pro-slavery elements, they made raids on western Missouri, often harassing families who had southern connections. The hate between Kansas and Missouri kept growing and finally reached its peak with the outbreak of the War between the States.

PART ONE

ONE

The town of Lawrence had wide streets lined with trees, numerous stores and fine attractive homes. It was known to be the most elegant town in the state of Kansas. The population had increased to twelve hundred, and the citizens of Lawrence were prosperous and happy. It had become a recruiting center for the Union Army, and the streets were filled with soldiers in their blue uniforms, many of them young and dashingly handsome.

The town of Lawrence, Kansas, was definitely not in Amelia Adams's thoughts as she stood in front of her bedroom mirror, examining her reflection. At nineteen, Amelia Adams was quite attractive, although she herself found her looks disappointing. She had always longed to have a voluptuous figure, but voluptuous she most assuredly was not. Her breasts were well formed, but small, and her hips were narrow. Amelia had always wanted to be tall, but she was petite and no taller than the average thirteen-year-old. She would have been pleased with her smooth and light complexion if it weren't for the freckles splashed across her nose. Freckles that did not fade with puberty, as she had hoped they would.

Peering more closely into the mirror, Amelia decided her eyes were acceptable. She would have preferred that her eyebrows not arch quite so prominently and that her eyes be more rounded instead of slanted. But she could find no fault with their color. They were neither blue nor green, but a mixture of both colors—which made them turquoise blue.

Taking a pink ribbon from her dresser, Amelia pulled her hair back from her face, securing it with the silk ribbon. She was completely satisfied with her hair, and, studying the long tresses, she tried to refrain from vanity. But it was difficult not to admire hair that was the color of gold, and so full that the natural curls fell into flowing waves, cascading down past her waist.

The ribbon perfectly matched the pink roses in her dress, and, lifting the long skirt, Amelia curtsied in front of her mirror. Smiling, she held out her hand. "Captain Bishop," she said demurely, "I would love to have this waltz with you." Humming, she danced gracefully across the bedroom floor. Absorbed in her fantasy, she sat on the edge of her bed, dreaming about the dashing Captain Bishop.

Although she had never been introduced to the captain, she had seen him in town, and once he had even come into her uncle's store to buy cigars. She had been at the rear of the store and hidden from view by all the filled shelves and tables loaded with merchandise. But by peeking around one of the shelves, she had seen him distinctly. He was taller than the average man, built with wide shoulders, slim hips, and strong muscular legs. His blue uniform was tailored to fit snugly across his shoulders, and his trousers clung skin-tight across his hips and down his legs, before being tucked securely into his black army boots. She had never seen him without his hat, but that day he had removed it as he conversed leisurely with her uncle. His dark hair was thick, and his moustache was fashioned to sweep toward his long sideburns. For the first time, Amelia had gotten a close look at the handsome captain, and in doing so, she had fallen hopelessly in love.

Sighing dreamily, Amelia rose from the bed and left the room. She knew her aunt was expecting her downstairs, and she had already kept her waiting longer than necessary.

Amelia's uncle was a merchant and owned a store in the middle of town. He and his wife had been among the first families to settle in Lawrence, and they had remained through the Wakarusa War and the pro-slavery attack of 1856.

Amelia was from a small town in Massachusetts. Her mother had died shortly after Amelia's birth. Like his brother in Lawrence, Amelia's father had been a storekeeper. Following a short illness, her father had died, and her uncle had traveled to Massachusetts to bring Amelia back to Lawrence to live with her next of kin.

Amelia had now been living in Lawrence for six months, and she found the town thrilling and exciting. But coming from a small and devout Methodist community, Amelia was totally innocent of life. She had hoped to make new friends with girls her own age, but it seemed that in Lawrence most "girls" of nineteen were married women. Amelia began to think of herself as a spinster, and the fear of being an old maid plagued

13

her continually. But she would not marry just for the sake of marriage! She would marry for love, and her husband would be a dashing cavalier; a man just like Captain Bishop!

The stairway was located at the rear of the store, and, hurrying, Amelia descended the flight of steps, rushing to the front counter. Her aunt was in the process of putting on her straw bonnet, pinning it to her gray hair so that it wouldn't blow off in the wind. Lillian Adams was a middle-aged, plump woman with a round face and rosy cheeks. Smiling, she said cheerfully, "Well, it's about time you came down."

Calvin and Lillian Adams were considered upperclass citizens, and Lillian had been invited by the mayor's wife to the mayor's home for a tea party. Amelia was to watch the store until her uncle returned. He had gone fishing with a friend.

"I'm sorry I kept you waiting, Aunt Lillian," Amelia apologized sincerely. It had been wrong to keep her aunt waiting, but when she started dreaming about Captain Bishop she always lost track of time.

"Calvin will be back fairly soon. Are you sure you can manage alone, my dear?"

Smiling, Amelia reassured her, "Of course, I can. Now, you run along and have a nice time."

Swiftly Lillian placed a light kiss on her niece's cheek, then in a flurry she left the store, the bell ringing loudly as the door was opened and closed.

Her thoughts returning to romance and Captain Bishop, Amelia sauntered to the fabric table and absent-mindedly folded some material that had somehow become rumpled. The bell rang clearly as the front door was suddenly opened. Not bothering to turn around, Amelia called out, "Did you forget something, Aunt Lillian?"

The door was closed, and the bell rang again. The footsteps crossing the floor were much too heavy to be her aunt's, and quickly Amelia whirled about.

Immediately a blush rose to her cheeks, and her heart began to pound rapidly. Removing his hat, the man smiled pleasantly, and, placing his arm across his chest, he bowed gallantly. "Miss Adams, I presume?"

Flustered, Amelia gasped, "Yes."

His smile broadened, putting a bright twinkle in his brown eyes. "Allow me to introduce myself." Standing erect, he clicked the heels of his boots together, as he announced, "Captain Bishop at your service, madam. Calvin told me he had a niece, but he failed to tell me you were so lovely. Had I known, I would have come here sooner to purchase my cigars."

"But you did!" Amelia blurted. "Three weeks ago last Monday!" Oh, why did I say that? she cried to herself. Now, he surely must know how I feel about him! He probably believes me to be a desperate spinster!

The captain laughed heartily, his laugh placing a deep dimple in each cheek. "Do you also remember the time?" he asked.

Blushing, Amelia answered breathlessly, "It was three-thirty in the afternoon."

Smiling appeasingly, he moved closer to Amelia, and, placing his hand under her chin, he tilted her face upwards. "Are you always so direct, Miss Adams?"

"Shouldn't I be?" she asked.

Removing his hand, he answered, "Well, most

ladies are, shall we say, more subtle. They would never admit to a man they had only met that they had counted the days since they last saw him."

"Oh, but I have seen you other times since you were last here!" Amelia cried, without thinking. "Four times to be exact, but twice I was on one side of the street, and you were on the other side."

Amused, he asked, "And the other two times?"

"You were riding into town with your troops."

"I must have been blind not to see such a beautiful angel with golden hair and enchanting eyes."

Amelia's heart was pounding heavily, and, finding it difficult to breathe, she feared she would surely swoon. Oh, it was all happening just as she had dreamed it would!

"Where is your uncle?" he questioned.

"He's fishing, but he should be back soon."

"Then I shall return in a couple of hours."

"Did you come to see Uncle Calvin?"

"No, I came to buy a box of cigars, but I'll wait and pick up a box when I come back." Nodding politely, he put on his hat, as abruptly he turned and hastened to the door.

"But Captain Bishop," Amelia called, "I can sell you a box of cigars."

Opening the door, he replied with a grin, "I'll wait and buy them from Calvin, because now I have something very important to ask him."

"May I ask what?" Amelia questioned, wondering how she could be so forward.

"I need to ask him permission to call on his beautiful niece."

Gaping, Amelia asked, "Me?"

Laughing, he inquired, "Does he have more than one niece?"

Her voice ringing with joy, she replied, "No, of course not!"

Giving her a wink, he walked through the doorway, allowing the door to slam shut behind him. As the bell clanged, Amelia hugged herself and skipped across the floor. Amelia Adams was head over heels in love with the man of her dreams!

TWO

Although Calvin Adams had his reservations, he gave Captain Bishop permission to court Amelia. Calvin had known Jason Bishop for years. Jason's family had moved to Lawrence in the year following the Wakarusa War. Calvin was a man of strict values, considering himself a devout Methodist. Jason's parents and sister had attended church regularly, but Calvin had never seen Jason in church. In his teens Jason had been rowdy and unruly, but Calvin didn't hold that against him. Remembering back, he had been a little rowdy himself in his younger days. Jason's parents had died, and his sister had married and moved away, but Jason had remained in Lawrence, joining the Kansas State Guard, which had now become part of the Union Army. Calvin liked Jason Bishop, but he questioned whether he was the right man for his niece. Amelia was so gentle and naive, and Jason was dynamic and experienced. But then, perhaps, Amelia's gentleness was what Jason needed to make him settle down and set aside his devilish ways.

Calvin had given Amelia permission to invite Jason

to dinner. Following the meal, Calvin decided to work on his books in the kitchen, with Lillian offering to assist him. Calvin suggested that Amelia and Jason retire to the parlor, and later he and Lillian would join them for coffee.

Walking into the parlor beside Amelia, Jason remarked lightly, "Your uncle and aunt are very nice, especially considering how they discreetly made sure we would have some time alone."

Blushing, Amelia gestured toward her uncle's chair. "Would you care to sit down?"

Taking her arm, he answered, "Yes, but on the sofa beside you."

Amelia had never had a beau as dashing, or as elegant, as Captain Bishop, and his mere presence made her feel flustered and tongue-tied. Oh, if only I were a little more experienced!, she thought desperately. She was sure her lack of knowledge would cause her to make a complete fool of herself.

Grasping her arm firmly, he led her to the sofa. As he sat beside her, he leisurely placed one arm on the back of the sofa, which almost placed her in his embrace. Amelia could feel nervous perspiration accumulating on the palms of her hands. Oh please, please! she prayed silently. Don't let him hold my hands, because he'll feel how moist they are, and it's so unladylike to perspire!

Amelia's dress was pale green, which made the green predominate in her turquoise-blue eyes. Gazing into her face, Jason said sensually, "Yesterday afternoon your eyes were blue, but now they are green. Are you an enchanting little witch who can make her eyes change colors?"

Never one to be anything but straightforward and totally sober, Amelia explained, "My eyes are actually turquoise blue, but if I wear green. the color seems to reflect in my eyes.

Amused, he laughed cheerfully, and Amelia grew flushed wondering what she had said that was so humorous. Oh, I am making a fool of myself! she thought, depressed.

He stopped laughing, and, smiling, he asked, "Tell me, Amelia, have you ever flirted with a man?"

Her eyes opened wide, and she exclaimed, "Heavens no! Back home, Reverend Black's wife had a serious conversation with me and some of the other girls in the parish, and she told us flirtation was much too forward. And it could very easily lead a man to believe a lady to be fast and promiscuous!"

Once again he guffawed loudly, and Amelia felt like dying of shame. Suppressing his mirth, he told her, "Fast you most assuredly are not, but Amelia, you are very innocently promiscuous."

She knew she should find his remark in bad taste and reproach him, but instead, she was thrilled. "I am?" she asked quickly.

"It's your eyes, your smile, and the way in which you move," he explained.

This time, Amelia's strict religious background took command, and sternly she objected, "But Reverend Black's wife said . . ."

Interrupting, he asked, "What did she look like?"

Puzzled, she stammered, "Wh . . . what?"

"Mrs. Black. Describe her."

"She was tall and quite skinny. She always wore matronly dresses that were either black or gray."

Amelia giggled childishly, "And she had a terribly long nose."

"And undoubtedly, she secretly despised you for your beauty. Amelia, pay no mind to advice you received from a straightlaced, homely old biddy. I want a wife who will keep her vanity and good looks, so I can display her proudly."

Gasping, she uttered, "Wife!"

"Why should my intentions surprise you? Do you think I'm spending my time sitting in this parlor for my health, when I could be doing something a helluva lot more exciting? Your uncle will no doubt insist that I court you for a reasonable amount of time before we announce our engagement. So I will abide by his decision. But I have only one motive in mind, my sweet, and that is to show you off as Mrs. Jason Bishop."

Amelia opened her mouth to protest his manners, but she was struck speechless.

Again he laughed, but Amelia was too innocent of life to detect the arrogance in his laughter. Finally, finding her voice, she stuttered, "But . . . what about . . . love?"

"You'll be my wife, and you will belong to me. Of course, I will love you."

If Amelia had been a little wiser, she would have been aware of the dominating implication in his statement, but all she had grasped were the words "I will love you."

She thought he would take her in his arms and kiss her, but instead, he got to his feet. "Give my apologies to your uncle and aunt, but I'm afraid I can't stay for coffee. My troops and I are riding out in the morning, and I need to retire early."

"How long will you be gone?" she cried.

"I'll be back before you know it, and then we'll continue this courtship. Because of the war, I'm sure your uncle will understand if we choose to cut it short."

Moving swiftly, he crossed over to the door. Taking his hat from the rack on the wall, he turned back to look at Amelia. "Good-bye, my sweet."

"Jason," she began apprehensively, "will you and your troops be in any danger?"

Impatiently, he answered, "We're crossing into Missouri. Of course, there will be danger."

Fearing for his life, she hurried to reach his side, but abruptly he opened the door and departed. Standing in the open doorway, she watched her gallant cavalier hurrying down the stairway. Sincerely, she cried, "God be with you, Jason Bishop!"

THREE

Captain Bishop and Amelia Adams's wedding was one of the most elaborate the townspeople of Lawrence had ever seen. They were married in the Methodist Church, the bride attended by four bridesmaids and two flower girls. It hadn't been difficult for Amelia to come by her attendants. As soon as her engagement to the dashing captain was announced, Amelia was immediately the most popular young lady in town. The single ladies befriended her enviously, and the married ladies welcomed her into their circle of young matrons.

When Amelia walked down the aisle of the Lawrence Methodist Church, she was a beautiful bride. Holding on to her uncle's arm, she looked neither left nor right to acknowledge the soft praises she was receiving from the congregation. Her gaze held steadfast on the handsome Jason Bishop, as he stood in front of the pulpit waiting for his lovely bride to reach his side.

Amelia's wedding gown was soft satin. The bodice had intricately woven seed pearls in a pattern of roses. The neckline was cut to barely reveal the slight swell of her breasts. The long sleeves had the intricate pattern of seed pearls sewn to the cuffs. The flared skirt was cut into scallops along the front, where again the seed pearls were repeated. The sides gently sloped back to a long train that was carried by one of the flower girls. Amelia's veil was made of fine silk trimmed in soft lace. The veil lay over her hair, which was piled high on her head, the golden tresses laced with white daisies.

Standing at the front of the church, Amelia turned from Jason to look at Reverend Humphry, and her breasts brushed fleetingly across Jason's arm. The intimate touch suddenly brought to her mind the talk she'd had the night before with Lillian.

On the eve of Amelia's wedding, her aunt had clumsily tried to explain to Amelia what to expect on her wedding night. But Lillian had found the task so embarrassing that she had blundered it miserably, leaving her niece more confused than if she had said nothing at all.

At nineteen, an age Amelia had considered dangerously close to spinsterhood, she was totally uninformed about the sexual act. In the small town where she had grown up there had been no older woman to explain marital relations to Amelia, and her girlfriends had been just as unenlightened as she. It had been a topic their mothers had left closed until it was time for their daughters to marry. Amelia had tried desperately to grasp what Lillian was awkwardly explaining, but, in the final analysis, all Amelia understood was that her husband would do something unpleasant to her body, but that it was her wifely duty to submit to him. This mysterious thing he would do to her would be painful, but only during the first time. From then on, it would be quite painless, but very degrading. But she must not be depressed, it was a cross all wives had to bear and it was the only way to conceive a child. If she were fortunate, she would soon become pregnant, and then her husband would respectfully make no more demands on her body while she was carrying his child.

Her extreme apprehensions over her wedding night caused Amelia to absently recite her marriage vows. Later, she would only vaguely remember saying the words that had made her "Mrs. Jason Bishop."

Walking swiftly down the aisle with his bride holding tightly to his arm, Captain Bishop made a dashing figure in his dress uniform, and Amelia's white satin wedding gown flowed gracefully with her light steps. They made a handsome couple, looking as if they had just stepped out of a fairy tale, destined to live happily ever after.

The wedding reception was held at the hotel known as the Eldridge House. The dining room was filled with officers of the Union Army and their wives, businessmen and their wives, and V.I.Ps. like Captain A.R. Banks, the provost marshal of Kansas, and George W. Collamore, the mayor of Lawrence.

If Captain Bishop sensed his bride's extreme fear, he did nothing to help lighten her apprehensions. He said very little to Amelia during the reception, appearing to be more interested in talking war and drinking an abundance of champagne.

It was Lillian who finally came to Amelia and discreetly told her it was time for her to retire to her room and wait for her husband. Captain Bishop had rented living quarters at the hotel. Actually, they were only a bedroom with an adjoining sitting room. But for the present, they would have to suffice as their home. They would simply eat their meals in the hotel dining room.

Amelia had been seated beside her husband at one of the dining tables. As she excused herself, the men promptly stood, bowing to her formally, before eyeing Captain Bishop with envious twinkles that Amelia was incapable of understanding. The wives at the table said their goodnights, some of them smiling romantically, the others wearing expressions so somber that Amelia felt as if she were going to the gallows instead of her wedding bed.

Captain Bishop had taken her hand, and, bowing gallantly, he had kissed it. Looking into his bride's eyes, he had smiled charmingly, causing Amelia's fears to vanish. She was being so foolish! To be married to a handsome man so dashing and wonderful as her husband was just too romantic! She must not let her aunt's old-fashioned beliefs upset her. Her wedding night would be pure poetry, and a night she would remember forever!

Trying not to blush too noticeably, Amelia inconspicuously followed her aunt out of the dining room, up the stairs, and to the rooms she would share with her husband.

Her nightgown was on the foot of the bed where she had placed it the day before. Yesterday her things had been moved to the hotel, and she and Lillian had come to the rooms to put everything neatly away.

Making small talk, Lillian helped her niece out of her wedding dress and into her nightgown. Going to the mirror, Amelia looked thoughtfully at her reflection. The gown was the palest of blue, and so sheer that it was almost transparent. Slowly she took the pins from her hair, freeing the long tresses. Radiantly, her golden curls cascaded down past her waist. She was breathtakingly beautiful, but Amelia could only see a woman she considered too slim, too short, and too small-breasted. Frowning at her not voluptuous figure, she asked herself for the hundredth time how she had managed to catch a man as handsome as Jason Bishop.

Walking to the large wardrobe, Lillian removed the blue dressing robe that matched Amelia's nightgown. She handed it to her niece, and, thanking her, Amelia put it on.

With sudden tears springing to her eyes, Lillian hugged her niece, whispering in her ear, "It'll be all right, my dear. The first time is always the worst."

With those words of warning, Lillian hurried out of the room. Once again, she had managed to instill fear in her niece's heart.

Captain Bishop's bride had been absent two hours before he finally remembered she was upstairs waiting for him. He had been so engrossed in talking war and drinking champagne that she had completely slipped his mind. He almost reproached himself for his rudeness, but instead, he simply shrugged it off, reminding himself that Amelia didn't especially have a buoyant personality that would cause one to immediately be aware of her absence. But although she wasn't by any means the most interesting or charming woman he had ever known, he was still well pleased with his choice of a bride. She would make a perfect officer's wife. In every respect, she was a lady, and she would be accepted by the stringent wives married to his superior officers.

Bishop was an ambitious man, hoping to someday go into politics. Perhaps, he would run for the Congress, or the Senate. And a wife like Amelia would be an asset to his career.

Taking another drink of champagne, Jason smiled slyly. Amelia was a lady, but she was also quite attractive, and he could feel his passion rising as he thought about the delights waiting for him upstairs in his room. He was intoxicated, but he believed an officer was a gentleman, and a gentleman always carried his liquor well. So, as he bid his fellow comrades goodnight, he appeared to be totally in control of his faculties. Crossing the large dining room, his steps were straight and smooth. He remembered to nod politely to the few people who were still at the reception. Most of the guests had already gone home. Calvin and Lillian had departed over an hour ago, puzzled and a little embarrassed that the groom had not retired to his rooms to be with his bride, but had seemed to be more interested in drinking and conversing with fellow officers.

Captain Bishop paused before attempting to climb the stairway, which looked to him, in his alcoholic stupor, extremely steep and precarious. But he could feel eyes on him, and he knew he was still being watched, so taking a deep breath he began to tackle the dangerous stairs that were strangely rocking back and forth. Placing his hand on the banister, he took each step carefully, remembering to keep his posture straight, but casual.

When he reached the top, he darted around the corner, and knowing he was now out of sight of the others, he leaned against the wall. Rubbing his hand across his brow, he released the breath he had been holding. He was beginning to perspire. God, he was drunk! Why in the hell had he let himself drink so much champagne? Damn, tomorrow he was going to have one helluva headache! His stomach began to churn. "Oh damn," he groaned, "I hope I don't get sick!" But as he continued wiping at the perspiration accumulating on his brow, he willed himself to dismiss the idea. Hell, he never got sick from drinking, but then he usually drank brandy or bourbon, not champagne. His stomach settled, and the nausea passed. Relieved, he began moving down the hallway, trying to remember which room was his. The numbers suddenly came to mind. Room 217.

He no longer felt sick, but another pressing urge was making itself known. Reaching for the doorknob to his room, he thought fleetingly, Damn, I need to take a leak!

He swung the door open wide, stepping into the room. The door led into the adjoining sitting room, where Amelia, her eyes red from crying, was on the sofa. Seeing her husband, she leaped to her feet. Oh, why had he left her alone for so long? She had spent the first hour pacing nervously, but she had passed the second hour crying, feeling terribly hurt and rejected. She tensed expectantly, waiting for her wonderful cavalier to say something thrilling and romantic.

"Where's the goddamned chamber pot?" he bellowed gruffly.

Amelia gasped. "Wh . . . what?"

Slamming the door closed, he repeated testily,

"Where's the chamber pot?"

Amelia was so shocked and embarrassed that she was struck speechless. But then, feebly, she managed to nod toward the bedroom.

Jason no longer cared about his deportment, and, giving in to his drunken condition, he stumbled into the bedroom. He didn't bother to close the door, and quickly Amelia moved away from the open doorway. With tears once again flowing, she walked to the window that overlooked one of the main streets in town. Although she looked outside, her stare was vacant. All at once, she heard her husband using the chamber pot, and, cringing, her hand flew to her mouth to hold back a gasp. Where was the romance? This wasn't how she had imagined their first moment alone. In her dreams, Jason had been so anxious to be with her that he had come to the room the moment Lillian left. He had a bottle of champagne, so they could have a private toast to their marriage. And then, he made her feel loved by lavishing her with adoring compliments. Then he would take her into his arms and confess his own love, telling her, if necessary, he would die for her. And then . . . and then? At that point, Amelia always drew a blank.

"Amelia!" Jason said firmly.

Startled, she whirled away from the window. She had been so absorbed in her reverie that she hadn't heard her husband returning.

Amelia's negligee temptingly shadowed her feminine contours, and Jason's eyes traveled hungrily over the silhouetted delights awaiting him. "Let's go to bed," he uttered, moving toward her.

In his drunken condition, Jason's steps were awkward, and his handsome face was distorted with animal lust. Instinctively, Amelia backed away from his clumsy approach. Quickly he reached out, grabbing her by the wrist. "I said let's go to bed!" he snarled.

All her life, Amelia had been taught to be docile, as befitting a lady, but docility was not in her true character, a fact she herself was as yet unaware of. But, jerking free from her husband's tenacious grip, Amelia got her first glimpse of who she really was, as she exploded furiously, "How dare you treat me as if I were a common woman of the streets! I am your wife, and you will show me respect!"

Surprised but impressed by his wife's outburst, Captain Bishop eyed her thoughtfully. So his timid bride had spunk, did she? Well, perhaps this marriage wouldn't be as dull as he had been led to believe. He smiled admiringly, causing Amelia to lose some of her tension. She had been shocked by her daring rebuke, but she wouldn't take it back. He had deserved it!

Carefully, he drew her into his arms. "I'm sorry, Amelia," he whispered.

Encouraged by his apology, she asked sharply, "Why did you leave me alone for two hours?"

Although he admired her spirit, he didn't relish being married to a nagging shrew, and menacingly he warned, "I will not tolerate insubordination!"

Astounded, she pushed out of his arms. "I'm not one of your soldiers! I am your wife!"

"I expect my wife to be obedient!" he said firmly. "Which is no more than any husband would demand! I apologized for my behavior, and now you will accept my apology and let it go at that!"

"If I don't?" she rebelled defiantly.

33

Roughly he jerked her into his arms, and, before pressing his lips to hers, he said demandingly, "But you will accept my apology, won't you, my sweet?"

During their short courtship, Jason had kissed her often, but they had been polite, dispassionate kisses, nothing like what he was doing to her now. His mouth on hers was rough, painfully bruising her lips. His breath smelled strongly of champagne. The odor was overwhelming, causing Amelia to feel slightly nauseous.

His kiss had awakened no passion in Amelia, but, thinking only of his own desire, Jason swept her into his arms, carrying her into the bedroom. Pausing beside the bed, he placed her on her feet. Breathing heavily, his mouth attacked her slender neck, leaving a trace of wetness where his lips traveled.

"My precious," he whispered hoarsely, "take off your gown and get into bed."

His lips had left her neck moist and slimy, and finding his drunken display of passion repulsive, Amelia shuddered. When she made no move to obey him, he became angered.

The rage in his eyes frightened her as he demanded, "Get undressed!"

Trembling, she began to unfasten the tiny buttons on her dressing gown. "The light," she pleaded modestly, nodding toward the lamp.

Captain Bishop was not totally without compassion, and, losing his anger, he stepped to the table beside the bed. As he extinguished the light, Amelia caught a quick glimpse of his handsome face, and once again his charming smile lightened her apprehensions and fears.

The lamp in the sitting room was still burning, and since the adjoining door was open it kept the bedroom from becoming totally dark.

Amelia wanted to ask Jason to close it, but, afraid the request would anger him, she decided to leave well enough alone. Thankful in part for the semidarkness, she continued to unbutton her dressing gown. She thought her husband would start to undress also, but he seemed to be more interested in watching her disrobe.

Wanting to get it over with quickly, Amelia slipped out of her dressing gown, placing it on the foot of the bed. Turning her back to Jason, she pulled the flowing nightgown over her head, dropping it to the floor. The covers were already pulled back, so instantly she was in bed, with the sheet jerked up to her chin. She kept her eyes glued to the ceiling, refusing to look at her husband.

She heard Jason laugh brusquely, the chuckle having a ring of cruelty to it, instead of humor. She could tell by the sounds that he had started to undress. He finished in a surprisingly short time, and before Amelia had time to adjust herself to the situation at hand, he was at her side of the bed. Flinging back the sheet, he told her to move over. With her vision still locked to the ceiling, she complied as she scooted across the bed.

Before she could reach the edge, he grabbed her around the waist, pulling her to his side. His hard, muscular body felt alien against her soft flesh. Immediately his mouth was on hers, as his hands began exploring her body. She shut her eyes tightly, wishing she could blot the terrible and shameful scene from her mind. When his hands touched the most intimate parts

35

of her body, she felt dishonored and degraded.

He grasped her breasts, his fingers bruising the nipples. Amelia sobbed softly, but he was unmindful of her whimpers. Moving his hand downward, he touched the most secret part of her body. Not caring if he hurt her, he probed at her cruelly.

Suddenly he took her hand, holding it to his hard erection. "Rub it, my sweet," he moaned fervently.

Amelia's eyes widened with shock. She wasn't completely ignorant of the male's genitals, having seen boy babies, but she had no idea that a man could grow to such size. She could feel him throbbing against her hand as she instinctively encircled her fingers around him.

For a moment, Jason became tender as he kissed her gently but passionately. Strangely, Amelia could feel her body longing for fulfillment. Putting her arms around his neck, she arched her thighs to his.

But Jason's lust once again took command, and his kiss returned to being rough, as he began caressing her painfully. His clumsy and cruel treatment, made Amelia quickly forget that, for a fleeting moment, she had wanted to respond.

Leaning over her, he used his knee to part her thighs. The sitting room lamp cast unnatural shadows across the bedroom, causing the man mounting her to appear grotesque. It was as if the Devil himself had taken over her husband's body. Her aunt's warnings about marital sex came frighteningly to mind. She now recalled Lillian's telling her about penetration, and how painful the first time would be. Apprehensive, Amelia grew rigid, causing Captain Bishop's entry to be excruciating.

The sharp pain made Amelia cry out, but her husband didn't try to ease her hurt with soothing words. He was only aware of his own urgent need, and, thrusting powerfully, he pounded away into the body beneath his.

If Jason had been tender and caring, he would have aroused Amelia's passion, but his continual and awkward thrusting was painful to her, making her despise what he was doing to her.

He climaxed quickly, and, had Amelia known that usually he lasted much longer, she would have sighed thankfully.

Breathing rapidly, he moved to his own side of the bed. He hadn't expected his wife to respond; wives weren't supposed to enjoy sex. When a man wanted a good tumble in bed, he paid a prostitute. But he had enjoyed taking Amelia, and he would continue to enjoy taking her. She was a real beauty, and she belonged unequivocally to him.

Satisfied with his choice of a wife, and happy with his present position in the Union Army, he rolled to his side. Sighing contentedly, he murmured, "Goodnight, my precious." Within minutes his spent passion coupled with his overconsumption of champagne sent him into a sound sleep.

For a long time, Amelia remained rigid, staring dully at the ceiling. Finally, the dampness between her legs became so uncomfortable that it brought her out of her apathy. She got slowly out of bed, her body aching from her husband's rough assault. Taking her dressing gown with her, she moved stiffly to the wash basin. She lifted the pitcher and filled the basin. Grabbing a wash cloth, she dipped it into the water, As she wrung it out, her thoughts began running fluently. Oh God, it had been horrible! Aunt Lillian had been right! The act had been degrading and painful! Why were women forced to undergo such misery? A wife's plight was indeed a terrible one!

Washing between her legs, she was horrified to find traces of blood. She almost panicked, but suddenly she remembered her aunt telling her that she would bleed, but only during the first time. Afterwards, there would be no more blood or pain. For that, Amelia was very grateful.

Finishing her ministrations, she put on the dressing gown. Hearing her husband's constant snoring, she looked to the bed. She couldn't return to his side! Not now! Later! Perhaps later, when she became so sleepy and fatigued that she would immediately fall asleep.

Quietly she walked into the sitting room. Turning down the lamp, she went to the front window. Pulling aside the curtain, she gazed down to the street. She recognized the couple strolling out of the hotel. They had been guests at her wedding and reception. She noticed how they had their arms entwined as they chattered happily. It was Lieutenant Coffman and his wife. They looked to be so much in love! Even from her second story window, Amelia could detect the adoration in the woman's eyes as she gazed up into her husband's face.

Amelia was naive, but she wasn't dense. She realized no wife could look at her husband with so much adoration, if the woman had constantly to endure what she had just gone through. Her eyes followed the couple until they were out of her sight. So love didn't have to be a man pawing and clutching at your body, invading you cruelly, then pounding away at you until he finally collapsed. It could be different! The lieutenant's wife was visible proof.

Turning from the window, Amelia sat in one of the large overstuffed chairs. Drawing up her knees, she snuggled into the deep contours of the chair. Different? she pondered. Different how? She didn't know. Placing her arms across her raised knees, Amelia leaned her head on her arms and cried.

FOUR

Amelia descended the hotel steps with a grace that came naturally. She made a pretty picture, wearing her favorite mint-green dress. Perched on top of her golden curls was a wide-brimmed bonnet adorned with a silk ribbon that matched the color of her dress. The green ribbon tied beneath her chin, making a smooth bow. Unaware of her charms, Amelia didn't notice the admiring glances she received from the hotel patrons as she left the stairway to enter the lobby.

Looking around, she wasn't surprised to find that Lillian hadn't arrived. She could always bank on her aunt's being habitually late. Lieutenant Coffman's wife had invited Amelia and Lillian to her house for an afternoon tea party. Lillian was supposed to come by the hotel for Amelia, so they could go to Mrs. Coffman's together. Amelia wasn't annoyed with Lillian; where her aunt was always late, she was always early.

Amelia smiled charmingly at Mr. Cramer, the desk clerk, as she passed the front desk to sit in one of the lobby chairs. She chose a chair positioned so that it faced the front door. She would be able to see Lillian as soon as she arrived. She was fairly close to the lobby desk, and, knowing Mr. Cramer was still watching her, she turned to him and nodded politely.

He was a small man, extremely thin, and his hairline was beginning to recede. Finding Captain Bishop's wife very attractive, he smiled admiringly. "Good afternoon, Mrs. Bishop. May I help you?"

"No, thank you. I'm merely waiting for my aunt," she answered, remembering to smile pleasantly, although she had lost the desire to smile along with her maidenhood.

She had now been Mrs. Jason Bishop for two weeks and was putting on a cheerful facade for her friends, family, and husband. They all believed her to be a happy bride. But Amelia wasn't happy. She had never been so far from being happy in her whole life. She didn't know why she was so depressed. Her husband didn't mistreat her, and, normally, he was very courteous and thoughtful. Amelia still despised the sexual act she was obliged to participate in nightly. But she could have resigned herself to a wife's terrible plight if only she could somehow forget the look of adoration she saw in Mrs. Coffman's eyes every time she looked at Lieutenant Coffman. That worshipping look was a constant reminder to Amelia that there was something drastically wrong with her own marriage. It never occurred to Amelia that she might not be in love with her husband. Immaturely, she still saw him as the dashing and elegant cavalier of her dreams.

Hearing the front door open, Amelia looked up, hoping to see her aunt. Disappointed, she saw two men entering. She noticed how the younger one remained by the door as the older one limped slowly to the desk.

Amelia watched as the man paused to talk to Mr. Cramer. "Howdy," he said cheerfully.

Nodding brusquely, Mr. Cramer replied, "Good afternoon. May I help you?"

The man chewed loudly on a wad of tobacco, as he drawled, "Well, that remains to be seen. My boy and me just got into town a couple of hours ago. We was lookin' for work. The blacksmith told me to come here to the hotel. He said you might be a needin' some help."

The man stopped speaking as he looked down at the floor, obviously searching for a spittoon. Spotting it beside the desk, he leaned over and spat tobacco juice into it. Continuing, he explained, "The blacksmith said your handyman just up and disappeared a few days ago."

"Yes, he did," Mr. Cramer confirmed. "It was very strange. He was here one day and gone the next. He didn't even take his clothes or belongings."

Leaning against the desk, the man eyed the clerk seriously. "Well, I'll be danged," he drawled. "Do you reckon somethin' happened to him?"

"With all that Missouri scum slipping into Lawrence, I wouldn't doubt that one of them murdered him."

"Now, why do you reckon they'd kill a hotel janitor?"

"They kill for the pleasure of it!" Mr. Cramer huffed.

"It ain't gonna be safe around here, 'til all them guerrillas are killed or run out of Missouri."

"My sentiments exactly," Mr. Cramer agreed. "To get back to your reason for being here. The hotel

43

is looking for a new janitor. Do you have any references?''

''Nope, don't reckon I do. My boy and me were farmers. I sold our little piece of land and we took off to join the Union Army. We felt it our patriotic duty to kill some of them Rebs. But the army wouldn't take me, 'cause of my lame leg.'' He leaned closer to the clerk, lowering his voice, but Amelia could still hear him. ''My boy joined up, but he was wounded. He got shot in the chest. The minnie ball almost shattered his lungs. He's a-healin' up real good, though. As soon as he's completely well, he wants to go back to fightin' them Rebs. That's why we want to stay in these here parts, so he can get right back into the army when he's feelin' fine again.''

He continued to talk to the clerk, but Amelia stopped eavesdropping as she looked at the man who had stepped away from the door to gaze out the front window. She wondered why his father insisted on calling him a boy. He was definitely a man. She noticed he was quite tall, built slim, but strong. She couldn't see his face because he had his back turned.

''Come on over here,'' his father called to him.

Complying, he moved toward the desk, taking long and sturdy strides. As he reached his father's side, he glanced at Amelia, and she could see that he had a short trimmed beard as black as his hair. For a fleeting moment, her gaze met his, and she was confronted by a pair of eyes that were strikingly blue.

''This is my son Jamie,'' the man said clearly. ''And I'm Sam Tyler.''

Moving her scrutiny from the son, Amelia studied the father. Both men were handsome, although there was little physical resemblance between them. Sam Tyler was of average height and sturdily built. His full beard and hair were a rich brown.

"Mr. Tyler," the clerk began, "the hotel needs only one employee. We cannot pay two wages."

"We don't need two salaries," he replied. "We'll work for one wage. You can't beat that. Two men for the price of one. And we'll be willin' to do most any kind of work you might have for us."

Mr. Cramer studied the men thoughtfully. With most able-bodied men in the army, help was hard to come by, and the hotel was in desperate need of a janitor. He wished the men had references; it would make his decision easier.

"Mr. Tyler," the clerk decided, "I will hire you and your son on a two-week trial basis. If you two prove to be conscientious and qualified employees, the hotel will be happy to keep you on."

Offering the clerk his hand, Sam Tyler said firmly, "It's a deal!"

Accepting his handshake, Mr. Cramer replied, "It's very fortunate for you that our janitor disappeared."

Smiling inwardly, Sam Tyler surmised, "Just a lucky coincidence, I reckon."

"Your room is in the rear of the hotel, off the kitchen. I will show you to your quarters." The clerk tapped the bell on his desk, and quickly a boy in his early teens came hurrying into the lobby. "Johnny, watch the desk while I show these men to their quarters."

"We have a wagon and a pair of horses out front. Where should we stable 'em?" Sam Tyler asked the clerk.

45

"The hotel has its private stable. You may use it."

Turning to Jamie, Sam Tyler ordered, "Take the wagon and the horses around back."

Jamie didn't answer his father, he simply nodded. Amelia watched him as he crossed the lobby in long strides. When he reached the front door, Lillian came bustling into the lobby.

Immediately, Amelia got to her feet. Rushing to her aunt, she asked breathlessly, "Are we going to be late?"

Giving her niece a light peck on the cheek, Lillian answered, "Only fashionably so, my dear."

Adjusting her bonnet, Amelia followed Lillian through the door and outside, where she saw the Tylers' wagon parked and Jamie standing at the rear. Apparently, he was in no hurry to obey his father.

As Amelia stepped down from the sidewalk to cross the street, she once again became aware of Jamie's good looks, causing her to miss seeing the gray cat that suddenly scurried past her feet. Trying to avoid stepping on the animal, Amelia tottered clumsily. Bounding right behind the cat was a large blue-ticked hound. The dog brushed roughly against Amelia's legs, and, losing her balance completely, she was knocked backwards. Vainly she reached out, only to grasp at thin air.

All at once, a strong arm grabbed her around the waist, preventing the fall that had seemed inevitable. Retaining her balance, Amelia looked at the man who had so gallantly come to her rescue.

"Jamie!" she gasped, without thinking.

His clear blue eyes stared into hers, sending an inexplicable thrill running through her entire being.

Slowly, almost reluctantly, he removed his arm from around her waist, and, composing herself, Amelia mumbled, "Thank you."

Clutching her niece's arm, Lillian encouraged, "Come on, my dear. We must not dally. We don't want to be so late that it is considered rude, instead of fashionable."

Allowing her aunt to lead her away, Amelia hurried her steps to keep up with Lillian's speedy pace. As they were crossing the street, her aunt reproached her, "Honestly, Amelia! Did you have to fall in that man's arms?"

Annoyed, Amelia answered sharply, "I didn't exactly plan to make a clumsy spectacle of myself."

As they stepped up to the sidewalk, Amelia glanced back at the Tyler wagon. She was surprised to find Jamie still standing in the same place, his eyes fixed on her. Quickly, she looked away. The knowledge that the man had been staring at her didn't upset Amelia. But, strangely, she could still feel the strength in the arm that had so alertly grasped her around the waist. She had found his touch exciting, and that piece of knowledge disturbed Amelia greatly.

FIVE

Trying to look preoccupied, Amelia busied herself by carrying a tray filled with empty cups and saucers into Mrs. Coffman's kitchen. Hoping to be the last guest to depart, she took her time removing the dishes from the tray and placing them on the kitchen counter.

Amelia wanted desperately to talk alone with Lieutenant Coffman's wife. She hoped to discreetly bring up the subject of "love," so they could discuss the topic together, as one married woman to another. Perhaps, if she could learn more about Mrs. Coffman's marriage, she could somehow find out what was wrong with her own.

When Amelia finally returned to the parlor, the other guests had left. Mrs. Coffman sighed with fatigue as she dropped gracefully into one of the chairs. Spotting Amelia standing in the doorway to the parlor, she smiled sweetly. "Amelia, dear, thank you for helping with the dishes. But I didn't invite you here to put you to work. Sit down, and let's talk for a moment."

Relieved that the woman apparently wished to chat

with her, Amelia hastened to the sofa. Mrs. Coffman's chair was placed close to the sofa, and as Amelia sat down, she reached over and patted Amelia's hand.

Cynthia Coffman was a pretty woman. She was tall and willowy, and she always moved gracefully. Her hair was chestnut brown, worn in a flattering style, piled high on top of her head, with tight ringlets framing her oval face. Her gray eyes were extraordinarily large, and she had a small upturned nose. Her lips were full and pouting, giving her a sullen expression that was definitely misleading. Cynthia Coffman was never sullen. She was too happy and too kind ever to be morose.

Cynthia waited patiently for Amelia to speak. She had sensed that Captain Bishop's wife wished to have a private conversation, and that had been her reason for dallying. She had no inkling what Amelia wished to discuss. Surely, she wasn't having marital difficulties. Why, Captain Bishop was so gallant, and such a gentleman, that Amelia must be ecstatically happy!

Feeling ill at ease, Amelia toyed with the folds of her long skirt as her eyes traveled over the room. Lieutenant Coffman's home was small and modestly furnished. But from the moment one entered the Coffman home one felt a sense of warmth and coziness. It's because love lives here, Amelia thought. The warmth and coziness is only a reflection of Lieutenant Coffman and Cynthia's love. Thinking how cold and formal the rooms were that she shared with her husband, Amelia frowned touchingly.

"Are you all right?" Cynthia asked.

Compelling herself to smile, she answered, "Yes, I'm fine." Trying to sound nonchalant, she added,

"How long have you known your husband?"

"David and I have known each other all our lives. We are from the same town. It's a very small town in Illinois."

"When did you and David fall in love?" Amelia asked.

Cynthia giggled merrily. "My goodness, David and I have always been in love. From the time we were children, we knew someday we would marry."

"How long have you been married?"

"A little over a year." Cynthia replied.

Amelia could feel her cheeks growing warm, and she knew the question she was going to ask was much too personal, but she had to know. She just had to! "Cynthia," she began hesitantly, forgetting her plan to be discreet, "do . . . do you like being married?"

Cynthia was puzzled. "What are you trying to say, Amelia?"

Amelia's face had turned scarlet with embarrassment, but she was determined to press the issue. "I mean . . . do you like . . . being a wife . . . at night?"

Cynthia's own face grew red, and breathlessly she exclaimed, "Why, Amelia Bishop!"

All at once, Amelia burst into sobs, and, instantly touched by her tears, Cynthia moved to the sofa, taking Amelia into her arms. The two women were the same age, but Cynthia crooned soothingly to Amelia as if she were years older and wiser.

"Oh Amelia, you poor darling! Sh . . . sh . . . you must not cry. Just give your marriage a little more time, and you'll learn to accept your husband with open arms."

Gently, Amelia pushed out of Cynthia's embrace. Desperately, she pleaded, "Please Cynthia! You must tell me! Do you enjoy that part of marriage?"

Once again, Cynthia blushed conspiciously. When she made no reply, Amelia grasped at Cynthia's hands. "Please!" she begged. "Tell me!"

"Why?" Cynthia cried. "Is marriage that terrible for you?"

"Yes!" Amelia shouted. "I hate it! I hate the way he paws at me! I hate having him . . ."

Interrupting, Cynthia said sternly, "You must not tell me these things!"

Returning to her senses, Amelia was shocked by her own distasteful conduct. Leaping to her feet, she apologized, "Oh Cynthia, I'm so sorry! Please forgive me!"

Embarrassed, Amelia whirled brusquely, rushing out of the parlor. As she reached the front door, Cynthia called, "Amelia!"

She turned to look back at her. Cynthia rose from the sofa, and wringing her hands nervously, she admitted, "I enjoy every part of my marriage."

"Why?" Amelia pleaded.

"Because I love David, and he loves me," Cynthia replied.

With fresh tears stinging her eyes, Amelia opened the door. She left Cynthia's home without further comment.

Walking swiftly, Amelia headed toward the hotel. Love, she thought. But I love Jason! He's so handsome and so wonderful! Of course, I love him!

Lifting the hem on her long skirt, she stepped from the sidewalk to cross the street. As usual the town was bustling with citizens, Union Soldiers, and traffic heading in different directions. Her thoughts in a turmoil, she entered the hotel and hurried up the stairs to her rooms. She was surprised to find the door to the sitting room standing open. Wondering if Jason had come home, she rushed anxiously into the room. Spotting Jamie working on the window in the sitting room, her steps halted abruptly.

Turning, Jamie looked at her. "Mr. Cramer said your window was stickin', and he told me to come up here and fix it," he explained.

Smiling pleasantly, Amelia replied, "Good! It's been so warm, and I haven't been able to open the window."

Jamie didn't answer. He turned away to continue working on the stuck window. She watched him as he finished with a tool and dropped it back into the tool box. Then, easily, he pulled the window wide open. Immediately a fresh breeze blew his black hair back from his forehead, and, once again, Amelia was amazed by his good looks.

Smoothly, he moved away from the window, his blue eyes meeting hers. She was surprised that a man who had been a farmer could move so gracefully. As though he had read her thoughts, he stiffened his lean frame as he lifted the tool box. Mumbling, he said, "The window is fixed, ma'am."

"I wish to thank you again for coming to my rescue this afternoon. My goodness, if it hadn't been for you, I'd have made a terrible spectacle of myself," Amelia said.

"You're welcome, ma'am," he replied.

Moving closer to him, she held out her hand. "I am

very pleased to meet you. I'm Mrs. Jason Bishop. My husband is a captain in the army.''

For a fleeting moment, she thought she detected a strange glare in his eyes, but the moment was gone so quickly that she wasn't sure if she had only imagined it.

Jamie hadn't accepted her handshake, and she was beginning to feel foolish when, all at once, he took her hand. "I'm glad to meet you, Mrs. Bishop," he replied, then, releasing her hand, he hurried out of the room.

SIX

Cursing under his breath, Jamie rushed down the stairs, through the lobby, and into the kitchen. Leaving the tool box by the pantry door, he went to the quarters he shared with Sam Tyler.

Stepping into the small room, he slammed the door shut behind him. His blue eyes shining with rage, he said to the man unpacking their battered suitcase, "I don't know if I can go through with this damned charade!"

The man known as Sam Tyler laughed heartily. "Calm down, James Henry. We got a job to do, and we'll do it. Hell, nobody said it was going to be easy."

Moving to the bed, James Henry sat on the edge. Reaching into his pocket, he brought out a small cigar. Looking at the other man, whose true name was Buford Stewart, he stated bitterly, "I just met Captain Bishop's wife."

Buford eyed him sharply. "James Henry, this is no time for personal revenge!"

Lighting the cigar, Jamie answered, "I know, and

don't worry, I'm not going to do anything rash.''

"We'll get our revenge on Bishop. We just have to wait for the right time and the right place.''

James Henry didn't comment. He was thinking about Captain Bishop's wife. He had found her enticing, and more beautiful than women more abundantly endowed.

Strolling to the door, Buford grumbled, "We got work to do, James Henry.''

"I'll join you in a few minutes,'' Jamie replied.

As Buford left the room, James Henry stretched out on the bed, and, leaning back against the headboard, he sat silently as he smoked his cigar. Staring vacantly at the closed door, his mind drifted into the past as he remembered the night he and Buford had ridden back to the old homestead in Western Missouri.

It had been two years since James Henry Stewart had been home to Clay County, Missouri. As he and his uncle rode steadily closer to the old homestead, he could see smoke from the stove chimney billowing briefly before disappearing into the dusky shadows of evening. The smoke was a welcome sight to James Henry; it meant they were arriving in time for supper.

The man riding at his side obviously felt the same way, because, smiling broadly, he remarked, "I'm so hungry, I could eat a damned mule.''

James Henry nodded in agreement, but he made no comment. He was wondering what his Pa would say about his oldest son's suddenly materializing on his doorstep.

Riding past the cornfield, the two men reined their

horses. Observing the trampled corn, James Henry asked, "What do you suppose happened?"

Spitting to the ground, his uncle grumbled, "Jay-hawkers!"

They continued toward the house, their tired horses plodding sluggishly. As Amelia had observed, there was little resemblance between the two men. James Henry was tall, slim but strong. His hair was coal black, and his complexion was a dark olive, contrasting elegantly with his blue eyes. His dark eyebrows and lashes made the blue in his eyes shine with a brilliant hue, and his close-trimmed beard was as black as his hair. At twenty-eight, James Henry Stewart was exceptionally handsome.

His uncle, Buford Stewart, was of average height. James Henry had taken after his mother's side of the family, the Henrys, but Buford was a true Stewart. His build was stocky, his full head of hair a dark brown, matching his eyes and thick beard. Buford Stewart was forty-two, but he carried the physique of a man ten years younger. He was a good-looking man, inheriting the Stewarts' well-chiseled and attractive features.

It was early summer in the year 1862. There was a border war between Missouri and Kansas. The Kansas troops were being led by men such as Jim Lane, Jim Montgomery, and Doc Jennison. Striking back at these Federal militia were Pro-Confederate bands, led primarily by William Quantrill.

The Stewarts and the Henrys were originally from Tennessee, but Paul Stewart and the former Sarah Henry had moved to Missouri a year after their marriage. Like most southerners, they had considered

Missouri a Southern frontier state, and, finding the land rich for farming, they settled in Clay County to raise their crops and their children.

Western Missouri had been settled mostly by Southern emigrants, many of them longing to remain neutral during the War between the States. But they refused to strike a blow against the South, making them targets of the Federal troops who continually crossed from Kansas into Missouri, harassing these families.

As they neared the house, James Henry found it unchanged. It was a log house, built with a loft that his father had made into one large room used as a bedroom for his sons. The main level consisted of the kitchen and living area, with two bedrooms at the back of the house.

The evening shadows were growing heavy, and they could see a lamp shining in the front window, but it was swiftly extinguished. The door was swung open, and the barrel of a rifle greeted them.

"Identify yourselves, or I'll blow you to smithereens!"

Recognizing the voice, James Henry grinned as he answered, "Is that any way to welcome your prodigal son's return?"

Astounded, the man exclaimed, "James Henry, is that you?"

As he and Buford dismounted, James Henry replied, "It sure is, Pa!"

Propping his rifle against the door, Paul Stewart stepped out to the porch, ordering briskly, "Ben, light the lantern; Luther put my gun away, and Anne get supper on the table! James Henry has come home!"

Hurrying out into the yard, Paul hugged his son before embracing his younger brother. Buford was aware that the embrace he had received had been less than enthusiastic. He knew Paul would never forgive him for taking his oldest son away from his family.

Placing his arm around his son's shoulders, Paul led him to the porch and through the doorway. His steps hesitant, Buford followed them into the house.

Immediately James Henry was met by his brothers and sisters shoving against one another to hug their long absent brother.

First, James Henry took Anne into his arms. She was only one year younger than James Henry, and he felt closer to Anne than to the others. For seven years there had only been the two of them.

Anne Stewart was pretty, her hair as black as James Henry's, but her eyes were Stewart brown. Embracing her brother warmly, she whispered, "Welcome home."

Before releasing her, he kissed her cheek. "You're looking beautiful, Sis."

Next, James Henry welcomed Becky into his arms. Rebecca Stewart was ten years old and the youngest child. Like the Henry women, she was small, but she had inherited the Stewarts' coloring.

Turning to Ben, James Henry shook hands with him vigorously before embracing him. Ben Stewart was twenty years of age. He was built solidly, slightly shorter than his brother. His hair was light brown and unruly, his most handsome feature being his eyes, which were hazel, with lashes so long that they were almost feminine.

Stepping to his youngest brother, James Henry was again welcomed by a robust hug. At sixteen, Luther

Stewart was still at that awkward age, somewhere between boyhood and manhood. He had received all the Stewart traits, his hair dark brown and his eyes the same shade.

Looking around the room, James Henry asked, "Where's Ma? Isn't she home?" He was answered by silence, as all eyes suddenly evaded his. Turning to his father, he asked, "Where is Ma?"

Paul Stewart was a tall man, but he appeared shrunken as his wide shoulders slumped, and, bowing his head, he answered, "Your ma is dead."

His voice strained, James Henry asked, "When did she die?"

"Two weeks past," his father replied.

"What happened? James Henry asked. "Had she been ill?"

To Buford and James Henry, Paul said gruffly, "Hang your hats and those gun belts you're totin' on the rack by the door. You're not out west among savages. You're in a civilized home!"

Hurrying, Luther took their gun belts, hanging them on the rack. The family was unaware that the two men felt naked without their revolvers fitting snugly against their hips.

"Let's sit at the table," Paul began, "and I'll tell you what happened."

James Henry followed his father across the room. The table was long and narrow, covered with a red-checkered tablecloth. There were no chairs, the table having been built with benches on all sides.

After the men were seated, Paul explained, "Ben and I went into town. While we were gone, a group of Jayhawkers came to the house. They barged into the house, demanding Quantrill's whereabouts.''

Interrupting, James Henry asked, "Why did they think any of you would know anything about Quantrill?"

"Wade Jarrette is riding with Quantrill," Paul answered.

"Wade!" James Henry exclaimed. "But why didn't they go to the Jarrettes' homestead? Why did they come here?"

Placing a plate on the table in front of James Henry, Anne answered, "Wade and I are engaged."

She took her brother totally by surprise. "You and Wade?" he gasped.

A flush rising to her cheeks, Anne replied, "James Henry, you know I have always been in love with Wade."

Wade Jarrette had been James Henry's boyhood friend. And although James Henry had always known that his sister had a crush on Wade, he had never believed anything would come of it.

As Anne returned to the stove to serve supper, Paul said pleasantly, "I know you remember Wade as being a wild, devil-may-care rascal, but he's a changed man."

James Henry waited until Anne had finished putting the food on the table. As she sat down beside Becky, he asked her, "When do you plan to marry?"

Shrugging, she answered somberly, "Because of the war, we haven't set a date."

To his oldest son, Paul ordered, "James Henry, you can say the blessing." When he didn't respond, his father snapped impatiently, "We're waiting!"

Bowing his head, James Henry mumbled, "Bless

61

this food. Amen.''

Reproachfully, his father complained, ''That has got to be the shortest blessing I've ever heard.'' Looking to Anne, he grumbled, ''Start passing the potatoes.'' As the bowl of potatoes was being passed around the table, Paul explained, ''When the Jayhawkers stormed into the house, your ma told them she had no idea where Quantrill and his men were hiding. Which was the gospel truth. We hadn't received word from Wade in weeks. They didn't believe your ma, so they decided to torture Luther, thinking that would make your ma or Anne tell them what they wanted to know. They dragged Luther outside. They ripped away his shirt and started whipping him with ropes.''

Accepting the plate of biscuits that was now being passed around the table, Paul continued, ''Your ma hadn't been well for a long time, the doctor said it was her heart. Seeing Luther being beaten was more than her health could take. She was struck with an attack. When the Jayhawkers saw what was happening to her, they rode off trampling the cornfield as they left. She died shortly after Ben and I returned home.''

James Henry took the platter of meat Buford handed him, but his appetite had vanished. He speared a slice of the ham, dropping it to his plate, then passed the platter to his father.

Clearing his voice, Buford spoke for the first time since entering the house. Gesturing to Ben and Luther, he asked his brother, ''How have you kept these two rascals at home?''

''It hasn't been easy,'' Paul answered. ''I had hoped to remain neutral through this war, but the Federals refuse to accept neutrality. All our young men are subject to military duty and ordered to report to the nearest military post." Angered, his voice grew stern. "Southerners are being ordered to fight for the Union! Men who have remained neutral are now telling their sons to join up with Quantrill. What other choice do they have? They can't tell their sons to join the Union and fight friends, relatives, and their own principles!"

"What advice did you give your sons?" Buford asked.

"Ben is leaving next week, along with some of the neighboring boys. A rendezvous with Quantrill has already been arranged. Ben will fight for his home and family. Not for the Union!"

"And Luther?" Buford questioned.

"He's too young," Paul answered.

"I'm not too young, Pa!" Luther blurted, his face red with rage.

"You're just turned sixteen! You're still a boy!" Paul insisted.

"I'm going, Pa!" Luther shouted. "When Ben leaves, I'm leaving with him!"

Resigning himself, Paul answered, but there was an unmistakable note of pride in his voice, "If you're determined to leave, I know there's nothing I can say to keep you here."

Dishing out a second helping of potatoes, Ben asked eagerly, "You're coming with us, aren't you, James Henry?"

Pushing aside his plate, from which little had been eaten, James Henry answered, "I won't ride with Quantrill."

Shocked, as well as disappointed, Ben demanded, "If you don't aim to fight, then why did you come back home?''

"To check on all of you," James Henry replied calmly.

"What are you going to do?" Ben raged. "Go back out west and turn your back on your home and kinfolks?"

Sighing, James Henry replied, "I intend to join the Army of Confederate States, even though I don't believe the South stands a chance of winning the war."

"James Henry!" Paul bellowed. "You're talking treason!"

"Calm down, Pa," James Henry coaxed. "Because I don't think the South can win doesn't make me guilty of treason."

"But Clay County is your home," Paul began. "If you're going to fight, why not fight here?"

"I won't ride under a man like William Quantrill. He has no dignity or integrity. If I must fight, then I'll surrender my services to a Confederate officer. A man who is fighting for a cause and not for personal revenge." Crossing his arms on the table, he proceeded to explain to his father and brothers. "Don't you realize Quantrill doesn't give a damn about Missouri or Southern sympathizers? He's using the war as an excuse to vent his own outrage against Kansas."

"Part of what you say may be true," Paul agreed. "But Quantrill is all we have. But since you apparently have all the answers, suppose you tell Ben and Luther what they should do. Do they betray their principles and their friends and join the Union, or do they abandon their neighbors and join the Confederacy?"

For a long time everyone remained silent. Standing, James Henry finally commented, "I don't have the answers, Pa. But I do understand why Ben and Luther feel it their duty to join Quantrill. I only want them to see this war and Quantrill for what they really are.''

"It's your duty too, James Henry!" his father replied firmly. "You were born here. You lived in Clay County for the first twenty years of your life, before you took to wandering with Buford. If you're going to offer your services, then you owe them to our Pro-Confederate bands, not to the Confederate Army! The Confederacy has other men to join the army, but all we have are our own, and whether you like it or not, James Henry, you are one of us!"

"The Confederacy doesn't even recognize Quantrill's men as Confederate soldiers," James Henry tried to explain. "They aren't even protected by the Code of War. As far as the Union is concerned, they are guerrillas and outlaws to be shot down in cold blood!"

Quietly, his father replied, "You don't intend to avenge your mother's death, do you, James Henry?"

"A small band of Jayhawkers caused Ma's death, not the entire Union Army. And I don't intend to avenge her by killing Federals at random.''

The two men's eyes met, their expressions resentful; then, turning swiftly, James Henry stalked out of the house.

Grumbling, Paul looked at Buford, "I've never been able to understand that boy.''

"James Henry hates this war," Buford replied quietly.

"But why?" Paul pleaded.

Rising, Buford's eyes scanned the people sitting before him. "I'll tell you why, but my words may as well be falling on deaf ears, because not one of you is capable of understanding. The majority of people in this state and all other states are incapable of comprehending what this war will mean to all of us. You question why men like James Henry and myself are not elated and filled with patriotism. The War between the States, and the border war between Missouri and Kansas, are tragedies that our country will never rise above. Your beloved Clay County and the South, as well as the North, will be stained by its men's blood, and its women's tears, for years to come. It will take at least two generations before the blood is finally cleaned from the land and the tears are dried.''

Eyeing Ben and Luther, Buford continued, ''Experience your excitement and patriotism now while you can, because if you live to see the end of this war, when it's over, you'll have nothing left to feel but bitterness and hatred.''

Slowly Buford walked to the front door. Turning, he faced the others. ''When the war is over, and western Missouri and the South are minus more than half of their young men, their families will turn to one another and cry, Why? That question will haunt us all until our dying day. Why? A small word, but someday it will echo across an entire nation.''

Opening the door, Buford stepped outside, but, as he had predicted, his words had not been understood.

The next day, Anne was deeply engrossed in her sewing when James Henry entered the house. Seeing his sister in the pine rocker that had been his mother's favorite chair, he commented, ''You look a lot like Ma, you know.''

Placing her sewing on her lap, she asked, ''Where

have you been?''

Crossing the room in long strides, he answered, ''I rode over to the Jarrettes'.'' Taking the chair across from hers, he asked, ''Where is everyone?''

''Pa and the others rode into town, and Becky is taking a nap.''

''What are you sewing?''

Smiling proudly, she answered, ''It's a shirt for you, and when I finish I'll start on one for Uncle Buford.''

Baffled, he questioned, ''Why are you making shirts for Buford and me? Do our clothes look that ragged?''

She smiled. ''Of course not.'' Lifting the partially finished shirt, she held it up for him to see, as she explained, ''It's a guerrilla shirt.''

''It's a what?'' James Henry snapped.

Dropping the shirt back into her lap, Anne replied hesitantly, ''Confederate uniforms are not available to our men.'' She lifted her chin haughtily, continuing, ''Besides, even if they were, I doubt it would suit our men to wear them. They have their own style of dressing. The shirts, like the one I'm making for you, are patterned after the hunting coats of the Western plainsmen. It's cut low in front, with the slit narrowing to a point above the belt and ending in a rosette. Your shirt will have four large pockets, two in the breast, and I will decorate it with needlework. Oh, James Henry, you will look so handsome. Although you told Papa you wouldn't join up with Quantrill, I knew you would change your mind!''

''Just what makes you think I'm planning to join the guerrillas?'' he asked impatiently.

Sudden tears sprang to her eyes. "Aren't you?" she cried.

"Is that what you want me to do?" he asked urgently.

"That's what Pa wants!" she answered.

"But what do you want me to do?" he insisted.

Crying, she covered her face with her hands, and between sobs she admitted, "If you refuse to join Ben and Luther, I'll be so ashamed!"

James Henry leaned back in his chair, stretching his long legs. He waited until his sister's sobs subsided, before commenting matter-of-factly, "I love you, Anne. You're always in my thoughts, even when I'm a thousand miles away."

"I love you too, James Henry!" she cried sincerely.

"I know you do," he murmured. "Sew the shirt, Anne. If I don't join up, you can always give it to Ben."

"Does that mean you're thinking about it?"

A slight nod was the only answer she received. Continuing her sewing, she dropped the subject. "James Henry," she began, "what do you and Uncle Buford do when you're out west?"

"Do?" he questioned.

"Yes, how do you make a living?"

"Different ways. Trapping, for one."

"What do you trap?"

"Mostly we trap muskrat and beaver."

"How far west have you traveled?"

"California," he answered.

Amazed, she exclaimed, "You have actually been in California?"

Grinning, he replied, "Once."

"But why in the world did you go to California?" she asked, astounded.

"Because it was there," he replied dryly.

"Oh, James Henry, when are you going to stop crossing mountains, only to see what is on the other side?" But, fascinated with her older brother, she pressed, "And what other exciting adventures have you had?"

"None I would care to tell my sister," he chuckled.

Stammering, and feeling a little self-conscious, she asked, "What do you think about Wade and me getting married?"

Mumbling, he answered, "I'm happy for you, Sis."

"You don't sound happy!" she retorted.

"I am happy for you, Anne. But it's this damned war. I just hope when it's over, Wade will still be alive to come home to you."

"How can you sound so bitter?" Anne asked harshly. "You should be proud of men like Wade and our brothers!"

"Pride can be a lonely word, when it's all you have to warm your bed and fill the two empty places at the table. This war you are so fascinated with may very likely take your future husband's and your brothers' lives. Then what will you have, Anne? Your damned pride, that's what you'll have!"

Before Anne could reply, Becky entered the room, rubbing sleep from her eyes. Holding out his arms, James Henry coaxed, "Come sit with your big brother, honey."

Pleased, Becky hurried to his side. Taking her into his lap, he placed a kiss on her forehead. Holding her close, he looked back to Anne. "Before this war is over, even children will suffer because of it. May God damn this war straight to hell!''

James Henry's thoughts returned to the present, and, rising abruptly, he smashed his half-smoked cigar into the ash tray. Thinking about Anne and Becky, he stomped to the door, and before opening it he swore, ''Someday, Bishop, I'm going to kill you for what you did to them!''

SEVEN

Walking down the hotel stairway at her husband's side, Amelia placed her hand in the crook of his arm. Studying Jason out of the corner of her eye, she admired his dashing appearance. He was dressed in his blue uniform, and his wide-brimmed hat was worn back from his brow, allowing his dark curls to fall attractively over his forehead. His heavy scabbard was strapped around his hips, the long sword flushed tightly against his muscular leg. Raising her gaze, Amelia looked at his handsome profile. His nose was straight and refined, his high cheekbones prominent, and his dark lashes were long, curling sensually over his brown eyes. Surely, she thought, he must sense that I am watching him, so why won't he turn to me and smile, the way I have seen Lieutenant Coffman smile at Cynthia? A loving secret smile that only lovers can share?

They reached the bottom of the stairway, but Jason continued to look straight ahead, his head held arrogantly.

As they headed toward the dining room for breakfast, Amelia saw Jamie in the lobby. There was a huge bucket at his side, and she watched him as he dipped a mop into the bucket. Wringing it out, he began to scrub the floor. The bucket was placed close to the entrance to the dining room, and Amelia found it easy to see, but Jason was still strutting haughtily, causing him to miss it entirely.

Before Amelia could grasp the opportunity to warn him, he walked straight into the bucket. As his shin hit the bucket sharply, the collision caused dirty water to splash onto his pants leg.

"Goddamn!" Jason shouted, losing his refined deportment.

Stopping his chore, James Henry turned around. He tried to keep his face expressionless as he got his first look at Captain Jason Bishop, but his jaws clenched tightly, and a nerve twitched at his temples. Quickly he looked away from the man and returned to scrubbing the floor.

His temper exploding, Jason kicked the bucket, as he raged, "Get that goddamned bucket out of my way!"

James Henry's hand grasped the mop handle firmly, and, turning back around, he faced Jason. "Sir?" he asked, but his inner rage was growing extremely dangerous.

"How dare you place a bucket of mop water where a man can stumble blindly into it!" Jason barked.

Timidly, Amelia touched her husband's arm. "Please Jason, it was only an accident."

Callously he shoved her hand away, continuing his ranting, "What is your name? I intend to report your negligence to Mr. Cramer!"

Coming very close to forgetting his reason for being in Lawrence, James Henry took a step forward, but at the same moment Buford opened the front door, stepping into the lobby.

Remembering to limp, Buford hurried to the scene. There were only a few patrons in the dining room, and all eyes were turned curiously to the lobby.

"What's the problem?" Buford asked, standing close to James Henry.

"That sonofabitch placed his dirty bucket right in the entrance to the dining room!" Jason bellowed.

Instantly James Henry lurched forward, but Buford stepped in front of him. "Captain, there ain't no reason for that kind of talk. Especially with a lady present."

"Who are you?" Jason demanded. "I've never seen either of you men before."

"We just started workin' here a couple of days ago. But just who in the hell are you?" Buford asked.

"I am Captain Bishop!" Jason announced.

Quickly Buford looked at James Henry, but, relieved, he saw that his nephew was remaining calm, playing his role to perfection. Buford turned his attention back to Captain Bishop. His tone mocking, he asked, "Did you do somethin' dumb, like walk into a bucket?"

"Hell man, just look at my trousers!"

Lowering his gaze, Buford looked casually at Jason's wet pants legs, then he looked at the bucket. Smiling shrewdly, he remarked, "It's a mighty big bucket. I don't see how you missed seein' it, unless you had your nose stuck up in the air."

Offended, Jason's face turned red with rage. "How

73

dare you be so insolent! What is your name?''

"I'm Sam Tyler, and this is my son Jamie,'' Buford answered calmly.

"I will report this incident to Mr. Cramer!'' Jason huffed.

James Henry's voice tinged with anger, he offered, "He's in his office. I'll be glad to show you the way. Or, if you'd rather, we can step outside.''

Quickly Amelia grabbed hold of Jason's arm. "Please Jason, let's forget the whole unfortunate incident. Let's have our breakfast. We haven't much time. You must leave soon.''

Becoming aware of Amelia's plea and the patrons in the dining room, Jason recovered his composure. He would be charitable. But not because of Amelia, but to impress others. "Very well,'' he said clearly. "I will not report you two to Mr. Cramer.''

Placing his hand on Amelia's elbow, Jason ushered her into the dining room, his posture once again straight and formal.

Going to their usual table, Jason pulled out Amelia's chair. Knowing people were staring at them, she blushed vividly as she took her seat. Quickly Jason was seated across from her. The waiter was an elderly man, but he hurried to their table and took their order.

Jason, still fuming, remained silent as they waited for their breakfast to be served. Toying with her napkin, Amelia tried to forget the ugly incident, but against her will she kept reliving it over and over in her mind. Oh, how could Jason have been so discourteous? No, she thought, not discourteous, but downright rude! Looking across the table, she studied him intently. Did she even know this man who was her hus-

74

band?

Feeling her eyes on him, Jason faced her. Smirking, he grumbled, ''Must you stare, Amelia?''

''I wasn't staring,'' she replied strongly, refusing to let him bully her.

Suddenly, Jason smiled. ''Let's not argue, my sweet. I will be leaving within the hour, and I won't be back for three maybe four weeks. Let's part on a pleasant note, shall we?''

Agreeing, Amelia nodded brusquely. She wondered why she wasn't upset by Jason's leaving for so long. She should be sad, as she knew Cynthia was sad over Lieutenant Coffman's departure, but instead, Amelia was only grateful for all those nights that she could sleep alone and undisturbed.

''What are your plans for today?'' Jason asked.

''Cynthia is to meet me here this morning, and after tea we plan to go shopping.''

Noticing the waiter pouring coffee at the next table, Jason impatiently called to him. ''Where is our breakfast? Good God, man, I don't have all day!''

Annoyed by Jason's rudeness, Amelia unconsciously wadded her napkin tightly in her hand. Much to her dismay, she was beginning to question if she liked the man she had married.

Sitting in the dining room, Amelia sipped on her second cup of tea as she waited for Cynthia's arrival. Jason had left only moments before, and she was grateful he was gone. She knew it was terribly wrong for her to feel this way, and she was abashed by her own feelings. Jason and his troops were riding into

Missouri, and he could be wounded, or worse, be killed. Oh, she didn't want anything bad to happen to him! He was her husband and she loved him! Truly she did! He had only been upset this morning. He wasn't usually so inconsiderate and short-tempered. But all the same, Amelia still knew she was relieved that he was gone. She smiled secretively, thinking about the long, peaceful nights she would have all to herself.

Absorbed in her thoughts, Amelia didn't see James Henry entering the dining room, but his eyes were immediately drawn to Amelia as he detected her mischievous smile. He paused abruptly, studying her curiously. He had heard that Bishop and his troops were heading into Missouri, and, raising his eyebrows questioningly, he wondered why she looked so pleased. Her husband had just ridden off to the wars, and she should be torn apart with grief and worry, not looking like the cat who had just swallowed the canary.

He continued to observe Amelia, his eyes taking in her innocent beauty. Her golden hair was pulled back from her face, secured with a blue ribbon that was the exact shade of her dress. A cluster of long curls was gathered at the back of her neck.

Unaware of being observed, Amelia's smile widened even more as she realized just how dearly she would relish her freedom.

Seeing her delightful smile, it became quite apparent to James Henry that Mrs. Bishop was not in love with her husband. He found the thought pleasing, and a slight smile crossed his own lips. Stepping to a nearby table, he picked up an empty tray, then he ambled over to Amelia.

Hearing his approach, her smile vanished. Raising

76

her gaze, she looked at James Henry as he stopped at her table. "Jamie," she said pleasantly.

"Excuse me, ma'am," he apologized, "but I need to clean off the table."

"Please don't let me stop you. I'm merely biding my time, waiting for a friend."

"Would you like another cup of tea?" he inquired.

"No, thank you, but when my friend arrives, I'd appreciate it very much if you would bring her a cup. I am sure she will need a relaxing cup of hot tea."

He looked at her as though he was puzzled, but secretly he was finding the freckles splashed across her nose attractive and downright cute.

"Her husband is Lieutenant Coffman," Amelia proceeded to explain. "He is leaving this morning to ride into Missouri. She will be very upset and worried." Amelia frowned briefly, sympathizing with Cynthia, but she was too happy to be sad for very long, and a playful smile once again tugged at the corners of her mouth.

Seeing her amusement, James Henry choked down the impulse to teasingly ask her if it had slipped her mind that her own husband was riding into Missouri.

All at once, as though she had read his thoughts, Amelia blushed conspiciously. Relieved, she suddenly saw Cynthia walking into the dining room. Following her gaze, James Henry said quickly, "I'll get that cup of tea, ma'am."

Cynthia took the chair across from Amelia, and instantly Amelia became aware of how her friend's eyes were red and swollen.

"Oh Cynthia!" she cried sympathetically. "You've been crying, haven't you?"

Cynthia nodded, and her chin quivered. "I love David so much. If anything were to happen to him, I couldn't bear it!" Admiring Amelia's courage, she exclaimed, "How can you be so brave? You must be as upset as I am, and yet one would never know by looking at you. Oh Amelia, I wish I had your strength!"

Feeling terribly guilty, Amelia lowered her gaze, and fiddling with her napkin she stammered, "Cynthia, let's not talk about it. Let's just pretend this day is like any other day."

"I'll try," Cynthia replied unconvincingly.

Reaching across the table, Amelia patted Cynthia's hand. "After you have a cup of tea, we'll go shopping. And, Cynthia, we'll have a marvelous time. I promise you."

Observing Jamie returning, Amelia exclaimed, "Ah, here's your tea. You'll see, Cynthia. There's nothing like a nice cup of tea to make one feel much better."

As Jamie placed the cup on the table, Cynthia sighed. "If only I didn't love David so much."

Her words struck Amelia profoundly. But she loved Jason, didn't she? So why wasn't she as depressed as Cynthia? What is wrong with me? she wondered.

Walking to another table, James Henry began placing used dishes on a tray. Believing him to be out of hearing range, Cynthia said to Amelia, "Dear, about the other day . . ."

Interrupting, Amelia pleaded, "I want to apologize for my unforgivable conduct."

James Henry's acute hearing picked up their conversation, and, his curiosity aroused, he eavesdropped.

"Oh no!" Cynthia protested. "You do not owe me

an apology! But, Amelia, I haven't been able to forget how upset you were. And . . . and I was wondering if you would still like to talk about it.''

Disheartened, Amelia sighed, ''Talking about it won't help. I suppose I am what is known as a frigid wife.''

Hearing Amelia's confession, James Henry held back the urge to laugh, causing him to drop the plate he was transferring to the tray, but quickly he caught it before it could hit the floor.

Totally unconscious of being overheard, Amelia continued bitterly, ''I despise that part of marriage!'' Deciding to be completely honest with Cynthia, she added, ''And I'm grateful I will have all these upcoming nights to myself!''

Astounded, Cynthia gasped, ''Amelia, how can you say such a horrid thing!''

Determined to remain honest, Amelia answered, ''It's true! But I can't help how I feel! I don't want anything bad to happen to Jason. He's my husband, and I love him.'' Amelia's eyes flashed indignantly. ''But, Cynthia, I hate marital relations. I find it degrading and . . . and just awful!''

Getting to her feet, Cynthia stuttered, ''Dear . . . don't . . . don't you think . . . we should do our shopping?''

Rising, Amelia apologized, ''I've shocked you, and I'm sorry.''

''That's all right,'' Cynthia replied faintly.

Stepping to Cynthia's side, Amelia gently touched her arm. ''I also shocked myself. I don't think I truly understood how much I dislike that part of marriage, until now.''

Wishing to change the subject, Cynthia began walking out of the dining room as she asked politely, "How is your dear Aunt Lillian?"

Following her out of the room, Amelia replied, "She's just fine, Cynthia Coffman, as you very well know."

The uneasy moment passed, and suddenly Cynthia and Amelia smiled at each other. Locking arms, they stepped into the lobby.

Turning from the table, James Henry watched the ladies leaving. He heard Buford walking up behind him, but his uncle's approach didn't stop him from smiling.

Buford looked at Amelia's departing back, and then to James Henry's cocky grin. "What are you thinking about, James Henry?" he asked in a lowered voice.

"You don't want to know," he assured him.

"I hope you didn't go and do something you haven't got any business doing," Buford replied with an undertone of warning.

James Henry's smile broadened as he thought about the frigid Amelia. "Not yet, Pappy! Not yet!" he remarked cunningly.

"Damn it!" Buford whispered gruffly. "Can't you call me Pa or Dad? I don't like being called Pappy!"

"Why not?" James Henry taunted. "You look like a Pappy."

Grumbling, Buford fussed, "I ain't even old enough to be your Pa, unless I sired you at the tender age of fourteen."

"Can I help it if you look old enough to be my Pappy?" James Henry baited.

"I'm not supposed to look older, you sonofabitch,

you're supposed to look younger!'' Buford scowled.

Laughing, James Henry picked up the tray of dirty dishes, as he replied loudly, ''Whatever you say . . . Pappy!''

EIGHT

Although the night was late, James Henry couldn't sleep. Visions of his family kept tearing into his thoughts as well as his heart. Leaving the room he shared with Buford, he left the hotel by the rear entrance. There was a small back porch with three steps leading up to it, and sitting down on the top one, James Henry sighed deeply as he gazed into the dark night. His thoughts returned to the Stewart family, as bit by bit he recalled the day that would haunt him for the rest of his life.

James Henry and Buford had ridden over to the Jarrettes' homestead with Ben and Luther. Carl and Norman Jarrette would be leaving with Ben and Luther in two days to join up with Quantrill's band of guerrillas. They were meeting with Carl and Norman to make their final preparations. One of Quantrill's men would be there to instruct them on procedures. James Henry knew Buford was considering joining the pro-Confederates, but as yet James Henry had not committed himself.

It was midafternoon, and the weather was extremely warm, causing Paul Stewart to seek shade on his front porch. Using his hat as a fan, he waved it in front of his face as he sat on the porch steps. Detecting approaching horses, he figured James Henry and the others were returning. Slowly he got to his feet, but listening closely, he realized the horses were coming from the wrong direction. Suddenly five riders charged from the woods, their horses running at a breakneck speed. Distinguishing their dress, Paul stepped off the porch to greet them. He could see that one of the riders was slouched over his horse and barely able to stay in the saddle.

Their horses stirring up loose dirt, the riders reined them to an abrupt stop. "Mr. Stewart!" the one in the lead called.

Recognizing him as one of the neighboring boys, Paul ran to the group of men. "What's wrong, Ralph?" he asked.

"Wade's been shot!" Ralph answered breathlessly. "We had a skirmish with some Feds, and Wade's hurt too badly to make it to the Jarrettes'. Can we leave him here?"

"Of course!" Paul answered automatically, willing to risk his own well-being to protect Wade.

Anne had heard the riders arrival and had rushed from the house, recognizing Wade. Quickly she was at her father's side, helping to assist Wade from the saddle.

Grabbing the reins to Wade's horse, Ralph said in haste, "We'll take his horse with us, so the Feds can't trace Wade to you. As soon as possible, find

84

Wade a place to hide out. Don't wait too long, Mr. Stewart! The Feds are close behind us!'' In a flash, the young guerrillas were gone as suddenly as they had appeared.

Paul and Anne helped Wade up to the loft, giving him Ben's bed. Examining the wound to his shoulder, they were relieved to find it wasn't as serious as they had at first believed. Fortunately, although the bullet had passed through and there had been a considerable loss of blood, he was still conscious. As Anne finished bandaging his shoulder, he said to Paul, "It's too risky for me to be here. You've got to take me to the woods and hide me out."

"No!" Anne objected. "You're too weak to be moved!"

Taking her hand, he told her gently, "Sweetheart, my being here puts all of you in danger." Wade was a handsome man, his hair a dark brown. He preferred to be clean-shaven, but in the bush he had had little opportunity to shave, so a full beard covered his face. He placed her hand to his lips, whispering, "I love you, Anne. If anything were to happen to you because of me, I couldn't stand it."

"I'll saddle my horse," Paul began, "and take you into the woods, then tell your folks where you are. Are you able to ride?"

"I can make it," Wade answered hastily. "Hurry, Mr. Stewart! You've got to get me out of here! Damn it, Ralph should never have brought me here in the first place!"

Becky was standing in the doorway, her eyes open wide with fright. Noticing her, Paul said lightly, "You can come with me, honey, and help me saddle my horse.''

Crossing the room, Paul suddenly heard the sounds of horses galloping into the yard. He grabbed Becky's hand, and together, they fled down the loft steps.

Terrified, Anne knelt beside the bed, clutching at Wade's hand. Wade didn't fear losing his own life, but he feared for Anne's. ''Sweetheart,'' he said tensely, ''whatever happens, don't get involved. They won't hurt you, if you stay out of the way.''

''Maybe they aren't Federals!'' she moaned. ''Oh please, please God, don't let them be Federals!''

Taking Becky with him, Paul rushed to the front window. Looking outside, he saw the dreaded sight of blue uniforms. Grasping Becky by the shoulders, he ordered, ''Run out the back door and hide in the barn. And don't come out until I call you!''

Becky had been a witness to the Feds' whipping of Luther, and since that day she had acquired an extreme fear of all men wearing blue uniforms. Her heart began pounding rapidly, and she was finding it difficult to breathe.

For a moment, Paul was afraid that she would go into convulsions. But turning quickly, she ran to the back of the house and out to the barn.

Going to the door, Paul flung it open. Standing proudly, he greeted the Union troops without flinching an eye. He watched as the twelve troopers dismounted. The officer in charge and five of his men barged up the porch steps and into the house.

''What is the meaning of this intrusion!'' Paul demanded.

Shoving him aside, the officer ordered his men,

"Search the house!"

Two soldiers hurried up the loft steps. Paul grieved for his oldest daughter. He knew the officer would probably order Wade to be taken from the house and shot.

"Up here!" one of the soldiers called out.

Immediately the officer rushed up the stairs. Slowly, Paul climbed the steps behind him, hating the Union a little more with each step he took.

Entering the loft, the officer smiled cleverly. Desperate to save Wade's life, Anne hurried to the officer. "Please!" she begged. "Don't hurt him! He's been wounded!"

Using his good arm for leverage, Wade sat up on the bed, leaning back against the headboard. "Anne!" he called. "Stay away from that damned, low-down, dirty sonofabitchin' Jayhawker!"

His stride slow and smooth, the officer moved to the foot of the bed. Pausing, he looked at Wade with an expression of pure hate. "You goddamned Missouri piece of scum," he sneered. "I'm goin' to enjoy blowing your brains out, personally!"

"Well, at least I have brains. That's more than I can say for you Yankees!" Wade replied, unafraid to die.

Standing in the open doorway, Paul regarded Wade admiringly, proud that he had almost become a member of his family.

"Where are the others?" the officer demanded.

"What others?" Wade asked innocently.

"The rest of you Missouri mules!" the officer replied, smirking.

"They're out there in the brush, gettin' ready to

kick all you Yankees' asses straight to hell!'' Wade retorted.

Stepping into the room, Paul said, ''Anne, come with me!''

Panicking, she yelled, ''No!'' Her heart thumping wildly, she fled to Wade. Anne didn't see the officer drawing his pistol, but Wade did, and urgently he shouted, ''Anne, stay back!''

It all happened so fast that not even the officer realized what had taken place until it was all over.

Sheltering the man she loved, Anne had thrown her body over Wade's at the same instant the revolver discharged. The bullet that had been meant for Wade struck Anne in the side of the head, killing her.

Wade had only enough time to call her name, before Captain Jason Bishop shot him between the eyes, silencing him forever.

The two soldiers gasped with disbelief, but, not caring that he had shot a woman, Captain Bishop sneered, ''Well, I guess that will teach these Missouri rebels not to mess with the Union Army!''

Swerving quickly, he left the loft, his two men following hastily. Left alone, Paul Stewart was numb with shock and grief. Tears rolled from his eyes, and down his face, as, trembling, he stared at his daughter and Wade sprawled on the bed. Both of them were now dead, with Anne's delicate body lying pathetically across her beloved's. Their blood mingled as it dripped soundlessly onto the white sheets.

The voice from outside carried into the house, ''Search the barn!''

Paul's sudden cry filled the deadly quiet of the loft, "Becky!"

Crazed with shock and grief, he fled from the room. He stumbled on the steps, and, losing his balance, he fell down the steep stairway. His head hit the floor solidly, the hard blow almost knocking him unconscious. Tense minutes passed before he was able to get back to his feet. Holding his hand to his head to blot the flow of blood, he hastened to the back of the house and outside.

The barn faced the rear of the house, and Paul began running toward it. There was a bare window in the barn loft for ventilation, and, glancing up, he could see Becky backing up towards it as a soldier cautiously approached her.

Freezing, Paul yelled, "Becky, stop! He won't hurt you!"

Becky had heard the shots in the house, and that coupled with her terror of blue uniforms caused the child to be terrified. The young soldier turned away, worried that she would fall, but Becky continued backing straight toward the open window.

Afraid for her safety, the soldier warned, "Little girl, stop!"

"Becky!" Paul shouted. "Becky, stop!"

Becky was too frightened to heed the soldier's warning, or her father's, and blindly the child stepped back into thin air, plunging to her death.

Paul's mournful outcry was so powerful it caused the birds in the surrounding woods to screech loudly. Startled, they flew from their nests, flying wildly around the cluster of trees.

Paul ran to his daughter. Kneeling beside her lifeless body, he lifted her into his arms. Her head dangled unnaturally. "Oh God!" he groaned. "Her neck! Oh God, her neck is broken!" He rocked the child back and forth, tears once again streaming down his face.

The young soldier ran from the barn and to the front yard to rejoin the others. That the child had fallen made him feel sick, but God, he had tried to warn her, hadn't he? It wasn't his fault!

Gently, Paul laid his daughter back on the ground. His grief driving him mad, he went back into the house. Going straight to the pantry, where he kept his rifle hidden behind the flour barrel, he grabbed the weapon.

Paul Stewart had no coherent thought as he stalked through the house and out to the front porch. The soldiers had mounted and were preparing to leave. Before anyone could stop him, Paul aimed his rifle and shot the man nearest him. The young soldier who had been in the barn fell from his horse, dead.

Paul never had a chance to fire a second time. Drawing his revolver, Captain Bishop shot him in the chest. Dropping his rifle, Paul collapsed to the porch.

Two troopers dismounted, and placed the body of their dead comrade across his horse. Quickly remounting, they and the other soldiers rode away from Paul Stewart's home, leaving a deathly silence behind them.

James Henry rose from the step to go back into the hotel, but suddenly, his grief hit him strongly. Doubling his hand into a fist, he slammed it against the porch railing. ''Bishop, you bastard!'' he raged. ''You goddamned murdering bastard!''

NINE

Jason had been gone three weeks, and with her husband temporarily out of her life Amelia quickly became light-hearted and buoyant. She faced each new day with a smile because she had spent the previous night in bed alone, without Jason's pawing at her and invading her body.

Her days were full and busy. Being Captain Bishop's wife, she was always obliged to attend social functions, and often she visited with her aunt, Cynthia, and other friends.

Returning to the hotel from one of her afternoon social engagements, Amelia bustled into the lobby. Her steps were lively, and her mood was gay. She was looking forward to an early dinner and retiring to her rooms with a good book. She would indulge herself in a hot, relaxing bath, then lie on her large bed and read herself to sleep.

Her long skirts swayed with her sprightly gait as she hurried to the lobby desk. She had expected to see Mr. Cramer, but, surprised, she saw Jamie.

Amelia's turquoise-blue eyes twinkled happily as

she smiled at Jamie. "Good afternoon," she said, her voice chipper.

James Henry's eyes hadn't left her from the moment she had entered the lobby. He had seen her often since her husband left town. But she was always so busy and preoccupied he never had the opportunity to say more to her than a quick hello.

"Good afternoon, ma'am," he said.

"Do I have any mail?" she inquired.

Turning, James Henry checked the mail rack, but the Bishops' cubbyhole was empty. Facing her again, he replied, "No, ma'am."

Her face glowing attractively, Amelia questioned, "When did you start watching the front desk?"

"I started today," he answered.

Smiling pertly, she asked, "It's much better than scrubbing floors, isn't it?"

Her smile was so charming, James Henry had an overwhelming desire to lean across the desk and kiss the lips that were so innocently driving him wild. "Yes, ma'am," he answered, keeping his tone even. "It's better than moppin' floors."

Tilting her head, Amelia studied Jamie. Oh, he's such a handsome man, she thought. She wondered how he would look if he weren't wearing his farmer's overalls but was dressed stylishly. Yes, he would make a dashing figure of a man. And even more handsome than Jason, she suddenly decided. Because Jamie would be rugged and masculine, whereas Jason is refined and elegant.

Shocked at herself for mentally comparing Jamie to her husband, she stammered, "May I have my key, please?"

Taking the key from the rack behind the desk, James Henry placed it in her palm, letting his hand remain over hers.

Amelia gazed down at their hands, and she was a little amazed at how small hers were compared to his. Strangely, Amelia could feel her pulse beginning to race, and although she knew she should remove her hand, she left it under his. Gently, he took her fingers and folded them over the key that was resting in her palm. His touch was tender, yet, for some unexplainable reason, she had never been more aware of his blatant maleness.

"Your key, Mrs. Bishop," James Henry said softly.

Composing herself, Amelia stepped back from the desk, and, smiling briefly, she replied, "Good day, Jamie." Turning swiftly, she walked away.

Leaning against the desk, James Henry watched her as she climbed the stairs to her rooms. When she disappeared out of his sight, he checked the lobby. Seeing that it was empty, he reached into the desk drawer, taking out Mr. Cramer's bottle of bourbon. Opening it, he tilted the bottle to his mouth, helping himself to a generous drink. Replacing the cap, he returned it to the desk.

Turning, he looked back at the stairs, and staring at the spot where Amelia had disappeared he swore under his breath, "Tonight, Mrs. Bishop! By God, it'll be tonight!"

As Amelia opened her bedroom window to let in the refreshing evening breeze, she yawned. The hot bath she'd had earlier plus two hours of reading had made her extremely sleepy. Walking to the bed, she slipped off the pink dressing gown. Placing it across a nearby chair, she yawned again.

Smiling contentedly, she drew back the covers, and, lifting the long hem on her sheer nightgown, she sat on the edge of the bed. Leaning over, she turned off the lamp on the night table. Lying down, Amelia covered herself with only a sheet, and, turning over, she snuggled her face into her pillow, totally unaware that downstairs in the Tylers' living quarters there was a man named James Henry Stewart, who had every intention of soon joining her in her bed.

James Henry was lying on his bed with his arms crossed under his head, staring at the ceiling. Although his expression was calm, his thoughts were turbulent. He would wait at least two more hours, he decided. He had to be sure she'd be asleep. He couldn't take the chance that she might see him entering her room.

Sitting up, he moved to the edge of the bed. He had exchanged his overalls for black pants and a blue shirt. The shirt was unbuttoned, revealing a mass of dark hair that grew abundantly across his chest and tapered down to his waist.

Reaching into his pocket, he brought out a gold watch. It was a pocket watch that his father had given him years before. It had once belonged to James Henry's grandfather. Opening it, he checked the time. Under the lid was a miniature picture of Anne. For a long time, he gazed down at the picture. Then suddenly, with his fingers tightening their hold on the watch, he snapped it shut. Quickly he shoved it back into his pocket.

"Anne," he groaned aloud. Leaning over, he placed his arms across his knees. Gazing down at the bare floor, his thoughts turned back to the day he and his brothers had ridden back to the farm after their visit to the Jarrettes'.

Before reaching the Stewarts' home, Buford had decided to ride into town, leaving the three brothers to journey the rest of the way by themselves.

As they rode past the trampled corn field, James Henry was the first one to notice their father. His whole body grew rigid, and sitting straight in the saddle, he arched his neck to get a better view.

Their gazes following James Henry's gaze, Ben and Luther were confronted with the sight of their father sprawled on the porch.

The veins in Luther's neck protruded, as fiercely he cried, "Pa! . . . Pa!"

Quickly the brothers broke their horses into a run, heading speedily to the house. Entering the yard, James Henry leaped from his mount before the animal had a chance to come to a complete stop. Swiftly he bounded up the porch steps. As he knelt beside his father, he prayed he would find a sign of life, but gazing down into Paul Stewart's sightless eyes, James Henry knew he was dead.

Running wildly, Luther stumbled up the steps. Collapsing to his knees, he took his father into his arms. Hugging the lifeless body, he groaned, "Pa! . . . Oh God, Pa!"

Gently, James Henry pulled their father from Luther's embrace. Climbing the steps, Ben knelt beside

Luther and took him into his arms. He pressed his younger brother's head tightly against his chest.

Lightly, James Henry brushed his fingers over his father's eyes, closing them forever. The initial shock passing, James Henry suddenly stiffened. Looking at Ben, he cried, "Anne and Becky!"

The man in Luther overcame the boy, and composing himself, he jumped to his feet along with his older brothers.

"Luther," James Henry commanded, "search the barn, Ben take the downstairs, and I'll look in the loft!"

Running into the house, James Henry took the loft steps in three bounding strides. As he rushed anxiously through the open doorway, his long steps came to an abrupt and awkward stop.

Usually, James Henry was a quiet man, and unemotional, keeping his feelings to himself. But as his vision fell upon his sister and Wade, tears sprang to his eyes, and his voice rose to a lamenting pitch, "Oh God! . . . Anne! . . . Anne! . . . Aw, God! . . . Anne! . . ."

Shocked, James Henry crossed the room. His movements were ungainly as he slowly approached the bed, and, pausing beside it, he reached for his sister. Lifting her in his arms, he carried her to Luther's bed. Sitting, he cradled Anne's fragile body in his lap. Pressing her head to his shoulder, he rocked gently back and forth.

James Henry had never loved anyone as dearly as he loved Anne. Her gentleness and kindness had always touched his heart, even when they had been children.

Tenderly, he moved her so that he could see her face. Her eyes were closed, but even in death she was lovely. Her beauty was marred cruelly by the blood and wound to the side of her head. His hand trembling, James Henry pulled out his shirt, using it to wipe away the blood from his sister's face.

Suddenly becoming aware of a movement at his side, James Henry turned. Standing motionless, Ben stared at his brother and dead sister, an expression of cold animosity glaring in his eyes. "Jayhawkers!" Ben raged. "Goddamn Jayhawkers!"

Before James Henry could reply, they heard Luther coming up the stairs. Rising, James Henry placed Anne on the bed. He moved across the room to meet Luther, hoping he had found Becky. He was worried the child would be half-crazed with grief and shock.

Before he reached the doorway, Luther stepped into the room with Becky held in his arms. Her head and arms dangled lifelessly, and her long hair was flung across her face.

Trying to take his grief like a man, Luther fought back tears as he moaned, "They killed her! Dear God, they killed our little sister!" Suddenly noticing Anne and Wade, Luther gave in to his distress, and, sobbing heavily, he cried, "NO! . . . Damn it, *no!*"

Ben turned away swiftly and, losing sensibility himself, he began hitting his fists against the wall over and over again.

Going to Luther, James Henry took Becky from his arms. Slowly, he carried the child to the bed and placed her beside Anne. For a long time, he simply stood at the bed, looking down at his sisters.

Controlling his emotions, Ben walked over to his older brother. Luther's shoulders shook with his deep sobs as he moved across the room to join James Henry and Ben.

James Henry being the oldest, the two brothers waited for him to tell them what to do, but instead, he only continued to stare at Anne and Becky.

Finally, leaning over the bed, James Henry placed a light kiss on Becky's lips, then on Anne's. Swerving, he walked over to Wade. Gently, he closed what was left of Wade's lifeless eyes.

Moving quickly, James Henry suddenly turned toward his brothers. His voice was strong and authoritative, "Luther, ride over to the Jarrettes' and bring them back with you, and Ben, stay here!"

"What are you going to do?" Luther asked.

"They haven't been dead very long. Whoever did this can't be far away. I'll pick up their tracks."

"James Henry," Ben objected, "you can't go alone!"

Refusing to comment on Ben's objection, James Henry answered, "If I'm not back by morning, don't wait for me. See that they are buried next to Ma." Without further words, he left the room.

There was no need for him to stop first and arm himself. His rifle was on his horse, his Colt revolver strapped around his hips, and his knife was tucked snugly into its scabbard.

Following the Jayhawkers' tracks would be easy for James Henry; he had once lived with the Comanche, and at times he could be more Indian than white man.

Blocking that day from his mind, James Henry rose from the bed and stepped across the small room. Going to the window, he looked outside. To his relief, the night was overcast. He didn't want any moonlight filtering through Amelia's window, making it possible for her to recognize him. As a precautionary measure, if her bedroom drapes were open, he would be sure to close them.

Smiling, James Henry recalled Amelia's conversation with Mrs. Coffman. A frigid wife, was she? With the stoical Bishop to teach her the pleasures of love, he didn't doubt it for a moment.

Thinking about Captain Bishop, James Henry's smile faded. Did he want to make love to Amelia because she was Bishop's wife? Did he long to taste Amelia's sweetness, or did he simply want the sweet taste of revenge? When the moment was right, would he tell Bishop that he had bedded his wife? Was he hoping he could tell him that Amelia had enjoyed it, and that she had wantonly begged him for more? Was he only wanting to insult Bishop in the worst way before killing him? Or did Bishop have nothing to do with his compelling need to take the beautiful Amelia? He had never wanted any woman as badly as he wanted her. Damn, how he longed to run his hands through her long golden hair, to kiss her sweet lips, to caress her breasts, and finally, to part her delectable thighs and take her completely. Which force was it that drove him? Revenge or desire? Deciding he was probably driven by both compulsions, James Henry suddenly shrugged as if it were of no consequence.

Stepping to the bureau, he picked up the key to Amelia's room, slipping it into his pocket. Working at the front desk, he'd had access to all the extra keys, and borrowing the key to room 217 had been simple. Later tonight, he would return it.

Going to the bed, he lay back down. He would get a couple of hours' sleep. James Henry smiled with anticipation. If all went well he would need the rest.

TEN

It had been easy for James Henry to slip up the back stairs and move silently down the dim hallway. Mr. Cramer had retired hours before, and Buford was watching the lobby in case a late customer should arrive. James Henry knew he was supposed to relieve Buford at the front desk, and quickly he took out his watch to check the time. He still had an hour before Buford would be expecting him.

Recalling Amelia's alluring beauty, he wished to hell he had more time. But if his plan was successful, it'd be an hour of ecstatic pleasure for Amelia as well as himself.

Nearing the door to room 217, James Henry reached into his pocket, withdrawing the key. He was surprised to see how his hand slightly trembled as he quietly inserted the key into the lock. Annoyed that the innocent little Amelia could affect him so strongly, he willed himself to forget desire and concentrate on revenge. It was Bishop's wife he intended to seduce. He must never allow himself to think of her as Amelia. She was only Bishop's wife, and nothing more!

Carefully he opened the door, stepping soundlessly into the sitting room. The drapes were closed, causing the room to be dark, but the dim light from the hall shone inside. Quickly his eyes shifted to Amelia's bedroom. The door was ajar, and even though the night was overcast, a shadowy path fell across her room. Quietly he closed the hall door, remembering to relock it, then he returned the key to his pocket.

His long strides were silent as he swiftly crossed the sitting room. Entering the bedroom, he headed toward the window to draw the drapes. He glanced at the sleeping Amelia, and, admiring her guileless beauty, halted abruptly.

She was lying on her back, with her long golden hair flowing across the pillow. Slowly he moved to the bed, his gaze never leaving the lovely vision. The soft light filtering through the open window fell across Amelia, making it easy for him to see her. She looked so tiny in the huge bed that she appeared to be no more than a child. He gazed down into her face, concentrating on the long lashes curling slightly over her closed eyelids, the freckles splashed here and there across her nose, and the lips that were innocently inviting. My God, he thought, it would be more like seducing a young virgin than a married woman! Studying Amelia's simple innocence, he had a quick impulse to return to his own room. But, all at once, she turned to her side, causing the clinging sheet to outline her feminine shape. His eyes traveled over her legs, up to her hips, and then to the slight swell of her small but firm breasts. She was lovely and so damned tempting. She was no child, or virgin, but a woman who was ripe for love. And, by God, he'd taste her sweetness, if it was the last thing he ever did in his life!

Swiftly James Henry went to the window, and as he drew the heavy drapes, the room became pitch black. The path back to Amelia's bed was clear, and easily he returned to her side. It would be hell making love to her in total darkness, but he had no other choice.

He sat on the edge of the bed, and it gave a little under his weight, causing Amelia to fret slightly as she slowly returned to consciousness.

Leaning over, James Henry placed his face close to hers, finding her lips with his.

His kiss was tender, bringing Amelia back to awareness. Vaguely, her thoughts were that Jason had come home, but suddenly she became aware that the lips caressing hers were gentle, tantalizing, and so different from her husband's. Frightened, a muffled cry came from her throat as her eyes opened wide, only to find the room completely dark. She could see nothing, not even the man kissing her! She turned her head, trying to break free, but his mouth conquered hers, making escape impossible.

Blindly she struck out at him, trying to shove him away, but keeping his lips locked to hers, he quickly seized her wrists, holding her arms over her head.

Squirming, she kicked wildly, hoping desperately to force him to turn her loose. In one swift move, he stretched out beside her, and placing his body over hers, he pinned her beneath him.

Amelia had never been so terrified, and yet as his strong frame covered hers, the feel of his body flush to hers excited Amelia in a way that was strange to her.

Confused, she stopped fighting, and once again became aware of the lips that had never left hers. She relaxed, making it possible for him to pry her mouth open as his kiss grew passionate. His tongue probed between her teeth, entering her mouth intimately. He pressed himself to her thighs, and his male hardness was thrust demandingly against her.

Cautiously, he removed his lips from hers. "Mrs. Bishop, if you promise not to scream, I won't gag you," he whispered, camouflaging his voice by keeping it gruff and hoarse. Menacingly, he added, "Gags are very uncomfortable and confining. But make no mistake, madam, if it becomes necessary I will stuff a gag in your beautiful mouth." He paused, before continuing, "But, of course, a gag would make it quite difficult for me to seduce you. To take you to love's highest rapture, I'll need to have your sweet lips at my disposal."

Amelia was shocked. This can't be happening! she thought. It must be a dream, a fantasy! This man hasn't come to my room to rape me, but to seduce me! But why? . . . Why? Dumbfounded, Amelia was speechless.

Understanding her silence, he whispered teasingly, "Mrs. Bishop, would you care to say anything before I help myself to your lovely body? Or would you rather I dispensed with formalities and got on with what I came here to do?"

"Wh . . . what?" Amelia stuttered, finding her voice.

He laughed, the tone low and brusque. She listened intently, trying to identify his laughter. Had she heard it before? Obviously, the man knew her because he had called her by name.

Whispering he told her, "I hope you make love better than you make conversation, otherwise, I may fall asleep from boredom.''

His insult angered Amelia, causing her to completely forget her fear. ''You contemptible beast! If you don't leave this minute, I'll scream!''

His tone became ruthless. ''Apparently, you haven't been listening. If you try to scream, I'm going to stuff a gag down your throat. And if you are fortunate, you might not choke on it!''

Her fear returning, Amelia pleaded, ''Why are you doing this? . . . Please leave me alone!'' Panicking, she tossed her head, begging, ''Don't hurt me! . . . Please! . . . Please!''

Soothingly, he murmured, ''I won't hurt you, Mrs. Bishop. I only want you to relax and give me a chance to awaken your passion. Later, if you still want me to leave, then I will. And I promise you, you won't be molested.''

Hopeful, she asked, ''I won't be hurt or . . . or violated?''

''I didn't come here to rape you,'' he answered calmly.

''Then why are you here?'' she cried.

''To try and seduce you,'' he replied, remembering to keep his voice disguised.

Desperately, Amelia tried to rationalize her turbulent thoughts. If she didn't respond to him, he would not force himself on her. All he wanted was a chance to make her want him, but if he failed, he would leave. It would be insulting and degrading to lie passively and let this man fondle her, but she would survive his detestable ministrations. She certainly wouldn't surrender to passion, because she hated a man pawing at her and brutalizing her lips with his. Yes, it would be best to yield to his wishes. If she refused to comply, it could anger him, and then he might do all kinds of terrible things to her.

Her voice trembling, Amelia pleaded, "I won't fight, if you promise not to hurt me."

Softly, he answered, "I don't want to hurt you, I only want to love you. You are so beautiful that you are driving me wild with desire."

Amelia was astounded. Why, this man she couldn't see, couldn't identify, was actually whispering endearments to her that she had always longed in vain to hear from her husband.

Carefully, James Henry released her wrists. Resigned, she moved her arms to her side. Taking her hand, he raised it to his lips, kissing it gently. She could feel his beard, and she tried to picture all the men she had seen in town who wore beards. But there were so many that it was an impossible task.

Slowly James Henry placed one of her fingers between his lips, moving it back and forth across his tongue. Amelia was startled by his sensual gesture, but she made no attempt to pull her hand free.

"I want to make love to you," he murmured, as his lips began to trail over her fingers.

Amelia could feel a strange sensation stimulating her senses. She couldn't quite understand what was happening to her, but she knew it was being caused by the warm lips gently touching her fingers that seemed to have the power to send exciting chills through her entire being.

Releasing her hand, he placed his face next to hers. Tenderly, he whispered, "I'm going to kiss you, and when I do, I want you to put your arms around my neck. Don't be afraid. Try to relax, and let me show you the ecstasy that can be found in a kiss.''

Very slowly, his lips touched hers. When she made no move to hold him, he took her arm and placed it about his neck. Then taking her into his embrace, he gently pried her mouth open with his own.

He kissed her softly, then he paused, keeping his lips as close to hers as he could without touching her. Then he kissed her again, before pausing to once again tease her by removing his lips from hers. He continued to kiss her in this fashion, until finally Amelia found herself anticipating his next kiss.

Amelia wasn't aware of how her hold had tightened about his neck, or that she had placed her other arm around him.

Feeling her respond, his kiss deepened. Lingering, he parted her lips and his tongue entered to explore her mouth. Entwining her fingers in his hair, she pressed him even closer, accepting his kiss completely.

Gently he moved his hand to her breast. His intimate touch brought Amelia back to her senses. Stiffening, she attempted to push away from him, but aggressively he locked his other arm around her waist. With his lips still on hers, he caressed her breast. Groaning, she tried to object, but he ignored her protest.

Placing his lips close to Amelia's ear, he murmured, ''Relax, little one, and let me love you.''

Once again his mouth was on hers, demanding her response. Amelia's conscience screamed at her to remain coldly passive, but for the first time in her life her passion was being awakened, and, against her own volition, she returned his kiss.

109

Raising up, he moved to her side. Oh, how she wished she could see this man who was making her feel so strange but so wonderful!

He drew back the sheet, then quickly he lifted her nightgown. Before she could utter a protest, he pulled her to a sitting position, removing the garment in one swift move. Easing her back down, he dropped the gown to the floor.

"No!" Amelia cried, as instinctively she grabbed for the sheet to cover herself.

Catching her hands in his, James Henry stretched out his long frame beside her. Placing one leg over hers, he held her to the bed. She thought he would again hold her arms over her head, but instead, he wrapped them about his neck as he began kissing her.

Easily, James Henry aroused her response, and, forgetting her reservations, Amelia kissed him back with a passion that came to her naturally.

His lips traveled to her neck, then down to the hollow of her throat, making Amelia moan with pleasure. Lowering his head, he found her breast, and his tongue circled her nipple, sending Amelia's pulse racing with desire.

"My little one, you're so warm and so beautiful," he groaned. Parting her legs, he placed himself on top of her. She could feel his hard erection pushed against her. She arched her thighs, wanting to get closer to him. Putting his hands under her hips, he lifted her until his manhood was pressed to her tightly, making her realize how good it could feel to have a man's hardness thrust between her legs.

Once more, his lips were on hers, and, hungrily, Amelia received his kiss.

Hoarsely, he whispered, "This is as far as I go. If I go any farther, I'll not be able to abide by my promise not to rape you."

"You're not leaving?" she cried, without thinking.

"It's up to you, sweetheart. If you want me to leave, then I will. But if I stay one moment longer, I'm going to take off my clothes and then make love to you completely."

Without waiting for a reply, he raised up, and instantly she missed the feel of him. Going against everything she believed in, Amelia pleaded, "Don't leave me!" James Henry couldn't see the tears that sprang to her eyes, as she cried, "I need you!"

"Aw, God!" he groaned, as his mouth came down on hers. Their kiss grew intense, causing Amelia to boldly pull him to her tightly.

Breaking their kiss, he said hastily, "I'll get undressed."

Quickly, he rose from the bed, and impatiently he began removing his clothes.

Amelia waited anxiously for him to return to her side. Her religious convictions and marriage vows were temporarily forgotten. She was conscious of nothing except an overwhelming desire to be in this man's arms.

Feeling the bed give under his weight, she reached for him. Taking her into his embrace, James Henry's frame covered hers. Willingly, she opened her legs, ready for him to take her to the ecstasy she now knew was awaiting for her.

As his mouth came down on hers, he penetrated her swiftly and deeply, causing Amelia to cry out softly.

"Are you all right, little one?" he asked tenderly.

"Oh yes!" she murmured, his entry making her tremble with longing.

"Put your legs around me," he whispered.

"Wh . . . what?" she stuttered, confused. Jason had never asked her to do such a thing.

"Put your legs around my back," he repeated patiently.

Although the request seemed unusual to Amelia, she complied. The position caused him to enter her more deeply, and, finding herself enjoying his deeper penetration, she locked her ankles firmly across his back.

"Now, little one," he began, "together we shall climb to love's highest peak."

Wanting to please Amelia, James Henry showed her how to match his rhythm, and, releasing her inhibitions, she followed his example, allowing herself to experience all the pleasures of love.

James Henry's passion grew intense, and with her own need building, Amelia met his demanding thrusts time and time again.

Climaxing, James Henry jerked her to him roughly. Moaning with satisfaction, she held her thighs against his as a tingling chill ran up and down her spine.

She thought he would immediately roll to his side, as Jason always had, but instead, he remained inside her. Tenderly, his lips found hers, and his hand gently caressed her breasts.

"Little one," he whispered, "making love to you has been wonderful."

Breathlessly, she demanded, "Who are you?"

"A secret admirer," he answered.

She tried to place her hand on his face to trace his features, but quickly he halted her. "No, you must never know who I am," he warned.

"But why?" she pleaded.

"I can't explain why," he replied, his voice remaining disguised.

"It isn't fair!" Amelia cried. "I have been closer to you than I have ever been to anyone, and I don't even know who you are! Dear Lord, I can't believe this is happening to me!"

"Believe it, little one," he chuckled, shoving his thighs against hers.

Soothingly, she ran her hand across his back and down to his smooth and muscular buttocks. Pressing him even closer, she murmured, "I believe it!" She sighed happily, adding, "Oh, how well I believe it!"

He began to move inside her, and she could feel him growing hard. She didn't know it was possible for a man to go twice, and, surprised, she exclaimed, "Again?"

He laughed. "You're damned right!"

Their lovemaking came to them slowly and gently, before climbing to its peak. Afterwards, Amelia was exhausted, for she had equaled James Henry's passion.

Placing her head on his shoulder, she snuggled close. "Tomorrow this will all seem like a dream," she whispered.

"A very beautiful dream," he replied.

Embarrassing herself, she stammered, "Is this . . . is this the only time we will be together?" She was shocked by her own boldness. What kind of mastery did this man have over her?

Rising, he answered, "I don't know."

"Are you going?" she cried.

Leaving the bed, he began to put on his clothes, finding the chore a little difficult in the dark. "I did what I came here to do," he replied.

"Seduce me?" she asked. Not waiting for a reply, she said harshly, "You make it all seem so cold and formal!"

"Cold and formal?" he questioned. "I didn't find it that way at all." He sat on the edge of the bed, putting on his boots. "Go back to sleep, Mrs. Bishop."

"Sleep!" she spat. "How can I sleep after . . . after what has happened?"

Chuckling, he leaned over, placing a light kiss on her lips. "Goodnight, little one."

Swiftly, before she could attempt to stop him, he moved quietly out of the bedroom. She heard the door to the sitting room open and then close.

Leaping from the bed, she lit the lamp on the night table. Hurrying to the wardrobe, she took out a dress. Going to the bureau, she grabbed her underclothes out of the drawer. As quickly as she could, she slipped into her clothes. Stepping into her shoes, she fled from the bedroom, running through the sitting room and out to the hall.

Hastily she descended the stairs, rushing to the lobby. Buford was seated behind the desk, and hearing someone approaching he got to his feet. Noting Mrs. Bishop's disheveled hair and flushed face, he asked urgently, "Is something wrong, ma'am?"

"Mr. Tyler," she began breathlessly, "did . . . did you see a man leaving the hotel?"

"Now?" he asked.

"Yes, now!" she snapped. Composing herself, she added, "Well, I mean a few minutes ago."

"No, ma'am," he answered. "I haven't seen any-one."

"How could he just disappear?" she cried irratio-nally.

"Has there been some kind of trouble, Mrs. Bish-op?" Buford asked.

Exasperated, she rubbed her hand across her warm brow. "Trouble? she asked vaguely. "No . . . no there's been no trouble."

He started to question her further when the back door to the lobby swung open and Jamie entered. He was dressed in his usual overalls and faded shirt.

"Jamie!" Amelia cried. "Were you at the back of the hotel?"

"Yes, ma'am," he answered.

"Did you see anyone go out the rear door?" she asked.

"Yes, I did," he lied, knowing it would be best to let her believe her admirer had slipped out the back door.

"A man?" she asked sharply.

"Yes'm," he nodded.

"Did you recognize him?" she asked quickly.

Shaking his head, he answered, "I only saw him from the back."

"How was he dressed?"

"He was wearing an army uniform."

"Uniform?" she repeated.

"Yes, ma'am," he replied.

Turning, Amelia began heading back to the stair-way. Apparently the mystery man was a soldier. A friend of Jason's perhaps?

Placing her hand on the banister, she climbed the

115

steps very slowly. Would she ever learn his identity? Or would she go the rest of her life longing for a man she had never seen?

When Amelia disappeared at the top of the stairs, Buford turned to James Henry. "You didn't see any man leaving this hotel!" he remarked gruffly.

Sauntering to Buford, James Henry leaned his elbows on the desk, commenting casually, "I had a feeling she'd come down here looking for her secret admirer."

"Damn it, James Henry! What have you been up to?"

Raising his eyebrows, he smiled shrewdly. "Need you ask?"

"It's because she's Bishop's wife, isn't it?"

"Maybe," he answered.

"Stay away from her!" Buford fumed.

Recalling how much he had enjoyed making love to Amelia, he replied honestly, "I don't know if I can."

Understanding James Henry's expression, Buford warned, "You don't want to start caring about her, James Henry, because if you do, she'll get you killed!"

Sitting behind the lobby desk, James Henry relaxed with a bottle of whiskey. A tender smile crossed his face as he thought about Amelia. He wondered if she would have trouble tonight falling asleep. It was just as well that he had to watch the front desk, because he knew if he were in bed thoughts of Amelia would be keeping him awake. His smile suddenly vanishing, he took a large swig of whiskey. What in the hell was wrong with him? His reason for being in Lawrence was vitally important. Too damned important for him to endanger his mission by becoming involved with Bishop's wife.

Purposely dismissing Amelia from his mind, he turned his thoughts instead to the day he had trailed the Union Troops from his father's farm.

Captain Bishop had ordered three of his men to take the soldier who had been fatally wounded back across the Kansas border. When James Henry came upon the set of tracks separating, he chose to follow the ones made by four horses. He planned to confront the soldiers, and confronting the smaller group of Jayhawkers would be child's play for an experienced man like James Henry.

The three soldiers had stopped to rest their horses and eaten a cold meal from their bland field rations. Remaining in the small clearing, they decided to have a smoke before continuing on to their destination. Sitting side by side, they leaned against the trunk of a tree, relaxing as they talked.

Quietly, James Henry dismounted. Moving with the silence of an Indian, he took off his boots to quiet his steps, then swiftly he slipped out of his shirt. He knew how easily a shirt could snag and rustle the brush, announcing his arrival as surely as if he had sent a calling card. Placing it across the saddle, he noticed Anne's dried blood on the shirt, standing out clearly against the light blue fabric. He ran his fingers across the smeared blood, his caress as tender as if he were caressing a woman.

117

Resolutely, he erased Anne from his mind. He had to keep his thoughts clear and alert. Later, there would be a time to grieve. Taking his kerchief, he tied it around his forehead to keep the perspiration from dripping into his eyes.

James Henry could foresee no problem in sneaking up on the soldiers, but he realized their horses were an entirely different matter. He checked which way the wind was blowing, then moved soundlessly to his right, knowing the wind would send his scent in the opposite direction of the horses.

Stealthily, he circled through the woods, bringing himself up behind the three soldiers. Quietly, he stalked closer to the large tree that shaded the men sitting leisurely, smoking their cigars.

Totally unaware of the approaching danger, one soldier ground out his cigar, remarking lazily, "Well, I guess we'd better head out."

Seeing no reason to hurry, the three men got slowly to their feet. The two older ones stretched, while the younger one ground out his cigar with the heel of his boot.

James Henry leaped out of the brush so swiftly and agilely that the two men stretching froze with their arms extended over their heads, and the other soldier stood motionless.

Shocked, the three men gasped, unsure if they were being confronted by a Confederate guerrilla or a wild savage.

James Henry kept his revolver in its holster, his hand held close to the weapon. "Make one wrong move," he warned, "and it'll be your last."

"What in the hell do you want?" the oldest soldier

asked.

"A name," James Henry replied calmly.

"Whose name?" he asked.

"The officer who was in charge when you raided the Stewarts' farm." James Henry answered shortly.

The three soldiers didn't detect the group of men slipping through the surrounding brush, but James Henry knew they were there. If they were the Union, he was as good as dead, but if they were guerrillas, they would do nothing but stay back and watch.

James Henry knew the two older soldiers were contemplating drawing their pistols. He wanted to warn them not to draw, but before he had a chance, they reached quickly for their guns. James Henry pulled his Colt revolver from its holster with lightning speed, and with perfect precision he killed one soldier by sending a bullet into his chest, then, as the other one cocked his pistol, James Henry killed him in one clean shot.

Staring in disbelief, the young soldier trembled in fear as he watched his comrades fall to the ground.

Slipping his gun back into its holster, James Henry stalked to the soldier. Taking his knife from its scabbard, he grabbed the young man, and, turning him, he held the knife to his throat.

Speaking softly, James Henry warned, "We're being surrounded, and it's not the Feds, or I'd be a dead man."

The soldier didn't believe him. If there were men out in the brush, he would have heard them.

"I'll ask them to let you go free," James Henry continued. "But first, you're gonna give me some information." He moved the blade closer to the man's throat, knicking his skin fleetingly. "Give me the officer's name, and tell me what happened at the Stewarts' farm. Why did the officer in charge allow a woman, a little girl, and an old man to be killed?''

Stammering, the soldier explained, ''We attacked a band of guerrillas. They got away but . . . but we knew one of them was wounded. We thought maybe . . . they would decide to leave him somewhere, and the Stewarts' home was on our list of Southern sympathizers. So we stopped at the farm.''

Gritting his teeth, James Henry demanded, ''The officer's name?''

Becoming a traitor, the soldier stuttered, ''Cap . . . Captain Jason Bishop. He told us to search the house, so me and two others went upstairs. The man we were looking for was up there in the loft. We called the captain, and he came upstairs.''

''Why was Wade killed in bed? Why didn't Bishop take him away from the house to have him killed?''

''The guy smarted off to the captain, and before anyone knew what had happened, Captain Bishop drew his pistol. He didn't mean to kill the woman, but she flung herself across the bed just as the captain pulled the trigger.''

''Did it bother him?'' James Henry asked.

Confused, the soldier stammered, ''Wh . . . what?''

''Did it bother him to kill a woman?'' James Henry repeated, his jaws clenched tightly.

''I don't know!'' the soldier answered hastily. ''He never said anything.''

''What happened to the little girl?''

''She was in the barn, and a couple of men were searching it. She was up in the loft, and I guess she was scared, because she kept backing up toward the window. The soldier closest to her tried to get her to stop, and so did the old man. He was in the yard. But the kid just kept on backing up and then she fell.''

"How did Paul Stewart die?"

"After the girl fell, I guess he went berserk. He ran into the house, and as we were getting ready to ride off, he came to the porch with a rifle. He shot one of us, then Captain Bishop killed him.''

Brusquely, James Henry released him. Now all the pieces fell into place. If Captain Bishop had behaved like a gentleman and an officer, Wade would have been taken from the house to be killed, and Anne would still be alive. His father and Becky? He believed their deaths could have been prevented if Captain Bishop had behaved as befitted an officer.

Slowly, James Henry moved away from the soldier. He knew their hidden audience would be making its sudden appearance at any moment. He hoped he could talk them into letting the youngster go free, but he seriously doubted it.

James Henry turned his back to the soldier, and because the young man didn't believe they were surrounded by guerrillas, he reached for his gun.

James Henry didn't have to see him going for his revolver to be aware it was happening. His instincts were as alert as an Indian's. He could sense it, he could feel it, and spinning on his heels, he sent his knife soaring through the air. Sharply, it penetrated the soldier's shoulder, and, dropping his pistol, he feel to his knees.

Returning to him, James Henry pulled out his knife, wiping the blood on the soldier's shirt. Groaning, the wounded man took his handkerchief, pressing it tightly to his bleeding shoulder.

Slipping his knife back into its scabbard, James Henry glanced around at the surrounding brush. "Gentlemen," he began strongly, "the show is over!"

"And a most entertaining one," a deep voice answered, as, standing, two men materialized from the thick brush. They were immediately followed by a small group of men, and then dozens of riders appeared from the dense woods.

The two men approached James Henry. They were both wearing Confederate uniforms. The one who had spoken continued, "Whom do we have the pleasure of addressing? A fellow Confederate, or a wild savage?"

James Henry smiled appeasingly at the older man. Minus shoes, shirt, and wearing a headband, he knew he probably did resemble a savage. "The name is James Henry Stewart," he replied.

The two men paused, studying him closely. "I am Colonel Garson," the man proceeded, "and this is William Quantrill."

"Stewart?" Quantrill pondered. "Are you kin to Paul Stewart?"

James Henry regarded the notorious guerrilla. He was tall and slim. His complexion was fair, and his hair and moustache blond with a reddish tint. He was an imposing figure, but his shifty eyes and stern lips revealed the latent cruelty beneath the man's well-mannered composure.

"Paul Stewart was my father," James Henry replied.

"Was?" Quantrill questioned.

"He's dead," James Henry answered unemotionally.

"I'm sorry to hear that. One of my men is engaged to your sister."

"Was engaged," James Henry corrected. Quickly he told the two men what had happened at the farm, explaining his reason for following the three Jayhawkers. Remembering the young soldier, he asked Quantrill to let him go free.

"Why should I?" Quantrill smirked.

"Why not?" James Henry remarked. "He's only a kid."

Amused, Quantrill answered, "Look around you, Mr. Stewart. Look closely at my men. Most of them are between the ages of sixteen and twenty. There are no kids in the Confederacy or the Union Army."

James Henry shrugged. The young soldier was as good as dead. He would liked to have saved him, but there wasn't a damned thing he could do. Turning, his eyes scanned the riders who had now completely circled the three of them and the wounded soldier. The majority of the guerrillas were too young to grow beards. They wore their hair long, some of them having let it grow to shoulder length. Mounted on fine horses, they wore "guerrilla shirts," and all of them were armed with Colt revolving pistols. Regardless of their youth, they made an awesome and threatening appearance.

"Mr. Stewart," Quantrill began, "your brothers are joining my band of Pro-Confederates. Will you be accompanying them?"

James Henry was hesitant about answering, but Quantrill was quite certain he understood his reason for refusing to commit himself. He could sense the man's dislike, but he needed men like James Henry

123

Stewart. Casually, he continued, "You'll never find Captain Bishop if you leave Missouri. If you desert your brothers, you'll be leaving them to avenge your father and sisters without you."

"Mr. Stewart," Colonel Garson spoke up strongly. "when your brothers rendezvous with Quantrill, be with them!"

Glaring at the colonel, James Henry said angrily, "I'm not one of your guerrillas! So don't give me orders!"

Explaining, Colonel Garson answered, "I am a colonel in the Confederate Army."

"Then what are you doing here?" James Henry asked.

"I am here on military business."

"Why do you want me to be at the rendezvous?"

The colonel smiled pleasantly. "Mr. Stewart, may I ask you a personal question?"

James Henry had no dislike for Colonel Garson, so he replied cordially, "Sure, as long as the question is just between the two of us."

Quantrill wasn't offended. That a man like James Henry Stewart resented him didn't bother him in the least. For every man who distrusted him, he had fifty who worshipped him. Bowing to the colonel, he said briskly, "Excuse me."

Leaving the two men alone, Quantrill walked to the wounded soldier, deciding to question him before having him shot.

"What's the question?" James Henry asked the colonel.

"Obviously, you have reservations about joining up with your brothers to fight for western Missouri. So

124

tell me, Mr. Stewart, exactly what are your plans?''

''Before my family was killed, I was planning to ride to Arkansas and join the Confederate Army.''

''And now?'' he asked.

James Henry studied the man closely. He appeared to be in his late forties. He was short and stockily built. He wore a full-length brown beard.

''I don't know what my plans are,'' James Henry answered honestly.

''If you had planned to join the Confederacy, why did you wait?''

''I was living out west,'' James Henry replied.

''Mr. Stewart, I want you to be at that rendezvous.''

''Will you be there?''

''Yes, and it is imperative that I talk to you.''

Skeptically, James Henry questioned, ''Does this have to with Quantrill's band or the Confederate Army?''

The colonel waited a moment before replying, then looking James Henry straight in the eyes, he said firmly, ''The Army of the Confederate States!''

Nodding, James Henry answered, ''I'll be there.''

''Thank you,'' the colonel replied sincerely.

''Now, if you'll excuse me,'' James Henry began soberly, ''I'm needed at home.''

''Of course,'' the colonel said quickly. ''And, Mr. Stewart, you and your brothers have my deepest sympathy.''

''Thank you,'' James Henry answered, walking away from him and toward the men still mounted on their horses. But the guerrillas made no attempt to move so that he could pass through.

William Quantrill stopped questioning the soldier to

turn and look at James Henry. For a brief moment their eyes met, and their mutual dislike for each other was obvious. Then, smiling, Quantrill ordered, ''Let this man pass!''

James Henry took one last look at the young soldier before leaving. He knew he would always remember the naked fear on the boy's face. He felt sorry for him, but as his thoughts returned to his father and sisters, the soldier faded from his mind.

As James Henry rode away, the colonel stepped over to Quantrill. Heartily, the colonel announced, ''Mr. Stewart is the kind of man I've been searching for!''

ELEVEN

It was past noon when Amelia finally awakened. The night before, her troubled thoughts had kept her awake until dawn.

Stretching, Amelia came slowly back to awareness. Turning to her side, she snuggled her face into her pillow. Her eyelids fluttered open, and noticing how the sun was shining across the room, she was amazed that she had slept so late. Her thoughts muddled, she looked toward the window. Puzzled, she wondered why the drapes were drawn farther back than usual.

Coming wide awake, she bolted straight up. The drapes! He had closed them, but before falling asleep she had reopened them!

Limply, she fell back on the bed. Dear Lord, it had happened! It had really happened! A man had come to her room and seduced her!

Her face growing flushed, her thoughts continued as she remembered how she had shamelessly responded. "Oh, how could I?" Amelia groaned. Tears filled her eyes, and, sobbing, she jerked the sheet up to her chin.

"What's wrong with me?" she gasped. Mortified, she gave in to her distress, and burying her face into the pillow, she cried.

Finally her tears subsided. Sniffling, Amelia sat up slowly, moving to the edge of the bed. She walked to the dresser and studied her reflection in the mirror.

Her long hair was mussed, and her eyes were red and swollen, but, peering closer, Amelia intuitively sensed there was something very different about her. It wasn't visible to the eye, but, all the same, it was there.

Inhaling deeply, she took a step backwards as her hand flew to her face. "I'm a woman who has known a man's love!" she cried. "I look different because, at last, I have experienced fulfillment! I gave love, and I received it!"

Her tears once again flowing, Amelia returned to the bed and sat on the edge. Oh, how would she ever endure Jason's clumsy fondling, now that she knew how beautiful love could truly be?

"It isn't fair!" she groaned. "Why? Why did he come to my room? If I had never experienced love, then I would never have known what I've missed!"

Will he return? she wondered. Is this it? Will I encounter complete fulfillment only once in my lifetime?

Standing, she began pacing the floor. Who is he? How did he get into my room? The door wasn't tinkered with. So how did he get in? I must have forgotten to secure the door, she decided. Unless he has a key! But how could he come by a key? No . . . no, I must have forgotten to lock up.

Concentrating deeply, she tried to recall if she had locked the door before retiring, but she couldn't be sure.

Slowly Amelia walked to the wardrobe, removing a dress. She began to put on her clothes, while her thoughts raced back to the night before. Is he handsome? Somehow, she instinctively knew that he was. Is his hair light or dark? Dark, she quickly decided. He is tall, dark, and handsome, Amelia concluded romantically. He's better-looking than Jason or Lieutenant Coffman. He's the handsomest man in town!

Suddenly, Amelia smiled dreamily. And he loves me! Surely he must! Why else would he have come to my room? A secret admirer! Yes, he has always admired me from afar. But, finally, his love became so uncontrollable that he threw caution to the wind, just to be with the woman he loves! Oh, it's all just too romantic!

Going to the dresser, she sat on the stool. Her earlier feelings of shame were completely forgotten, and, wrapped up in a fairy tale romance, she smiled happily. Arranging her hair in a flattering style, she pulled it back from her face with two pearl-clustered combs. Would he be in town today, watching her from afar? Would he find some excuse to speak to her? Perhaps to inquire about Jason? Would she know him if he were to talk to her? Yes! Yes, she'd know it was him! Somehow, she would know! She was sure of it!

Standing, she examined her full appearance. Her dress was beige, with brown lace trimming the short puffed sleeves and high neckline. It had a dark brown sash to fit neatly around her waist, tying at the back in a large smooth bow.

She had promised Lillian that she would help her in the store this afternoon, because Calvin had gone fishing again. But first she would go downstairs to the hotel dining room and have lunch.

Hurrying, Amelia left her rooms. She moved quickly down the hallway, and as she descended the stairway her full skirt swayed with her rapid steps. Passing through the lobby, she hastened into the dining room, going to the table she usually occupied. As she pulled out her chair, she caught a glimpse of Jamie. He was busy cleaning off one of the tables. Catching his eye, she smiled charmingly.

Leaving the tray of dirty dishes, he hurried to Amelia, his strides long and sturdy.

Touching the back of her chair, he said, "Let me help you, Mrs. Bishop."

"Thank you," she gleamed. She sat down, and gently James Henry positioned her chair.

Standing to where he could see her face, he asked, "Are you all right, ma'am?"

"Why, yes!" she answered pertly. A secret smile tugged at the corners of her mouth as she added, "In fact, I have never felt better!"

Observing her tiny smile, James Henry fought the impulse to bend over and kiss her sweet lips. By God, she wasn't the only one who had never felt better! He felt pretty great himself.

"When you didn't come down for breakfast," he began, "I thought maybe you were sick."

She looked at him with fondness. "I'm fine, really I am."

"Did you find the man you were lookin' for last

night?''

A sudden flush rose to her cheeks. "No . . . no, I didn't find him," she stuttered.

"Why were you lookin' for a man, Mrs. Bishop?" James Henry asked seriously, wondering with amusement how she was going to answer his question.

Embarrassed, she gulped. "Well . . . well, it's a little difficult to explain. But it wasn't important, so let's forget it, shall we?"

"Yes, ma'am," he answered, holding back a grin.

"Thank you, Jamie," she replied.

"Well," he began hesitantly, "I guess I'd better get back to work."

He turned to leave, but impulsively, she called out, "Jamie!"

"Yes, Mrs. Bishop?" he answered, looking back at her.

"Is . . . is the extra key to my room still behind the lobby desk?"

"Yes, ma'am," he replied, appearing to be surprised. "Did you think something happened to it?"

Vaguely, she whispered, "Then I did forget to lock my door."

Pretending he hadn't heard her, James Henry asked, "What did you say, Mrs. Bishop?"

"Nothing," she answered quickly.

"Well, good day, ma'am," he mumbled, and, holding back a grin, he returned to the other table.

"Honestly, Amelia!" Lillian complained. "Why are you so . . . so jittery?"

Busying herself, Amelia straightened a few of the

canned goods on the shelves behind the counter. If she didn't answer Lillian, then perhaps she would let the subject drop, but she couldn't blame her aunt for being perturbed. She had already broken two glass jars because twice a bearded soldier had come into the store. The first time she had been in the process of placing extra jars of preserves on a shelf, when she heard the bell over the door ring. Turning, she had seen a young, tall, and bearded lieutenant entering. She didn't know his name, but she had often seen him talking to Jason. He had met her intense gaze, and immediately he had smiled quite roguishly. His knavish expression made Amelia believe him to be her secret admirer, and, going limp, she had dropped the jar of strawberry preserves. It hit the floor and broke into little pieces, and the thick mass of jelly splashed across the hem of her dress. Hastily, Lillian and the lieutenant had come to her aid. As they helped her pick up the broken glass, Amelia had studied the soldier. But quickly she had come to the conclusion that he wasn't her secret admirer. His hands were too short and delicate; her mystery man's hands were slender and strong.

Composing herself, she had returned to filling the shelves with jars of preserves. A few minutes later, the bell over the door clanged again, but this time Amelia didn't bother to turn around.

Picking up a jar, she had lifted the hem of her long skirt, and then she climbed the short stepladder so that she could reach the top shelf.

"Mrs. Bishop," a deep voice called.

Placing her free hand on the shelf to steady herself, she turned to look at the man who had addressed her.

Recognizing him, she had automatically smiled. He was a close friend of Jason's, and she had spoken to him on more than one occasion. He was a captain, and he was tall, slender, and bearded. She suddenly wondered if he could be her admirer.

Finding Captain Bishop's wife delightfully attractive, he had said quietly so Lillian wouldn't overhear, "Mrs. Bishop, you are a vision of loveliness."

His secret message caused Amelia to totter precariously as, once again, she dropped a jar of preserves. Alertly, the captain had hastened around the counter, reaching Amelia just in the nick of time to keep her from falling. As he helped her down from the ladder, she had placed her hands on his arms, and immediately she became aware that he wasn't her secret admirer. The muscles in his arms hadn't been nearly strong enough to belong to her mystery man.

Fortunately for Amelia, he had been the last bearded soldier to come into the store, but her nerves were stretched to their limit, and Lillian's constant whining wasn't helping matters.

"I have never known you to be so clumsy," Lillian rattled. "Two jars in one afternoon. And, Amelia, broken jars of preserves make such an untidy mess. It's a wonder we haven't cut our hands cleaning up all those pieces of glass." Huffing, she continued, "Oh dear, I do feel a splitting headache coming on. Maybe I should go upstairs and make myself a cup of hot tea. This afternoon has been too disorderly."

Holding her patience, Amelia replied, "I'm sorry, Aunt Lillian, if I have upset you." Wanting her aunt to leave so she could be alone, Amelia added, "Why don't you have your tea? I'll watch the store."

Eyeing her dubiously, Lillian questioned, "Are you sure you can manage?"

"Yes," Amelia sighed. "And I promise not to break anything."

"Very well," Lillian responded.

The moment her aunt was gone, Amelia burst into tears. Crying heavily, she knew she couldn't go on this way. She had to stop searching for her secret admirer. Somehow she had to find a way to erase him from her mind. If she kept on in this fashion, she would soon become a bundle of nerves.

Suddenly the front door opened, and the bell rang. Hastily Amelia wiped at her tears as she tried to calm herself.

Entering the store, Jamie strolled to the counter. Smiling, he said, "I'd like to buy some cigars, please."

Sniffling, Amelia picked up a box of cigars from the end of the counter. Fighting back tears, she handed the box to Jamie.

Accepting it, he asked tenderly, "Ma'am, are you cryin'?"

Her chin quivering noticeably, she replied, "No, of course not."

"If you aren't cryin', then why do I see tears in your eyes?"

"Well," Amelia conceded piteously, "maybe I am crying, just a little."

Touched, James Henry wished he could take her into his arms and kiss away her tears. Instead, he asked hesitantly, "Is there anything I can do to help, ma'am?"

Incapable of controlling her distress, she bawled

134

dramatically, "There is only one person who can help me, and I don't even know who he is!"

Placing the box of cigars on the counter, he asked, "The man you were lookin' for last night?"

"Yes!" Amelia cried.

"How could he help you, Mrs. Bishop?" he questioned gently.

Intuitively she sensed she could trust Jamie, and she exclaimed, "I need to see him so desperately!"

"Do you, Amelia?" James Henry whispered, before catching himself. Quickly he looked at her, but she was so distressed that she hadn't recognized his sensual tone. Inwardly, he gave a sigh of relief. In the future, he had to be more careful.

Without thinking, Amelia reached across the counter, and her hand grasped his. "Oh Jamie, I feel as though my whole world has turned upside down!"

All at once, Amelia began crying uncontrollably. Acting a little self-conscious, James Henry moved around the counter to stand at her side, and instantly, she flung herself into his arms. Amelia's shoulders shook with her deep sobs. Tightening his hold, James Henry pulled her close, and, mustering all his will power, he continued to be Jamie. "Mrs. Bishop," he began, "this mornin' you were so happy. What happened to make you change?"

Her voice tremulous, she cried incoherently, "Twice . . . I thought . . . I thought . . . I had found him!" Then suddenly, she blurted out illogically, "Oh Jamie, I broke two jars!"

Because he was holding her, she didn't see his tender smile. "You're cryin' because you broke two jars?" he asked, although he knew differently.

"Oh, it was a terrible mess!" she cried miserably. "Broken glass everywhere and splattered preserves all over my skirt! And . . . and Aunt Lillian was so upset . . . and . . . and it's all his fault!"

"His fault?" James Henry asked. "But, Mrs. Bishop, I thought you said you broke the jars."

"But I did!" she exclaimed.

Although he had mentally unraveled her dilemma, he continued to question her, so she would remain in his arms. "Then why do you blame him?" he asked, sounding totally confused.

"Amelia!" Lillian shrieked.

Instantly, Amelia flew out of James Henry's embrace. Her face red with embarrassment, she stammered, "Aunt Lillian . . . I didn't . . . hear you come downstairs."

"Obviously!" her aunt huffed.

James Henry found it very difficult to keep a straight face, but remaining impassive, he paid for the cigars. Picking up the box, he hurried from the store, forcing himself to restrain his laughter until he had stepped safely outdoors.

The moment he was gone, Lillian folded her arms under her large breasts, and, glaring at her niece, she scolded severely, "Amelia Bishop, how could you? I saw it with my own eyes, but I still can't believe it! You were actually in that . . . that man's arms!" Placing her hand over her fluttering heart, she gasped breathlessly, "What if someone else had seen you? Oh my goodness, what a scandal it would have caused." Sternly, she ordered, "Amelia, I want you to stay away from that man! Don't even speak to him!"

Lillian's attitude annoyed Amelia, and, for the second time in her life, she refused to be docile. Allowing her true character to surface, she whirled away from the counter, and, stomping to the front door, she said crisply, "I most assuredly will speak to Jamie! Whenever and wherever I feel like it!" She swung open the door and striding outside she deliberately let it slam behind her.

As Amelia paced across the bedroom floor, her sheer dressing gown flowed with her steady gait. Wringing her hands nervously, she wished her heart would stop pounding so rapidly. But she had never been so apprehensive. Tonight, if he came to her room, she would find out who he was. She had it all strategically planned.

Scurrying to the bed, she knelt beside it. A sly smile came to her lips, as she touched the box of matches placed on the floor between the bed and night table. Rising, she hurried to the window, opening the drapes only wide enough that he would find it necessary to close them. The narrow slit would only let in a stream of moonlight but, all the same, she knew he would never allow even that much light to be in her room. When he went to the window to close them, she would be feigning sleep. Then as soon as she heard him draw the drapes, she would grab the matches.

Pretending to be her mystery man, Amelia imagined the room to be dark as she stepped quietly toward the bed. Taking long, manly strides, she mentally counted, One, two, three, four, five, six. "Six!" she said aloud. "On the sixth step, he will be beside my bed. So when I hear him close the drapes, I must count to six, before I strike the match." Amelia giggled victoriously. "And the light will shine right into his face!" Hugging herself, she exclaimed, "And then I will know who he is!"

Her steps lively, Amelia rushed to the door in the sitting room. Unlocking it, she patted the doorknob as she smiled triumphantly. "There!" she cried. "He thinks he is so shrewd, but he has met his match in Amelia Adams!" Tossing her head smugly, she headed back to the bed, completely unaware that she had unconsciously refused to use her married name.

Flinging back the covers, she got into bed, reciting the cliché, "He will need to rise early in the morning to pull the wool over my eyes!"

Turning down the wick of the lamp until it was out, she snuggled under the covers. Her eyes wide open, she stared into the surrounding darkness, and fretfully waited.

Later that night, Amelia didn't detect the doorknob turning, nor did she hear the man's soft chuckle when he found it to be unlocked.

James Henry had had no intentions of visiting Amelia, but his curiosity had made him stop at her room to see if she had left the door unlocked. Grinning, he wondered what kind of trap she had set for him. It was very tempting to find out, but his mission in Lawrence was more important than playing games with the beautiful little Amelia. Still smiling, he walked away from her door.

By using pure will power and determination Amelia had stayed awake until dawn, but finally, exhausted and disappointed, she had fallen asleep, her last conscious thought being that she would set the trap again . . . and again . . . and again . . . until, at last, she had snared him!

After checking Amelia's door and finding it unlocked, James Henry had gone downstairs to relieve Buford at the front desk. In the solitude of the lobby, Buford had been leisurely enjoying a bottle of whiskey. As his uncle bid him goodnight, James Henry told him to leave the bottle.

Taking the chair behind the desk, James Henry sat casually, stretching out his long legs. Uncapping the whiskey, he took a large drink. He glanced at the marble stairway leading to the rooms upstairs. Damn, it was tempting to go back up those stairs and to Amelia's bed. Recalling her charms, he could literally feel his desire rising. Suddenly, growing angry, he helped himself to a big swig of whiskey. He should take Buford's advice and stay away from the beautiful little vixen.

Crossing his legs on the desk top, he leaned back in the chair, and in the quietness of the deserted lobby, James Henry relived the days that had inevitably led him and Buford to Lawrence, Kansas.

Quantrill's new recruits, James Henry, his brothers, and Buford among them, sat apart from the others at the guerrilla camp. The recruits were overly anxious to take the oath and become legitimate Pro-Confederates. Ben and Luther were as impatient as the others, eager to get on with the war so they could kill some dirty

Federals. That James Henry obviously didn't share their keenness didn't annoy Ben and Luther. They had stopped trying to understand their older brother, and the fact that he was at the rendezvous was more than they had hoped for. They had decided to leave well enough alone and not anger James Henry by reproaching him for his lack of enthusiasm.

Hearing riders arriving, the guerrillas and the recruits got to their feet, their eyes glued to the horses breaking through the surrounding brush. William Quantrill sat proudly on his white stallion. His head was held high, and his shoulders straight as his eyes regarded the men who had been waiting for him to make his appearance. Finding him impressive, some of the recruits caught their breaths sharply. Most of them were seeing the famous William Quantrill for the first time.

Quantrill and Colonel Garson dismounted. Quantrill spoke hastily to one of his men before falling into stride beside Colonel Garson. Together they walked across the campground to stand close to James Henry and Buford.

"Mr. Stewart," Colonel Garson said politely to James Henry. "I'm glad to see you showed up."

He nodded brusquely to the colonel. "I said I'd be here."

Colonel Garson smiled shrewdly. "Are you a man of your word, Mr. Stewart?"

"I try to be," James Henry grumbled, aggravated by the man's question.

Stepping quietly, William Quantrill moved so that he stood at James Henry's side. He nodded at the man he had spoken to earlier.

The man acknowledged Quantrill's nod with one of his own, and, reaching into his pocket, he brought out a folded piece of paper. Speaking commandingly, he ordered: "All you recruits line up here in front of me, and you'll be sworn in."

Anxious, the young men obeyed as they rowdily shoved against one another to be the first to arrive.

James Henry had to force himself not to restrain his brothers and advise them to wait. But he knew it would be useless to try and stop them. Noticing that Buford had remained, he looked at him and asked, "Aren't you taking the oath?"

Scowling, Buford replied, "I'm not taking any damned oath, until I hear it first."

William Quantrill snickered and said, "You'll take my oath or be shot!"

Stepping to Quantrill, Colonel Garson placed his hand on the man's arm. "Not so fast, Quantrill! I may be interested in both of these men!" Looking to James Henry and Buford, he said crisply, "You two will come with me, please!"

The colonel led them into the brush, and when they came upon a small clearing, he paused. Keenly, he looked from one man to the other. Finally, he offered Buford his hand. "I am Colonel Garson of the Confederate Army."

Accepting his handshake, Buford replied, "I'm Buford Stewart, James Henry's uncle."

"It is quite apparent," Colonel Garson began, "that you are both opposed to taking Quantrill's oath. But are you opposed to taking an oath to the Confederacy?"

Both men shook their heads, answering no.

"Good!" the colonel remarked. "I will swear you both in myself!"

"Now?" Buford asked.

Nodding vigorously, Colonel Garson replied, "Yes, now! Later, I want you both to tell me as much as you can about yourselves. I need to be sure my instincts concerning you two are correct."

"And after we tell you our life stories?" James Henry questioned.

"You will be taken to a guerrilla hideout, and you will stay there under Captain Anderson's command until I've checked out your stories. If all goes well, I will then tell you what your mission will be."

Colonel Garson looked at James Henry and Buford questioningly, waiting for their answers. Smiling slightly, both men nodded their agreement.

Within an unbelievably short time, Colonel Garson had both men signed up and sworn into the Confederate Army. Folding their enlistment papers, he placed them into his coat pocket. Immediately, his deportment became totally military as he told them, "You are now in the Confederate Army, and at the present I am your commanding officer, and I order you both to return to Quantrill's camp and take his oath!"

Incredulous, the two men stared at him. But showing the colonel the respect due him, James Henry asked, "Sir, may I ask you why you want us to take the oath?"

Cordially, the colonel answered, "Yes, I suppose I owe you two that much. That you men are in the Confederate Army must be kept under cover. Only a selected few will know the truth."

"Is Captain Anderson one of the selected few?" James Henry asked.

"Yes, he is. For appearance's sake, you two will have to ride with him on occasion, but he will not order you to accompany him on skirmishes that are connected with too much danger. His orders will be to keep you two alive and well." Seeing their indecision and irritation the colonel continued almost apologetically, "I'm sorry, but for the time being I can tell you no more. But soon, everything will be explained to you."

Obeying their commanding officer, James Henry and Buford returned to the guerrilla camp, where they reluctantly took Quantrill's oath.

James Henry hadn't wanted to become a Pro-Confederate guerrilla, and in his opinion pretending to be one came awfully damned close to being the real thing. But since joining Captain Anderson's band he hadn't come into contact with William Quantrill, and with Quantrill out of the picture, James Henry began to see the courageous and impetuous guerrillas in a different light.

The Pro-Confederates, most of them extremely young, believed wholeheartedly that they were fighting for their homeland and their rights, which, indisputably, they were. The Union had refused to accept their neutrality, forcing many of them into war. The question of slavery and secession didn't even seem to be the vital issue between western MIssouri and Kansas. During the lawlessness and horror of the Missouri-Kansas warfare of the fifties, the two opposing sides had already developed an unnatural hate for one another. Although very few Missourians had actually taken part in the Kansas outrages of the fifties, their state had acquired a reputation in the North as a hotbed of radical, violent, pro-slavery people. Many Kansans considered all Missourians ruffian slaveholders, and Missourians despised "Abolitionist Yankee Kansas."

James Henry and Buford were ordered to accompany Captain Anderson on multiple excursions to destroy railroads, burn bridges, and tear down telegraph wires. So, wearing the shirts that Anne had so proudly made for them, James Henry and Buford rode with Bill Anderson and his band of roving guerrillas. If they were fired upon, Anderson immediately ordered James Henry and Buford to be surrounded by their fellow comrades, the young guerrillas unquestioningly protecting the two men by sheltering them with their own bodies.

To be sheltered during warfare deeply bothered both James Henry and Buford, but they were soldiers, and they had no alternative but to obey Anderson's command. But living in the midst of the guerrillas, James Henry found himself admiring and respecting these brave Missourians, who, through no fault of their own, had become involved in the ominous war between Kansas and Missouri.

James Henry refrained from forming an opinion of Captain Anderson, who would gain the name of "Bloody Bill." Northerners would label him a sadistic, cruel, and brutal demon. But, then, it all depended which side you were on, as to how you judged a man.

For nine long and hard weeks, James Henry and

Buford rode with Anderson's band, before Colonel Garson finally returned to instruct them on their mission. On the evening of the colonel's arrival they met with him and Captain Anderson a short way from the guerrilla camp. The setting sun cast a radiant orange glow across the horizon as the four men made themselves reasonably comfortable beneath the large trees that shaded the secluded area. James Henry and Buford were impatient for Colonel Garson to speak. At last, they were to learn what they had been recruited for.

Clearing his throat, the colonel began, "First, I want to tell you that I have received permission to grant you both field commissions. You will become captains in the Confederate Army."

Surprised, James Henry and Buford looked at each other. They hadn't expected to be promoted to officers.

Captain Anderson smiled broadly. He liked James Henry and Buford, and he was pleased for them. "Congratulations!" he said cheerfully.

They both nodded to the captain, and James Henry mumbled, "Thanks."

Anderson was sitting close to James Henry, and he patted him fondly on the back as they shook hands. Captain Anderson was a young man, still in his early twenties. He was exceptionally handsome. His hair was dark brown, and worn in the guerrilla fashion, and his beard was full and tastefully trimmed.

Continuing, Colonel Garson explained, "I will begin by making this as short as possible. Later, we will go into it in depth, and you will be free to ask questions. The Confederacy has an 'informer' in the Union

Army. You will not be told his name. You will learn his identity when he comes to you. You are both being sent to Lawrence, Kansas. You will reside in Lawrence under assumed names."

Spies! James Henry cringed inwardly. My God, we're going to be spies!

But Colonel Garson had spotted James Henry's initial reaction, and commandingly he stated, "I will not force you two men to take this assignment. So if you have any reservations, speak them now! Otherwise, hold your peace and obey my orders without question!"

Both men remained noncommittal. "Very well!" Colonel Garson said shortly. "Later, your names and identities will be explained to you. We don't want the Union to question why you aren't in the army. So, Buford, you will pretend to have a lame leg, and, James Henry, you have seen action, but at present you are recovering from a chest wound." Reaching into his pocket, he brought out an envelope. Handing it to James Henry, he explained, "This is your medical discharge. I want to make it very clear to both of you that you must do nothing to draw attention to yourselves. If the Union was to get suspicious, it would take one good look from a doctor to know that both of you are perfectly healthy." He paused a moment, then continued. "The informer will eventually arrive in Lawrence, and he will relay information to you that will lead to a great victory for the Confederacy. It will be a battle like none other, with the Confederate Army the winners!"

"Sir, may I ask a question?" James Henry asked.

"Yes," the colonel replied.

"Why will the informer be in Lawrence?"

"There is to be an important military conference. Some of the highest brass in the Union Army will be gathered in Lawrence to attend this meeting."

"The informer must be a very influential man to be sitting in on an apparently vital military discussion," James Henry surmised.

The colonel smiled shrewdly, refusing to comment.

"Sir," Buford began, "why did you choose us for this assignment?"

"Very simple. You are both from Missouri, and you caused no suspicions among the men when you were sworn into the Pro-Confederate bands. If I had brought two of my own men into Missouri, the guerrillas would have known that something vitally important was taking place. Under pressure, to save their lives, one of them may have told the enemy."

"They already know we're here for a special reason," James Henry pointed out.

"Yes, but they think you are guerrillas, so they have no inkling you will be spying for the Confederacy. They are completely unaware that they have any information that the Union would be interested in knowing."

"When we leave this camp, they're going to wonder where we're going," James Henry said.

"They'll simply be told that you are joining another guerrilla band."

"What happens after we get the information from the informer?" Buford asked.

"You'll return to this hideout. I will be here waiting for you."

"That means slipping through enemy lines and back

into Missouri," James Henry stated gravely.

Once again, the colonel smiled. "That should cause no problem for two men who once lived with the Comanche."

"When this mission is completed," James Henry began, "will we ride with the Confederate Army?"

Colonel Garson shook his head, his expression apologetic. "You will return to riding with the guerrillas, until your next assignment."

"If we live in Lawrence as citizens, some of the soldiers will come to know us," Buford began. "Then if we are captured later as guerrillas, they'll know we're spies."

It was Captain Anderson who commented bitterly, "Guerrillas are not taken alive. You will be shot down in cold blood, before anyone has a chance to recognize you."

"And if by some remote chance you aren't," Colonel Garson ordered, "you will take your own life before being captured. By then, you will know the informer's identity, and you must protect him at any cost!"

"Our lives for his," Buford uttered matter-of-factly. Shrugging, as if it were merely incidental, he continued, "Sounds good to me. What about you, James Henry?"

James Henry grinned. "It's as good a way to die as any, I guess."

Removing his legs from the desk top, James Henry stood and walked over to the stairway. Placing his hand on the banister, he gazed up the steps. He hoped the informer's expected arrival would be soon. If he had to wait much longer to complete his mission, he knew he would find his way back to Amelia's bed, regardless of the danger involved.

TWELVE

Opening the door to the hotel, Calvin placed his hand on Amelia's arm as he escorted her into the lobby. Pausing, he gazed down into her strained face. She had been looking peaked for the past two weeks, and he was worried about her. He wondered if Amelia was in the family way, but surely, if she was, she would have told Lillian. And his wife would have informed him of Amelia's delicate condition.

Smiling, Amelia said, "Thank you, Uncle Calvin, for inviting me to dinner."

"Honey, your aunt and I always enjoy having you at home. We only wish you would visit us more often."

She looked at him with a deep fondness. He reminded her so much of her own dear father. They had the same thick gray hair, twinkling eyes, and warm smile.

"I'm sorry, Uncle Calvin. I didn't mean to slight you or Aunt Lillian . . . but . . . but I haven't been feeling well."

"Are you ill, dear?" he asked, concerned.

"No, I'm fine. But I haven't been sleeping very

well.''

"Why?'' he inquired.

Blushing, she stammered, "I . . . I have a lot on my mind.''

Instantly sympathetic, he replied, "Of course—Jason.''

"Jason?'' she repeated vaguely.

"You must be very worried about him,'' he answered. "He's been gone longer than expected.''

"Oh, yes, of course,'' she said, guiltily dropping her gaze to the floor.

Worried about her listlessness, he decided to tell her the information he had heard from the mayor. He knew he should keep it quiet, but Amelia needed cheering up. And, after all, tomorrow the whole town would know.

"I have some news that will lift your spirits,'' he told her brightly.

"News?'' she asked, looking at him.

"I understand that Lawrence is going to be visited tomorrow by some high brass in the army, and Jason more than likely has been ordered to return home.''

"High brass?'' she questioned, confused.

"Some type of military meeting is on the agenda, I suppose.'' He thought the news would make her happy, and, puzzled by her lack of response, he questioned gently, "Honey, don't you want Jason to come home?''

"Of course,'' she mumbled, lowering her head.

He placed his hand under her chin, tilting her face upwards. "Amelia,'' he began sincerely, "I love you very much. And, honey, I'll always be here for you if you ever need me.''

"I know, Uncle Calvin," she answered, loving him almost as much as she had loved her father.

"Do you want to talk about what is bothering you?" he asked tenderly.

She shook her head. How could she conceivably tell her uncle that she was miserable because she was longing for a man who had slipped into her room and seduced her? She couldn't very well tell him that for the past two weeks she had lain awake at night, waiting for him to come back to her. She had even stopped planting the matches by the bed. She had lost the desire to trap him, she only . . . she only wanted to be in his arms.

Noting her uncle's worry, she said reassuringly, "Tonight I'm so tired, I'm sure I'll fall asleep the moment my head hits the pillow."

"It is fairly late," he observed. "Do you want me to walk you to your room?"

"No, that won't be necessary." On tiptoes, she placed a kiss on his cheek. "Goodnight, Uncle Calvin."

"Goodnight, dear," he replied.

Compelling herself to smile, she turned away and began walking to the stairway. Noticing Sam Tyler behind the lobby desk, she nodded politely to him before climbing the steps.

Opening the drawstrings on her cloth purse, she took out her key. Stopping at her door, she inserted the key, and leaving the door ajar, she stepped inside.

Walking farther into the room, she suddenly became aware of how dark it was. She had left the drapes open, and the room should be shadowy, not pitch black! But the only light filtering into the room came from the hallway.

Cautiously, she started to turn around to look behind her, but before she could move, the door was firmly closed, followed by total silence.

Feeling faint, she dropped her purse as her hand flew over her pounding heart. Staring into the thick blackness, she cried weakly, "You came back!"

"Yes, little one," he whispered hoarsely.

She didn't hear him moving toward her, and she cried out with surprise when he suddenly pulled her into his arms.

Immediately his lips were on hers. She wrapped her arms about his neck, drawing him even closer. Hungrily, she opened her mouth beneath his. Oh, I could become lost in his kiss! her heart cried.

His arms seized her around the waist, forcing her small frame against him. She could feel the wonderful hardness of him through her skirt and petticoats, and she pressed her thighs to his.

Removing his lips from hers, he groaned, "I have missed you, little one."

"Why did you wait so long?" she cried, not caring how wanton it sounded.

"I didn't relish walking into your little trap," he answered, keeping his voice disguised.

Astounded, she stammered, "But . . . but how did you know?"

"Leaving your door unlocked for two weeks straight made it quite obvious. Weren't you afraid that the wrong man might walk into your room?" he asked lightly, wishing he could tell her that as Jamie he had kept a vigil watch on her unlocked door.

"I was willing to take my chances. But the door was

154

locked tonight, so how did you get in?''

"How do you think?" he asked, his voice remaining rasping.

"The window?" she guessed.

"Sounds good to me," he replied, refusing to tell an outright lie.

"But this is the second floor, and my window faces the street. How did you manage to climb up to the window without being seen?"

Thinking about the key hidden snugly in his pocket, he chuckled gruffly. "Where there's a will, there's a way."

"How can you just come and go without a trace?" Exasperated, she sighed, "Perhaps you aren't even real, but only a figment of my imagination."

Taking her hand, he placed it on his hard erection. "Does that feel like a figment of your imagination?"

"No!" she gasped, pressing her hand tightly against him.

Her touch was electrifying, causing him to moan with desire. Covering her hand with his, he moved her hand up and down his male hardness.

As she felt him grow even more erect, Amelia rose to her tiptoes, and, finding his mouth with hers, began kissing him. Boldly her tongue darted between his lips, probing deeper and deeper.

"Aw, God!" he groaned, lifting her in his arms. Knowing there were no obstructions in their path, he carried her straight to the bed.

Placing Amelia on her feet, he helped her to undress, wishing he could light the lamp and view her delectable body.

Impatiently, Amelia pulled at her restricting

clothes, flinging them to the side. Quickly she removed the last undergarment, then drawing back the covers, she got into bed.

Hastily James Henry rid himself of his own clothes. As he joined her she flung her arms around him, wanting so desperately to be with him. Oh God, how was it possible to love a man she had never seen? She didn't know, she only knew that she loved him! She had thought herself in love with Jason because he was so dashingly handsome, but she didn't know, or care, if this man was good-looking.

"Amelia," he groaned, calling her by name.

Only fleetingly did it register with Amelia that he had used her first name. It didn't matter! Obviously he knew all there was to know about her. Every day she probably passed him on the streets, never imagining that she was so close to the man she loved.

"I want you," she murmured, placing her lips to his. Feeling a warm longing between her legs, she moaned deeply, kissing him passionately.

Taking his mouth from hers, he let his lips travel across her shoulders, then down to her breasts, kissing first one and then the other, making the throbbing between her thighs become even more feverish.

He moved over her, and, wanting his entry, she opened her legs. He thrust into her deeply, and, crying out with pleasure, she locked her ankles across his back.

"Amelia," he whispered raspingly. "You feel so wonderful."

"Love me," she murmured seductively. "Please love me!"

Crushing his mouth to hers, he put his hands beneath her hips, pulling her to him so that he could penetrate even deeper.

He began thrusting against her powerfully, and, meeting his passion, she dug her fingers into his shoulders. Together, they took each other to the highest peaks of rapture until, at last, their climax came to them with a kind of demanding ecstasy.

Breathing heavily, James Henry kissed her lips lightly, before moving to lie at her side. Going into his arms, she placed her head on his shoulder.

"You aren't going to believe this," she began softly, "but I used to think I was frigid."

Grinning, he replied innocently, "No?"

"Yes, I did!" she replied firmly. "I hated sexual relations!"

"Really?" he whispered as though he was surprised.

She sighed discontentedly. "I suppose I will still hate it with Jason."

James Henry's jaws clenched tightly as he suddenly envisioned her in Captain Bishop's arms. Hell, she was Bishop's wife, wasn't she? So why should he give a damn if Bishop made love to her? After all, she wasn't anything to him, except a means of revenge.

"He'll be returning home soon," she stated sadly.

"Hasn't he already been gone longer than he planned?" James Henry asked.

"Yes," Amelia sighed. "But tonight my uncle told me that some high army brass are coming to town. He said he thinks there's going to be an important military meeting. And Jason has probably already been ordered to return."

"Did he say when the high brass are expected?"

James Henry asked urgently.

"Tomorrow," she answered.

"How in the hell did your uncle hear about this?"

"He's good friends with the mayor, and he probably learned about it from him," Amelia said.

So the informer will be in Lawrence tomorrow, James Henry thought. Thank God, I can soon stop playing at this ridiculous charade and return to Missouri! The fact that he wouldn't see Amelia again started to gnaw at him, but he refused to let himself think about it.

Suddenly they heard the sounds of horses galloping down the street. Quickly James Henry leaped from the bed. Walking swiftly through the darkness, he went to the window. Turning his back to Amelia, he made a narrow slit in the drapes. He looked down to the street, then, releasing the drapes, he returned to the bed.

"Who are they?" she asked, although she had a sinking feeling she already knew.

"Your husband and his troops," he answered, slipping quickly into his clothes.

"Oh, no!" Amelia cried.

"Don't worry," he assured her gently. "He rode past the hotel, but I'm sure he'll be returning very shortly."

James Henry had spoken quietly, but he had forgotten to keep the gruffness in his voice.

"I know you!" she exclaimed, sitting straight up.

"Wh . . . what?" he asked.

"Your voice! I've heard it before! I've spoken to you, haven't I? But . . . but I can't place you!"

Hurrying, he pulled on his boots. Would she connect his voice to Jamie? He seriously doubted it. She

158

believed her secret admirer to be a soldier. Bending over the bed, he found her lips, kissing her quickly. "Goodbye, little one," he whispered hoarsely.

"When Jason rides out again, will you come back?"

"Sorry, little one, but I'll be riding off to the wars myself."

Although she couldn't see him, she knew he was leaving. Rising from the bed, she started to beg him to wait, but the plea died on her lips as she suddenly heard the door in the sitting room open and then close.

She went to the lamp by the bed and lit it, her hands trembling. "He's gone!" she cried. "He came into my life, stole my heart, and now he's gone!"

She wanted to cry, she longed to cry until she had no tears left to shed. But her tears wouldn't bring him back.

Moving as though in a trance, she picked up her clothes and placed them in a chair. Going to the wardrobe, she removed her dressing gown. Slowly she walked to the wash basin to take a sponge bath.

Jason would be arriving at any moment. She shuddered, thinking about the sexual act she would soon be obliged to participate in with her husband.

Blocking it from her mind, she reached for the wash cloth and said numbly, "My husband has come back, and the man I love is gone."

THIRTEEN

The Eldridge House provided an outstanding dinner followed by a ball to honor the high-ranking army people visiting Lawrence. The hotel was filled with Union officers, all of them dressed handsomely in their blue uniforms with gold braid, many of them displaying polished medals pinned neatly to their jackets. Their wives were also elegantly attired in their prettiest formal gowns.

Because of the special occasion the hotel dining room was closed to the general public, and open exclusively to the army and government officials. The abundant spread of food was set up buffet style, so that the majority of the tables could be removed, making space for a dance floor and a five-piece orchestra.

Mr. Cramer, whose duty it had been to oversee the elaborate festivities, had asked James Henry and Buford to work as waiters. They were more than willing to accept the extra work. It would give the informer a good opportunity to contact one of them. They would know him by the words "Colonel Garson is a friend of mine." They would simply reply, "He told me that he knew you.''

The spacious room hummed with voices, as the orchestra played waltzes and reels. Everyone present was enjoying the social occasion to the fullest; everyone, that is, except Amelia Bishop.

Standing apart from the others, Amelia kept rising on her tiptoes, trying to catch a glimpse of every soldier wearing a beard. Oh, why must I be so short! she thought glumly. If only I were a little taller, then I could see over people's shoulders.

Amelia was not aware that her anguish was visible on her worried face. Walking past her, James Henry noticed her torment, and, curious, he paused close to her as he pretended to be busy gathering used glasses.

Frowning miserably, Amelia continued straining her neck, desperate to eye every bearded soldier within her sight. But there were so many, and any one of them could be the man she loved.

Returning to the dining room from the ladies' powder room, Cynthia immediately became aware of her friend's apparent distress. Worried, she hastened to her side.

Touching Amelia's arm, she questioned urgently, ''Amelia, dear, what's wrong?''

James Henry, gathering glasses, listened attentively.

Turning to Cynthia, Amelia's eyes filled with tears, and her chin quivered piteously. ''Oh, Cynthia!'' she said forlornly.

Alarmed, Cynthia's heart seemed to skip a beat. What had happened to her dearest friend? Should she send for Jason or a doctor? ''Darling, what is wrong?'' she asked pressingly.

Amelia's tears streamed from her eyes, and, puckering her face into a childish pout, she cried wretchedly, "Oh Cynthia, half the men here are wearing beards!"

Poor Cynthia was totally dumbfounded, but James Henry had to turn away to conceal his mirth. His shoulders shaking, he placed his hand over his mouth to muffle his deep laughter. He wished he could simply walk over to Amelia, sweep her into his arms, and tell her how damned sweet she was!

He moved back to the table to remove the glasses, intending to continue eavesdropping. Suddenly a hand touched his shoulder, and, looking at the man standing behind him, James Henry instantly forgot Amelia and Cynthia's conversation.

"Yes, sir?" he asked. James Henry had never before spoken to the Union officer who was now regarding him, but he knew who he was. The man's name and reputation were public knowledge.

He spoke quietly to James Henry. "Colonel Garson is a friend of mine."

James Henry was completely awed. He had never imagined that the informer would be a man so well known, a man surrounded by so much prestige and nobility.

"He told me that he knew you," James Henry replied softly, trying to keep the shock out of his voice.

Removing his coat, the officer spoke audibly. "I spilt champagne on my coat. Would you mind taking it to the lavatory and cleaning the spot before a stain can set in?"

"Yes, sir," James Henry answered. "I'll be glad to clean it for you."

Pointing to the wetness, the officer explained, "The spot is on the left side, and it has probably soaked all the way through the material, so be sure to clean the inside as well."

Accepting the coat, James Henry could feel the envelope concealed in the left inside pocket. "Yes, sir, I sure will," he replied hastily.

Quickly James Henry took the coat to the men's room. Entering, he looked around, making sure he was alone. Then he went to the door and locked it. Removing the envelope, he opened it, taking out a slip of paper. Although he read the information in haste, he memorized every word. He returned the paper to the envelope, shoving it deep into his pocket. Then, hurrying, he washed the stain on the coat.

Leaving the lavatory, he slipped unseen to his room. Taking the envelope out of his pocket, he struck a match, setting the paper aflame. He dropped it into the ashtray and watched it until it burned down to ashes. Picking up the ashtray, he went to the open window, scattering the ashes into the evening breeze. Replacing the ashtray, he hurried out the door and back to the dining room.

Locating the informer, he hastened over to him. He was busy conversing with fellow officers, but, seeing James Henry bringing him his coat, he spoke clearly to him. "Thank you for cleaning my coat."

Handing it to him, James Henry replied, "You're welcome, sir. I cleaned the stain as you asked."

"You did get rid of it, didn't you?" he said, emphasizing the word "it."

"Yes, sir. There's no sign of it," James Henry answered.

The man nodded brusquely, then he turned his attention back to the other officers.

Dismissed, James Henry walked away. Glancing around the room, he tried to find Buford, but he was nowhere to be seen. But he did catch sight of Amelia. She was dancing with her husband. Seeing her in Bishop's arms made James Henry's nerves grow taut. "Thank God this mission is completed," he mumbled under his breath. "Even if it means coming into contact with Quantrill again. Anything is better than seeing her in that sonofabitch's arms!"

When Jason returned to Lawrence, he had been ordered to make all necessary preparations in regard to the military officials' expected arrival, leaving him no time to bed his wife. Amelia had been thankful for the twenty-four-hour reprieve. Submitting to Jason on the same night she had willingly given herself to another man would have been heartbreaking to her.

But Amelia's reprieve was short-lived, and the next night Jason made up for it.

Amelia and Jason remained at the ball until it had come to an end. The moment they retired to their bedroom, Jason ordered her to remove her clothes. Complying, Amelia undressed, and, trying not to think about her mystery man, she got into bed.

Impatiently, Jason rid himself of his uniform. When he was completely stripped he flung back the covers. Without a word, he placed himself on top of her. He lifted her legs, and his forced entry tore into her. The sharp pain made Amelia cry out, but Jason had been heedless of her discomfort.

As her husband thrust into her time and time again, Amelia tried not to cry, but tears streamed from her eyes. Jason was unmindful of her distress. He was aware only of his own urgent need. While her husband demanded his marital rights, Amelia cried for the man she loved but had never seen.

Jason climaxed quickly, and, rolling to his side of the bed, he immediately fell asleep. Burying her face into her pillow, Amelia continued to cry. Her tears finally subsided, and she tried desperately to fall asleep, but, emotionally tormented as she was, sleep evaded her, causing her to toss and turn fretfully.

Swinging her legs over the edge of the bed, she got to her feet. Stepping to the wash basin, she scrubbed her body clean, then, going to the wardrobe, she took out her gown and dressing-robe. Putting them on quickly, she slipped into her cloth shoes. She entered the sitting room, and, restless, began pacing back and forth.

Deciding fresh air might help her to sleep, she went to the door. She knew Jason would be extremely angry if he were to learn that she had left their rooms. But with all the liquor he had consumed, there was little chance that he might awaken.

Stepping into the hall, she closed the door quietly. At this time of night, there was only a slim chance that she would run into anyone. Knowing that either Sam Tyler or Jamie would be watching the front desk, she decided to use the back stairway. Going to the rear entrance, she walked out onto the porch. Pausing on the top step, she folded her arms across her chest and lifted her face to the soothing breeze drifting through the quiet night.

Moving down the steps, she strolled to the hotel's private stable. Entering, she went to the stall occupied by Jason's chestnut gelding. Hoping she had a cube of sugar, the horse nuzzled her shoulder. Smiling, she reached over and gently patted him. "I'm sorry," she murmured, "but I don't have anything to give you."

Realizing he wasn't going to receive a tidbit, the horse snorted loudly before turning away. Gathering the folds of her dressing gown protectively close, Amelia walked across the dark stable. Pausing in front of an empty stall, she postponed returning to her room. Recalling Jason's cruel abuse of her body, she shuddered as, once again, tears filled her eyes. Giving in to her distress, she began crying heavily. "Oh God!" she sobbed desperately. "I hate being married to Jason!"

The man's steps were silent, and Amelia wasn't aware of his presence until, suddenly, he grabbed her shoulders, thrusting her back against his hard chest.

"Don't turn around, little one," he warned gruffly.

Amelia's knees gave way, and she would have fallen if he hadn't been holding her. "What are you doing here?" she gasped.

His voice disguised, he replied, "Like you, little one, I couldn't sleep. So I decided to take a walk. Perhaps it was fate that led me here." Sensing her sorrow, he whispered tenderly, "You need me, don't you?"

"Oh yes!" she cried with a heartbroken sob.

Securing her with one arm, he reached into his pocket and removed a plain white linen handkerchief. "Amelia," he explained, "I'm going to cover your eyes."

He tied the blindfold securely but gently. Easing his hands down to her shoulders, he turned her around so that she was facing him. "Little one," he whispered in his disguised voice, "promise me you won't try to remove the handkerchief."

"I promise," Amelia sighed, knowing she would keep her word. Apparently it was vitally important to him that she not learn his identity. She would respect his wish, although it took all the will power she possessed to not jerk off the blindfold and look into the face of the man she loved.

Leading her into the unused stall, he assisted her down to the floor. Sitting beside her, he drew her into his arms. Resting her head on his shoulder, she welcomed his tender embrace.

"I understand why you were crying," he said hoarsely.

She didn't answer, but, involuntarily, she moaned deeply.

"Is marriage with Jason that bad for you?" he asked sympathetically.

"Yes," she groaned.

"I'm sorry," he whispered.

Amelia's hands found his, and grasping them tightly, she admitted, "He makes me feel unclean and cheap! And . . . and he hurts me!"

Pulling her closer, he rasped, "Amelia! Amelia, I wish there was something I could do to help you."

She knew he hadn't planned this rendezvous, and, after tonight, he would vanish from her life. This was her last chance to feel love, to take love, and to give love. "But you can help me!" she exclaimed.

"How, little one?" he asked.

"Love me!" she cried. "One last time, make love to me! Please!"

Groaning, he eased her down onto the soft straw. "I want you, Amelia. But are you sure this is what you want?"

Wrapping her arms about his neck, she replied from the bottom of her tormented heart, "Yes! Oh, yes! I want you!"

Easily, he helped her to remove her nightclothes, and when she lay revealed he wished the confining stall wasn't so dark. He could barely see her beauty. Damn, why must he always make love to her in an obscure blackness!

He longed to be completely rid of his own clothes, but if someone were to come into the stable, it would be difficult enough to get Amelia dressed before they could be discovered.

Unfastening his trousers, he slipped them past his hips. He moved over her, and wanting him desperately, she spread her legs. Feeling his hard desire touching the softness between her thighs, Amelia gasped with longing, then entwined her fingers in his hair to press his lips down to hers.

Kissing her passionately, James Henry placed his hands beneath her hips, pulling her upwards to meet his arousal. He entered her quickly, and instantly Amelia's legs were crossed over his back, wanting his deepest penetration.

His movements were slow and tantalizing, and, following his guidance, Amelia swiveled her hips gently. He took his mouth from hers long enough to whisper her name before, once again, he was kissing her sensually, almost teasingly.

Suddenly he pulled away, and, afraid he was going to desert her, Amelia cried, "Please don't leave me!"

"I'm not leaving, little one. I'm just going to show you another way to love." Putting his hands on her slim hips, he urged hoarsely, "Roll over, Amelia."

"Wh . . . what?" she stuttered, totally confused.

Gently, he turned her over, then, placing one arm around her waist, he lifted her to her knees. Kneeling behind her, he eased into her awaiting warmness.

At first, Amelia was too shocked by the position to respond. But as he began to slide in and out of her, Amelia found herself pushing back against him, taking all he had to offer. Her passion building, she moved back and forth, loving the feel of him entering her womanhood deeper and deeper. Controlling their rhythm, James Henry would allow her wonderful excitement to last only temporarily, before firmly grasping her hips to slow her down. Then he would move inside her circularly and gently, before, once again, encouraging her to release her feelings and let her passions soar.

Amelia's fulfillment came to her suddenly and explosively, causing her to cry aloud as a glorious sensation flooded her entire being.

James Henry was still aroused, and quickly he turned her onto her back. Lifting her legs, he entered her swiftly. Wanting him again, Amelia equalled his driving power until they climbed together to mutual satisfaction.

Spent, James Henry rolled to her side. Breathing heavily, he murmured, "Little one, I'll never forget you."

Tears came to Amelia's eyes, but the blindfold hindered them, and instead of rolling freely down her cheeks they were absorbed by the confining handkerchief.

Sitting up, James Henry refastened his trousers. It was dangerous to linger. Taking her gown, he helped her slip into it. Before he could finish helping her dress, she reached out blindly, finding his arms. Clutching them she pleaded, "Come back to me!" Someday, please come back!"

"I can't," he groaned.

"I'll leave Jason!" she promised desperately. "We can run away together!"

Gently, he took her hands, holding them in his. "You don't even know who I am."

"I don't care who you are! . . . I don't care!" she cried.

Caressing her cheek with his fingertips, he replied, keeping his voice disguised, "Believe me, if you knew, you would care."

"Why?" she pleaded.

Briskly, he muttered, "I must go."

Resenting him for coming into her life only to leave her, she blurted angrily, "Damn you! Damn you for the pain you have brought me!"

"Little one," he said sympathetically. He attempted to take her into his embrace, but, pushing him away, Amelia fell back on the strewn straw.

Standing, James Henry looked down at her. He could barely make out her small frame in the darkness inside the narrow stall. Dear God, how he longed to lift her into his arms and carry her away from Bishop. But there was a war raging, and he was in the midst of it.

Sighing, James Henry ran his hand across his brow. He didn't want to leave her but, damn it, he knew he had no other choice. Why in the hell had he been so foolish as to let himself become involved with Bishop's wife? But at the beginning he hadn't known it was going to hurt him so badly to let her go. He had only inflicted more unhappiness upon himself. First his family, and now Amelia.

Their impending separation tore painfully into his heart, and he spoke so softly that Amelia barely heard him. "Sometimes, I think the only reason God gave me a heart is so that it can ache."

She didn't reply because she knew he wouldn't hear her words. He was gone, silently and swiftly. Reaching up, she undid the blindfold. Clutching the handkerchief, she buried her face into it and cried.

The following morning, before the Eldridge House had time to return to normal, the army high command departed, as the citizens of Lawrence turned out to cheer them on their way. In the midst of the vociferous hubbub, no one took notice of the Tylers' old battered wagon as it inconspicuously left town.

Using the excuse that she preferred to sleep in late, Amelia didn't join her husband in the farewell celebration. Believing she was tired from the previous night of dancing and dining, Jason didn't insist that she accompany him.

Depressed, Amelia had lain in bed for hours, longing for the man who had mysteriously slipped into her life and taken complete control of her young heart.

Finally, forcing herself to rise, Amelia dressed and went downstairs for brunch. Noticing that Mr. Cramer seemed more upset than usual, she asked him if anything was wrong. When he informed her that the Tylers had left without bothering to give adequate notice, Amelia rushed back to her room. Throwing herself across the bed, she cried.

That Jamie could leave town without telling her goodbye hurt Amelia, and she felt depressingly rejected. She had believed them to be friends.

Amelia didn't stop to question why losing Jamie added to her already broken heart. If she had, she might have realized that love was such a strong emotion that it could not be deluded. She would have intuited then that Jamie was not who he had pretended to be. But, foolishly, Amelia didn't try to analyze her dilemma, so her mystery man and Jamie remained unconnected.

With her husband back in her life, Amelia's days were unhappy, and her nights were even worse. But as the weeks passed, she submissively resigned herself to living with Jason.

She believed her secret admirer to be a part of her past, gone without a sign that he had ever been in her life, leaving nothing behind except her broken heart. But, shockingly, Amelia soon realized that he had left much more behind, and that her mystery man would never be completely out of her life. She was pregnant! Quick calculation assured her that the baby couldn't possibly be Jason's.

Her initial reaction was one of panic. She was going to have a child, and it didn't belong to her husband. What should she do? Leave Jason? Move back to Uncle Calvin's? But what would the scandal do to Calvin and Lillian? They would be so ashamed and embarrassed that they wouldn't be able to face their friends.

No, she couldn't put such a terrible burden on them! There was one thing for certain, she couldn't go to the baby's father and ask him for help. How do you find someone you don't even know? It was too ironic! She was going to have a child, and she had never even seen the baby's father. How could it be true? But it was!

Knowing she had no other alternative, Amelia allowed her husband to think that the child was his. But even her deceit had its consolation. In consideration for her now delicate condition, Jason respectfully left her alone.

PART TWO

FOURTEEN

Jason rented a small frame house at the edge of town. It was an attractive home with a large yard surrounded by a white picket fence. Amelia planted flowers alongside the walkway that led up to the house, and on the front porch was a swing built to accommodate two people. The Bishop's home was the ideal cottage for a young wife happily awaiting the birth of her first child. But although Amelia kept her home neat and meticulously clean, her heart was not with her home or her husband. It still belonged to the man she loved but had never seen.

As Amelia's pregnancy progressed and she became more conscious of the child growing in her womb, her unborn baby became the center of her life. She prayed it would be a boy. If she couldn't have the man she loved, at least she could have his son. And, oh, how she hoped he would resemble his father! If he did, would his hair be dark or light? And what color eyes would he have? She already knew he would grow to be tall and slender. But if he took after his real father, would Jason suspect the truth? She had no way of knowing, but she didn't really care. She wanted the baby to be a perfect replica of his father, regardless of the consequences.

For the first time since she had married Jason, Amelia came close to being happy. Anticipating her baby's birth filled her days and nights with motherly joy. She was visited often by friends, but it was Cynthia's visits that she enjoyed the most. Cynthia was sincerely happy for Amelia, and she looked forward to the birth of Amelia's child. Although Cynthia was envious, longing for her own child, her envy didn't take away from the joy she had in her heart for Amelia. Cynthia and Amelia spent many afternoons together, sewing for the baby and talking to each other. Their friendship grew even deeper. Often Amelia would find herself longing to tell Cynthia about the man she loved and confess the secret of her baby's parentage, but, afraid that Cynthia wouldn't understand, Amelia didn't reveal her secret.

Amelia was six months pregnant when Jason returned one morning from one of his missions into Missouri. Barging into the kitchen where Amelia was eating breakfast, Jason coldly informed her that Lieutenant Coffman had been killed in a skirmish with Missouri guerrillas.

Jason hadn't meant to be cruel, but being self-centered he judged others' reactions by his own. Amelia's overwhelming grief surprised him, and, worried that she would lose the baby, he tried to calm her. But avoiding his attempt to console her, Amelia stormed out of the house. Hurrying to the Coffmans' home, she found it to be filled with concerned friends. When she asked about Cynthia, she was told that she was alone in her bedroom. Amelia went straight to Cynthia's room, opened the door, and without bothering to announce her arrival walked inside. Cynthia had been lying on the bed, and, rushing to her side, Amelia took her into her arms. For hours she remained in the bedroom sharing her friend's grief. Although Jason came over and demanded that Amelia return home, she refused to comply. Finally, losing his patience, Jason left. Brooding, he wondered what had become of the timid woman he thought he had married.

It was Amelia's friendship that carried Cynthia through her grief. And the friendship didn't end only with consolation. Amelia also went to Calvin and Lillian and asked them to offer Cynthia employment so that she could remain in Lawrence. Thankful for the opportunity, Cynthia accepted the Adams' offer.

Cynthia Coffman had an inner strength that gave her the will to pick up the pieces of her life and go on living. But she knew that without Amelia she would never have found that inner strength. Grateful to Amelia, Cynthia became totally devoted to her dearest friend, loving Amelia as if they were sisters.

Amelia was on the front porch sitting on the swing and sewing a gown for her baby's layette, when, unexpectedly, Jason came home with Lillian. Holding politely to Lillian's arm, Jason led her up the walkway and onto the porch.

Placing her sewing on her lap, Amelia smiled. "Aunt Lillian, what a pleasant surprise."

Sitting beside her, Lillian asked, "How are you

feeling, dear?''

"I'm fine, thank you," Amelia replied.

Lillian's eyes inspected Amelia's pregnancy, and, inwardly, Amelia gave a sigh of thankfulness that her baby was apparently going to be small. She was a month farther along than anyone suspected.

Sitting on the porch steps, Jason lit a cigar, then said, "I asked your aunt to come home with me for a very special reason, Amelia."

"Oh?" she questioned, looking at Jason. "Is anything wrong?"

Impatiently, he snapped, "You know very well what is wrong!"

Amelia knew exactly what he was referring to. Perturbed, she replied firmly, "No, Jason! I have already told you that I have every intention of nursing this baby myself!"

Placing her hand over her heart, Lillian gasped, "Oh, Amelia! Darling, ladies do not . . . they . . . well, my dear, they hire a wet nurse!"

Frowning, Amelia fumed, "Jason, how dare you bring my aunt into this!"

"Somebody has to talk some sense into you!" he raged.

Taking Amelia's hand, Lillian kept patting it as she pleaded, "Darling, your own dear mother isn't here to reason with you, so you must take my advice. Amelia, you and Jason have a certain prestige in Lawrence that you must uphold."

Short-temperedly, Amelia replied, "My goodness, Aunt Lillian, you speak as if a mother nursing her baby is indecent!"

"No . . . no," her aunt protested breathlessly.

"But, darling, the upper class consider it very poor taste when one of their own kind does not hire a wet nurse to take over the unpleasant task. Oh dear! A woman with your high status allowing her child to . . . to . . . ! It's unheard of!" Becoming desperate, Lillian exclaimed, "Do you want to have your lovely figure completely ruined?"

"My figure will not be ruined!" Amelia insisted.

Rising, Jason began pacing the porch. "The subject is closed, Amelia! Lillian will start immediately to try and locate a woman who will be able to nurse our child!"

Amelia leaped to her feet, and the small gown she had been sewing fell to the porch. "No! Jason, please! Please!" she cried.

"I will not be shamed by my wife!" he bellowed.

"Shamed?" Amelia pleaded pathetically. "Oh Jason, how can it be wrong for a mother to want to feed her baby?"

Concerned, Lillian rose quickly. Grabbing Amelia's arm, she warned, "Darling, you must not get upset! Don't forget your condition!"

Angrily, Amelia flung off her aunt's hand. "How dare either of you tell me what I shall and shall not do with my own baby!"

"It's my child, too!" Jason yelled.

Instantly, Amelia fell silent. She didn't in any way think of the child as being Jason's. Always, in her mind, the baby belonged unequivocally to her.

"I don't care what either of you says!" Amelia insisted. "I intend to nurse my child!"

Sneering, Jason's hand clutched Amelia's arm. Glaring into her eyes, he whispered gruffly, "Don't count on it, Amelia!''

Her pregnancy making her move awkwardly, Amelia pulled away from her husband and hurried into the house. Going to the bedroom, she fell across the bed. She would nurse her baby! She would! She would! . . . And she didn't care what anybody said!

But, much to Amelia's dismay, she did not nurse her child. Following the baby's birth, Jason explained Amelia's foolish desire to the doctor, convincing him to tell Amelia that her breasts were too small to adequately nourish an infant. Although to Amelia it had seemed that her breasts were overflowing with milk, she believed the doctor knew best, and, disappointed, she accepted his decision.

Amelia had been denied the joy of feeding her baby, but she hadn't been denied a son. He was a small baby, causing no one to question that he could be a month premature. Amelia and James Henry's son was a beautiful child. He had been born with a head full of black hair, and even though Amelia knew all newborns had blue eyes, she was certain that her baby's eyes would remain blue. They were too dark and clear to ever change color. Apparently, the man she loved had dark hair and blue eyes, and he had passed those physical traits down to his son.

The fact that the child didn't resemble either Amelia or Jason didn't arouse Jason's suspicions. After all, a baby's looks usually changed, and besides, Jason's father had been dark.

The child was two weeks old before Jason decided it was time to give his son a name. He joined Amelia in their bedroom, where she was lying on the bed holding the sleeping infant in her arms.

Closing the door behind him, Jason fussed, "You're going to spoil the child, Amelia. When he's asleep, let him remain in his crib."

Her face glowing, Amelia murmured, "I love holding him! He's so beautiful, isn't he?"

Walking over to stand beside the bed, Jason answered tediously, "I suppose, if it's possible for babies to be beautiful."

Piqued, she snapped, "Jason, is it impossible for you to love anyone but yourself?"

He smiled smugly. "Don't be ridiculous, my sweet. He is my son, of course I love him. But babies are a woman's business. When he grows older, then I will take an interest in him."

Amelia felt a cold chill. Would her husband's influence on her son turn him into a man like Jason Bishop?

Continuing, Jason said, "I have decided the child will be named for my father, especially since it does appear that he will have a strong resemblance to his paternal grandfather. But I don't want Calvin to feel as if we have slighted your side of the family. So he can have your father's name as well."

Jason's arrogance made Amelia long to tell him exactly what she thought of his insolence, but wishing to avoid an altercation, she suppressed the urge.

"Your father's name was James, wasn't it?" she asked, remembering Calvin mentioning the name on different occasions. But Jason seldom spoke about either of his parents. He seldom talks about anyone, she thought, but himself!

"Yes," he replied. "And your father's name?"

She smiled bitterly. "We have been married a year, and you don't even know my father's name. That's because you never cared about my life. You care about nothing except yourself!"

"Amelia, you do try my patience!" he snapped.

She shrugged. Why argue with him? He would never change. "My father's name was Henry," she replied.

"Very well, the child will be christianed James Henry," Jason announced.

Turning brusquely, he strutted to the door. Opening it, he said firmly, "I will send the nurse in to relieve you of the child. You need your rest." As his eyes raked over her, it was obvious what was on his mind. Smiling, he added, "I want you to get well soon, my precious."

When the door closed behind him, Amelia looked down at her sleeping child. "James Henry," she said softly. "Yes, I like the name, and somehow it seems to suit you." Whispering lovingly, she repeated, "James Henry."

FIFTEEN

Shortly following the birth of Amelia's child, rumors were being heard that Quantrill planned to attack Lawrence to slaughter the citizens and burn the town. Guards were stationed at all the roads leading into town, and Jason remained in Lawrence with a full battalion of troops. If Quantrill should attack, they would be ready for him.

Believing William Quantrill to be capable of the most barbaric of crimes, the citizens of Lawrence were petrified. They were aware that Quantrill had a personal grudge against Lawrence, because years before the town had found him to be an undesirable citizen and had ordered him to leave. Would he now return to Lawrence and vent his outrage? The question traveled from one citizen to another, adding to the town's extreme fear.

Amelia was so terrified that she refused to leave her home. If the rumors were true, then even her son's life was in danger. Quantrill planned to kill everyone! No one would be spared! Men, women, and children would all be murdered! Afraid for her child's life,

Amelia kept her baby close to her side, refusing to leave him alone even in the safety of their home.

Her overprotection of the child angered Jason, and they continually argued about it. Jason would rage that her constant hovering would spoil the child, but Amelia would retaliate by telling him he would have to physically restrain her to keep her from sheltering her baby.

After three months passed, and nothing happened, the citizens of Lawrence laughed at their fears. It had been a ridiculous rumor and nothing more. Not even Quantrill would have the outrageous gall to attack the town of Lawrence.

With the passing of time, Amelia also believed the rumors insignificant, and she stopped being so protective of her son, letting a superficial peace be restored between herself and Jason.

The child's nurse, a woman named Addie, was relieved that the Bishops had ceased their feud. Their continual bickering had been almost more than she could bear. She was a quiet, matronly woman in her early thirties. Her husband had been killed in the war when she had been eight months pregnant. Her child had been stillborn a week before Amelia's baby arrived. When Lillian heard of the woman's tragedy, she had offered her the position as wet nurse to the Bishops' child. Destitute, with no means of support, Addie thankfully accepted the job.

Jason was once again ordered to ride into Missouri, leaving Amelia, the baby, and Addie alone. The Union officials believed Lawrence to be safe, and the guards were no longer stationed, and only seventy soldiers remained in Lawrence. So it was that when

Quantrill rode into Lawrence on that fatal morning of August 21, 1863, he found no guards, and the town totally at his mercy!

The earliest rays of dawn were filtering into Amelia's bedroom when, for some reason, she woke up. The baby! Had she heard him cry? Quickly she got out of bed.

Slipping on her dressing gown, she stepped into her house shoes and hurried to the room across the hall. Opening the door she rushed to her son's crib. Relieved, she saw that he was sleeping peacefully.

Addie slept in the same room with the baby, and, hearing Amelia's intrusion, she sat up on the bed, coming slowly awake.

"Is anything wrong, Mrs. Bishop?" she asked sleepily.

Speaking softly, Amelia apologized, "I'm sorry, I woke you."

"That's all right. What can I do for you?"

"Nothing," Amelia replied. "I . . . I don't know what awakened me. I thought maybe I had heard the baby cry."

"Why, no," Addie said pleasantly. "He slept like a little angel all night."

Smiling, Amelia looked down at her son. "He is an angel, isn't he?"

"Yes, ma'am, that he is," Addie agreed.

Whispering, Amelia told her sleeping child, "I love you, Hank." Jason despised the name Hank, insisting that the child be called James, but Amelia always used the nickname when Jason wasn't around. Looking at

Addie, Amelia said quietly, "Go back to sleep. It's too early to get up. I think I will return to bed myself."

"Yes'm," Addie answered.

Amelia turned to leave when, all at once, she heard horses coming down the road. Wondering if Jason had returned home, she went to the window. The bedroom faced the front of the house, and, looking outside, she saw a large group of Missouri guerrillas charging down the street. Suddenly they broke into demonic yells as some of them dismounted, while others continued to head farther into the town.

"Oh, dear God!" Amelia cried. Temporarily frozen, she could only watch as four raiders barged into the home across the street. Immediately they dragged Amelia's neighbor outside. He was an old man, in his middle seventies. Throwing him to the ground, one of the guerrillas drew his pistol, and placing it to the man's head, he shot him.

Addie rushed to Amelia's side just in time to see the old man's fourteen-year-old grandson be shot down in the same way.

Screaming, Amelia ran to her son's crib. As she gathered him into her arms, he began crying. He waved his small fists in the air, angry at being so abruptly awakened.

Amelia's screams became more terrified as she heard the front door being forced open. Oh God, they were going to kill her baby!

Weakening, she fell to her knees, hugging the crying child to her bosom. Protectively, Addie knelt in front of them, sheltering Amelia and the baby with her own body.

Crying convulsively, Amelia could hear the intruders storming through her home, searching the rooms. When the bedroom door flew open, she dropped to the floor, pinning her child beneath her. She didn't even look up as she begged, "Please . . . please don't hurt my baby! Please! Oh God, have mercy!"

Three guerrillas walked into the bedroom. Two of them were young, but the other one was a man in his forties. The older one hurried across the room and roughly flung Addie to the side. Pausing, he stared down at Amelia.

"Are there any men in this house?" he asked gruffly.

Looking up at him, Amelia gasped, "No . . . no . . ."

"Where's your husband?" he demanded.

"He's in the army, but he isn't here!" she replied breathlessly. Hugging her child closer, she begged, "Oh, please don't hurt my baby! . . . Please . . . Please!"

"Ma'am, we ain't here to kill no babies or woman," the man answered. "But we're goin' to kill every sonofabitchin' male who's big enough to carry a weapon!" He whirled to leave, but pausing momentarily, he said with a compassion that was ironic in the situation, "Don't worry, ma'am, ain't no one goin' to hurt that little baby of yours. The men have done been ordered not to kill no children or women."

As the guerrillas stormed out of the house, Addie helped Amelia back to her feet. Crying heavily, Amelia kept repeating over and over, "Hank is safe! Hank is safe!"

Gently, Addie took the child from Amelia's arms, and, trying to soothe the baby's cries, she sighed,

"Thank God!"

Amelia grew limp with thankfulness, and for a moment she could think of nothing except that her child wouldn't be killed.

Then, slowly, she became conscious of pistol shots, screams, and the sounds of panic. Stiffening, she cried, "Uncle Calvin!" Firmly she placed her hands on Addie's arms, as she ordered, "Stay here with Hank! Don't even leave this room!"

"Oh, Mrs. Bishop!" Addie exclaimed. "You can't go out there! It's too dangerous!"

"I must go!" Amelia cried. "Aunt Lillian and Uncle Calvin must be warned!"

"But, Mrs. Bishop, there's no time to warn them! It's too late!"

Whirling, Amelia ran from the bedroom, shouting, "Take care of Hank! I'll be back as soon as I can!"

The guerrillas had left the front door open. Lifting the hem on her dressing gown, Amelia fled outdoors. She hurried across the porch and to the street. Running, she began heading in the direction of her uncle's store.

Later, Amelia would wonder how she had found the strength and the courage to make it to the center of town. The closer she got to Calvin's store, the more horrible was the chaos that she witnessed. Raiders dragged husbands, fathers, and sons from their homes and shot them down in sight of their loved ones. Women begged for their men's lives, but their pleas fell on deaf ears and unfeeling hearts. The death-dealing maniacs ravaged the town, killing men and boys, showing no mercy. Businesses, stores, and homes were set to the torch, the glaring flames

190

streaking toward the early morning sky.

Amelia tried to blot the horrifying sights from her mind as she continued to run wildly toward her uncle's store. The Missouri guerrillas ignored her, obeying the explicit order that no women were to be killed or hurt.

She paused at the Methodist Church to catch her breath. Spotting an elderly man stumbling across the street, she ran to him. Supporting him, she yelled, "You must hide! They'll kill you if they see you!"

Gasping for breath, he answered, "The church . . . please help me to the church! They are hiding us in the storm cellar."

Amelia placed her arm around his waist, and, leaning against her, he tried to make it to the church, but he was an old man and his strength was gone. His knees buckled, and his weight pulled Amelia down to the street beside him.

Hearing horses bounding behind them, Amelia saw a small group of guerrillas heading in their direction.

"Run, young lady!" the old man warned. "Run before you get hurt!"

Amelia's first impulse was to leave the man to his fate and flee, but with a bravery she had never known she possessed, she remained at the old man's side. She knew she couldn't save him, but at least . . . at least he wouldn't be alone!

Only one guerrilla dismounted, as the other four remained on their horses. The guerrilla approaching Amelia and the old man was young. He was nice-looking and clean-cut. He certainly didn't look like a murderer, but Amelia knew that he was.

Pulling the old man into her arms as if he were a child, she prayed, "God have mercy!"

"Thank you, ma'am," the old man replied, his voice surprisingly strong. "And God bless you!"

Without flinching, Amelia looked up at the young guerrilla standing before them. "Well?" she sneered. "What are you waiting for? Kill him and get it over with! You . . . murdering . . . sadistical . . . monsters!"

The guerrilla smiled, and, tipping his hat, he answered, "I'm going to help him, ma'am."

Bending over, he grasped the old man's arm, pulling him to his feet. "Were you taking him to the church?"

Amelia refused to answer, believing it to be some kind of trick, but at that moment, Reverent Humphry appeared on the church steps, calling, "Good, you found another one! Bring him over here, young man!"

"Another one?" Amelia cried. "You've helped others? But why?"

"I don't kill men who aren't in uniform," he answered simply.

"But you're a guerrilla!" she screamed angrily.

"Yes, ma'am!" he replied firmly and proudly. Without further explanation, he led the old man to the church.

Turning, Amelia looked at the four horsemen. They were also guerrillas, but apparently they had no wish to slaughter innocent people. "Then you aren't all heartless monsters!" she stated, without realizing what she had said until the words were spoken.

When they refused to comment, she desperately cried out to them, "If you didn't come to Lawrence to kill innocent people, then why are you even here?"

"To burn the town," one man answered calmly. Then spitting to the ground, he added, his tone so cold that it sent chills up Amelia's spine, ''And to kill god-damned Federals!''

Noticing that the men's eyes had traveled down to her breasts, Amelia suddenly became aware that her dressing gown had come open, and underneath she wore only a sheer nightgown. Under less traumatic circumstances she would have been embarrassed, but instead, she continued her flight to her uncle's store, remembering to fasten the buttons on her dressing gown merely as an afterthought.

As she got closer to the center of town, she saw buildings burning, and the sidewalks were filled with dead bodies. Most of them were elderly men, but some were boys in their teens. There were women wandering aimlessly, many of them crying and screaming hysterically, while others remained by the dead body of their loved one. The Missouri guerrillas were everywhere, drinking, plundering, and murdering whenever and wherever the notion struck them.

Entering the street where Calvin's store was located, Amelia arched her neck, trying to see if her uncle's business and home were burning. Relieved, she saw that they had not been set to the torch. Hurrying her steps, she fled down the sidewalk. She forcibly shoved her way past the guerrillas who were plundering merchandise from businesses along the street.

As she neared Calvin's store, she saw Lillian lying on the sidewalk covering a form with her own body. At first, Amelia couldn't distinguish who was beneath her, but as she drew closer, she realized it was her uncle.

Crying, Amelia ran wildly to her aunt. Kneeling beside her, Amelia pulled her away from Calvin.

Flinging herself into her niece's arms, Lillian sobbed, "They killed him! Oh, dear God, they killed him!"

Forcefully, Amelia held back her hysteria. As she hugged her aunt, she thought she was murmuring, but her voice shrieked, "Oh no! . . . Oh, dearest God, no! . . . Oh, Uncle Calvin!"

Suddenly, Lillian pushed out of Amelia's arms. She grabbed her niece's shoulders, as she cried, "What are you doing here? The baby! . . . Oh God . . . they . . . they didn't kill the baby?"

"No!" Amelia quickly reassured her. "No, Aunt Lillian! He's fine!"

Lillian's eyes rolled wildly, as she pleaded, "Oh Amelia, you must hurry home! Don't leave the baby! Don't leave him!"

"He's with Addie!" Amelia replied loudly.

Lillian's fingers dug into Amelia's shoulders. "You shouldn't have left him! Go back to your baby!"

"I can't leave you here alone!" Amelia cried. "You must come with me!"

"And leave Calvin's body at the mercy of those animals?" Lillian screamed.

Amelia had refrained from looking at her uncle, because she didn't want to see him this way, but now, dropping her gaze, she stared down at him. She could tell he had been shot in the chest by all the blood on the front of his shirt. His eyes were closed, but his face had the look of death.

Placing her hand over her mouth, Amelia groaned, "Oh, Uncle Calvin!"

Lillian's hands were still on Amelia's shoulders, and, shaking her roughly, she insisted, "Go home! Go

194

home, Amelia!"

"But . . ." Amelia objected.

"I'll be all right!" Lillian shouted. "Hurry, darling! Hurry back to your baby!"

Amelia was reluctant to abandon her aunt, but she knew it would be useless to try and persuade Lillian to leave with her.

"Are you sure you're all right?" Amelia cried.

"Yes!" Lillian exclaimed.

Taking one last look at her uncle, Amelia got to her feet. It was on her lips to beg her aunt to come with her, but she realized why it was vital to Lillian to remain with Calvin's body.

Whirling, she began running down the sidewalk. Lillian would be safe! The guerrillas weren't killing women! Or babies, Amelia's heart cried thankfully.

Hurrying, Amelia kept her eyes on the ground, trying to avoid seeing the horrible sights. Moving through the burning town, she blocked the living nightmare from her mind, concentrating only on reaching the sanctuary of her home. Fighting back tears, she refrained from thinking about Calvin. She would think about him later, when she was safely home, with her baby close at her side.

Reaching the Methodist Church she paused to cross the street, when suddenly she remembered Cynthia. She was living alone, and she must be terrified.

For a moment, Amelia was undecided. Should she go straight home, or should she go to Cynthia's house and tell her to come stay with her and Addie? Amelia's concern for her friend made the decision for her, and, changing course, she headed toward the narrow street where Cynthia had her home. Except for the guerrillas

195

the town was now practically empty; most of the surviving men and boys of Lawrence were safely hidden in homes and churches.

As Amelia turned the corner to enter Cynthia's street, she heard a woman's piercing screams, and looking to her left she saw a small group of raiders dragging Mr. Holt out of his house, as his wife held tenaciously to her husband's arm. Mrs. Holt and Lillian were good friends, and, wanting to help her, Amelia crossed the street. She called the woman's name, but Mrs. Holt didn't even hear Amelia. She kept screaming and begging for her husband's life.

Mr. Holt was a middle-aged man. He was kind and generous and had never intentionally hurt his fellow man. He tried to plead with the guerrillas not to kill him in front of his wife, but ignoring his plea they callously shoved him to the ground.

Immediately Mrs. Holt fell across her husband, protecting him with her own body. The guerrillas had their pistols drawn, but it would be impossible to kill the man without taking a chance on hitting the woman instead.

As Amelia reached the Holts' front yard, one of the guerrillas leaned over, and, grabbing Mrs. Holt with one hand, he pulled her away from her husband. Then he placed his pistol to Mr. Holt's head and shot him. His blood splattered across his wife's bosom. Giving one prolonged scream, she fell back across her husband's body.

Amelia's stomach churned. Turning, she vomited onto the ground. The guerrillas pushed past her, mounted their horses, and rode away from the Holts' home.

Having witnessed the murder from their windows, neighboring women came rushing from their houses. Going to Mrs. Holt, they tried to console her.

Amelia's nausea passed, and slowly she began moving down the street. She wanted to flee, but her legs were so weak and wobbly that she could barely keep her balance.

Amelia heard a rider approaching, but she didn't bother to turn around. If he was a guerrilla, she didn't want to see his face. She never again wanted to see a Missouri guerrilla, unless she could have the pleasure of seeing him dead. Amelia had never been a vindictive or malicious person, but she could feel her heart growing cold with hate. Dear God, this wasn't war! This was slaughter of innocent people!

The rider drew closer, and, seeing Amelia, he quickly reined his horse.

It was on the tip of Amelia's tongue to tell the guerrilla to go straight to hell, but, whirling to look at the rider, she saw he wasn't a guerrilla. It was Mr. Cannon, who owned a barber shop in town. Amelia had spoken to the man a couple of times, but she had never found him to be very pleasant. Jason had seemed to like him, but Calvin had always said he was the kind of man who couldn't be trusted.

He dismounted hastily, and cautiously Amelia questioned, "What do you want?"

Mr. Cannon was a huge man, but, moving quickly, he lifted Amelia in his arms. Fighting and kicking wildly, she cried, "Put me down! Put me down!"

Roughly he flung Amelia on his horse, then, still holding on to her, he pulled himself into the saddle. Grabbing the reins with one hand, he placed his large arm around her waist, keeping her trapped against his powerful chest.

"Why are you doing this?" she shrieked.

"I'm going to ride out of this town," he began gruffly, "and you're riding out with me. If I've got a woman with me, it won't be so easy for them to shoot me! They ain't killing no women!"

"They'll still kill you!" Amelia cried.

Mr. Cannon tightened his arm around her waist so powerfully that she could barely continue to breathe. "You shut up!" he demanded. Jerking the reins, he headed his horse down the street, making the animal flee at a breakneck speed.

Within minutes they were at the edge of town, and it was beginning to appear as if Mr. Cannon was going to escape. But as the horse left the street to enter the road that led out of town, five mounted guerrillas were waiting for them. Amelia recognized them as the same men who had killed Mr. Holt.

Abruptly, Mr. Cannon pulled his horse to a stop. Drawing his pistol, he held it to Amelia's head. "Let me through, or I'll kill the woman!" he warned.

The guerrillas laughed, their laughter sounding so cynical that Amelia grew weak, and her head fell forward. Cruelly, the man jerked her head back up, and, pressing the pistol barrel against her temple, he repeated his warning, "I'll kill the woman!"

Again the guerrillas simply laughed. Amelia knew they wouldn't let Mr. Cannon go free to spare her life. If they were the same men who had helped the old man to the church, then perhaps they would protect her, but not this ruthless group of raiders!

The middle guerrilla moved his horse forward. He

had his revolver in his hand, but it was resting across the front of his saddle. He drew perilously closer, and Amelia shut her eyes. Terrified, she began silently to pray.

"That's far enough!" Mr. Cannon yelled.

Carefully, the guerrilla halted his horse in front of them. Opening her eyes, Amelia looked at him. Meeting her gaze, he smiled, and ironically, his smile was tender. He was a nice-looking man in his early twenties. His hair was dark brown, worn to shoulder length. He had a moustache that curled attractively at the corners of his mouth. He was dressed in the customary guerrilla shirt.

"Quantrill said he didn't want any women killed!" Mr. Cannon reminded him.

"How do I know this ain't some kind of trick?" the guerrilla asked. "As far as I know, she might be your wife."

"I swear I'll kill her!" Mr. Cannon swore.

The guerrilla nodded casually. "Yeah, I think maybe you would. But Quantrill's orders were for his men not to kill any women." His voice became hard, and a coldness appeared in his eyes, as he continued, "It won't be us killin' her, you sonofabitch, it'll be you!"

"But you guerrillas will get the blame!" Mr. Cannon reasoned.

Once again, the young man nodded. "All right, you woman-killin' bastard, you can go."

Amelia could feel Mr. Cannon relax. He moved the pistol from her temple, but he still kept it aimed at her head.

Everything happened so fast that it was over within

a matter of seconds. The instant that Mr. Cannon re-laxed, the young guerrilla, moving with practiced speed, had his revolver grasped and ready to fire. Using perfect precision, he sent a bullet into Mr. Cannon's head.

The force behind the bullet knocked Mr. Cannon sideways on the horse. Panicked by the pistol shot, the animal leaned back on his haunches, and his eyes rolled wildly. Amelia almost lost her balance, but, grabbing tightly to the horse's mane, she stayed in the saddle. But Mr. Cannon's lifeless body fell to the ground.

Amelia was not an experienced rider, and incompetently she tried to calm the nervous horse, as the guerrilla, riding over to Mr. Cannon's body, once again fired a bullet into his head. The sudden shot sent Amelia's horse into a run, and, bounding down the street, he charged out of town. Amelia attempted to restrain him, but the bridle reins were trailing the ground, and it took all her strength just to remain mounted. Grasping the saddle horn, she could only hold on for dear life, as the frightened animal carried her farther and farther away from Lawrence.

SIXTEEN

Amelia's entire body was jarred with the hard pounding of the horse's hooves as he sped across the fields and into the woods. If she had been an experienced rider she would have relaxed and allowed her body to flow with the horse's steady gait, but her inexperience caused her to remain rigid. The wind whipped at her long hair, blowing it across her face, but she was too scared to let go of the saddle horn to push the flinging hair out of her eyes. Her dressing gown had worked its way up to her thighs, and the leather flap on the saddle was chafing her bare legs.

As Amelia and the horse plunged farther into the woods, the brush began to thicken. Limbs from bushes slapped against her ankles, cutting into her skin, making jagged and bleeding scratches.

Carefully, Amelia removed one hand from the saddle to push her hair out of her eyes. Looking over the horse's head, she saw that the frightened animal was running straight toward a large oak tree. She considered jumping, but there wasn't time. Ducking, she leaned over, placing her face against the horse's neck.

Avoiding the tree, the animal made a sharp turn to the left, but one of the lower branches struck across Amelia's shoulder. As the limb ripped through her gown and into her skin, she cried out with pain.

She wanted to raise up and examine her wound, but she couldn't. She had lost her hold on the saddle and was now clutching the horse's mane.

Amelia could feel herself falling dangerously to one side, but her legs were too short to reach the stirrups, and the reins were still dragging on the ground. There was no way she could regain her balance.

Suddenly the horse made another quick turn, sending Amelia plunging to the hard ground. The fall was so severe that for a moment it knocked the breath from her. She rolled to her side, and, placing her arm under her head, she took deep breaths, filling her lungs with needed air.

Cringing, she got slowly to her feet. Examining her shoulder, she saw that the branch had made an ugly cut, but it didn't appear to be bleeding too badly. Grasping the torn material on her gown, she ripped at it until she had a piece large enough to use for a bandage. Awkwardly, she managed to tie it over her shoulder. Lifting the hem on her dressing gown, she looked down at her ankles. The scratches were still stinging, but at least they had stopped bleeding.

Trying to get her bearings, Amelia glanced around at her surroundings. Where was she? It had seemed as if she had been on the horse for hours! But surely it couldn't have been more than fifteen minutes . . . thirty minutes . . . an hour? How long?

She decided to call out for help, hoping there might

be soldiers somewhere close by. Amelia started to yell when, suddenly, her hand flew to her mouth. No! She couldn't! She might not be heard by Union Soldiers, but Missouri guerrillas! She had no other choice, she must find her own way out of the woods and back to Lawrence. But which way should she go? The sun! She would use it as a guide.

Amelia hadn't realized how much the fall had bruised her until she began to walk. There wasn't a part of her body that didn't ache. Suddenly a sharp twig dug into her house slipper, causing her to stumble. Oh Lord, how long would her cloth slippers hold up? If she didn't soon find her way out of these woods, she would be forced to walk barefoot.

Quickly Amelia's injured body grew fatigued. Her shoulder ached terribly, and her stomach had begun to gnaw with hunger. The summer day was hot, but it was relatively cool in the dense woods, the coolness preventing Amelia's throat from becoming parched.

Tired, she slowly made her way to a thick cluster of bushes. She would rest for a moment before continuing. Sitting, she removed the slippers from her sore feet. The soles of her shoes were full of holes and snags. They wouldn't last much longer. She placed them at her side. Then she gently massaged her aching feet before putting the slippers back on.

All at once, Amelia's chin began to quiver, and, sniffling, she tried to hold back the urge to cry. The day was still early, and already she had lived through more nightmares than she should have experienced in a lifetime! Giving in to her distress, she fell to the ground, and, pillowing her head in her arms, she wept.

She cried until her tears ran dry; then, shocked, injured, and exhausted, she went to sleep.

The three riders halted their horses close to where Amelia lay sleeping. The cluster of bushes hid her presence from their view. Unaware that there was anyone within hearing distance, they began to speak to each other. If Amelia hadn't been so exhausted, she most likely would have awakened. But, remaining totally unconscious of her surroundings, she continued to sleep.

Two of the men had just returned from Cincinnati, Ohio. They had already given the third man the information they had acquired in Cincinnati. Now they had stopped their horses to wait for their expected escort, who would be arriving at any moment. The oldest man in the group, never imagining that he could be overheard, mentioned the name of the Confederate spy in the Union Army as he conversed with the other two men. Then, reaching over, he shook hands with his comrades, saying, "James Henry and Buford, I congratulate you both on the fine job you are doing."

James Henry started to reply when, suddenly, he noticed a robin land on a nearby bush, then immediately fly away, as if it had been startled.

Cautiously, James Henry dismounted. Keeping his voice low, he told the others to continue talking as if nothing had happened. Then, audibly, he announced that he needed to step into the bushes to relieve himself. Walking swiftly, James Henry moved to his left, disappearing into the surrounding thicket. Quietly, he stalked through the woods, circling back to his right.

The robin, wishing to eat the berries hanging on the bush next to where Amelia slept, dived back down toward it. Seeing that the woman was still there, he flapped his wings and shrieked loudly, then flew up to perch on a tree limb.

The bird's sudden screech awakened Amelia, and, alarmed, she quickly sat up. The fast movement caused her shoulder to ache, and, groaning, she pressed her hand to her wound. As the pain subsided, she became aware of voices close by. Frightened, she lowered herself back to the ground. Her hand trembling, she tried to part the heavy bush so she could see on the other side. But it was so thick that it was impossible.

She listened closely to pick up the conversation, but before she had a chance to detect what was being said, a deep voice called her name.

"Amelia!"

Turning swiftly, Amelia stared at the man standing so near to her that, for a fleeting instant, she wondered how he had come so close without her hearing him.

Recognizing the man, she got clumsily to her feet, gasping, "Jamie! . . . Thank God, it's you!" Amelia was so thankful to see someone she knew that she threw herself into his arms. "Oh Jamie! Jamie!" she cried, holding him tightly.

Instinctively, James Henry pulled her close, relishing the pleasure of her soft, clinging body. It had been a year since he had last held her in his arms. But he had never forgotten the wonderful feel of her.

As Colonel Garson and Buford hurried toward them, James Henry reluctantly released her. Stepping back, Amelia looked at the two men approaching, and then to James Henry. Frowning, she questioned, "Jamie?" She turned her gaze to Buford. "Mr. Tyler?"

Something was terribly wrong. Why would Jamie and Mr. Tyler be with a Confederate officer? And why wasn't Mr. Tyler limping? And Jamie! Why did he look so different?

Amelia's long hair was falling across her face, and, flinging it back, she studied the man she thought to be Jamie Tyler. The loose overalls and faded shirt were gone, replaced by tight tan trousers and the customary guerrilla shirt. A holster with a Colt revolver was strapped around his hips, his hand resting familiarly on the butt of his pistol. She raised her gaze to look into his eyes, and, feeling a sense of forboding, Amelia placed her hand over her heart as she cried, "Who are you?" Panicking, she accused, "You're a spy!" Her vision flew to Buford. "And so are you! Oh, dear God, you are both spies! You're working for Quantrill!"

As her dead uncle and the Lawrence massacre flashed vividly across her mind, Amelia went berserk. Her small fists floundered wildly across James Henry's chest. Screaming, she raged, "You murderers! You raving maniacs! How could you? How could you kill old men and young boys? You heartless, cruel monsters!"

Easily, James Henry grabbed her fists, holding them in his hands. "Amelia!" he yelled. "Calm down, damn it!"

But Amelia was beyond comprehension, and, furiously, she continued her ranting, "I hate you both! I wish you were dead! You killed Uncle Calvin! And all

206

those young boys! You murderers! You killers! I hate you! Oh God, let me go! I want to go home! I want my baby! My baby!''

Knowing there was no other way to calm her, James Henry secured her fists in one hand, and then with his other hand he slapped her across the cheek.

The unexpected sting shocked Amelia, and she abruptly ceased her incoherent rambling. Crying piteously, she moaned, ''I want to go home to my baby.''

''Baby?'' James Henry questioned sharply. ''Amelia, do you have a child?''

Suddenly, Amelia's whole body stiffened, and, jerking her hands free, she stepped back. All at once, she knew the truth! Oh God, it had been Jamie! Jamie! Jamie was the man who had slipped into her room and seduced her! How could she have been so foolish not to have known? But she had always believed her mystery man was a soldier!

James Henry started to question her again, but before he could Colonel Garson demanded, ''What in the hell is going on?''

Quickly James Henry told him who Amelia was, and that he and Buford had known her when they worked at the Eldridge House.

Eyeing Amelia, Colonel Garson asked sternly, ''Young lady, what are you doing out here in the woods dressed the way you are?''

Sneering, she replied sarcastically, ''You dirty lowdown pieces of filth attacked so early this morning that I wasn't given adequate time to dress properly for the occasion!''

''Amelia!'' James Henry raged. ''What in the hell are you talking about?'' His eyes examining her injuries and disheveled appearance, he continued in a gentler tone, "What happened to you?"

Looking at him with open contempt, Amelia replied, "You know very well what I am talking about! William Quantrill and his raiders attacked Lawrence this morning! They burned most of the business district and murdered men and young boys!" Not believing James Henry's look of surprise, she added, with hate, "And you were probably the one who laid out his plan of attack for him, since you are so familiar with the town! Is that why you came to Lawrence, so that . . ."

Interrupting her, James Henry gritted his teeth as he warned menacingly, "Shut up, Amelia! You don't know what you're talking about!"

Before Amelia could come back with an angry reply, Colonel Garson asked demandingly, "Young lady, did you say that Quantrill attacked Lawrence?"

"Yes!" she shouted angrily. "He ordered his raiders to murder men and teen-age boys!"

"My God!" Colonel Garson groaned. "How many citizens were killed? Do you have any idea?"

"I don't know!" she cried. "A hundred . . . maybe two hundred! God, I don't know!"

"Quantrill!" James Henry snarled. "You sick sonofabitch!"

His voice breaking with emotion, Buford moaned, "God have mercy!"

Amelia didn't believe them. For some reason, they were only pretending innocence and compassion. The two men she knew as Jamie and Sam Tyler were wearing guerrilla shirts, so obviously they were part of Quantrill's raiders, and they had probably even been at

208

the Lawrence massacre!

Shaking his head, Colonel Garson replied sorrowfully, "Quantrill isn't under my command, but I wish he was. I'd have him executed." Composing himself, he looked at James Henry and asked, "How much do you suppose she heard?"

"I don't know," James Henry answered gravely.

Puzzled, Amelia's gaze darted from one man to the other. "What do you mean?"

"Our private conversation, while you were hidden behind the bushes," Colonel Garson explained. "How much of it did you hear?"

"I heard nothing!" Amelia snapped. "I was asleep!"

"Was she sleeping when you found her?" the colonel asked James Henry.

For a moment, James Henry hesitated, but it wasn't in him to lie to his commanding officer. "No," he answered.

"I see," the colonel replied. "James Henry, I need to speak to you alone. Buford, stay here with the lady."

"Wh . . . what?" Amelia stammered. "What did you call him?"

Confused, the colonel questioned, "James Henry?"

Looking at the man she had known as Jamie, she asked, "Your name is James Henry?"

"Yes," he answered.

Thinking of her baby's name, Amelia began laughing hysterically, as she rambled, "James Henry! It's too ironic! Too unbelievable! Dear God, will I ever awaken from this crazy nightmare!"

Roughly, James Henry grasped her shoulders, his

grip tearing painfully into her wound. Shaking her, he shouted severely, "Damn it, Amelia! This is no time for hysterics!"

Pushing away from him, she stopped her laughter, and cried angrily, "Don't touch me, you dirty, murdering guerrilla spy!"

Quickly Buford stepped to her side, and gripped her arm firmly. "Just calm down, Mrs. Bishop. I don't want to hurt you."

Scowling, she looked up at him. "Oh, you Missouri guerrillas are so brave! You murder unarmed men and boys, and take full advantage of a woman's inability to defend herself!"

Studying her closely, James Henry wondered what had become of the timid and innocent Amelia he had once known. Had the Lawrence massacre done this to her, or had more happened to her in the past year? And what in the hell was she doing out here in the middle of nowhere?

"James Henry!" Colonel Garson said sternly.

"Yes, sir!" he replied.

"Come with me," he ordered.

James Henry followed the colonel over to the horses. Pausing beside his own mount, Colonel Garson turned to look at James Henry. Firmly, he stated, "She must have heard the informer's name."

"We can't be sure," James Henry replied quickly. "She may have been asleep."

"But she wasn't sleeping when you saw her. No, I'm sure she knows who he is." Seeing James Henry's concern for Amelia, he continued almost apologetically, "If she were aware only of your identity and Buford's, we could simply hold her captive until Buford completes his mission in Lawrence. Afterwards, we could let her go free. What she knows couldn't endanger either of you, because you'll both be leaving Missouri for good.'' Clearing his throat, he added authoritatively, ''But she has heard the informer's name! We must protect him at any cost!''

''Her life?'' James Henry asked, his voice suddenly weak.

Watching James Henry carefully, he questioned, ''If I were to order you to carry out her execution, would you obey my order?''

''No, sir!'' James Henry answered.

''Would Buford?'' the colonel asked.

''No, sir!''

''Disobeying an order is a court-martial offense.''

His jaw set firmly, James Henry stated, ''I won't kill a helpless woman!''

Taking his gaze from James Henry, the colonel patted his horse's neck as he asked casually, ''Are you in love with her?''

''No,'' James Henry answered quickly.

The colonel looked at James Henry again. ''What happened between you and the lady?''

''Sir?''

''Last year, in Lawrence, how well did you know her?''

''I'd prefer not to answer that question, sir!'' James Henry replied.

''She's a very attractive young woman. Are you quite sure you didn't fall in love with her?''

''Yes, I'm sure.''

''Buford called her Mrs. Bishop. Is she married?''

''Yes,'' James Henry replied quietly.

"Bishop?" the colonel pondered. "Is she by any chance married to Captain Jason Bishop? The officer who raided your father's home?"

Bitterly, James Henry answered, "Yes, sir!"

Studying James Henry thoughtfully, Colonel Garson asked, "If you were in my place, what would you do under these circumstances?"

"If we kill an innocent woman then, in my opinion, that makes us no better than Quantrill."

"But this is war!" the colonel answered sternly.

"War is no excuse to slaughter the innocent," James Henry replied.

"She isn't innocent. She knows the informer's identity."

"But it wasn't intentional!"

Sighing deeply, the colonel said, "Your sisters were also innocent, yet they died."

"What are you trying to say? Do you want me to kill Mrs. Bishop to avenge my sisters?"

"No, of course not. I am only pointing out that, during war, the innocent are sometimes killed." Eyeing James Henry seriously, he continued, "Compared to the informer's life, Mrs. Bishop's life does not matter!" Demandingly, he asked, "Do I make myself clear?"

"Yes, sir!" James Henry answered.

Hearing horses, the colonel looked at the large group of guerrillas approaching. "My escort is here."

"Sir!" James Henry said. "If you order them to execute Mrs. Bishop, you will have to order my execution, as well!"

"What!" Colonel Garson bellowed.

"You'll have to kill me, because I'll try to save her

life!''

"Goddamn!" the colonel uttered angrily. Colonel Garson liked James Henry, and he sure as hell didn't want to order his death! Waiting until his escort brought their horses to a stop, he commanded, "You men stay mounted. I'll be ready to leave in a few minutes." Looking to James Henry, he said in a lowered voice, "If you'll give me your word that you'll hold Mrs. Bishop captive, I'll temporarily place her in your custody. When I get to Texas, I'll report this incident to my superiors. And, damn it, James Henry, what happens to Mrs. Bishop will be their decision. Maybe they'll simply order her to be taken somewhere safe and kept a prisoner for the duration of the war."

"Or they may order her execution!" James Henry replied irritably.

"Do I have your word that you won't let her escape?" Colonel Garson asked impatiently.

For a moment, James Henry's expression was indiscernible, then, nodding, he replied, "You have my word!" Shaking hands with the colonel, he added, "Thank you, sir."

"Take her to Captain Anderson's camp, and explain to him what has happened. I should be back within a month, two at the most." He paused. "I need to talk to Mrs. Bishop and Buford, then I'll be on my way."

Together, they walked over to Amelia and Buford. Standing close to Amelia, the colonel eyed her severely. "Mrs. Bishop," he began, "you will be taken to Captain Anderson's camp. I'm sending explicit orders to Captain Anderson that you are to be immediately executed if you mention the informer's name to any of his men."

Shocked, Amelia stared at him. "What are you talking about? I don't know anything about an informer! And how dare you kidnap me!"

"Mrs. Bishop," the colonel warned, "your life is hanging on a very thin thread, so I suggest that you tread lightly!" Turning sharply, he regarded James Henry. "If she gives the informer's name to anyone, she is to be killed! And, goddamn it, if I find out you didn't give this order to Captain Anderson, I'll take great pleasure in personally ordering your court-martial!"

Incredulous, Amelia cried, "I don't know anything about an informer!" Suddenly, becoming aware of how serious her situation was, her knees grew weak. "Dear God!" she gasped. "He must be someone very important!" Remembering Jamie and Sam Tyler had disappeared on the same morning that the Union officials left Lawrence, Amelia speculated, "He's an officer in the Union Army, isn't he?"

Buford was standing close to her, and, grabbing her wrist, he jerked her toward him. Under his breath, he grumbled, "Shut up, you little fool!"

James Henry could see the colonel's indecision, and quickly he reminded him, "Sir, I gave you my word. Surely, I also have yours!"

Colonel Garson nodded brusquely. "Very well, James Henry. We will both uphold our agreement." Looking at Buford, he ordered, "Wait a few days before you go to Lawrence. It would be best that you don't arrive too soon after Quantrill's raid."

"Yes, sir," he replied.

First the colonel shook hands with James Henry, and then with Buford. "I'll see you two in a few weeks." Turning to Amelia, he said stiffly, "I'm sorry, ma'am!" Quickly he went to his horse, mounted, and, along with his escort, he rode into the woods.

Buford was still holding Amelia's wrist, and pulling her hand free, she blurted resentfully. "When Jason finds out what has happened, he'll kill you both!"

"Mrs. Bishop," Buford began calmly. "I'm going to give you some advice, and I hope you take it. Don't mention your husband in my and James Henry's presence."

"Why?" Amelia demanded. "Are you two that afraid of him?"

Buford chose to ignore her accusation. Walking away from Amelia, he told James Henry, "I'll find a safe place to camp for a few days, then go to Lawrence."

James Henry nodded. "Take care, Buford."

Pausing at James Henry's side, Buford shook hands with him. "I will, and you do the same."

Silently, they watched Buford as he went to his horse. He waved to James Henry as he rode away.

Turning to Amelia, James Henry ordered gruffly, "Let's go!"

"I'm not going anywhere with you!" she shouted.

Sighing impatiently, he replied, "Aw, hell, Amelia, don't give me a hard time. I don't like this situation any more than you do."

Without stopping first to think, she yelled, "I hate you! You're a murderer and a rapist!"

Casually, he responded, "So you know it was me."

"Yes!" she cried.

"Your child," he began carefully, "who's the father?''

She would rather die than admit to a damned guerrilla that he had fathered her child. "Jason!" she said firmly.

"Are you sure?" he insisted.

"Of course, I'm sure!" she shouted.

James Henry's look of relief was so obvious that Amelia was actually startled. Apparently, it had meant a great deal to him not to be her baby's father. For a fleeting moment, she wondered why.

Stepping to her side, he asked, "How in the hell did you come to be in these woods?"

She raised her chin defiantly, refusing to give him the satisfaction of an answer. He simply shrugged, as if her explanation was of no importance. Taking her by the arm, he tried to lead her to his horse, but, roughly, she pulled back.

Grinning as though he was amused, he lifted her in his arms. She fought against him, but her futile attempts only caused him to hold her tighter. Still smiling, he gazed down into her face. "I missed you, little one."

She hadn't expected such a confession, and, surprised, Amelia stopped fighting him. His clear blue eyes stared into hers, and she felt as if she could become lost in his piercing gaze. Remembering how he had once taken her to such wonderful heights of passion, tears sprang to her eyes, and she mumbled unconvincingly, "I hate you."

Seeing her sadness, he said tenderly, "I'm sorry, Amelia."

She almost believed him, until, suddenly, she remembered he was a Missouri guerrilla and a despicable spy! He was the enemy! "When Jason kills you, it'll be no less than you deserve!"

His strong arms gripped her so powerfully that she cried out. His eyes flickered with a silent rage. Determined not to be intimidated, she taunted him flippantly. "You cowardly guerrillas definitely fear a man who is capable of defending himself, don't you?"

"I don't fear your husband!" he said coldly. "But, someday, I'm going to kill him!"

Shocked, she cried, "Why?"

"It's a personal matter!"

"But he's my husband!"

Carrying her to his horse, he remarked sourly, "That, madam, is your problem!" Placing her on the saddle, he lifted himself up behind her. Taking the reins in his hand, he asked lightly, "Tell me, little one, do you still despise Bishop's sexual advances?"

Conscious of his arms encircling her and his hard body so close to hers, she stammered, "No . . . no . . . of course not."

Placing his lips next to her ear, he whispered, "You're lying."

She hated him! He was a spy and a guerrilla! Yet, she could feel herself responding to his nearness. Fighting her desire, she said peevishly, "You contemptible, low-down, Missouri piece of scum!"

He laughed heartily. "You've become quite spirited since I last saw you. This time, it's going to be a helluva lot more fun seducing you."

"You'll have to rape me, because this time there'll be no seduction!"

"Seduction?" he questioned humorously. "But only a few minutes ago, you called me a rapist. Are

217

you admitting that I never raped you?''

Confused, she snapped, ''I'm admitting nothing, except that I hate you!''

''If it wasn't imperative that I get you to Anderson's camp as soon as possible, I'd lay you on the ground and take you here and now. And we both know, it wouldn't come to rape.'' Lightly, his lips brushed her cheek. Sensually, he whispered, ''Little one, I have never forgotten you.''

She wanted to cry out that she had easily forgotten him! But she hadn't forgotten him, not for one moment! He had continued to exist in her memories and through their son. Thinking of her child, Amelia began crying.

''What's wrong?'' he asked gently.

''I want to go home to my baby!'' she cried pathetically.

Pulling at the reins, James Henry encouraged the horse into a brisk walk. Leaning her head against his chest, Amelia continued to cry for her child. James Henry had to force himself not to turn the horse around and take her back toward Lawrence. But, by God, he had given his word, and he would remain true to his promise, even if it meant Amelia's death, as well as his own!

SEVENTEEN

The sun had begun to set when James Henry and Amelia arrived close enough to Anderson's camp to be halted by his guards. Recognizing James Henry, they gave him permission to continue.

The hideout was located in a secluded valley, surrounded by steep, rolling hills. There was a brook flowing beside the crowded camp. It was filled with men bathing, or kneeling at the bank washing their clothes. Seeing a woman approaching, the ones bathing quickly ducked under the water.

As James Henry guided the horse toward the center of the camp, the guerrillas stared at Amelia with astonishment. What was a woman doing at a guerrilla hideout?

There was a tent erected in the middle of the camp, and when they reached it, James Henry reined his horse. Immediately, the front flap was pushed aside.

Observing the man stepping out of the tent, Amelia instinctively caught her breath. He was young, but maturely handsome. He wasn't dressed exclusively as a guerrilla or a Confederate, but he wore a combination of both kinds of clothes. He projected an aura of refinement that she found overwhelming. She was completely awed and captivated by his presence. Surely this man couldn't be Bill Anderson, known among the Union as "Bloody Bill" because it was rumored that he had never spared a captured soldier's life.

James Henry dismounted. Walking to the man, he shook hands with him, saying cordially, "Hello, Bill."

Dear Lord!, Amelia thought. He is Captain Anderson! I never dreamed he was so young! Or so good-looking, she admitted to herself reluctantly, but truthfully.

"James Henry," Anderson replied, shaking his hand firmly. He glanced up at Amelia.

She met his eyes, and she was surprised to find them warm.

Looking back at James Henry, he said clearly, "I suppose you have an explanation for the lady's presence."

"Yes, let's step inside where we can speak privately."

The captain nodded, stepping back for him to enter. James Henry moved forward, then, hesitating, he said, "You'll have to post a guard on her."

It was apparent that Anderson found his request unusual, but without question, he immediately commanded two of his men to stay with Amelia.

The guerrillas Anderson ordered to guard Amelia were young. The moment their commanding officer and James Henry disappeared inside the tent, one of them asked her politely, "Ma'am, would you care to dismount?"

She regarded him curiously. He wasn't very tall. He was towheaded and clean-shaven. His smile seemed to be genuinely friendly. "No, thank you," she replied softly.

"Would you like a drink of fresh water?" the other one asked.

She looked at the man who had spoken. His hair and beard were bright red. She was sure underneath his beard there must be freckles galore. "Yes," she answered. "A drink would be nice."

Moving quickly, as if waiting on a lady was a great honor, he hurried to the water bucket that was placed beside the tent. Filling the dipper, he brought it to Amelia, who drank and returned the dipper, thanking him.

"You're welcome, ma'am," he replied.

As he returned the dipper to the water bucket, she looked from one man to the other. It had been men like these who had raided Lawrence. How could they be capable of so much violence, yet, under different circumstances, behave like gentlemen? Oh, it was all too confusing, and she was so weary! And hungry! She hadn't eaten all day. Unknowingly, she sighed deeply with fatigue.

Returning, the one with the red hair asked, "Are you tired, ma'am?"

The other one offered her his hand. "Let me help you down, ma'am. We'll make you a comfortable place to rest."

Accepting his hand, she allowed him to assist her from the horse. The other man moved away but returned promptly with a blanket. Spreading it on the ground, he gestured toward it, telling her to sit down.

As she made herself reasonably comfortable on the spread blanket, the one with the red hair introduced himself and his friend. "Ma'am, my name is Pat, and this is Gary."

She almost told them that her name was Mrs. Bishop, but cautiously she caught herself. Her husband was their enemy, and they might have a personal grudge against him. "My name is Amelia," she replied.

"Miss Amelia," Gary began, "could I get you something to eat?"

"Food?" she gasped hungrily. "Oh yes, that would be wonderful!"

"I'll be right back, ma'am," he promised, before leaving to fetch her dinner.

Absent-mindedly, Amelia glanced down at her dressing gown, and, suddenly, she became embarrassingly aware of how she was dressed. Quickly she looked at Pat, but if he found her attire peculiar, he was too polite to let on.

Returning with her food, Gary knelt beside her, handing her a plate of steaming rabbit stew.

"Oh, it smells delicious!" she cried. She devoured the food ravenously, not caring what her guards thought of her manners.

When she finished Gary took the empty plate. "Could I get you some more?" he asked.

Before Amelia could answer, the flap on the tent was once again pushed open, and James Henry and Captain Anderson stepped outside.

At once, Anderson dismissed her guards. Walking over to Amelia, he knelt beside her. "Mrs. Bishop," he began, "James Henry has told me of your circumstances. First, I want to say that I profoundly regret that a lady like yourself had to become involved in this war. But, madam, whether we like or not, you have become very deeply entangled. The information you overheard today has placed you in a very perilous situation.''

"But I don't know the informer's name!'' she pleaded. "Captain Anderson, please believe me! I don't know!''

He slowly shook his head. "Perhaps, but your speculation in Colonel Garson's presence only placed you in more danger.''

Frightened, Amelia looked over at James Henry. "Am I going to be executed?'' she cried piteously.

In two long strides, he was on the blanket kneeling at her other side. "Amelia,'' he whispered sympathetically.

Tears filling her eyes, she returned her gaze to Captain Anderson. "Am I going to be killed tonight?'' she asked, her voice breaking with a heartrending sob.

He smiled tenderly. "No, Mrs. Bishop. Not tonight or at daybreak. My orders are to hold you captive. But, ma'am, if you know the informer's identity, please don't tell any of my men who he is, because if you do, I'll be forced to order your immediate death.''

Burying her face in her hands, she gasped, "But I don't know his name!''

Rising, Captain Anderson spoke to James Henry. "There's a cave at the foot of the hill on the west side of the camp. She can have privacy there. The hill is too steep for her to climb, and the only other way out is back through this camp. I'll have some of my men bring you blankets and supplies.'' Observing Amelia's apparel, he added, "I'll also see if we can find her some clothes. But she's so tiny that it isn't going to be easy to scrounge up something that will even come close to fitting." To Amelia, he said compassionately, "Mrs. Bishop, I am truly sorry about everything that has happened. I will try to make your stay at this camp as pleasant as possible."

Looking up at him, she answered sincerely, "Thank you, Captain Anderson."

Taking her hand, James Henry helped her to her feet. As he began leading her in the direction of the nearby cave, Amelia asked, "Is it true that Captain Anderson carries a silk cord, and for every Federal he himself kills he ties a knot in the cord?"

"Yes, it's true," James Henry answered.

Abruptly, Amelia halted. "But he seemed to be a man of compassion!"

"He has no compassion for Jayhawkers!" James Henry answered coldly.

"Why? Because they are his enemy?"

Gripping her arm, he continued their pace. "They murdered his sister!" he explained bluntly, understanding exactly how Anderson felt.

She longed to question him further, but she had a feeling he would refuse to answer her questions.

The interior of the cave was small, but the walls were high, making it possible for James Henry to maneuver without being forced to stoop.

The cave was dark and damp, compelling Amelia to cross her arms as she involuntarily shivered. "It's so gloomy in here," she remarked.

"I would make a fire, but in this weather we sure don't need any extra heat. When the men bring the supplies, they'll have a lantern. Maybe it'll help to lighten the gloom."

Moving to her side, he attempted to take her hand into his. Recoiling, she stepped away. "Don't touch me!" she demanded.

Startled by her response, he asked, "What's wrong?"

She laughed bitterly. "Wrong?" she repeated. "I have been kidnapped by a spy, and I'm being held captive at a guerrilla camp! And you ask me what is wrong?"

With ill temper, he replied, "Amelia, the circumstances cannot be altered, so why don't you just make the best of them!"

"How?" she snapped. "By being nice to you?"

"That would be a good place to start!" he said firmly.

"Oh, you would like that, wouldn't you?" she raged. "Your own private mistress at your disposal!"

Moving swiftly, he reached out to grab her. Changing his mind, he doubled his hands into fists, letting them remain at his side. "Damn it, Amelia! I don't like this situation any more than you do!"

"Why? Am I keeping you from your dirty business of spying on Union towns, so that Quantrill can raid them and kill innocent people!"

"I had nothing to do with the Lawrence raid!" he yelled.

Raising her chin obstinately, she replied unyieldingly, "I don't believe you!"

Detecting the cold fury in his eyes, she shrank back

225

from him, afraid that he might strike her.

Swerving, he stomped out of the cave. Sitting by the entrance, he took out a cigar and lit it. Amelia watched him as he sat silently smoking. She had a sudden impulse to go to him and tell him she was sorry. But was she sorry? No, not if he was involved in any way with the attack on Lawrence. She could never forgive him for such an evil act.

Finding her emotions confusing, Amelia walked to a corner of the cave and sat down. Leaning back against the cave wall, she continued to study James Henry. His back was facing her, but for a moment he turned his head, and she could clearly see his profile. His black hair was falling across his forehead. Casually, he brushed it back from his face as he placed the cigar between his lips. He rested his arms across his raised knees, and Amelia could hear him sigh deeply. He turned his head to look in front of him, and she could no longer see his face. She wondered what he was thinking. What kind of man had fathered her child? Would her baby inherit his characteristics? It was apparent that her son had already inherited his father's looks.

Thinking of her baby, Amelia snuggled closer into the corner. Would she ever see her child again? Captain Anderson had seemed to be a gentleman, but it could be nothing more than a facade. He most likely could order her execution without giving it a second thought. What was one more death to him when he had ordered so many? And James Henry? Would he attempt to save her, or perhaps help her escape? No! If he had wanted to protect her, he would never have brought her here! He would have taken her close to

Lawrence and then set her free.

She suddenly felt terribly alone, and, lying down, she muffled her cries. The dirt rubbed into her cheek, and placing her arm under her face, she kept her sobs hushed, hoping that James Henry wouldn't hear.

Against her will her shoulders began shaking as with a chill, and, surrendering to her sorrow, she missed detecting James Henry's hurried entrance. Sitting beside her, he placed his hand on her long disheveled hair, pushing it back from her face. His unexpected touch startled Amelia, and quickly she sat up.

"Little one," he murmured lovingly.

Heedlessly, she flung herself into his arms. Clinging to him, she cried, "Will I ever see my baby again?"

Groaning sympathetically, he held her tightly. "Amelia . . . Amelia," he whispered.

"Answer me!" she begged, her arms still holding onto him tenaciously. When he made no reply, she unconsciously dug her fingers into his skin as she demanded, Answer me! . . . Will I ever see my baby?"

Placing his hand on her hair, he nestled her head to his shoulder. "I don't know," he admitted. "But I promise you, Amelia, if it's within my power, you'll see your child again."

"Why did you bring me here to be killed?" she cried. "My God, what kind of man are you?"

"Amelia," he sighed, "how can I make you understand?"

She wanted to push out of his arms and continue her verbal abuse, but she was too physically and emotionally exhausted to find the needed strength. Relaxing, she permitted him to place her on his lap as if she were

227

a child. Keeping her head on his shoulder, she sniffled, then hiccuped as her sobs quietened.

"Do you have a daughter or a son?" he asked gently.

"A son," she murmured.

"How old is he?"

She almost revealed that he was three months old, but alertly she replied, "Two months." She wondered if he was doing a quick calculation. Well if he was, let him! He would come up one month short.

"What's his name?" he asked.

"His . . . his name?" she questioned. "It's . . . it's Hank." There had been no reason to avoid her son's Christian name, after all, it had only been an honest coincidence that he had received James Henry's name. But as a precautionary measure, she would keep it to herself.

"Do you think Bishop will have any problems finding the baby adequate nourishment?"

Confused, she asked, "What do you mean?"

"Aren't you nursing your child?" he questioned.

His intimate inquiry caused Amelia's cheeks to grow warm, and she was thankful that her head was on his shoulder, and he couldn't see her face. "No . . . he has a wet nurse," she stammered.

"Didn't you want to nurse your child?" he asked. "A mother should share that special closeness with her baby."

Finding his attitude insufferable, she said irritably, "Of course, I wanted to be the one to feed him, but the doctor said . . . he said . . ."

"He said what?" he coaxed.

Flustered, Amelia began to fidget. How could she

228

conceivably tell him that her breasts had been too small without dying from embarrassment?

"Well?" he insisted.

"I wasn't physically able," she replied.

"Had you been ill?"

My goodness, would he never stop asking questions? she wondered. "No, I hadn't been ill," she answered.

"Then what was wrong?" he pressed.

Piqued, she lifted her head, and, her eyes flashing indignantly, she blurted, "I wasn't large enough!"

Holding back the urge to grin, he kept his face sober. "Amelia, it's not a mother's size, but how much milk she has."

"And how would you know?" she asked doubtfully.

When he made no reply, Amelia frowned. Thoughtfully, she said, "But I had plenty of . . ." Inhaling sharply, she suddenly became aware of the truth. "Damn Jason! He convinced the doctor to be a part of his deceitful conspiracy! Oh, he can be so arrogant! I'll never forgive him! Never!"

"Apparently, your husband preferred that his wife not be physically tied to his child."

"His child!" she huffed impulsively. "He's my child!"

"What?" he questioned suspiciously.

Realizing what she had said, she explained hurriedly, "Jason takes no interest in Hank. He believes a baby is strictly a woman's business. I'm sure when Hank is a little older, Jason will be more of a father to him."

Agreeing, James Henry replied, "Bishop doesn't

229

especially strike me as the type who would enjoy bouncing a baby on his knee.''

Amelia didn't realize she was smiling as she answered, ''He would be too worried that the baby might burp and stain his immaculately clean uniform.''

James Henry chuckled. ''He'd probably order the poor kid to his crib for insubordination.''

Giggling, Amelia replied, ''Ten days detention, at the very least.''

Laughing, they looked into each other's eyes, but, suddenly, their laughter ceased. The unexpected magnetism between them was electrifying, causing Amelia to gasp for breath.

Reading his thoughts, she whispered pleadingly, ''No . . . no . . .''

''Why not, Amelia?'' he asked sensually.

Furiously, she cried, ''No!'' She tried to push away from him, but easily, he kept her in his embrace.

''I want you, little one,'' he murmured.

His voice and confession sent chills up her spine. Oh why? Why did this man hold such a strong mastery over her?

''If you have any compassion at all, you'll leave me alone!'' she pleaded.

''Why? Tell me why, damn it?'' he demanded.

''Have you no mercy?'' she cried. ''Today, I witnessed men and boys being murdered! I saw Uncle Calvin dead! I was abducted by Mr. Cannon, and then trapped on a runaway horse! As if that wasn't enough, I became lost in the woods, only to be abducted by you!'' Overwrought, she began hitting her fists against his chest, as she ranted, ''I can't take any more! Do you understand? I can't take any more!''

Clutching her hands in his, he crooned soothingly, "Don't, little one . . . Don't . . . it'll be all right . . . Sweetheart, everything will be all right. . . ."

Falling into his arms, she allowed him to hold her securely, and, listening to his soothing words, she drifted into sleep.

Gary and Pat had gone through the camp thoroughly, locating everything that they were sure Amelia would need during her stay at the hideout. Anderson's raiders, most of them taught from early childhood to honor and protect a lady, were willing to share part of their meager belongings to help a lady in distress.

Proudly, Gary and Pat displayed the Pro-Confederates' gifts to Amelia. Two of the smallest guerrillas, both boys of sixteen, had sent her a pair of trousers and a shirt. Because it was a guerrilla shirt, she was tempted to refuse it, but, swallowing her pride, she accepted it. Anything was better than wearing a torn dressing gown. Had Amelia known that the boy who had sent the shirt only had two shirts to his name, her heart would have softened, but she had no way of knowing this.

Her gifts consisted of ribbons that one raider had acquired for his wife, and perfumed soap that another had planned to give his mother. Captain Anderson sent her a brush and comb set that had belonged to his sister, a sentimental treasure he always kept with him.

When Pat and Gary embarrassedly showed her a pair of ladies' lace "undies," Amelia was shocked. How in the world had they found such feminine apparel in a guerrilla camp? They explained to her that the gift was from a man called Bulldog. "Bulldog"? she questioned. Laughing, they told her when she saw him, she would understand how he came by the nickname. But Bulldog had refused to tell them why he had a pair of ladies' underwear among his possessions, and they hadn't insisted. No one pressed Bulldog about anything, unless they be willing to forfeit his life.

Apologizing, they told her they hadn't been able to find her a pair of boots. A couple of the men actually owned an extra pair, but they were much too large to even stay on Amelia's dainty feet. But, if she would give them her ragged slippers, they would try to repair them.

Captain Anderson, conscious of her wounds, had sent a medical kit, but when Gary offered it to Amelia, James Henry had insisted that he give it to him instead.

The moment Pat and Gary said their goodnights, leaving with Amelia's slippers, James Henry picked up an empty pan and, without an explanation, he left the cave.

He returned momentarily, and as he approached Amelia, she saw that he had filled the pan with water. He placed it at her side, then he fetched the medical kit. Sitting beside her, he reached over, touching her wounded shoulder.

Finding his touch and nearness disturbing, she moved back a little, trying to avoid him.

"Amelia," he said tenderly, "let me tend to your shoulder."

"I can do it!" she replied frigidly.

Losing his patience, he warned, "If you don't stop acting like a child, I'm going to treat you like one, and take you across my knee and spank you!''

Her eyes widening, she stared at him, gasping, ''You wouldn't dare!''

''Oh, wouldn't I?'' he replied, his gaze penetrating hers with such an intensity that Amelia questioned if he would actually stoop to such uncouth brutality.

''You're not only a contemptible spy and murderer, but also a bully!'' she sneered.

''This is my last warning,'' he told her, his voice dangerously menacing. ''If you don't stop this childish hostility, I'm going to spank your very attractive bottom!''

How dare he speak to me in such a manner! she fumed silently. He is worse than Jason! Men! I detest all of them! They think they are so superior, because they are physically stronger than women!

Her temper flaring indignantly, she scowled angrily, ''I hate you!''

''Damn it, Amelia!'' he cursed. ''You have told me you hate me one time too many! Apparently, you have to be taught a lesson the hard way!''

He moved so quickly that Amelia wasn't aware of what had happened until she found herself across his knees. Before she could protest, his hand came down on her buttocks so sharply that she cried out.

''Oh, you beast!'' she shrieked. ''Let me go! How dare you! Let me up this minute!''

''Not until you tell me you don't hate me,'' he responded.

''But I do hate you!'' she blurted.

Again, his hand slapped her on the bottom, causing Amelia to try and squirm off his lap, but he kept her pinned against him. ''You don't hate me, little one,''

233

he said tolerantly. "Admit it!"

"Yes, I do!" she cried, but her voice lacked conviction.

"Have you forgotten the passion we once shared?" he asked sensually. When she didn't reply, he insisted harshly, "Have you forgotten?"

"No . . . no," she whispered faintly. Dear Lord, how could she have forgotten? Her son had been conceived from their passion.

Tensing, she waited for him to ask her again if she hated him. Unexpectedly he turned her, and, cuddling her in his arms, brought his mouth down against hers.

She didn't want to respond to his kiss. He was not only a spy, but a Missouri guerrilla! He was her enemy! It was wrong to desire him! So very sinfully wrong! But God forgive her, deep in her heart, she still loved him!

Wrapping her arms around his neck, she parted her lips beneath his. James Henry's kiss grew intense, stimulating all the passion in Amelia that had remained unawakened since the night he had walked out of her life.

Slowly, he removed his lips from hers. "Now," he challenged, "tell me you hate me."

"I can't," she whispered reluctantly.

He released her, and moving to his side, she remarked, "But I hate what you are!"

"What am I?" he asked gently.

"The enemy!" she stated bitterly.

Sighing, he replied, "I'm sorry."

Amelia didn't know how she had expected him to respond, but she certainly hadn't been expecting an apology. Her brow furrowing with puzzlement, she studied him closely. Oh, he was so complex, this man she loved with all her heart!

Without further comment, he opened the medical kit. Passively, Amelia permitted him to clean her shoulder and the scratches on her ankles. When he applied the antiseptic it stunged, causing her to bite into her bottom lip. But she wouldn't cry out and have him accuse her again of acting like a foolish child!

When he finished, Amelia sighed miserably, "If only I could take a bath. I feel so unbearably filthy."

Standing, James Henry reached down and picked up the lit lantern. He ordered, "Get two blankets and the bar of soap."

Doing as he requested, she asked, "Where are we going?"

Smiling, he answered, "Follow me, madam; your bath awaits."

Walking out of the cave at his side, Amelia's bare feet caused her to step cautiously. The rocks and broken twigs were hurtful, but she would take the pain. She sure wouldn't go so far as to ask him to carry her!

Turning to the right, James Henry led her to the far side of the cave, where she saw a small waterfall cascading down the side of the cliff.

Gesturing toward the rippling pool at the bottom of the cliff, he said, "Your bathtub, Mrs. Bishop."

Happily, Amelia murmured, "Oh, it looks so inviting! I can hardly wait!"

Stepping to the pool, James Henry set the lantern on the ground. Then picking up a stick, he shoved it into the bushes, rustling the shrubbery.

"What are you doing?" she asked.

"I wouldn't want you to get snake bit," he answered matter-of-factly.

Amelia gulped. "Oh?" she choked faintly.

Pitching the stick, he returned to her side. "The terrain is free of snakes, madam."

She waited, but he made no move to leave. "Well?" she questioned.

"Well, what?" he asked harmlessly.

"Will you please go away!" she demanded.

Grinning slyly, he replied, "But I was planning on taking a bath."

"Not with me!" she snapped.

The glow from the lantern made it easy for Amelia to see his face. His eyes were strikingly blue, his black hair and trimmed beard ruggedly attractive, and his smile roguish. Taking in his handsome features, her pulse began to race, and her heart began to beat rapidly.

"Oh, please go away!" she pleaded, afraid she would shamelessly throw herself into his arms if he remained.

"For various reasons, Amelia, it would be unwise to leave you here alone. But I will step back a few paces and turn my back. But that, little one, is as far as I will go to protect your modesty."

"You promise you'll keep your back turned?" she asked.

Humorously, he replied, "You have my word as a gentleman."

"Gentleman!" she scoffed. "A Missouri guerrilla a gentleman! That's a laugh!"

"Believe it or not, Amelia, there are gentleman among Pro-Confederates."

It was on the tip of her tongue to argue the point, but suddenly she remembered the young guerrilla who had helped the old man to the church. Had he been a gentleman? Oh, it all went beyond her comprehension. How could any woman be expected to understand what compulsions governed men?

Wishing he knew what Amelia was thinking about, James Henry walked a short distance away. Keeping his back turned, he lit a cigar. As he smoked it, he listened to the sounds Amelia made as she bathed in the pool.

When the splashing finally ceased, it was very tempting to swerve and look at her. He could picture her stepping out of the water. The light from the lantern would make her easy to see, and, with the dampness dripping from her soft, bare skin, she would be breathtakingly beautiful. He had touched the most intimate parts of her body, but his eyes had never beheld her beauty.

Hearing her steps, James Henry turned. She had a blanket wrapped securely around her, and her long golden hair was falling over her shoulders.

"Amelia," he pleaded, "take off the blanket and let me look at you."

His eyes bore into hers with an intensity so strong, that Amelia could actually feel an enticing warmth filling her senses and spreading downward to her thighs. She longed to throw off the blanket and beg him to make love to her. No! No, she mustn't! She couldn't let herself fall even more in love with him! He would only leave her again! And this time . . . this time, her broken heart would never mend!

Shoving the bar of soap into his hand, she fled to the

cave, completely unmindful of the small rocks and sharp twigs digging into her bare feet.

The interior of the cave narrowed down to a smaller opening that traveled farther back and underground. Returning from his bath, James Henry wasn't surprised to see this was where Amelia had decided to sleep. He knew she would attempt to stay as far away from him as was possible.

Adjusting the blanket she still had wrapped around her, Amelia lay down on the cover that she had spread on the ground. Becoming aware of James Henry's entrance, she had every intention of looking at him with mild indifference, but the effect his presence had on her was far from that of tranquility or detachment. In his hands he carried the lantern and his boots, and his clothes and Amelia's were gathered under one arm. He was completly naked, except for a blanket tied around his hips. The thick hairs on his muscular chest were still damp, and his black hair, wet from his bath, was falling carelessly across his forehead. He set the lantern down, then simply dropped the clothes and boots. Finding extra cover, he placed it on the ground close to the lamp. Noticing that Amelia was watching him, he grinned humorously as he undid the blanket tied at his hips.

Gasping, she quickly shut her eyes. Men had absolutely no modesty!

"You can open your eyes now, Amelia. I am decently covered." James Henry chuckled.

Peeking cautiously from under her half-closed eyelids, she saw that he was lying down with the blanket placed over him.

Trying to sound unruffled, she replied, "Goodnight, James Henry."

"Goodnight," he murmured. "By the way, Amelia," he began, as though it were merely an afterthought, "if you hear any flapping sounds coming from inside that opening you're lying so close to, don't be alarmed."

"Flapping?" she questioned.

"Bats," he explained casually. "I'm sure farther back this cave is full of them. But they probably won't come too close to the opening, and even if they should wander out, chances are they will choose to ignore you."

Sitting up, Amelia eyed the dark hole leading underground. "Bats?" she repeated shakily.

Looking at her, he nodded. "Yes, bats."

Fiddling with her blanket, she tried to act as if she couldn't care less, but vividly she was envisioning bats attacking her as she slept.

"You know," Amelia replied, attempting to sound totally collected, "it's terribly stuffy back here. I think I'll sleep closer to the entrance, so I can feel the evening breezes."

Holding back a pressing urge to laugh, he agreed, "That's a good idea."

Gathering up her blanket, Amelia hurried to the front entrance. As soon as she was once again settled down for the night, James Henry told her calmly, "Amelia, if I were you, I'd make sure the cover was tucked in securely."

"My goodness, James Henry," she sighed, exasperated. "It's too hot! Why in the world would I want to completely enclose myself in a blanket?''

''Snakes,'' he answered dispassionately.

''Wh . . . what?'' she stammered.

''Don't worry, Amelia. If they should crawl to the mouth of the cave, they won't venture in very far. The light from the lantern will dissuade them.''

''But the lantern is over there by you!'' she exclaimed.

Grinning, he answered, ''Yeah, I know.''

''James Henry, you're impossible!'' she remarked peevishly. Snakes! she fumed inwardly. He's only saying that to frighten me! Well, I'll show him that I don't scare so easily!

Turning to her side, she fixed her gaze on the ground outside the cave. Squinting, she examined the rocky terrain. Was that long, narrow object a stick, or a snake? It's only a stick, of course! Did it move? She couldn't be sure!

Sitting up rigidly, she ordered resentfully, ''James Henry, give me that lantern!''

''Come and get it,'' he baited.

Tossing her head smugly, she replied, ''All right, I will!''

Strutting, she crossed the span that separated them. As she leaned over to pick up the lantern, he reached out, grasping her around the waist. Pulling her down beside him, he teased, ''I got you, you little vixen!''

''Let me go!'' she demanded.

In one swift move, he had her pinned next to him. ''I'll let you go, under one condition.''

''What is that?'' she questioned.

''If, after five minutes, I have failed to seduce you, you can take the lantern and return to the front of the cave."

"Oh, James Henry, not again!" she sighed, knowing full well she would succumb to his advances as easily as she had surrendered that first night in her hotel room.

"Yes, little one, again," he whispered, before his lips were on hers.

Amelia's loyalties to the Union demanded that she remain unresponsive, but as his mouth possessed hers the war and everything it represented was completely forgotten. She was conscious of nothing, except the burning desire flowing hotly through her veins. With tears stinging her eyes, Amelia resigned herself to being in love with James Henry. How could she ever refuse him? She loved him with all her heart.

Impatiently, he pulled at the blanket covering her until he had it removed. Then flinging it to the side, he raised up to look at her. Hungrily, his eyes devoured her small, firm breasts, her tiny waist, and the golden hair between her thighs.

"You're so beautiful!" he moaned. "I have waited so long to see you as you are now."

Aggressively, she threw off the remaining cover between them. As he moved over her, she opened her legs, welcoming him. Feeling his erection thrust between her thighs, she placed her hand on the back of his head, pressing his lips down to hers. Kissing him boldly, she arched her hips, waiting for his penetration.

"Not so fast, little one," he murmured, running light kisses across her neck and then down to her breasts. His tongue teased one nipple and then the other, making Amelia moan with pleasure.

Lowering his body, he moved his mouth to her stomach, kissing her smooth flesh. Amelia gasped when his lips traveled farther downward. As his warm mouth began stimulating the most secretive part of her body, she felt as if she would swoon with ecstasy.

"Oh, James Henry!" she pleaded. "Please . . . please take me now! I want you inside me!"

Positioning himself, he entered her swiftly. "Oh, yes!" she murmured seductively, his penetration making her tremble with longing.

Placing his hands under her hips, he lifted her thighs to his, and, locking her ankles across his back, she willingly accepted his probing manhood.

Oh, how had she survived a whole year without experiencing this wonderful rapture that only James Henry had the power to awaken in her?

Wanting him desperately, Amelia met his powerful thrusting time and time again. Clinging to him, she equaled his passion with a boldness that aroused James Henry, causing him to take them ecstatically to love's highest peak.

Afterwards, Amelia was totally drained, but she had never felt so physically content. Placing the blanket over them, James Henry moved to her side. He took her into his arms, and, resting her head on his shoulder, she whispered, "What will happen to me?"

"Don't think about it, Amelia," he answered gently.

"Why did you bring me here?" she pleaded. "Oh, James Henry, why didn't you let me go free? Don't you care about me at all?"

"I don't want to discuss it," he answered. "I could never make you understand.

"James Henry," she began cautiously, "will I eventually be executed?"

She could feel him stiffen, as he replied, "Not if I can help it." Pulling her close, he told her, "Amelia, I swear I had nothing to do with the raid on Lawrence."

Sighing deeply, she replied honestly, "I believe you."

Silence fell between them for a long time, and James Henry believed her to be asleep. When she spoke, it surprised him. "If I should be killed," she said, her voice trembling, "promise me when my son becomes a young man, you'll find him and tell him how much his mother loved him."

"Amelia, don't," he pleaded.

"Promise me!" she insisted. "I can't trust Jason to tell him about me!"

Kissing her forehead, he said curtly, "Go to sleep, little one."

Depressingly, Amelia wondered why he refused to grant her wish. She had no way of knowing that James Henry planned to be executed with her. If she had to face a firing squad, she would not be alone. She would be in his arms.

EIGHTEEN

The Eldridge House hadn't been burned during Quantrill's raid, but Buford seriously doubted if he could get his old job back. Mr. Cramer was probably still angry because he and James Henry had left without giving proper notice. Remembering Amelia had said that her uncle had been killed, Buford decided to try and seek employment at Lillian's store. With her husband dead, she would most likely be in need of a man's assistance to help operate the business. He hoped the store was still intact. Amelia hadn't said anything about Calvin's business being destroyed.

Riding into Lawrence, Buford was astonished at the devastation. Quantrill's raiders had demolished the best buildings in the business section and much of the residential districts. Buford knew the people of Lawrence would clean up the rubble and rebuild, as they had once reconstructed their town following the pro-slavery attack of the fifties. The town could restore its material losses, but not the men and boys who had been murdered. The citizens' hatred for Missouri guerrillas was so strong that Buford could sense it in the air.

Entering the street where Lillian's store was located, Buford was relieved to see that the store was still standing undamaged. Halting his horse in front of the building, he dismounted, flung the reins across the hitching post, and remembered to limp as he approached the front door. Taking the role of Sam Tyler, he opened the door wide and stepped inside.

As he looked toward the counter, he saw Cynthia Coffman. Hearing his entrance, she looked up. Immediately, she smiled, "Why, Mr. Tyler! What a pleasant surprise."

Buford remembered Cynthia. He had seen her often at the Eldridge House. He had been quite taken with her, admiring her graceful and gentle manner. It had been apparent to Buford that she was deeply in love with her husband.

"Howdy, Mrs. Coffman," he said politely, limping to the counter. "Are you working here now?"

"Yes, I am," she replied.

"Is Mr. Adams around?" he asked.

"Mr. Adams was killed during the raid, but Mrs. Adams will be returning very shortly, if you'd care to wait."

"Well, ma'am, if you don't mind, I think I will."

"Of course, I don't mind. I'm happy to have the company."

Noticing that she was wearing black, Buford asked carefully, "Mrs. Coffman, are you in mourning?"

"Yes," she whispered, dropping her gaze.

"Your husband, ma'am?" he asked gently.

"He was killed six months ago," she replied sadly.

"I'm sorry, ma'am," he answered.

She compelled herself to smile, as she asked, "Do

you mind if we don't talk about it?''

"Of course not,'' he responded quickly.

Trying to make conversation, she inquired, "Is Jamie with you?''

"No, I left him with relatives in Springfield.''

"Are you only passing through, Mr. Tyler?''

"No, ma'am. I thought I might stay.''

Puzzled, she questioned, "Why would you want to remain in a town that was almost destroyed? There's nothing left in Lawrence but bitterness, hatred, and grief.''

"How many men and boys were killed? Do you know?''

"A hundred and eighty-five,'' she answered somberly.

"Good God!'' Buford exclaimed, astounded. "Did General Lane get killed?''

"No. He escaped,'' she replied.

"Did Mayor Collamore survive?''

"The mayor, and his friend Mr. Keefe hid in the mayor's well, but they were suffocated by the dense smoke from all the burning buildings. It was so tragic, and so ironic.''

"Why wasn't the Eldridge House destroyed?''

"The provost marshal, Captain Banks, opened a window and displayed a white sheet. He told Mr. Quantrill that he would turn the hotel over to him and asked that the people inside it be spared. Quantrill accepted his surrender. I suppose he needed a place to stay while his men raided the town.''

"That doesn't make any sense. If Quantrill wanted the hotel, why didn't he just take it on his own terms?''

Cynthia shrugged. "Who knows? How can one be

expected to understand a man like William Quantrill? If you ask me, he's the personification of the Devil!''

"That day must've been terrible for you, ma'am.''

Slowly she walked out from behind the counter, and, going to the front window, she looked outside. Sighing deeply, she replied, ''That day was terrible, yes, but Mr. Tyler, I am a coward. I stayed in my home, too frightened to take a step outdoors. There were men and boys who needed to be sheltered. I should have searched for them and taken them to my house to hide them.'' Bitterly, she continued, ''But I didn't! I was too afraid for my own safety!''

"Don't be so hard on yourself, Mrs. Coffman. Your reaction was normal.''

"Why was it normal?'' she questioned sharply, turning to face him. ''Because I'm a woman?''

"Yes, ma'am,'' he answered.

"And so is Amelia!'' she cried. ''Yet she left the safety of her home! She came here to the store to try and help Lillian and Calvin But when she got here, her uncle was dead. Lillian sent her back home, but she never reached her house. She disappeared!''

"Disappeared?'' he repeated, trying to sound surprised.

"So far as we know, Lillian was the last person to see her. Captain Bishop is beside himself with worry and grief. He swears if she is still alive, he will find her and kill whomever is responsible for her abduction.'' Taking a step away from the window, she continued, ''Jason and Amelia have a child, and the baby and nurse are staying here with Lillian.''

"The baby,'' he began, ''is it a boy or girl?''

"A boy,'' she answered.

248

Buford had been aware of the two nights that James Henry had gone to Amelia's room, and, pretending to be mildly interested, he said, "I've always liked babies. Do you reckon I could see the little guy?"

Nodding, Cynthia replied, "I'll check and see if he's sleeping."

Gracefully, she moved toward the rear stairway. Pausing momentarily, she glanced back at Buford. "You know, Mr. Tyler, I never thought of you as the kind of man who would love babies." Smiling, she remarked, "Underneath that gruff exterior, you must be as gentle as a lamb."

Guiltily, Buford offered no comment. Babies! Why, he'd never had anything to do with babies! They were so tiny and fragile that he hadn't been at ease the few times he had been forced to actually hold one.

Cynthia was only gone a few minutes before she returned with the baby. He was wrapped securely, but Buford could see the infant's black hair peeking over the edge of the blanket.

Going to Buford, Cynthia said, "Since you are so fond of babies, I'm sure you would like to hold him."

"Hold a baby, ma'am?" he choked.

Carefully, she handed him to Buford. Trying to appear experienced, he cradled the child in his arms.

"Isn't he beautiful?" Cynthia marveled.

"Black hair and blue eyes," Buford commented. It sounded like a casual observation, but his speculation was far from incidental. He knew beyond a doubt that he was holding James Henry's son.

"He doesn't resemble Mrs. Bishop or her husband," Buford remarked.

"No, he doesn't. He has looks and a personality that

are all his own.''

"What's his name?'' Buford asked, wishing she would take the baby. What if he wasn't holding him right? But surely he was, or else, she would have said something. He must remember to keep the little fellow's head supported. It seemed he had heard somewhere that supporting a baby's head was important.

Gently, Cynthia took one of the baby's hands into hers, caressing his tiny fingers. "His name is James Henry,'' she replied.

"Wh . . . what?'' he stammered.

"He was named after his grandfathers. James on Jason's side of the family, and Henry on Amelia's side.''

"Well, what do you know,'' Buford grinned. "If that ain't somethin'.''

Suddenly the baby began to coo, and, afraid he was getting ready to cry, Buford began to fidget. What was he supposed to do if the little guy started bawling? But looking down at the infant, Buford wasn't confronted by tears, but a smile so beautiful that Buford grinned from ear to ear. "James Henry,'' he whispered, "you're quite a boy.'' To himself, Buford added, Your papa would be proud.

Hearing the bell ring over the door, they both turned to look. Lillian bustled into the store.

"Mr. Tyler!'' Lillian remarked. "When did you get back to town?''

"Just a short while ago, ma'am,'' he answered, handing the baby to Cynthia.

"Mr. Tyler has been waiting to speak to you,'' Cynthia explained.

"Oh?'' Lillian questioned, moving to stand at Cynthia's side. "What can I do for you, Mr. Tyler?''

"I'm lookin' for a job, Mrs. Adams," he answered.

"With Calvin gone, I do need a man to help run the store. I remember Mr. Cramer saying that you were a conscientious employee. But, Mr. Tyler, you quit without giving the poor man adequate notice. You won't leave without giving me proper notice, will you?"

Knowing full well that he would run out on her without giving any kind of warning, he mumbled, "No, ma'am. I aim to stay right here in Lawrence for a long time."

"Very well," Lillian decided. "The job is yours. There is a small room at the rear of the store. It has a bed and a bureau. You are welcome to stay there."

"Thank you, ma'am. I'm obliged."

"When can you start to work?" Lillian asked.

Removing his hat, he replied, "Right now, Mrs. Adams!"

Without thinking, Cynthia reached over and squeezed his arm. "I'm glad you're going to be working here, Mr. Tyler."

Gazing down into her face, Buford noticed how her dark lashes curled over her large gray eyes. Wondering how it would feel to have her pouting and sensual lips responding beneath his, he smiled expansively as he answered, "I'm glad to be here too, Mrs. Coffman."

Becoming aware of how ruggedly handsome he was, Cynthia blushed noticeably.

NINETEEN

Standing close to the cave, Amelia looked over at the guerilla camp. It was a distance away, so it was a little difficult to pick out the men she knew by name. Amelia had now been a prisoner for eight days, and during that time she had been befriended by quite a few of Anderson's men.

Shading her eyes with her hand, Amelia tried to see James Henry, but if he was walking through the camp, she was unable to spot him.

Thinking about James Henry, she sighed despondently. Sitting on the ground, she crossed her legs Indian fashion, then, placing her elbows on her knees, she cupped her face in her hands. James Henry! She was so desperately in love with him! But was her love returned? She seriously doubted it. He had never said one word to lead her to believe that he was in love with her. He was always thoughtful, considerate, and a passionate and tender lover, but James Henry had built an impregnable wall around him that she couldn't even begin to penetrate. She knew nothing about his personal life, and whenever she tried to inquire about his life, he would rudely shut her out. Why? Why was the man she loved so secretive?

Once again, Amelia sighed unhappily. She was hopelessly in love, she missed her baby, and she was married to a man she didn't even like. And to top it all off, she would most likely be executed! Smiling bitterly, she muttered, "Even death has its brighter side; I won't be married to Jason!"

"Did you say somethin', Miss Amelia?" Gary asked.

Turning her head, she looked at Gary, who was standing by the cave's entrance. "No," she denied. "I didn't say anything."

Changing position, Amelia folded her arms across her raised knees. Vacantly, she gazed toward the camp. For some reason, that hadn't been explained to her, Captain Anderson had given strict orders that Gary, Pat, or Bulldog was to be in her company when James Henry wasn't with her. One of them accompanied her at all times. She was never allowed to talk alone with any of the men, except for her personal guards. She didn't mind having Gary or Pat following every step she took, because she had grown quite fond of them. Who could help but like Gary and Pat? But Bulldog! Just thinking about him made Amelia shudder. She had never seen a man as ugly as Bulldog. He wasn't very tall, but he easily weighed over three hundred pounds. His black scraggly hair was worn to shoulder length, but he was clean-shaven. Amelia often wondered why he didn't camouflage his homely face with a beard. Perhaps he wanted people to feel threatened by his appearance. Well, if that was his intention, he had certainly succeeded with Amelia. His brown eyes were beady, sunk into his loose skin. His nose was broad and hideously crooked. Apparently, it had been broken more than once. His lips were full, framing a mouth that was exceptionally large. His fleshly jowl hung grotesquely down his thick neck. The man was powerfully built. His shoulders were extraordinarily wide, his waist thick, his legs short and stocky. Eut if his looks were awesome, his personality was even more so! Bravely, Amelia had tried to talk to him a few times, but he had never responded. He would only glare at her, his eyes expressing a callousness that was frightening. Once, Amelia had attempted to confide in James Henry that she was horrified of the man, but he had simply laughed, telling her that Bulldog would never hurt a lady. Insult a lady, yes; but he would never harm one.

Spotting Captain Anderson walking in her direction, she quickly dismissed Bulldog from her thoughts. Why would Captain Anderson be coming to see her? She had seen him a couple of times during the past eight days, but he had only inquired politely about her health and then brusquely departed.

Nearing Amelia, Captain Anderson smiled at her as one would smile at a child, Dressed in trousers and a shirt three sizes too large, and wearing her hair in braids, Amelia did resemble a child.

At his approach she started to rise, but he promptly waved her back down. Immediately he ordered Gary to leave them alone. Walking to Amelia, he sat beside her. Making himself comfortable, he raised his knees, resting his arms across them.

"How have you been feeling, Mrs. Bishop?" he asked.

Amelia regarded him skeptically. "Captain Anderson, you didn't come here to ask about my health. So why are you here?"

He smiled pleasantly. "Mrs. Bishop, I have no ulterior motive. I should have paid my respects sooner, but I'm a very busy man."

Respects! she thought resentfully. You'd think I was entertaining him in my parlor! Turning to face him, she studied him intently, and, once again, she became aware of his good looks. He's almost as handsome as James Henry, she decided.

"Have the men treated you kindly?" he asked.

"Yes," she answered. "But . . . Captain?"

"What?" he coaxed.

"Why must I be guarded all the time?"

"I wouldn't want you to try to escape," he replied.

"Is that the only reason I am continually guarded?" she questioned.

He waited briefly before answering, "No. Mrs. Bishop, you are a very attractive young lady, and I must consider the possibility that you might use your feminine wiles to persuade one of my men to help you escape."

"How do you know I won't tempt Gary or Pat?"

"My dear, I'm sure you could be a big temptation to them, but they will remain loyal to me."

"And Bulldog? I could attempt to persuade him."

He threw back his head, roaring with laughter. Understanding his reason, Amelia suddenly found herself laughing with him. Bulldog being tempted was so unbelievable that it was humorous. Even the Devil probably kept a safe distance between himself and Bulldog.

Suddenly becoming aware that Captain Anderson was no longer laughing, Amelia's laughter ceased abruptly. "What is it?" she asked cautiously, wondering if she had done something wrong. Did he resent her laughing at one of his men?

For a moment his eyes seemed to become misty, but, blinking, he turned his face from hers. "Mrs. Bishop," he began somberly. "It seems as if an eternity has passed since I last heard a woman's laughter." Slowly he turned back to face her, and his eyes looked deep into hers.

"I'm sorry," she murmured.

"No, don't be sorry. Your laughter was beautiful." He paused, then added sadly, "It brought back memories."

Remembering James Henry had said that Anderson's sister had been killed, she asked, "Your sister?"

He nodded, answering softly, "Yes."

"James Henry said she was killed by Federals."

"Murdered!" he corrected angrily. "She was murdered!"

"Oh, Captain Anderson, are you sure?" she cried. "I can't believe the Union would murder women!"

"Believe it, madam!" he remarked coldly.

"But why would they murder her?" she pleaded.

He remained silent so long that Amelia believed he wasn't going to explain his sister's death. When he suddenly spoke, his voice startled her. "I had three sisters. Molly, Janie, and Josephine. The Federals arrested my sisters and held them prisoners. They were to be banished from Missouri. They were imprisoned in a dilapidated jail in Kansas City, with other women and girls being held for eventual banishment."

"But why were the women to be exiled from Missouri?" Amelia asked.

Anderson shrugged. "They were all connected in some way with Pro-Confederates. Sisters, wives, sweethearts, or relatives. To run our womenfolk out of the state seemed like a good way to punish us. I suppose that was their reasoning." He paused, then continued, "I believe three of the ladies were imprisoned because they had witnessed soldiers murdering a civilian. I'm sure the Federals wanted to get the ladies out of the state before they could testify."

"Why was your sister killed?" she asked gently.

"When the soldiers discovered that the Anderson girls were among their prisoners, they decided to kill them simply because they were my sisters. They wanted them dead, Mrs. Bishop, for no other reason except that they were my kin. My cousin, Mrs. Duke, owns a boardinghouse on Oak Street and Independence Avenue. Some of the soldiers were boarding with her, but they were unaware that she was related to my family. She overheard them plotting to kill my sisters. It was merely incidental to the soldiers that other prisoners would also be killed. They decided to undermine the old jail building, instead of simply burning it. If they burned it, the adjoining buildings would be endangered. They thought if would be much wiser to let the jail cave in on the women prisoners. My cousin, and some friends, rushed to the military headquarters and begged to have the girls removed from the jail."

Once again, Captain Anderson became quiet. Clearing his throat, he began to speak, but Amelia could sense how difficult it was for him to continue. "The commandant said he didn't believe my cousin. The sorry bastard was probably in on the plan! The soldiers removed the girders under the jail structure, and it collapsed into a deadfall. Molly and another woman were in the hallway. They escaped safely. Janie tried to get through a window, but there was a large cannonball chained to one of her ankles, so she was helpless!''

Doubling his hand into a fist, he raged, ''My God, they had tied a cannonball to a ten-year-old child!'' His voice breaking, he continued, ''Because of the cannonball, Janie could only get halfway out an open window. Her legs were crushed by the falling debris!''

''Oh, I'm so sorry,'' Amelia groaned.

He spoke quietly, but Amelia could detect an undertone of rage as he said, ''Josephine was killed by a pile of bricks that fell on top of her.''

''How old was she?'' Amelia asked.

''Eighteen,'' he whispered.

''Were the soldiers responsible punished?''

''Of course not! It was an old jail. It just happened to collapse. An accident, the officials ruled; a terrible, tragic accident. All the victims went down in the ruins, my sister among them, and not one man was arrested or punished for their deaths.''

''Are you sure it was murder and not truly an accident?''

''My cousin wouldn't lie about something like that!'' he answered firmly. Irritably, he raged, ''Damn woman! You can easily believe the worst about Missouri guerrillas, but you refuse to accept the worst in your own kind! Pro-Confederates are devils and Federals are saints! Is that how you see this war, Mrs. Bishop?''

''You forget, Captain Anderson, that I was a witness to Quantrill's slaughter of men and boys," she reminded him crossly.

Smirking, he replied, "And who do the Federals punish? Once again, they lash out at our families."

"What do you mean?" she asked.

"General Ewing has ordered Missourians residing in Pro-Confederate counties to leave their homes. Madam, the roads and highways are filled with fugitives, decrepit old men and women, little children, and entire families. What few belongings they can take with them are being carted by old oxen and mules—animals that the Federals have no use for. Most of their cows and sheep have been confiscated by soldiers. Their homes are being set to the torch. They are being punished because Quantrill raided Lawrence. Mrs. Bishop, I ask you, what in the hell did they have to do with Quantrill's massacre?"

She didn't answer his question; instead, she asked, "Where will these families go?"

Anderson shrugged. "That, madam, is a good question."

They sat silently for a few minutes, both buried deeply in their thoughts. Placing her elbows on her raised knees, Amelia once again cupped her face in hands. "Both sides have been terribly wrong," she mumbled more to herself than to Anderson.

Looking at her, he simply smiled. Continuing, she asked, "It's been that way since the beginning of the war, hasn't it? Both sides venting their personal revenge." When he didn't reply, she said disapprovingly, "You avenge your sister every time you tie a knot in that silk cord you carry into battle."

"Perhaps," he answered, undisturbed. "But, Mrs.

Bishop, I hated Jayhawkers before Josephine was murdered.''

"They also hate you," she stated calmly.

He laughed thickly. "Hate is putting it mildly. I think they hate me more than William Quantrill.''

"But you aren't like Quantrill!" she decided quickly. "You would never massacre civilians and teenage boys!''

"Why should you think that?" he asked lightly.

"You wouldn't, would you?" she questioned, her expression innocently trusting.

Admiring her guileless beauty, Captain Anderson found her irresistible. "Mrs. Bishop, you are very charming," he mused, smiling handsomely. "I think I have become captivated by your loveliness.''

Amelia studied him questioningly. Was he flirting with her? She believed he was, but harmlessly so. Smiling saucily, she responded to his frivolous mood. "Captain Anderson, you are quite charming yourself." Teasingly, she taunted, "If I didn't know better, I'd think you were trifling with my affections.''

"If we had met in another time, perhaps . . . ." His voice faded.

"Perhaps what?" she pressed.

He chuckled brusquely. "Well, Mrs. Bishop, war does make strange bedfellows, does it not?''

Sighing deeply, she looked over toward the guerrilla camp. Losing her gaiety, tears filled her eyes. "I have come to know quite a few of your men, and . . . and I like them. I don't think of them as the enemy. To me they are . . ." her voice dropped to a whisper, ". . . my friends.''

"I am sorry, madam, that you had to find yourself in

261

the midst of this war. If you had remained in Lawrence, surrounded by your own kind, you would have continued to think of Pro-Confederates as nothing more than the enemy. But, now, you have come to know us as individuals. Men with personalities, faces, and names.''

''But, captain, my loyalties are still with the Union!'' she stated firmly.

It surprised Amelia when he reached over, took her hand in his, squeezed it, and then released it. ''You are a compassionate and honest lady. Mrs. Bishop, I like you, and I also respect you very much.''

Encouraged by his words, she pleaded, ''If you truly feel that way, then you must believe me when I swear to you that I don't know the informer's identity!''

His eyes looked into hers, and Amelia met his stare, her eyes locked to his without wavering. Her heart began to beat rapidly as she realized he was trying to read the truth on her face.

At last, he broke their intense gaze. Amelia sighed deeply, releasing the breath she had unknowingly been holding.

''Instinctively, Mrs. Bishop, I believe you,'' he commented.

''Thank you!'' she cried, relieved. ''Does that mean you'll help me?''

''What can I do?''· he asked, sounding frustrated. ''You are not my prisoner, but Colonel Garson's.''

It was on her lips to beg him to let her escape, but she suppressed the impulse. He couldn't let her go free! He had his orders, and he would obey them, even if it meant her ultimate execution.

''Dear God!'' she groaned helplessly. ''Compared

to the informer's life, my life means nothing to you and the others!''

He remained silent for a long time, staring into the distance. Then slowly, he turned and faced her. ''Your life means a great deal to me, Mrs. Bishop. I am not a killer of women. Even when the Federals murdered Josephine, I didn't seek revenge by killing Union women.''

Unconsciously, she touched his arm, and her voice quavered as she asked, ''If Colonel Garson orders my execution, will you carry it through?''

Looking her straight in the eyes, he answered evenly, ''Yes, I will.'' But his tone hardened as he added, ''God help us!''

Since the day she was captured, Amelia had known that she might be killed, but until now the possibility had never seemed real. It couldn't happen! Not to her! Executions happened to other people! Deserters, spies, and traitors! People who were guilty of some crime, and she wasn't guilty of anything! She had done nothing! She was innocent!

Amelia had never been more frightened. Her tears came in a gush, and, crying, she pleaded, ''I don't want to die! I have a baby! I want to live to hear him say his first word and see him take his first step! I'm a mother, and my son needs me! Oh God, I don't want to die!'' Beside herself, she frantically clutched at his arm, and, looking up at him, she cried pathetically, ''Oh Captain Anderson, I don't want to die!''

Gazing into her upturned face, he was touched by her tears and her piteous pleas. Gently, he took her into his arms, and, placing her head against his chest, she wept uncontrollably.

Fleetingly, it dawned on Amelia that she was being consoled by the man who would give the final order for her execution. It was so ironic that she wanted to laugh, but she knew that if she did, she would laugh herself completely and hopelessly insane!

It was late evening before James Henry returned to the cave. Amelia was lying on her blankets, her back turned to the entrance, but, hearing his steps, she turned over swiftly, sitting straight up.

"Where have you been?" she demanded. "You were gone all day!"

He pushed his black hat back from his brow, causing his dark hair to fall attractively across his forehead. His steel-blue eyes penetrated hers with intensity. Was he angry? Why was he looking at her so strangely? Oh, if only she could understand him, this man she loved so dearly!

Her gaze traveled over him admiringly. He wasn't wearing his guerrilla shirt. He was dressed in black skin-tight trousers, matching vest, with a cream-colored shirt. His holster was strapped loosely across his slim hips, the pistol flush against his hard thigh. Examining him, Amelia suddenly noticed the pair of boots he was holding in his right hand. She looked at them questioning, and then up at James Henry.

Moving lithely, he crossed over to her. He handed her the boots. Taking them, she asked, "For me?"

He gazed down at her. God, she was beautiful! Her golden hair was cascading past her shoulders, falling softly across her breasts. She had the blanket wrapped around her securely, and he wondered if underneath it

264

she was completely nude. Suppressing the impulse to remove the blanket so he could admire her naked flesh, he swerved stiffly and stepped away from her.

"The storekeeper said they are the right size to fit the average ten-year-old boy, so they should be small enough for you."

Amelia couldn't have been more elated if he had just given her diamonds. "Oh, James Henry!" she gleamed. "Thank you! It has been so uncomfortable for me to walk outside in my cloth slippers. I don't know how many times I have bruised my feet on stones and sharp branches."

"Don't you think I know that?" he spat.

His abrupt vexation surprised Amelia. He is angry, she thought. But why? Why? Dropping her gaze to her lap, she placed the boots at her side. Demurely, she asked, "Is that where you've been all day? Trying to find me a pair of boots?"

Being extremely worried, James Henry didn't even hear Amelia's question. Restlessly, he began pacing. Amelia's fate had been gnawing at him for hours. He couldn't get it out of his mind. Would Colonel Garson return with orders for her execution? Envisioning his little Amelia standing before a firing squad, he cringed. He knew she would face her executioners bravely. Amelia had an invincible courage that she herself was not even aware of. She had told him about Quantrill's raid and how she had left the safety of her home to help her uncle. James Henry had admired her bravery, but his admiration had grown even stronger when she told him about the old man in the street, and how she had remained with him so he wouldn't have to die alone. She had to be aware of how perilous her present situation was, but still her bravery hadn't faltered.

Slowly he walked to the entrance of the cave and, pausing, he stared out into the darkness.

"James Henry, what's wrong?" she asked beseechingly.

He shook his head, refusing to answer. What could he say? I don't want you to die? If they kill you, they're going to have to kill me also?

His jaws clenched tightly. Should they try to escape? He smirked bitterly. Escape from Anderson's camp? A rabbit couldn't enter or leave this camp without being spotted. Anderson's men were trained too well. Besides, he had given Colonel Garson his word that he would keep her a prisoner. But was his word worth more than Amelia's life?

"James Henry," Amelia pleaded. "Please speak to me!"

Smoothly, he turned toward her. The glow from the lantern was falling across her face, illuminating her turquoise-blue eyes. He could detect the freckles on her small nose, and her lips were pursed innocently but invitingly. She was lovely!

"What are you wearing under that blanket?" he asked.

"Wh. . . what?" she stammered.

"You heard me," he replied impatiently. "What do you have on?"

"Nothing," she admitted shyly.

"Take off the blanket?" he ordered vehemently.

She gathered the blanket even closer, protesting, "But the lantern is burning. What if someone were to come to the cave? Except for that first night, the lantern has always been turned down before we remove our clothes.''

''I know!'' he fumed. ''And I'm getting sick and tired of making love to you in the dark!''

''But, James Henry,'' she began hesitantly, ''what if someone . . .''

Interrupting, he snapped, ''You know damned good and well that no one comes here after dark!'' Quickly he removed his hat, flinging it to the side. In one swift move, he unbuckled his holster, placing it on the ground. Moving toward her, he said between clenched teeth, ''Madam, I suggest you dispense with your modesty along with your blanket.''

When he reached her side, he didn't kneel. Instead, he stood in front of her, watching her with an expression she couldn't understand.

Flustered and embarrassed, she murmured self-consciously, ''Please turn down the lantern.''

''Why?'' he demanded.

''Please . . .'' she whispered.

''You tell me why, and then I might consider it!''

He was surprised to see tears in her eyes, as she confessed humbly, ''I am ashamed because I'm not . . . not voluptuous.''

Her sweet humility made him long to smile, but he knew now was not the time to make light of her confession. She was somberly serious. Kneeling, he took her hands into his. ''Amelia,'' he whispered lovingly, ''I thought you always wanted the lantern extinguished because you found our lovemaking sinful, and you were ashamed of your passion. I believed it was your religious convictions and marriage vows that placed the darkness between us.''

267

"Oh no!" she exclaimed. "No! James Henry, I'm not ashamed! When I'm in your arms, I'm so happy! But . . . but, I'm so . . . so undesirable."

"Why do you think that?" he asked tenderly.

"If only my breasts were fuller and my hips more rounded." Frowning childishly, she pouted, "Why can't I be more abundantly endowed?"

"Amelia," he began earnestly, "you are beautiful. I have enjoyed making love to you more than any woman. Your body is so soft, warm, and whether you believe it or not, you have everything it takes to drive a man wild with desire. A woman doesn't have to be voluptuous to be desired."

Carefully, he reached for the blanket, sliding it past her shoulders. Leaning over, his lips sought her bare flesh. Lightly, he ran fluttering kisses on her neck and down to the slight swell of her breasts. His warm breath sent exciting chills through Amelia's entire being, causing a moan to escape from deep in her throat.

Slowly, he pulled the blanket farther down, until her breasts were revealed. Tenderly he cupped them in his hands. His tongue circled the nipples, and he caressed each breast with his lips.

Rising, he drew her to her feet, causing the blanket to fall away. Placing his arms around her tiny waist, he molded her small frame to his. She could feel his belt buckle digging into her bare skin. Flinching, she stepped back.

"What's wrong?" he asked urgently.

"Your belt," she whispered.

Hurriedly he removed it, dropping it to the ground. Instantly, he had her back in his embrace. "I'm sorry," he murmured, his lips next to her ear. "I would never want to hurt you."

Almost painfully, Amelia was struck anew with how much she loved him. If only he loved her in return! But even if he did, there was no future for them. If she was set free she would have to return to Jason. He was her husband, and the vows she had shared with him had chained her to him for life. She was legally and morally shackled to Jason. But her love for James Henry was so free and unchained. It came from deep within her heart, not from a sense of duty.

Needing him desperately, she clung to him tightly. Feeling her soft thighs pressed against his male hardness, James Henry placed his hands to her rounded bottom, pressing her even closer.

As he bent his head over hers, she raised up on her tiptoes, meeting his lips with hers. Putting her hand on the back of his neck, she forced his mouth against hers as her tongue darted between his teeth. Oh, she loved him so much! But he could never truly be hers! Their love could never be more than a moment in time! She must cling to him tightly and put a lifetime of memories into the short time he would belong to her!

He released her gently, stepping back to look at her. As his eyes examined every inch of her, he whispered, "How can you think you aren't beautiful? Your breasts are perfectly formed, your waist is so tiny that I can easily encircle it with my fingers, and your thighs are soft and delectable." Suddenly he knelt in front of her, and, as his lips touched her stomach, she gasped, but with pleasure more than surprise.

Teasingly, his tongue flickered across her warm flesh as his hand touched the softness between her thighs. His fingers probed gently, entering her warmness.

"Oh, James Henry!" she groaned, her voice tremulous with longing.

He lowered his mouth, and when his lips and tongue replaced his hand, Amelia gasped feverishly. She weakened beneath his touch, and, clutching her buttocks, he held her firmly.

Only James Henry had ever loved her so intimately, and, surrendering to her fiery passion, she entwined her fingers into his black hair as a feeling of ecstasy began flowing between her legs.

Bringing her to a climax, James Henry felt her trembling beneath his lips and hands. She was so beautiful and desirable, he could make love to her for an eternity and still want more of her.

Rising, he quickly began slipping out of his clothes. Loving his handsome physique, Amelia watched him disrobe. The muscles on his chest rippled as he took off his shirt. He was lean, but so strong. Hurrying, he removed his boots and trousers. When he stood before her completely unclothed, she lowered her eyes to his maleness. Seeing his hard erection, she gasped, "I want you inside of me."

Easing her down on the spread blanket, she thought he would place himself on top of her. But, instead, he placed his hands on her waist, positioning them so that he was on the bottom.

"Sit up straight," he instructed, "and slide down on me. It won't hurt, Amelia. You're ready for my entry."

Following his guidance, she eased herself to him, accepting his initial penetration. Lowering herself inch by inch, she could feel him entering her deeper and deeper, until he was all the way inside her.

"Oh, my darling!" she cried ecstatically.

"Little one," he murmured. "You feel so wonderful; so hot!"

With his hands on her waist, he eased her up and down, until, taking the initiative, Amelia controlled their rhythm. As she released the last of her inhibitions, Amelia's natural passion excited James Henry beyond his own expectations. His climax came to him suddenly and uncontrollably. He groaned aloud, as his body was racked with spasms.

Gently, he placed her on the blanket by his side. "Amelia, you definitely know how to make a man feel good."

"Do I, James Henry?" she asked happily. "It means so much to me to please you."

He drew her into his arms. "You're so damned sweet," he said tenderly.

She sighed, but she was strangely discontent. She had been hoping he would tell her he loved her. Perhaps, if he knew they had a son, he would begin to love her. Should she tell him? Remembering how he had apparently been relieved when he thought that he hadn't fathered her child, Amelia quickly dismissed the idea.

Kissing the tip of her nose, he murmured, "Don't go to sleep, little one."

"Why?" she asked, looking up at him.

"Because as soon as I'm able, I want to make love to you again."

Putting aside her feeling of melancholy, she smiled at him flirtatiously. Moving her hand down his chest and past his stomach, she suggested, her tone purring seductively, ''In that case, why don't I help you become able?''

TWENTY

Lillian opened the front door. Pausing, she looked back at Cynthia and Buford. They were standing behind the store counter, waiting patiently for her to leave. This was already her third trip to the door, but each time she had bustled back to Cynthia and Buford, remembering some last minute instruction she had forgotten to tell them.

"Mr. Tyler, please don't forget to unpack the crates in the storage room," she reminded him.

"No, ma'am," he assured her.

"Cynthia, dear, the cologne Mrs. Kelley ordered is in the glass case beside the register. She'll be stopping by this morning to pick it up," Lillian told her again, for the fourth time in the past fifteen minutes.

"Yes, Lillian," Cynthia replied, an amused smile tugging faintly at the corners of her mouth.

Straightening her plump frame, Lillian asked dubiously, "Are you quite sure you can manage without me?"

They both nodded in unison. "Run along, Lillian," Cynthia encouraged, "and have a pleasant visit with

Mrs. Holt and the other ladies. Heaven knows, all of you deserve a nice time."

"Stay as long as you want," Buford added. "Mrs. Coffman and I will take care of everything just fine."

Adjusting her black bonnet, Lillian smiled at both of them, but the smile failed to freshen her features. Calvin's death had taken its toll on Lillian, and her grief had aged her considerably. With an abrupt nod, she left the store.

Shaking his head, Buford remarked, "You'd think she was goin' to be gone for weeks instead of hours."

"Yes," Cynthia agreed, "but Lillian is a gem, and I'm very fond of her. Losing Calvin, and Amelia's disappearance, have been very difficult for her. Under the circumstances, she has held up very courageously."

"Sometimes I think women are a lot stronger than we men give 'em credit for bein'."

"I never believed I could survive without David, but I did and I am. Perhaps women do have an inner strength."

Cynthia's expression became somber, and he knew she was thinking about her husband. Knowing her thoughts were on another man disturbed Buford. He had been back in Lawrence two weeks, and, since Cynthia also worked for Lillian, she and Buford had spent a lot of time together. Buford was fully aware that he was falling in love with Cynthia. He didn't want to be in love with her, and if he had any control over his emotions, he would have completely dismissed her. But how could he put her aside? She was so lovely, gentle, and kind.

Bringing herself out of her reverie, Cynthia said briskly, "Well, I suppose we had best get to work."

"Yep," Buford agreed, wishing he didn't have to keep up Sam Tyler's dialogue. If only he could be himself with Cynthia, then maybe she would see him in a different light.

Deciding to tidy some of the shelves, Cynthia turned swiftly to fetch the feather duster, but accidentally her elbow brushed a box of cigars, knocking them to the floor.

Both intending to pick up the cigars, she and Buford knelt at the same time. Their hands touched as they reached for the box.

Gently, he circled his fingers around her slim hand. Cynthia was too stunned to try and free herself from his grasp. Very slowly, she raised her gaze to his. She hadn't been this close to a man since her husband. His mouth was so near to hers that she could feel his breath on her face. Against her own volition, she studied his masculine features, feeling a hungry longing arousing her senses. Oh, it had been so long since she had been in a man's comforting arms.

She had always been aware that Sam Tyler was a nice-looking man, but she had never thought of him romantically, until now. His thick hair was the same shade of brown as his eyes. His nose and cheekbones were finely chiseled, and his lips were full but firm. His beard was heavy and neatly trimmed. Sam Tyler was indeed a handsome man, and so different from David, who had been fair and clean-shaven. He had been tall and slim. Sam Tyler was of average height, and solidly built.

She gazed down at their hands, comparing Sam Tyler's to David's. Her husband's hands had been long and slender, but Sam Tyler's were wide and visibly strong.

What was wrong with her? Why was she testing David against this man? Feeling terribly guilty, she pulled her hand free. She rose quickly, and, trying to compose herself, she nervously patted at her hair as if it had somehow become disheveled.

Getting to his feet, Buford placed the box of cigars on the counter. He turned as though he was going to leave, but then, pivoting smoothly, he grasped her around the waist. In one quick move, he had her pinned against him. Bending her over his arm, his mouth came down on hers before she even had a chance to protest.

At first, Cynthia was too astounded either to fight or respond. But Buford was well experienced when it came to arousing a woman's passion, and, effortlessly, he pried her lips open beneath his. Tightening his hold on her, he pulled her soft thighs against him so firmly that she could feel his solid erection through her clothes.

His tongue probed between her lips, touching her teeth, and the roof of her mouth, causing Cynthia to surrender to his dominant aggressiveness. David had never kissed her like this! She had enjoyed his kisses, they had always been so loving and tender. But Sam Tyler's kiss! Oh, it was so . . . so exciting! Instinctively her arms went around Buford, and she yielded to him completely.

Suddenly the front door opened, and the bell rang out loudly. Instantly, Cynthia and Buford broke their embrace, but not before Mrs. Kelley had had an opportunity to view their union. Hastily, Buford excused himself and hurried to the storage room to unpack the crates.

Eyeing Cynthia disapprovingly, Mrs. Kelley strutted to the counter. She was a middle-aged woman, short, and extremely thin.

Blushing, Cynthia tried not to be intimidated by the woman's hard scrutiny. "Mrs. Kelley," she began breathlessly, "I have your cologne for you."

Standing beside the counter, Mrs. Kelley disposed of her heavy purse by placing it next to the cigar box. Then, folding her arms beneath her small bosom, she exclaimed, "Cynthia Coffman, shame on you! Poor David has only been gone six months, and you are already throwing yourself at another man! Where is your decency and your self-respect? Your time of mourning has not passed. And of all men! Sam Tyler! Why, he's old enough to be your father!" Not giving Cynthia a chance to defend herself, she continued rapidly, "Cynthia, you are too good for him. He has no class or education! Why, the man probably can't read or write. I'm sure he's an illiterate!"

Holding up her hands in an effort to ward off the woman's words, Cynthia pleaded, "Please, Mrs. Kelley! I agree that most of what you say is true."

Mrs. Kelley's thin eyebrows arched sharply. "Most?" she questioned, offended.

"My time of mourning hasn't passed, and I was being unfaithful to David's memory. I agree Sam Tyler is old enough to be my father." Meeting the woman's arrogant stare, she continued icily, "But, Mrs. Kelley, Sam Tyler is not an illiterate. And I am not too good for him or anyone else. You are being a very mean and malicious person to say such cruel things about Mr. Tyler!" Whirling stiffly, she removed the bottle of cologne from the glass case. Setting it on the counter, she said crisply, "Your cologne, Mrs. Kelley!"

"Well!" the woman huffed. Quickly she paid Cynthia for the cologne, then left the store in a great flurry. As the door closed behind her, Cynthia broke into tears.

Having heard Mrs. Kelley's departure, Buford left the crates to return to Cynthia. Finding her crying, he hurried to her side. He tried to take her into his arms, but she pushed him away.

"Don't touch me!" she shrieked.

Surprised by her reaction, he asked sharply, "What did that scrawny busybody say to you?"

"Mr. Tyler, please!" Cynthia reproached him. "Don't insult Mrs. Kelley!"

"Insult her?" Buford mocked, grinning. "It sounded like a good definition to me. She's scrawny and she's a busybody, ain't she?"

Dabbing at her tears, Cynthia suppressed the urge to smile. What Sam Tyler said was quite true. But then, Mrs. Kelley had also spoken the partial truth. Her time of mourning hadn't ended, and it was wrong for her to want another man. So terribly and sinfully wrong!

"Mr. Tyler," she proceeded, turning to face him. "What happened a few minutes ago must never happen again."

His expression was handsomely cunning as he asked her, "Are you referring to our kiss?"

Her cheeks flushing scarlet, she stammered, "Yes . . . it . . . it should never have happened."

"Why?" he asked simply.

Flustered, she replied, "Mr. Tyler, you know I am

still in mourning.''

''You didn't kiss like you were mournin'!'' he retorted.

Spontaneously her hand flew up to strike him, but alertly he grabbed her wrist. His fingers gripped her so tightly that she winced. ''If you want to slap me, Mrs. Coffman, then I'll let you. But before you do, I think it's only fair to warn you that I hit back.''

Gaping, Cynthia's mouth dropped open. ''Are you threatening me?'' she exclaimed.

''No, ma'am. I'm just tellin' you how it is. I ain't no West Point graduate like your husband was. He was a refined, self-made gentleman, but madam, I ain't refined and I ain't no self-made gentleman. Thank God!''

''Exactly what are you?'' she asked, pulling her wrist free.

''A man,'' he answered. Raising his eyebrows, he grinned slyly, adding, ''And, madam, if I ever saw a woman badly in need of a man, it's you.''

''How dare you!'' she gasped.

''You daring me?'' he smiled.

''Wh . . . what?'' she stuttered.

He had her in his arms so suddenly that she was unaware of what had happened until she felt his mouth taking possession of hers.

He broke their kiss so abruptly that she tottered clumsily as he released her. ''Mrs. Coffman,'' he said, his expression serious, ''take that kiss to bed with you tonight. And when you lie there all by yourself longin' for a man, remember where you can find me.''

Finding his attitude insulting, she spat, ''You . . . you are an insufferable beast!''

He chuckled. "Well," he drawled, "I've been called a lot worse."

Remembering to limp, Buford headed back toward the storage room. Pausing shortly, he looked back at her. Leisurely he commented, "You can relax, Mrs. Coffman, I won't be tryin' to take advantage of you. If we should ever kiss again, it will be because you instigated it." His eyes twinkled amusedly as he added, "But once again, madam, I think it only fair to warn you that next time I won't stop with a mere kiss." Swiftly he left the room, closing the storage room door behind him.

Shocked beyond belief, Cynthia could only stare increduously at the closed door through which he had so quickly departed.

TWENTY-ONE

Although Amelia missed her baby very much, and Colonel Garson's imminent return was always on her mind, basically, she was happy at Anderson's camp. She liked and respected many of the guerrillas, and they in turn were quite taken with Amelia's kindness and integrity, so that friendships developed naturally between her and some of the men.

Captain Anderson frequently visited with Amelia, and, on occasion, they even spent hours conversing quietly in private. Amelia was uncertain of how she felt about Bill Anderson. The Union believed him to be a sadistical demon, and if the rumors she had heard concerning him were true, then he was a man without mercy or a sense of fairness. But it was so hard to believe the rumors when he was sitting at her side talking to her as one friend to another. To Amelia he revealed a compassionate side to his nature that was very different from his reputation.

Often Captain Anderson and the majority of his men would ride out and be gone two and three days at a time. James Henry was always ordered to accompany them, leaving Bulldog, Pat, and Gary to guard her. Amelia had asked James Henry why he was commanded to leave her to ride on these skirmishes, when she was supposed to be in his custody. As usual, he had refused to give her a satisfactory answer. He seemed determined to disclose nothing to her, even when it had to do with Amelia herself. Perturbed by James Henry, she had decided to go to Captain Anderson and demand an explanation from him. When she did so, he told her that it was so obvious he wondered why she hadn't thought of it herself. The reason he refused to leave James Henry with her when the camp was minus half its men, was because if James Henry wanted to help her escape, that would be his opportune moment. Amelia was shocked. Surely Captain Anderson knew James Henry had no intention of helping her escape! When she told Anderson in all sincerity that James Henry would never try to help her get away, the captain had merely smiled at her lack of perception, and ordered Pat to take her back to the cave.

Amelia had now been a captive for five weeks. She had awakened early this crisp morning. The night before it had rained, and the trees still had drops of water on their leaves, the terrain was damp, and small puddles of water had formed randomly.

Walking at her side, James Henry accompanied Amelia to the camp for breakfast. In the aromas reaching her Amelia could detect the wonderful smells of coffee and of bacon frying, mingling with the fresh smells of morning.

Amelia's thoughts were on a cup of hot coffee and a hearty breakfast, and she missed seeing the puddle of water in her path. She would have stepped blindly into it, but James Henry halted her.

"You'd best pay attention to where you're going. Where are your thoughts, little one?" he asked casually.

She smiled brightly as she looked up into his face. "On breakfast!" she replied hungrily.

Recalling their hours of lovemaking the night before, he stated good-humoredly, "Passion does give one a ravenous appetite. I'm famished myself."

Tugging at his arm, she encouraged, "Well, let's not just stand here and talk about it. Let's go find some food."

Laughing, he swept her into his arms, carrying her over the puddle. Crossing it, he placed her back on her feet, then, taking her hand, he began leading her to the camp.

Looking at him, Amelia studied his handsome profile. She was suddenly reminded of another moment in time, when Jason had escorted her down the hotel stairs to the dining room for breakfast. She had hoped then that her husband would sense her eyes on him and turn his face to her with a secret smile that only lovers could share. But he had arrogantly refused even to acknowledge her gaze. And, now, James Henry must also feel her eyes on him, but he continued to ignore her. Disheartened, Amelia started to turn her gaze from his face when, suddenly, James Henry's eyes penetrated hers. His scrutiny was intense, sending a longing flowing through her entire being. Gently, he squeezed her hand, and a sensual smile appeared on his lips. Oh, he does love me! Amelia thought happily. I can see it in his smile! He does! He does love me!

Halting her steps, Amelia gazed up at James Henry. Her face glowing with love, she murmured, "Please tell me you love me, James Henry. Please!"

He placed his hands on her small shoulders. His expression became serious, as he silently watched her. Amelia's knees weakened, and her heart began pounding rapidly. Waiting for his reply, she pleaded inwardly, Tell me you love me! Please, my darling! Please!

But Amelia was not to know if James Henry would have confessed his love, because, at that moment, a large group of men rode into the camp. Hearing their arrival, James Henry brusquely released her.

"Who are they?" she asked.

"Some of Quantrill's men," he answered. Recognizing one of the riders, James Henry smiled warmly. Grabbing Amelia's hand, he forced her to keep up with his long strides as he hurried towards the visitors.

Reaching Bulldog, who was standing by a campfire looking over the visiting guerrillas, James Henry told Amelia to stay with him.

She didn't want to remain with Bulldog, she wanted to be with James Henry. Rebelliously she attempted to follow him, but Bulldog clutched her arm, making her stay at his side.

Finding his touch repulsive, Amelia pulled away from him. Her feelings were obvious, and had she been more observant she would have recognized Bulldog's resentment. All ladies treated him the same! Because he had had the misfortune to be born homely, ladies shunned him. He had hoped Amelia would be different. She was kind and friendly to the other men, but she continually avoided him. He shrugged, telling himself he didn't care. Ladies! Who needed them? For the right price, he could bed a prostitute, and what he got from a whore was all a man needed from a woman.

Curiously, Amelia watched James Henry hurrying to the riders. Hastily one of the men dismounted, stepping to James Henry. It surprised Amelia when James Henry embraced the younger man. With their arms over each other's shoulders, they strolled away from camp and toward the cave.

"I wonder who he is," Amelia mumbled vaguely.

She hadn't expected Bulldog to speak, and his deep voice startled her. "His brother," Bulldog explained.

"I didn't know James Henry had a brother," she remarked, but then she knew nothing of James Henry's personal life. She didn't even know if Buford was any kin to James Henry. How was it possible to know so little about the man she loved? And why did James Henry insist on being so secretive?

"Do you know his name?" Amelia asked, turning to face Bulldog.

"Luther," he grumbled.

So James Henry has a brother named Luther, she thought. Well, at least I know that much about him! She wondered if she'd get a chance to talk privately with Luther. Maybe he wouldn't be quite as close-mouthed as James Henry.

"How long do you think they will stay?" she asked.

"Not long," he replied.

"Why did they come here?"

He didn't answer verbally, he simply shrugged his huge shoulders. Amelia decided not to press him any further. He had already spoken more words to her at one time than he had for the duration of her captivity.

Leaving well enough alone, she looked back at the group of riders. They remained mounted, so apparently their visit was going to be very short. She wondered if their only reason for coming here was so that Luther could talk to James Henry. And if so, what did Luther want to tell his brother that was so vitally important that he had made a trip to Anderson's camp?

Leaving his tent, Captain Anderson walked to the mounted guerrillas and began conversing with them. Watching, Amelia suddenly recognized one of the men. He was the raider who had helped the old man to the church during Quantrill's raid. Sensing her gaze, he glanced in her direction. Meeting her eyes, he touched the brim of his hat as he smiled politely. Apparently, he remembered her. If he was surprised to find her in a guerrilla camp, she couldn't tell by his expression. Amelia nodded to him, acknowledging his smile. Then, abruptly, he broke their gaze to begin a conversation with Captain Anderson.

Getting Bulldog's attention, she unconsciously touched his arm. Nodding toward the young guerrilla, she asked, "Do you know him?"

"He's Quantrill's right-hand man," he answered, surprised that she had actually touched him.

Still staring at the guerrilla, she exclaimed, "Quantrill's right-hand man! But if that's true, why would he help . . ." Catching herself, Amelia paused quickly. She couldn't tell Bulldog that the young man had helped men and boys in Lawrence. He had disobeyed Quantrill's orders, and if Quantrill were to learn of his disobedience he might order the man's execution. No! She wouldn't betray him! He was her enemy, but, all the same, she would protect him, she decided, unaware that in the near future she would be chained by another loyalty to her enemy, and one so perilous that it would inevitably change her whole life.

"What's his name?" she asked, still looking at the young guerrilla. "Do you know?"

"Cole Younger," he answered.

Losing interest in the guerrilla, she stepped over to the campfire, and, sitting beside it, she poured a cup of coffee. Turning to where she could see the cave, she saw James Henry and his brother entering it. Worried that Luther had brought bad news, Amelia waited anxiously for them to return, her earlier feelings of hunger completely forgotten.

Amelia was on her second cup of coffee, when Luther suddenly appeared at the mouth of the cave. Slowly, she rose to her feet as she observed him pausing to look back inside. She wondered if he was speaking to James Henry. Luther was too far away for Amelia to be able to tell if he was saying anything.

Evidently Luther was in a hurry, because, finishing his business with James Henry, he moved swiftly away from the cave. Amelia fixed her gaze on him, watching attentively. She wished she could speak to him. He was part of James Henry's family, and he played an important role in the life of the man she loved.

Setting down her coffee cup, Amelia inched her way closer to the guerrillas who were waiting for Luther. Maybe she couldn't talk to him, but at least she could get a good look at him.

Before she could reach the group of guerrillas, Bull-dog encircled her arm with his thick fingers. "That's

287

far enough!'' he warned gruffly.

Amelia had never been one to lose her temper, but, exploding peevishly, she jerked free, fuming, ''I'm sick and tired of being bullied by you men!'' Stomping her foot angrily, she flung her long hair back from her face and looked up at Bulldog's threatening stare.

The men within hearing distance were watching Amelia's tantrum with amusement. But their humor changed rapidly to surprise, when Bulldog suddenly grinned. Bulldog smiling was a novelty.

''You got a lot of spunk, ma'am,'' Bulldog praised.

Flattered by his compliment, Amelia lifted her chin and straightened her five-foot frame to its full height. ''I wasn't going to speak to him,'' she admitted proudly. ''I only wanted to get a good look at him.''

Nodding toward Luther, Bulldog told her, ''Here he comes.''

Swerving, Amelia watched Luther as he stopped to speak with Captain Anderson. She couldn't see any family resemblance between Luther and James Henry. Oh, how she wished she could hear what Luther was telling Anderson. And why had James Henry remained in the cave?

Captain Anderson shook hands with Luther, then patted him on the shoulder in a consoling fashion. Quickly Luther was mounted, and, turning their horses, Quantrill's guerrillas rode out of the camp.

Returning to his tent, Anderson spotted Amelia. Changing directions, he sauntered to her saying cordially, ''Good morning, Amelia.''

''Captain Anderson,'' she began, ''why did James Henry's brother come here to see him?''

''Don't you think you should ask James Henry?''

"Perhaps. But I'm asking you, aren't I?"

He nodded stiffly, then hastily he turned away to walk to his tent. Halting, he pivoted back in her direction. "Yesterday afternoon, James Henry's brother Ben was killed in a skirmish with Federals."

Hoping desperately that James Henry would need her, Amelia fled from the camp and to the cave. Rushing into the dark interior, she saw James Henry standing close to the cave wall, with one arm resting across it. He had his back turned, and she couldn't see his face.

Amelia hurried to his side. She wanted to take him into her arms, but afraid that he would balk at her attempt to console him, she murmured, "Captain Anderson told me what happened. I'm so sorry."

Removing his arm, he stood erect looking down into her eyes. She had thought she would see grief on his face, but she could see only anger.

"When this war started," he sneered savagely, "there were seven in my family! Now, there's only two of us left!" Raising his voice, he raged, "How many Stewarts have to die because of this crazy, goddamned war!"

"Seven!" she cried. "Wh . . . what happened to all of them?"

Suddenly, his blue eyes became so frighteningly cold that Amelia instinctively took a step backwards. Grabbing her by the shoulders, he jerked her close. His grip was so tight that it was painful. His voice tinged with madness, he raved, "My mother died of a heart attack, brought on by a group of Jayhawkers who barged into our home and dragged Luther outside to beat him . . . my sister, Anne, was engaged to Wade

Jarrette. He had been wounded in a skirmish with Federals. He was brought to my father's home. Before Pa could take him into the woods, Union soldiers came to the farm looking for him. Wade was upstairs in bed, and the officer in charge didn't even have the common decency to arrest him and take him away from the house before killing him. He pulled his pistol to shoot Wade, but Anne threw her body across his, and the bullet that had been meant for Wade killed Anne. Not giving a good goddamn that he had killed a woman, the officer fired his pistol a second time and killed Wade as he lay beneath Anne's dead body! My ten-year-old sister, Becky, was hiding in the barn. She was terrified of blue uniforms, and I'm sure she was frightened by the shots inside the house, and she backed blindly out the loft window and fell to her death! My father went berserk. He ran inside the house, got his rifle, and rushed out to the front porch. He shot one soldier before the officer killed him.''

Releasing her, he shouted, ''If the officer in charge had acted in a military manner, Anne would still be alive, and most likely Pa and Becky would also be alive!''

Amelia wanted to defend the Union officer, but how could she? James Henry was right. It had been the officer's fault.

''When did this happen?'' she asked.

''Before I came to Lawrence,'' James Henry answered.

''Were you riding with Captain Anderson when they were killed?''

Yelling, he replied, ''I wasn't even in this damned war!''

"Is that why you became a Missouri guerrilla? Are you seeking your own personal revenge against Federals?"

"Federals?" he questioned angrily. "Only one Federal!"

"The officer?" she asked.

"Someday, I'm going to kill him!" he swore.

Her eyes widening, Amelia's hand flew to her mouth. She had heard that same threat once before. "Jason!" she gasped.

"Yes!" he admitted. "Captain Jason Bishop!"

Clutching his arm, she cried wildly, "When you slipped into my room to seduce me, it was because I was married to Jason, wasn't it? You didn't want me, you only wanted revenge! You didn't come to me out of love, but hate!" When he didn't deny her accusation, she continued angrily, "Do you plan to tell him about us before you kill him?"

Callously he flung her hands off his arm. He shoved her backwards, causing her almost to lose her balance. "Get out of here!" he roared. "Get out!"

Frightened, Amelia ran from the cave. With tears blinding her vision, she stumbled toward the waterfall. Reaching the bank, she fell to the ground, burying her face in her crossed arms. He didn't love her! He had never loved her! He only wanted revenge, and he was using her to get what he wanted!

Sobbing heavily, she didn't hear the man's footsteps approaching. She was unaware of his presence until he gently touched her shoulder. Alarmed, she sat up quickly, coming face to face with Bulldog, who was kneeling at her side.

"What happened?" he asked, his tone surprisingly

tender.

Responding to his tenderness, she cried impulsively, "He doesn't love me!"

"You're wrong, ma'am," he replied firmly.

"H . . . how would you know?" she stammered, sniffling. She looked at him closely, wondering why she didn't find him repulsive. But he seemed changed somehow.

"If you don't know that James Henry is in love with you, then you're the only one in this whole camp who ain't aware of it. The captain don't even trust James Henry where you're concerned. Why do you think he don't trust him, huh? Because Anderson knows how James Henry feels about you."

"No, he doesn't love me," she insisted, pouting childishly.

Sitting beside her, he asked, "Do you want to talk about it? I promise you, whatever you say won't go no further."

Amelia's first thought was to tell him no, but quickly she suppressed the impulse. She had never talked to anyone about James Henry. She remembered how many times she had longed to tell Cynthia about the man she loved, but she had been forced to remain silent. If she should return home, she would once again be compelled to keep her love for James Henry a secret. For once, just once, she wanted to tell someone how much she loved James Henry. But Bulldog? Amelia smiled faintly, shrugging her shoulders. Why not?

Starting at the very beginning, Amelia told Bulldog about her relationship with James Henry, without revealing that he was the father of her child. That was one secret she dared not tell anyone. She even explained what had happened when she went to the cave hoping to console him.

"If you went to James Henry to console him, then why didn't you?" Bulldog asked crossly.

"What do you mean?" she questioned, baffled.

"Instead of consolin' him, you accused him of usin' you to avenge your husband. Ma'am, if you ask me, that's a helluva way to console a man."

"But . . ." she began.

Interrupting, he remarked, "It don't make no difference if he was usin' you or not. You went to him to help him. So why didn't you?"

"I . . . I don't know," she stuttered, suddenly feeling ashamed.

"It's because you got your feelings hurt, ain't it? Leave it to a woman to be dumb enough to think about her vanity when her man's a-needin' her love. Ma'am, he just learned that his brother is dead. He needed your arms around him and your understanding. Instead of lovin' him, you bitched at him. Never met a lady yet who wasn't a damned nag."

"But, Bulldog," she began, trying to defend herself, "what he did to me is unforgivable! And he's *still* using me!"

"You don't know that," he grumbled. "Besides it don't make no never mind. If you love him like you say you do, you'll go back inside the cave and let him know you care."

"Oh, I do love him!" she exclaimed. "Truly, I do!"

He grinned slyly. "Go on, ma'am. I'll make sure you two ain't disturbed."

"Do you really think he wants me?" she asked, her eyes shining with hope.

"Of course he does. James Henry ain't no god-damned fool!"

Smiling, she leaped to her feet. She took one step toward the cave before she remembered to thank Bulldog.

Pacing the confining interior of the cave, James Henry angrily reproached himself. Why had he yelled at her, ordering her to leave? Was it because her accusations had hit their mark, and the truth hurt? Was it his guilt that had lashed out at her? Had it truly been revenge that had sent him to Amelia's bedroom? Damn! He hadn't been sure at the time, and he still couldn't be sure!

He never should have told her about his family and Bishop. But he had been so upset over Ben's death that all his pain had spilled out before he could stop it. Why? Why had he confided in her?

Clenching and unclenching his fists, James Henry reluctantly admitted the truth to himself. He had revealed his deepest pain to Amelia because he had needed her! He had needed her arms around him, and, most important, he had needed to feel loved.

Maybe it hadn't been his guilt that had forced him to send her away, but his frustrations. But why should he need Amelia? He had never needed anyone! No! No, he thought, that it isn't true. I always needed Anne. Even when I was over a thousand miles away from her, she was in my thoughts.

His pacing stopped abruptly. For the first time, he

realized how much Anne and Amelia were alike. They had the same gentleness, integrity, and innocence.

Continuing his pacing, he told himself it made no difference how much similarity there was between Anne and Amelia. Amelia was married to Bishop, and she had a child with him. She was Bishop's property, not his!

Against his will, possibilities rushed fleetingly across his mind. When he killed Bishop, Amelia would be a widow! She would be free! Then he could claim her as his own!

Suddenly, he smiled bitterly. Oh, that would be just great! When her son got a little older and asked how his father had died, he could tell him how his stepfather had blown him away! Hell, there was no way he could help raise Amelia's son, knowing he was the man who had killed the boy's father.

Once again, his steps abruptly halted. Why was he even wasting his time thinking about his and Amelia's future? They would both die facing a firing squad. Colonel Garson's return would end their future permanently.

Amelia's entrance was silent and hesitant, but James Henry's acute instinct sensed her presence. Turning, he saw her pausing at the cave's opening. She looked so small and helpless. Her borrowed clothes were much too large, making her appear even tinier than she was. Her long golden hair cascaded past her shoulders and down to her waist. She was watching him warily, as though she wasn't sure if she should come inside. Was she afraid of him? God, he hoped not! He never wanted her to fear him. She was so sweet and vulnerable that he could never intentionally hurt her.

A tender smile tugged vaguely at his lips, and, holding out his arms to her, he murmured, "Amelia, come here."

Instantly she ran to him, throwing herself into his outstretched arms. Enclosing her in his embrace, he sent fleeting kisses across her forehead and down to her cheeks.

"Oh, James Henry!" she cried. "I'm sorry! Please forgive me!"

"Forgive you?" he questioned gently. "I'm the one who should be apologizing."

Stepping back so that she could see his face, she argued, "No! I was wrong! I shouldn't have accused you the way I did. Even if my suspicions were true, I chose the wrong time to confront you with them."

He agreed with her, but he found it hard to believe that someone as hurt and as upset as Amelia had been could have come up with such logical reasoning.

"Who have you been talking to?" he asked curiously.

"Bulldog," she answered, wondering how he had known that she had been talking to someone.

Smiling amusedly, he repeated, "Bulldog?"

"I certainly had the wrong impression of him. Behind that gruff facade, he's very kind and understanding."

"Amelia," he marveled, "you're so damned sweet and lovely, you could melt a heart made of stone."

Suddenly believing she had unraveled Bulldog's erratic behavior, she met James Henry's gaze, saying firmly, "It's you who Bulldog likes, not me! His concern was for you."

Brushing his fingertips across her cheek, he answered, "Don't underestimate yourself, little one."

She smiled happily. "It doesn't matter who he wanted to help. But he did promise me that you and I won't be disturbed."

He raised his dark eyebrows questioningly. "Oh? Are we in need of privacy?"

Slipping off her boots, she answered pertly, "Yes, unless you want witnesses to your seduction."

"My seduction?" he asked, chuckling.

Removing her shirt, she replied, "James Henry, it's about time you got a taste of your own medicine."

"I can hardly wait," he said, smiling with anticipation.

Quickly she rid herself of her remaining clothes. Moving sensually, she swayed against him, pressing her hips to his as she began unfastening his shirt. She slid it past his shoulders, and with his slight assistance it was dropped to the ground.

Next, he pulled off his boots, then patiently waited for her to continue. Rising on her tiptoes, she kissed his mouth passionately, then playfully ran kisses across his ears and then to his shoulders.

Kneeling, she unbuckled his holster, placing it at their feet. Reaching for his belt with one hand, she used her other hand to fondle his male hardness. At her exciting touch, he moaned, "Ah, Amelia! You do know how to please your man."

Delighted by his response, she boldly undid his trousers, tugging at them gently until they were past his muscular thighs.

Becoming impatient, James Henry helped Amelia rid him of his clothes. Examining his masculine frame, Amelia caught her breath with admiration. Oh, he was so handsome, this man she loved so much!

"Lie on the blanket, little one," he said fervently.

Lying down, she held out her arms to him, welcoming him into her embrace. As his mouth found hers, she dug her fingers into his bare skin, drawing him even closer to her.

Moving to her side, he placed her leg across his hip. Positioning himself, he entered her warmness, penetrating her quickly and deeply.

"Amelia," he murmured, his lips on her ear. "I could never get enough of you."

"Oh, my darling!" she confessed, "I need you! I need you!"

Their passions building ecstatically, they met each other's exciting thrusts. His mouth possessed hers as he effortlessly slid her small frame beneath his.

Lifting her legs to deepen his entry, James Henry removed his lips from hers as he groaned, "Love me, Amelia . . . Little one, love me!"

Putting her hand on the back of his head, she pressed his mouth to hers. Amelia's kiss came from deep within her heart and was filled with all her love.

Holding her tightly, he molded her body so close to his that Amelia felt as if she had become an inseparable part of him. Clinging to him, she equaled his driving passion until, at last, they attained love's most ardent bliss.

Relaxing, James Henry remained inside her, enjoying her pleasurable warmth. Burying his face in her long silky tresses, he placed his lips against her ear. For a few wonderful moments, she had helped him to forget his heartache. As his family came to mind, he whispered humbly, "Thank you, Amelia."

She held her face to his shoulder so that he wouldn't see her tears. If Colonel Garson were to set her free, how could she return to being Mrs. Jason Bishop, after sharing her life with James Henry? Tightening her arms around him, she cried silently, I love you! Oh, James Henry, how dearly I love you!

TWENTY-TWO

True to his word, Buford made no more advances to Cynthia. He behaved as if nothing had happened between them, resuming his usual friendly but impersonal demeanor.

Cynthia tried desperately to forget how it had felt to be in his strong arms, as his lips awakened her deepest passion. But the moment had not been so easy for Cynthia to dismiss. Three weeks had gone by since the morning Lillian had left them alone, and not a day had passed that Cynthia didn't recall how she had so freely responded to Sam Tyler. Her brazen behavior disturbed Cynthia. She had acted like a common trollop, not a lady.

When she recalled their union during daylight hours, she would blush shamefully, reminding herself that it would never happen again and that she must disregard the entire incident. Sam Tyler might not be a refined gentleman, but, all the same, he was well-mannered, and she need not worry that he would think her fast and try to take liberties with her.

But, at night, lying alone in her bed, Sam Tyler's

words would race across her thoughts: "Take that kiss to bed with you, and when you're lyin' there all alone longin' for a man, remember where you can find me." Restlessly, Cynthia would toss and turn, as Sam Tyler's image flashed vividly in her mind. Fighting the desire to forget propriety and flee to his arms, she would severely reprimand herself. Had she no shame? No decency?

She wished she could leave Lawrence and run away from temptation. But where would she go? Her parents were dead, and she had no close relatives. No! She must remain. Her home and all her friends were here in Lawrence.

With one quick breath, Cynthia would pray that Sam Tyler would return to Illinois, but, drawing a second breath, she'd pray that he'd never leave Lawrence.

For three weeks, Cynthia went to bed longing for Sam Tyler but determined to do nothing about it.

Lillian, Addie, and the baby had gone to Jason's home for dinner, leaving Cynthia and Buford to close the store. It had been awkward for Cynthia, because it was the first time she had been alone with Buford since the day he had kissed her. But if Buford felt self-conscious, it hadn't been noticeable. Helping Cynthia, he had rambled about nothing in particular in his usual drawling dialogue. But Cynthia had been ill at east, and, hurrying nervously, she left the store as quickly as possible. It wasn't until she was back at home that she realized she had left her knitting at the shop. She was making a sweater for little James Henry, and, knowing she would need something to help her get through the lonely hours before bedtime, she decided to return to the store.

It was dark when Cynthia reached the shop. Reaching into the pocket of her dress, she took out a key. Unlocking the door, she stepped inside, slipping the key back into her pocket. She started to light the lamp, but changed her mind. She was familiar with the interior, and she had left her knitting behind the counter. There was no need to take the time to light a lamp. Besides, Sam Tyler was probably in his room, and it would be best if he didn't know she was there. The mere thought of his close presence sent her pulse racing. Oh, she didn't want to be alone with him! What if he should try to kiss her? What would she do? Afraid she would behave like a loose woman, Cynthia quickly made her way to the counter. Stepping behind it, she felt for her yarn and needles.

Suddenly the door to Sam Tyler's room opened. Alarmed, Cynthia stepped back into the shadows.

She was surprised to see that Sam Tyler was not alone. She didn't recognize the man walking at his side. She was sure she had never seen him before.

The light from the small bedroom shone into the store, making it easy for Cynthia to see the two men, although the darkness behind the counter made her obscure.

Sam Tyler was dressed leisurely, his brown shirt unbuttoned and hanging loosely over his trousers. She saw him turn his face to the other man and smile. Watching him, Cynthia's heart seemed to skip a beat at the sight of his handsome smile.

As they drew closer, Cynthia could see Sam Tyler's full physique, and brazenly she lowered her gaze to his strong, muscular legs. Suddenly catching her breath, she placed her hand over her mouth to quiet her gasp. Sam Tyler wasn't limping! Good Lord, he was walking as well as any man! But Sam Tyler had a pronounced limp. His leg was so badly injured that it had kept him out of the army!

Cynthia felt faint, and her heart pulsated irregularly. Something was wrong! Terribly wrong! Who was Sam Tyler? Why did he only pretend to have a lame leg?

Spy! she cried inwardly. Dear God, he must be a spy! No! Oh, no!

Trying to remain calm and unseen, Cynthia's eyes followed the two men as they approached the front door. Shaking hands, they spoke in hushed tones, and she was unable to detect their words. Was the man with him a spy also? He must be!

Opening the door, Sam Tyler stepped forward, looking to his left and then to his right. Seeing that there was no one close by, he ushered the visitor through the doorway and outside.

Quickly he locked up, then returned to his bedroom, closing the door.

Relieved that she hadn't been spotted, Cynthia released the breath she had been holding. She wasn't sure of what she had just witnessed, but she knew she was in danger. She must not let Sam Tyler find her! She had to slip out of the store without her presence being detected. Forgetting her knitting, she moved swiftly, her thoughts only on escaping. Stepping out from behind the counter, she turned the corner so sharply that she nearly lost her balance. Steadying herself, she clutched at the top of the counter, accidently knocking the box of cigars to the floor.

Not waiting to see if Sam Tyler had heard the box fall, she lifted the hem of her black dress and ran toward the front door. Terrified, she heard his door being swung open, and she saw the light from his bedroom filtering across the floor. Frantically she grabbed for the doorknob as she shoved her hand into her pocket, searching for the key.

His large hands grabbed her shoulders roughly, swinging her around. Holding her forcefully, he demanded, "What are you doing here?"

Gasping, she stammered, "M . . . my knitting. I . . . I forgot it."

His fingers dug into her so strongly that Cynthia moaned. "Damn it!" Buford cursed. "Why in the hell did you have to come back here!"

"Please!" she pleaded. "Please let me go! You're hurting me!"

His grip lessened, but he still kept his hands on her shoulders. "How much did you hear?" he asked sharply.

"Nothing!" she cried. "I heard nothing!"

"Did you stand at my door and listen to what we were discussing?"

"No! Please believe me!" she begged.

He wanted to believe her! God, how he wanted to believe her! But, all the same, she now knew he wasn't simply a farmer from Illinois. His mission in Lawrence was almost completed. If he could somehow persuade her to keep quiet until he left, then there would be no harm done. Damn! What in the hell was he thinking about? He couldn't take her word for it that she hadn't heard the military secrets that had been discussed in his room. And just how in the hell could he

305

expect a Union widow to protect a Confederate spy?

Wondering how in the hell he could bring himself to kill a woman, let alone one that he loved, Buford unconsciously removed his hands from her shoulders, setting her free.

Instantly Cynthia grabbed for the doorknob, but, easily, Buford jerked her back. She tried to scream for help, but quickly he had his hand over her mouth, muffling her cries.

Panicking, she fought against him, finding a strength that only comes with desperation. She kicked wildly at his shins as her fists pounded across his chest and then to the side of his head.

Trying to dodge her blows without hurting her, Buford shook her roughly. Losing her footing, Cynthia dropped to the floor, pulling Buford down with her.

Landing on top of her, Buford captured her wrists in his hands, pinning her arms over her head. Shoving his legs against hers, he had her physically restrained, so that she couldn't move.

She opened her mouth to scream, but before she could utter a sound, he seized her wrists in one hand, covering her mouth with his other hand.

"Be quiet!" he warned hoarsely. "Damn it, Cynthia, don't make me hurt you!"

Cautiously, he removed his hand, but foolishly she attempted to cry out. Despising himself, Buford slapped her face sharply. "I told you to be quiet! I don't want to hurt you! Please don't force me to hit you again!"

Her cheek stinging, she sobbed, "I won't scream! Please . . . please don't hit me!"

Seeing her tears, Buford cringed. He felt sick inside.

306

He had never struck a woman before in his life. Gently, he stroked her cheek with his fingertips. "I'm sorry, Cynthia," he whispered.

The light filtering in from his bedroom shone on Buford's face, and, seeing his concern for her, Cynthia's fears began to dissolve. He wouldn't harm her. She didn't know who he was, or even if his name was really Sam Tyler, but she understood the man. And he was not capable of harming a woman.

Cynthia relaxed, and as she did she became conscious of Buford's weight pressing her to the floor. His body on hers was heavy, but, surprisingly, not uncomfortable.

Inadvertently, she shifted her hips, and his hardness slid naturally between her legs. Becoming aware of their intimacy, Cynthia began breathing deeply. Part of her conscience demanded that she push him away, but another part, and one she had no control over, forced her to look at him with such seductiveness that Buford groaned passionately.

Carefully he released her hands, and immediately her arms were around him. Drawing him closer, she parted her lips, waiting for his mouth to take possession of hers.

"Cynthia," he asked intensely, "are you sure?"

No, she wasn't sure! Where Sam Tyler was concerned, she would never be sure of anything!

Her voice trembling, she confessed submissively, "I want you. I've wanted you since that moment you first kissed me."

"I'm warning you, Cynthia. This time I won't stop with a kiss," he told her evenly.

She believed him. Oh, should she insist that he leave

her alone? All at once, David's image came to mind and she almost found the strength to demand that he let her up, but, suddenly, his lips were on hers. Yielding to his thrilling kiss, her husband's form vanished from her thoughts.

Cynthia had never kissed any man but David, and she innocently believed all kisses were basically the same. Never in her wildest dreams could she have imagined that a man's warm mouth on hers could stimulate so much passion within her. David's kisses had always been so tender, almost as if he had been afraid that he might hurt her. But the lips that were now on hers were insistent and demanding. Surrendering to his male dominance, Cynthia opened her mouth under his, accepting his kiss completely.

Without removing his lips from hers, Buford caressed her breasts, admiring their fullness. Hastily he unbuttoned her bodice, slipping his hand under the confining chemise, touching her bare flesh. As his strong hand cupped her breast, Cynthia moaned with pleasure. Her passion soaring, she placed her hand beneath her large breast, lifting herself to his touch.

Breaking their kiss, Buford moved his lips to her shoulders. Tugging at the dress and chemise, he forced them down past her breasts. Releasing her voluptuous mounds, he ran his tongue over one nipple and then the other.

Pulling at her skirts, he jerked them up to her hips. Running his hand on the inside of her long, slender leg, he moved his fingers upward until he reached the softness between her thighs, but her cotton undergarments prevented him from feeling the warmth he knew was awaiting him.

Vehemently, he groaned, "Damn! You women wear too damned many clothes!"

Standing, he reached for her hand, pulling her to her feet. Placing one arm around her waist and the other one behind her legs, he easily lifted her. Holding her firmly against his chest, he began carrying her to his bedroom.

His strength amazed Cynthia, and, impressed by his male aggressiveness, she wrapped her arms around his neck, relishing his closeness.

Entering the room, he kicked the door shut with the heel of his boot. Taking her to the bed, he gently laid her down on it. Then, turning quickly, he returned to the door and secured the bolt. Passing the lamp, he dimmed the flame, making the room less bright.

Taking long, even strides, he moved to the bed where she lay waiting for him. Sitting on the edge, Buford reached for her dress, and unfastened the remaining buttons. He lifted her long skirts, admiring her shapely legs. "Stand in front of me and undress," he ordered thickly.

Suddenly feeling terribly shy, Cynthia made no move to obey him. Before she knew what had happened, he had her jerked from the bed and onto her feet. Moving to the very edge of the bed, he positioned her between his spread legs.

"Undress!" he told her forcefully.

"B . . . but," she stammered.

He looked up into her face, and the undisguised passion she saw in his eyes sent her pulse racing. "Take off your clothes, and don't move away from me while you undress. I want you close."

His ardent expression and sensual request excited

309

Cynthia beyond reason, and, caught up in the romantic moment, she began to disrobe. She removed her clothes slowly and seductively. She could see in his eyes how much he admired her full breasts, small waist, and long, slim legs. As she temptingly took off the last remaining garment, Buford's breathing deepened so rapidly that she could hear his uncontrolled passion.

Placing his hands on her waist, he eased her down on the bed next to him. He stretched out beside her, and his lips found hers as his hand began exploring her intimately. Trembling with longing, Cynthia arched her breasts to his touch, and when he moved his hand downward, she willingly parted her legs, welcoming his fingers entering her warm flesh.

Rising, Buford hurriedly removed his clothes. Beyond her control, Cynthia watched him as if she were in a trance. She couldn't take her eyes from his masculine physique. His chest was wide, filled with dark hair, his waist slim, and his legs solid and firm. But it was his male hardness that she found most captivating. He was so large! For a moment she questioned if she was woman enough to accommodate him.

Spreading her thighs, he leaned over her. Grasping her ankles, he bent her legs to where her knees were touching her breasts. Conscious of his size, Cynthia was alarmed, but, before she had a chance to protest his entry, Buford slid into her swiftly. Surprisingly, his penetration wasn't painful but thrilling. Exciting chills ran over her fleetingly as she enclosed him into her embrace.

Locking her legs across his back, she matched his driving force, her thighs converging powerfully with his. Writhing and thrusting passionately, they reached for ecstatic fulfillment. Climaxing in unison, they both moaned with pleasure as they clutched frantically at each other.

Buford kissed her tenderly before moving to lie at her side. Breathing heavily, he murmured, "I have never enjoyed making love to a woman as much as I enjoyed having you."

"No woman?" she questioned skeptically, modestly covering herself with the crumpled sheet.

"No woman," he repeated firmly. "And I was once married."

"Jamie's mother?" she asked automatically, but quickly she dismissed the question. "Of course not. You aren't Jamie's father, are you? Is he also a spy?"

Sitting up rigidly, he moved to the edge of the bed. Placing his arms across his knees, he stared down at the floor.

"Who are you?" she asked. "Is your name really Sam Tyler?"

"You ask too damned many questions!" he sneered. Turning stiffly, he faced her, and the glare in his brown eyes was frightening. He showed her his strong hands. Menacingly, he warned, "With these I could silence you forever! All I need to do is wrap them around your neck and squeeze until I cut off your last remaining breath."

Cowering, Cynthia instinctively inched her way to the far side of the bed. She was terrified of him. Had she been mistaken? She had believed him incapable of harming a woman.

Seeing her fright, he said tenderly, "Don't be afraid, Cynthia. I'm not going to hurt you. I'm not that damned loyal to any cause. I can't kill a woman, especially you." But, unexpectedly, he grabbed her by the wrist, pulling her toward him. His fingers gripping her tightly, he demanded, "Look me in the eyes and swear that you didn't hear anything that was said in this room between me and the man you saw leaving this store!"

Meeting his hard stare, she answered strongly, "I heard nothing! I swear it!"

Brusquely, he released her wrist, and she fell back limply on the bed. Silently, he weighed the consequences. Even if she had listened to the conversation, the informer's name had never been spoken, nor any information concerning him. His visitor had already left Lawrence, and he wouldn't be returning. If he let her live, the only life in jeopardy was his own. He could always tie her up and skip town tonight. But no, he couldn't do that. He had one last contact to make early in the morning, before leaving for Anderson's camp. Damn! What in the hell was he going to do with her?

Standing, he walked over to the bureau and lit a cigar.

Regarding him, Cynthia was a little embarrassed by his nudity. She had seen David without his clothes, but he had never boldly walked around their bedroom without covering himself. But her modesty didn't keep her from admiring his naked flesh. She wondered how old he was. He had to be in his forties, but his physique was that of a man much younger. Who is he? she pondered. Apparently, he isn't the simple farmer he pretends to be. Now, that he was being himself, his drawling and uncultured way of speaking was gone. He might not be a man of high education, but he was far from being an illiterate.

Feeling her eyes on him, he turned to look at her. Leaning against the tall bureau, he unexpectedly smiled.

His winning smile went straight to her heart. Responding, her lips curled slightly as she asked carefully, "May I get dressed?"

He nodded agreeably. Watching her slip hurriedly into her clothes, he knew what had to be done. There was no other logical choice.

As Cynthia hastily pinned her hair up into its original state, Buford ground out his cigar in the ashtray. Stepping over to his clothes, he began putting them on, as mentally he mapped out his plan. He would gag her, then slip her out of the store and to the stable in back. Then he'd take her deep into the woods. He'd stay the night with her, then in the morning tie her securely to a tree. He'd return to town, see the contact who was expecting him, then go back to Cynthia and set her free. By the time she could walk back to Lawrence, he would be far into Missouri.

But Buford's plan was crushed when, suddenly, he heard a carriage stopping in front of the store. He reached over to seize Cynthia, but she was too far away. Before he could stop her, she had the door flung open. Slamming it closed behind her, she darted into the outer room at the same moment that Lillian inserted her key into the lock. Unsure of what she should do, Cynthia made a mad dash for the counter. Hurrying behind it, she began gathering the yarn and knitting needles.

Entering the store behind Lillian, Jason headed straight for the lamp. Lighting it, he said to Addie, who was standing in the open doorway holding Amelia's son, "I'll help you upstairs with the baby."

Jason took one step toward Addie when, all at once, he caught a glimpse of Cynthia. "What are you doing here?" he asked with surprise.

Lillian turned to Cynthia, looking at her with a questioning expression. "Cynthia dear, what are you doing here so late? And in the dark, no less."

Stammering, Cynthia answered, "I . . . I forgot my . . . my knitting."

"But, darling," Lillian continued, "why were you in the dark?"

Cynthia shrugged, saying evasively, "I saw no reason to light a lamp."

Lillian found her reasoning unusual, but, deciding not to press the issue, she asked Cynthia casually, "Do you know if Mr. Tyler has retired?"

"I . . . I don't know," Cynthia replied breathlessly.

Lillian was not aware of Cynthia's uneasiness, but Jason had detected her nervousness and her flushed cheeks. He also noticed that her hair had been pinned up untidily, as if she had been in a hurry. Smirking, he knew beyond a doubt that Sam Tyler hadn't retired. So the rumors Mrs. Kelley had been spreading about Cynthia and Sam Tyler were true. Well, apparently the prim Mrs. Coffman was not so prim after all. If she would stoop to someone as common as Tyler, then she would spread her legs for any man. Thinking Cynthia quite attractive, he was tempted to bed her himself, but, picturing her in Tyler's arms, he decided against it. He'd be damned if he'd take a dirt farmer's leftovers! He shrugged smugly, believing that not having

314

him as a lover was Cynthia's great loss.

Looking at Jason, Lillian said, "I'll see if Mr. Tyler is still awake."

She took a step toward his room, but quickly Jason halted her. "That's all right, Lillian. I'll get him out here."

Shouting severely, Jason demanded, "Tyler! I want to talk to you!"

"My goodness!" Lillian gasped. "Jason, you must not be so rude!"

Closed inside his room, Buford had heard Bishop's furious yell. So Cynthia had told Bishop about him! He wondered why her betrayal should hurt him so deeply.

The room was minus any windows, and the only way out was through the door. Stepping to the bureau, Buford opened the bottom drawer. Taking out his Colt revolver, he held it flush to his leg. Going to the door, he opened it slowly. Cautiously, he limped through the doorway. Keeping his pistol hidden behind his leg, he regarded the four people waiting for his entrance. Halting, his eyes examined Jason. If Cynthia had told him what happened, it wasn't apparent in his stony expression. Quickly his vision went to Cynthia. If she sensed his eyes on her, she made no attempt to acknowledge him, instead, she kept her gaze on Jason.

"Tyler," Jason began, "Mrs. Adams has informed me that you are very good with your hands, and are quite adept at making minor repairs. The lock on my front door is jammed, and if you'll go to my home in the morning and fix it, I will pay you a small sum for the job. It'll give you an opportunity to earn yourself a little extra income."

Buford sighed with relief. So Cynthia hadn't told

him! Grinning, his contempt for Jason was disguised as he drawled, "What if I can't fix it? Do I get paid for my trouble?"

Finding his attitude disrespectful, Jason replied huffily, "Men like you are always wanting something for nothing. Of course you don't get paid if you don't do the job correctly."

"Well, in that case," Buford said slothfully, "why don't you get yourself a locksmith?"

"Tyler, your laziness has just cost you a chance to make yourself some extra money."

Still grinning, Buford replied evenly, "I'm not too lazy, captain; I'm just too damned contrary."

Lillian, finding their bantering upsetting, declared breathlessly, "Gentlemen, please!" To Jason, she continued, "Perhaps Mr. Tyler is right. I think you should hire a locksmith."

"They overcharge!" Jason huffed.

"No . . . no, my dear!" Lillian quickly reassured him. "I know a locksmith who is very reasonable."

Eyeing Buford coldly, Jason told him, "That's all, Tyler!" But unable to let such an opportunity pass him by, he turned to Cynthia and said leadingly, "Cynthia, I'll give you a ride home. I see you have your knitting, so I'm sure you're ready to leave." As though it were merely an innocent afterthought, he added, "You didn't leave anything in Tyler's bedroom, did you my dear?"

Embarrassed, Cynthia blushed furiously. Fuming, Buford took a step toward Jason, his grip tightening dangerously on the butt of his pistol.

"Jason Bishop!" Lillian scolded severely. "How dare you speak so crudely to poor Cynthia! You apologize to her immediately!''

"That's all right! I can do without his apology!" Cynthia uttered, breathing rapidly. Flustered, she clumsily moved out from behind the counter. Determined to keep her dignity, she didn't hurry her steps as she walked past Addie. Pausing in the open doorway, she lifted her chin proudly, and, looking back at Lillian, she calmly bid her goodnight. For a fleeting instant, her eyes met Buford's, then she quickly departed.

Buford had his old battered suitcase packed, when he heard a timid knock at his door.

Closing the suitcase, he shoved it under his bed. Going to the door, he opened it. Overjoyed to see that Cynthia had returned, he had her jerked into his room and in his arms in one swift move.

Holding her tightly, he whispered, "Cynthia, I'm so glad you are here."

Startling him, she pushed out of his arms roughly. Looking at her, Buford was shocked to see she had a small derringer pointed at him. His initial reaction changing to humor, he asked, "Is that toy loaded?"

"Believe me, Mr. Tyler, you don't want to find out!" she cautioned.

"What are you planning to do, Cynthia? Are you taking me to Bishop?"

She shook her head. "Not unless you force me to. Mr. Tyler . . ."

Interrupting her, he remarked brusquely, "Don't call me Tyler. My name is Buford."

"And your last name?" she asked.

"You're asking too many questions again," he grinned.

"I didn't come here to ask questions. I came here to tell you that you have until tomorrow morning to leave town. If you are still here after noon, I will go to Captain Bishop and tell him everything I know about you."

"Everything?" he questioned cunningly, raising his eyebrows.

Blushing, she replied firmly, "I meant what I said!"

"Why are you doing this?" he asked.

"Mr. Tyler, I mean Buford, my loyalties are with the Union. I don't know what part you are playing in this war, but I do know you are not working for the Union. And regardless of what happened between us tonight, I will report you as the spy I believe you to be!"

"I have until tomorrow morning?" he asked.

"No later than noon," she replied.

Buford smiled casually. Her ultimatum fit right into his plans. "I promise you, I'll be gone before noon."

"Don't ever come back to Lawrence!" she warned.

"But I will," he assured her. "When this war is over, I'm coming back."

"Why?" she questioned.

"To ask you to marry me," he answered calmly.

Her gray eyes widened with astonishment. Although a part of her was thrilled by his promised proposal, her loyalties to the Union and her late husband held steadfast. "I could never marry a man who hadn't fought for the North!"

"Don't be so sure, Cynthia," he answered evenly. His calmness deceived her, and before she realized

318

what had taken place, his strong hand seized her wrist, forcing her to drop the derringer.

Suddenly he had her in his embrace, his mouth crushing against hers. She tried not to respond, but she had no defense against Buford. Giving in, she parted her lips beneath his as her arms went around him, gathering him even closer to her.

Releasing her, Buford placed his hands on her shoulders. He gazed down into her face trying to memorize her lovely features. He knew he wouldn't be seeing her again for a long time. He wondered how many times he would recall this moment, visualizing her large gray eyes and full, pouting lips. Touching her hair, he curled one of the tight ringlets around his finger. "I promise you, Cynthia, if I'm still alive when the war ends, I'll come back for you."

"I won't marry you!" she insisted.

Deciding not to pressure her, he leaned over, picking up the derringer. Handing it to her, he said, "Your weapon, madam."

Accepting the pistol, she took one last look at him before saying with finality, "Goodbye, Buford!" She left his room, closing the door behind her.

TWENTY-THREE

Standing at a safe distance, Amelia watched as Anderson's guerrillas practiced with their firearms. While some of the men remained unmounted and fired at stationary targets, others galloped on their horses, shooting while riding at breakneck speed.

The Missouri guerrillas were outnumbered by Union soldiers. The Pro-Confederates' success in combat, aside from their guerrilla tactics, lay in the Colt revolving pistol; and Anderson's men were accurate and deadly shots with these weapons. The revolvers, which could rapidly fire five and six shots, gave the guerrillas a tremendous volume of fire power. The Union soldiers patrolling the Kansas and Missouri border were armed with singe-shot muzzle-loading carbines, and only a small majority of the Union officers carried superior weapons.

As Amelia watched the guerrillas on horseback, they let loose with terrifying rebel yells, sending cold chills up her spine. Placing their bridle reins between their teeth, they carried a revolver in each hand, and, with increasing speed, they fired a barrage of heavy caliber bullets. They carried several loaded cylinders tied to their saddle horns or secured in their pockets, and, when a pistol was empty, they expertly knocked out the empty gun cylinder and swiftly injected the loaded one. Their aims were uncannily precise, and Amelia had a sickening feeling that most of their victims died shot through the head.

Out of the corner of her eye, she caught a glimpse of Buford walking in her direction. Buford had arrived at Anderson's camp the night before, and the moment Amelia saw him, she anxiously asked if her baby, Lillian, and Cynthia were well. Her husband's health slipped her mind entirely.

"Good morning, ma'am," Buford said politely, pausing to stand at her side.

Smiling, she replied, "Good morning."

Observing the guerrillas' expertise, he said impressively, "They're so good at what they do that it's almost unbelievable."

"Yes, but awesome," Amelia said.

He nodded, understanding what she meant. Touching her arm, he got her attention. "There's James Henry."

Rising on her tiptoes, Amelia arched her neck, trying to get a better view. Seeing James Henry riding speedily toward the guerrillas, she wondered if he intended to join the men who were drilling. She was surprised to see that he had tied a band around his forehead and removed his shirt.

Vaguely, she remarked, "If it weren't for his beard, he'd look just like an Indian."

"Comanche," Buford stated.

Facing him, she questioned, "What?"

322

"James Henry and I lived with the Comanche," he explained.

Astonished, she asked, "When?"

"Years ago," he mumbled.

"Are you kin to James Henry?"

"I'm his uncle. Paul Stewart was my brother."

"How in the world did you two come to live with Comanches?"

"I left my home in Tennessee when I was twenty-two and headed out west to seek adventure." He smiled pleasantly, reminiscing. "Well, I won't bore you with my life story. But I was befriended by the Comanche, and I lived with them for awhile. About that time in my life, I got to thinking about my family and how I hadn't seen them in years, so I went back home. I learned that my parents had died, and I knew my brother had moved to western Missouri. I paid an unexpected visit to Paul and his family. James Henry was twenty years old, and I could tell he was restless and anxious to sow his wild oats. I told him about how I had lived with the Comanche. From his reaction, it was obvious that he was impressed. Well, I was quite taken with my nephew, and I found myself growing fond of him. So when I decided to head back out west, I asked him if he wanted to go with me." Buford paused to chuckle. "He jumped at the opportunity. Paul and his wife Sarah were strongly opposed to the idea. But there was no stopping James Henry. Hell, there was nothing to keep him in Missouri, and he sure wasn't cut out to be a farmer."

"Did you take him to the Comanches?" she asked.

"The Comanche are a nomadic people, and it took me a while to find them. But, eventually, I located the tribe that had befriended me. The chief's son was the same age as James Henry, and, right off, they took a likin' to each other. The young warriors welcomed James Henry, and, in no time at all, he became like one of them.''

''How long did you stay with the tribe?'' Amelia asked, giving Buford her undivided attention. At last, she was learning about the man she loved.

''Well, while James Henry was sowing his wild oats with the young braves, I was spending most of my time with the chief's niece.''

''Aha!'' Amelia exclaimed good-humoredly. ''An Indian maiden!''

''She was a pretty little thing, but she was sickly. She was dyin'. She knew it, and I knew it.''

When Buford became quiet, she asked gently, ''What happened?''

''I married her,'' he answered.

''You must have been very deeply in love with her,'' Amelia speculated romantically.

Surprising her, he replied, ''No, not really.''

''Then why did you marry her?'' she asked.

Buford shrugged casually. ''It was the least I could do for her. I knew she didn't have much longer to live.''

''If she had been in good health, would you still have married her?''

He shook his head. ''I wasn't a Comanche; I was a white man. I had no hankerin' to live with Indians permanently.''

Wisely, Amelia stated, ''You married her because she was hopelessly in love with you.''

''Why do you think that?'' he asked.

Looking him in the eyes, she answered, "Because you and James Henry are too much alike, and if a woman loved you, her love could never be merely lukewarm."

Stepping to a large oak, Buford leaned against the trunk of the tree as he leisurely lit a cigar. He took a long drag from it, before continuing, "She died seven months after we were married. A few days later, James Henry and I left."

"Where did you go?" she asked.

"We traveled a lot, did some trapping. We came back to Missouri periodically so that James Henry could visit with his family. A couple of years ago, we decided to go to California and try our luck in the goldfields. There wasn't too much gold left to be found, but we staked a small claim. Fortunately for us, it paid off."

"Did you become rich?" Amelia asked enthusiastically.

Laughing, he answered, "We weren't that fortunate. But with the money we had saved from trapping, and with what we made off our claim, we had enough money to buy some land in northern Texas."

"Why did you want to own land in Texas?"

"Ranching," he explained. "We divided the property. There's enough land for both of us to have a fairly good-size ranch. We made plans to build our houses and buy our herds. We helped each other put up crude cabins close to where our homes will someday be built. The war had been goin' on for about a year before we decided to get involved. So we buried our money in a safe place and came back to Missouri."

"To become Missouri guerrillas," Amelia finished

for him, her voice tinged with unintentional bitterness.

They both fell silent, returning to watching the guerrillas and James Henry practice warfare.

Eyeing her carefully, Buford cleared his throat before saying, ''Your son is a beautiful baby.''

Facing him, Amelia's cheeks glowed, as she agreed, ''Yes, he is beautiful!''

''Have you told James Henry?'' he asked bluntly.

''Wh . . . what?'' she stammered.

''Have you told him the truth about your son?''

Her heart sinking, she sighed, ''Then you know.''

''I took one look at him and knew James Henry was his father.''

Glumly, Amelia informed him. ''No, I haven't told James Henry.''

''Why?'' he asked.

''I don't know why,'' she replied despondently. ''But I have a feeling he doesn't want to be my baby's father. I suppose that's why I haven't told him.''

''You're right not to tell him. James Henry has suffered too much tragedy since this war started, without adding an estranged son to the list.''

Before they could further discuss her son and James Henry, they were suddenly interrupted by a large group of men riding into the camp. Seeing that some of the riders were wearing Confederate uniforms, Amelia's heart began pounding with fear. ''Who are they?'' she asked, although she already knew the answer.

''Colonel Garson,'' Buford answered gravely.

Instantly Amelia's vision flew to James Henry. He had spotted the visitors and was riding speedily toward Amelia and Buford. Fleeing, she ran to meet him.

Nearing her, James Henry abruptly reined his horse.

Leaping from the saddle, he held out his arms, and, as she threw herself into his embrace, he grasped her tightly.

Clinging to him, she sobbed convulsively, "Oh, James Henry! I'm so afraid! Dear God, am I going to be killed?"

Placing his cheek on the top of her head, he held her as close as he could. "It'll be all right, Amelia. It'll be all right, sweetheart," he murmured soothingly, wishing he believed his own words.

Entering Anderson's tent, James Henry and Buford came to attention as they saluted Colonel Garson and Captain Anderson.

After returning their salute, the colonel sat in the chair placed behind a small table. "At ease, gentlemen," he said.

Slowly, Captain Anderson moved to stand beside Colonel Garson's chair. Desperately, James Henry tried to read Amelia's fate in the colonel's expression, but his face was set.

Looking at Buford, the colonel asked, "When you were in Lawrence, did everything go as planned?"

"Yes, sir," Buford answered.

Colonel Garson nodded brusquely. "Good! We'll talk about it later. First, I have a couple of other matters I need to discuss with you both. I'll be leaving in the morning at daybreak, and you two will accompany me. Your work here in Missouri is hereby terminated. Our destination is Mineral Springs, Texas. You will both be issued Confederate uniforms and receive your field commissions. You will then join our Confederate

327

troops.''

Leaning his elbows on the table, Colonel Garson folded his hands, placing them beneath his chin. Sternly, his eyes looked into James Henry's. "How is Mrs. Bishop?" he inquired.

"She's fine, sir," he answered, his concern for Amelia hitting him so severely that he felt as if his breath had suddenly been cut off. Was Colonel Garson going to tell him that Amelia was to be executed? James Henry was not a praying man, but inwardly, he prayed, Please God, don't let her die! Please!

Colonel Garson regarded James Henry closely. He had spotted Amelia running to James Henry, and he had seen the way he had held her in his arms. He's in love with her, the colonel decided. He may not be aware of it himself, but he loves her.

Unfolding his hands, the colonel placed them on the table, and, leaning back in his chair, he smiled. "I have good news for you, James Henry. Mrs. Bishop is to be set free.''

Noting James Henry's overwhelming relief, Colonel Garson knew he was right. James Henry was very much involved with the young lady. Continuing, he explained, "The informer died four weeks ago. Her knowledge can no longer be a threat.''

"Dead!" James Henry exclaimed. "But he was a very influential man. Why hasn't anyone heard of his death?''

"He was discovered to be a spy by the Union, and they murdered him. It would be very embarrassing for them to let it be publicly known that they had a Confederate spy in their midst, and a Union officer no less. I imagine they will soon report that he died heroically in battle."

"How were you able to learn all this?" James Henry asked.

"I have my ways," Colonel Garson answered evasively. Before James Henry could question him further, he said crisply, "In the morning, after we leave, Captain Anderson will see to it that Mrs. Bishop is escorted to the Kansas border. She will soon be back home." Sitting straight, he ordered in a friendly tone, "You're dismissed. I'm sure you're anxious to tell Mrs. Bishop the good news."

Smiling happily, James Henry replied, "Yes, sir!" He remembered to salute the colonel before darting out of the tent.

Elated, James Henry ran every step to the cave. As he rushed inside, he saw Amelia sitting on a blanket. Her arms were resting across her raised knees, and she had her head nestled on her folded arms.

Hearing his entrance, she glanced up. James Henry knew he'd never forget how vulnerable she appeared at this moment. Her extremely long hair was falling in disorderly fashion across her shoulders, with a few strands clinging to her cheeks. Her eyes were opened wide, pleading with his. She seemed so small and helpless.

Going to her, and taking her hands, he drew her to her feet. Placing his hand under her chin, he tilted her face upwards. "Amelia," he whispered lovingly, "you are to be set free. Tomorrow morning, you will be safely escorted to the Kansas border."

For a moment, she could only stare at him, her face expressionless. Her smile began faintly at the very corners of her mouth, and spread beautifully. "James

Henry!'' she cried ecstatically. "I'm not going to be executed! I'll see my baby again! Oh, thank God!''

Whooping boisterously, he placed his hands on her waist, twirling her around vigorously. Putting her arms about his neck, she threw back her head, laughing with joy.

Having completed his report to Colonel Garson, Buford was brusquely dismissed. The moment he left the tent, the colonel ordered Anderson to be seated. Pulling an extra chair up to the table, he sat down.

Taking his time, the colonel reached into his jacket pocket and removed a cheroot. Taking a box of matches off the table, he lit the small cigar. Blowing out the match, he returned the box to its original place. Looking across the table at Anderson, he stated calmly, "The informer is not dead."

Captain Anderson nodded slightly. "I didn't think that he was."

"You understand why I had to lie to James Henry, don't you?"

"Yes, sir," Captain Anderson answered quietly. "But eventually he'll have to be told the truth."

"I'll tell him when we are in Mineral Springs."

"And Mrs. Bishop?" he asked.

"You will take two of your most trusted men with you and escort Mrs. Bishop from the camp. After you have traveled a reasonable distance, she is to be executed. It is imperative that you swear your men to secrecy. Killing a woman is an ugly business. The Confederacy wants it kept confidential. Bury her body where it is not likely to be found. Then camouflage the grave by riding your horses back and forth over the site.''

When Captain Anderson didn't comment, the colonel said severely, ''This is an order! And the order is not exclusively mine! It also comes from my superiors!''

''But why me?'' Anderson pleaded.

''There is no one else,'' the colonel replied gravely. Knowing he had placed a terrible burden on Anderson's shoulders, he added apologetically, ''I'm sorry.''

Solemnly, Captain Anderson murmured, ''So am I, Colonel Garson. So am I.''

Amelia hadn't intended to fall asleep. She didn't want to spend her last night with James Henry in a state of unconsciousness. But following two hours of rapturous lovemaking, she had unwillingly drifted into sleep.

Amelia awoke with a sudden start. She didn't know what had awakened her. Perhaps, somehow, her subconscious had refused to let her waste her last moments with James Henry and had ordered her to open her eyes.

She was lying at his side, her head nestled on his shoulder. He had one arm around her, and distractedly he was brushing his fingers through her long hair.

The lantern had been extinguished and the cave was dark. ''What time is it?'' she asked.

Taking his arm from around her, he pushed aside the blanket, sitting up. Reaching for the lantern and the matches, he quickly lit the lamp. He adjusted the flame, then, picking up his trousers, he dug into his pocket. He removed his watch, then, lying beside Amelia, he opened it, checking the time. "Four-thirty," he answered, placing the blanket back over them.

"It'll soon be daylight," she murmured sadly.

He started to snap the watch closed when, suddenly, Amelia caught a glimpse of Anne's picture. Placing her hand on his to keep him from closing the case, she questioned, "Who is she?"

"Anne," he answered.

"She was very pretty," Amelia whispered. "You loved her very much, didn't you?"

Gazing at Anne's picture, he answered somberly, "Yes, but then she was very easy to love. Anne was gentle, kind, and totally unselfish."

"And Jason killed her," Amelia stated regretfully.

At the mention of Jason's name, he snapped the watch closed. As he put it back into the pocket of his trousers, Amelia cried sincerely, "James Henry, I'm so sorry! I feel so bad about what happened to your sisters and father!"

"There's no reason for you to feel bad. It wasn't your fault. You aren't responsible for your husband."

"Killing Jason won't bring them back!" she cried forcefully, not wanting James Henry to commit murder. She believed his act of revenge would inevitably destroy him.

Mistaking her motive, he replied unfairly, "Now, that you know you are returning to your husband, you've decided to resume your wifely role. Do us both a favor, Amelia, and don't start begging for his life."

She wondered what she had said to make him react

so unjustly. "But James Henry . . ." she began.

Abruptly, he cut her off, "Don't, Amelia! I won't discuss your husband!"

Deciding it would be best not to pressure him, Amelia let the subject drop. Snuggling up close to him, she asked, "Will I ever see you again?"

"I don't know," he answered. "But I seriously doubt it." Enjoying her naked flesh rubbing against his, James Henry placed his arm around her shoulders, drawing her intimately close.

Amelia longed to cry out to him that she couldn't go on living without him, but she choked back the words. She would continue to live. No one died from a broken heart. And she had their son! He would be her reason to want to go on living! Losing James Henry would break her heart, but her baby would heal it for her. She would dedicate her life to her child, and, through him, she would find happiness.

Turning to her, James Henry placed his hand under the blanket, finding her breasts. He caressed her gently, and Amelia could feel a tingling sensation spreading downward between her thighs. Oh, he can so easily arouse my passion! she thought. Suddenly, realizing it would soon be Jason's hands on her body, fondling her inconsiderately, Amelia involuntarily shuddered.

"What's wrong?" he asked urgently.

Believing it would be a mistake to bring up Jason, she denied, "Nothing. Nothing is wrong."

"Are you sure?" he insisted gently.

"Yes, I'm sure," she murmured, burying her face in his shoulder so that he couldn't see her tears.

Slowly he moved his hand down to her waist, and

then to her stomach, until at last his hand came to rest between her legs. Pressing his lips to hers, his fingers readied her for his entry.

With his mouth still on hers, he moved over her. Knowing their separation was only moments away, James Henry entered her swiftly, almost frantically. Believing this was the last time he would make love to Amelia, James Henry's inner turmoil caused him to cling and take her urgently.

Crossing her legs over his back, Amelia met his demanding thrusts. He came to her so powerfully that, at times, his deep penetration was painful. But Amelia welcomed the pain, it seemed to help her to forget the hurt tearing into her heart. The man she loved was leaving! She had lost him, and she would probably never see him again! Amelia clung tightly to him, holding him as close as she could. Oh, I love him! she cried silently. I love him so much!

Desperately, they clutched at each other as their passions exploded desperately. Achieving sexual fulfillment, James Henry held her tightly, spilling his life-giving seed deeply into her.

Startling Amelia, he moved brusquely away from her and reached for his clothes. She watched him as he stood to dress. Implanting his image into her mind, she wondered how many times she would close her eyes envisioning him as he was now, or remember that special little gleam that came to his eyes when he smiled. How often would she recall the sound of his deep voice and his laughter? In time, would her memories of James Henry fade? No! She would never forget him! If she lived to be a hundred, she'd still be able to flawlessly reproduce his image in her mind.

"You'd better get dressed," he told her. "It's getting light outside, and you'll be leaving soon."

Despondently, she began putting on her clothes. Was he going to leave her without telling her that he loved her? Did he feel about her the same way Buford had about his wife? Was it only compassion that had caused him to be kind and loving to her? Valuing her pride, she knew she would rather his emotions had been ruled by revenge than by pity.

Amelia was dressed and she was slipping on her boots when Gary's voice sounded from outside, announcing his arrival. "James Henry, the colonel is ready to leave."

"Come on inside," James Henry told him.

Appearing at the mouth of the cave, Gary smiled at Amelia. "Good morning, ma'am. Captain Anderson wanted me to tell you that you'll be leaving as soon as the colonel and his men ride out."

"Thank you, Gary," she murmured, getting to her feet.

His smile broadening, Gary remarked, "I guess you're looking forward to seeing your baby."

"Yes . . . yes, I am," she replied, forcing herself to return his friendly smile.

Fidgeting uncomfortably, Gary said none too discreetly, "Well, I reckon I'll head on back to camp, so that you two can be alone."

"That won't be necessary," James Henry spoke up. "Just wait out front, so you can walk Amelia to the camp. I'll be leaving immediately."

Nodding, Gary left the cave, and, walking out of hearing range, he waited for Amelia.

James Henry extinguished the lantern, and the cave

335

became as gloomy as Amelia's mood. Picking up his hat, he turned to face her. With a casualness he was far from feeling, he said, "Well, I guess this is goodbye."

He's going to leave me without telling me he loves me! she cried inwardly. Once again, he has come into my life, stolen my heart, and now he's deserting me just as he did before.

Stepping to her, James Henry took her hand into his. "Take care of yourself, little one," he said tenderly.

Is that all he's going to say? she thought desperately. He is leaving me as if we were nothing more to each other than casual friends! Tell me you love me, James Henry! she pleaded silently. Let me hear you say those three words, so I can treasure them for a lifetime!

Placing his hand under her chin, he tilted her face up to his. Leaning over, he kissed her lips softly. "Goodbye, Amelia." Abruptly he turned, picked up his saddle bags, and, without further words, strode out of the cave.

Her heartache coming to her in a mad gush, she ran after him. Darting outside, she spotted him walking swiftly toward the camp. "James Henry!" she cried frantically.

If he heard her, he didn't bother to turn around. She couldn't let him go! He was her heart! She loved him!

"James Henry!" she called again. She attempted to follow him, but suddenly Gary's hand was on her arm, halting her.

Sympathetically, he said, "Miss Amelia, how many times do you want to tell him goodbye? Don't you realize you'll only be making it harder for yourself and for him?"

Defeated, Amelia resigned herself to James Henry's departure. Standing beside Gary, she allowed her tears to roll unhindered down her cheeks as she observed the man she loved preparing to leave.

Unknowingly, she clutched at Gary's hand, her fingers digging into his flesh. Mounting his horse, James Henry rode over to Colone Garson and Buford. Amelia gasped when suddenly he turned in the saddle to look at her, and, smiling tenderly, waved. Amelia released Gary's hand to raise her arm, but abruptly Colonel Garson gave his sergeant the preparatory command to move out. Before she could return James Henry's wave, he had turned away from her and was riding out of the camp and out of her life.

Letting her arm fall limply to her side, Amelia whispered tearfully, "Goodbye, James Henry."

Touching her elbow, Gary encouraged gently, "Let's go, ma'am. It's time for you to leave."

Wiping at her tears, she permitted Gary to escort her to camp. The men she had come to know the best were gathered together, waiting to tell her goodbye.

Suddenly remembering that she had forgotten the brush and comb that Anderson had loaned her, she asked Gary, "Will you please go back to the cave and get the brush and comb? I want to return them to Captain Anderson."

As Gary left her to hurry to the cave, Amelia was immediately surrounded by her admiring friends. Some of them simply shook her hand to tell her goodbye, but others boldly kissed her on the cheek. Studying Anderson's men, Amelia knew she would miss them. Aside from being separated from her child, the weeks she had spent at Anderson's camp had been the happiest time in her life.

Spotting Bulldog and Pat standing beside the horse that had been saddled for her, she excused herself and walked over to them.

"Would you like some breakfast before we leave?" Pat asked.

Her stomach felt as if it were tied in knots, and quickly she refused, "No, thank you. I couldn't eat a thing." Noticing that the captain's horse was saddled and standing next to Gary and Pat's mounts, she asked with surprise, "Is Captain Anderson going with us?"

"Yes, ma'am," Pat answered.

"But why?" she insisted.

Pat shrugged. "Last night, he told Gary and me that he was ridin' with us. But I don't know why he's determined to go," he answered honestly. He and Pat had not yet been informed that Amelia was to be executed.

"Isn't it dangerous for Captain Anderson to ride with only two of his men? What if we should run into Union soldiers?"

"If you do, there's one thing for certain," Bulldog grumbled, "with only two men to protect the captain, he'll be taken alive. Then the goddamned sonofabitches will have a party at the captain's expense." Gravely, he added, "And they'll make sure he don't die none too fast."

Alarmed, Amelia exclaimed, "You must insist that he stay here!"

Shaking their heads, Pat and Bulldog looked amusedly at Amelia. "Ma'am," Pat explained, "we don't insist that a captain do anything."

"Oh, of course," she answered demurely, feeling foolish.

338

Returning from the cave, Gary handed Amelia the brush and comb. Accepting them, she was getting ready to thank him when, all at once, Captain Anderson stepped from his tent.

As usual, Amelia found his appearance overwhelming and impressive. He looked over at her, and it was on her lips to smile at him, but noting his angry expression, the smile failed to materialize.

"Mount up!" he ordered gruffly.

Hurrying, Amelia placed the brush and comb into the saddle bags on her horse. She would give them to him later, when his disposition was a little more pleasant.

As Pat and Gary moved to their horses, Bulldog helped Amelia to mount. Looking down at him, she said softly, "Goodbye, Bulldog."

"So long, ma'am," he replied, stepping back.

Captain Anderson rode his horse next to Amelia's, with Pat and Gary following close behind. "Are you ready?" Anderson asked her sternly.

Wary of his foul mood, she nodded, answering timidly, "Yes, I'm ready."

Encouraging her horse into a steady walk, she rode away from the camp at Anderson's side. Watching him out of the corner of her eye, she wondered why he was being so curt. Knowing there was nothing she could do about his bad temper, she decided simply to ignore him. Surely, later, he would regain his usual agreeable humor.

Suddenly, James Henry came to her mind, but resolutely she cleared him from her thoughts. If she started thinking about James Henry, she'd only begin crying.

Concentrating wholeheartedly on her baby, Amelia

could actually feel her arms aching to hold him. Thinking how wonderful it was going to be to see her son again, Amelia smiled.

PART THREE

TWENTY-FOUR

Amelia tolerated Anderson's stony silence for one hour, before her patience finally gave way. Eyeing him sharply as he rode beside her, she asked fretfully, "My goodness, Captain Anderson, did I say or do something to offend you?"

At the sound of her voice, he turned his head stiffly, looking at her as if he had completely forgotten that she was there. Suddenly his jaws clenched tightly, and his hard expression puzzled Amelia. "Guide your horse into the brush!" he ordered gruffly, nodding to their right.

"But why?" she asked, finding his command strange.

Anderson jerked his reins to the right, causing his large stallion to force Amelia's small mare into the dense thicket.

Gary and Pat were bewildered by Anderson's conduct, but, without question, they followed their commander.

Shortly, they came upon a clearing, and Anderson ordered everyone to dismount. Gary and Pat quickly swung from their saddles, then rushed to help Amelia.

Dismounting, Anderson handed the bridle reins to Pat, telling him to secure the horses.

After the animals were tied to a large tree, Anderson stood silently, his eyes seriously regarding each individual. He studied Amelia last.

She didn't like the way he was staring at her. Something was wrong! But what? . . . What?

Anderson took a step toward Amelia as if he was going to touch her, but, changing his mind, he abruptly halted. His expression became coldly indifferent and his voice authoritative as he said, ''Amelia Bishop, I received orders from Colonel Garson that you are to be executed.''

''What!'' Gary and Pat yelled in unison.

''No!'' Amelia shouted. Panicking, she raved, ''What kind of cruel joke are you playing on me! Colonel Garson said I was to be set free!''

''It is no joke, madam,'' Anderson answered impassively. To Pat, he ordered, ''Tie her hands!'' When Pat didn't obey the command, Anderson bellowed, ''Damn it, man! Are you hard of hearing? I said tie her hands!''

Reluctantly, Pat went to his horse, and, taking a strip of rope from his saddle bag, he returned to Amelia. Gently, he pulled her arms behind her back, tying the rope around her small wrists.

''Why are you doing this?'' Amelia pleaded. Anderson made no attempt to answer her, causing Amelia's fear to spread uncontrollably. Dear God, he was going to kill her! The man had no feelings or compassion! The Union was right! He was a sadistic demon! Pathetically, she cried, ''I thought you were

344

my friend!''

Captain Anderson turned away sharply, so she couldn't see his grief. Her pathetic plea had gone straight to his heart. But he had his orders! He had to execute her! It was her death or, inevitably, his own! If the Confederacy was to find out he had refused to carry out an order as vital as this one, they would demand his own execution. The informer's identity had to be protected. The informer's life was more valuable than Amelia's. Anderson sighed deeply. He really didn't believe that Amelia knew the informer's name.

Controlling his emotions, Anderson ordered Pat and Gary to draw their pistols. Then he moved to Amelia, and, placing his hands on her shoulders, he positioned her so that she was facing her two intended executioners. ''Do you want a blindfold?'' he asked.

Looking up into his face, tears streamed from Amelia's eyes. ''No, I don't want a blindfold!'' she cried. ''I want to live!''

Whirling swiftly, he walked back to Gary and Pat, as Amelia's heart-rending pleas followed him. ''Please Captain Anderson! Oh God, please! Don't kill me! Please! I haven't done anything! Why are you doing this? Why? Captain Anderson, why?''

Pausing beside Gary and Pat, Anderson ordered harshly, ''Prepare to fire!''

''B . . . but Captain,'' Gary stammered.

''Do as I say!'' Anderson shouted, his face red with rage.

''NO!'' Amelia begged. ''NO! Don't shoot me! Please!'' Dear God, if only she could faint, so she wouldn't hear Anderson's final command! Or die suddenly from a heart attack! Anything would be better than just standing here waiting to die!

"Ready!" Anderson ordered. "Aim!"

Trembling, Gary and Pat pointed their pistols at Amelia.

"NO!" Amelia screamed.

All at once, Anderson stepped in front of his men, knocking their guns to the side. "You damned fools!" he raved. "The way your hands are shaking, you're not going to kill her! What do you want to do, wound her, so you can shoot her again and again, until she finally bleeds to death? My God, you wouldn't be that cruel to a rabid dog!"

Drawing his revolver, Anderson whirled smoothly, aiming his gun at Amelia. She could read in his eyes that he intended to mercifully kill her in one clean shot. Accepting death courageously, Amelia bowed her head and prayed.

The seconds that ticked by seemed interminable to Amelia. Dear God, why was he waiting? Cautiously, she raised her head. She expected to see Anderson's pistol pointed at her heart, but instead, his revolver was at his side hanging loosely in his hand. She brought her gaze up to his face. Meeting her eyes, he groaned, "I can't! I can't shoot you any more than I could have ordered Gary and Pat to fire."

Amelia's relief came to her so powerfully that her legs buckled, and, dropping to the ground, she fainted.

Returning his gun to its holster, Anderson hurried to Amelia. Kneeling, he lifted her in his arms. Rising, he glared at Gary and Pat. "Well, don't just stand there!" he demanded, flustered. "Do something!"

"What should we do?" Pat asked. He had never seen a woman faint before.

"I don't know!" Anderson barked impatiently.

"I'll get some water!" Gary offered, rushing to fetch his canteen.

Carrying Amelia to a tree, Anderson gently laid her down on a bed of leaves. Joining them, Gary gave the canteen to the captain. Opening it, he poured a small amount into his hand. Gently, he rubbed the water across her forehead.

When this failed to bring her to, he asked, "Do either of you have any whiskey?"

"Captain," Pat began seriously, "you know you don't allow us to carry any spirits when we're on military business."

"I didn't ask you what I do or don't allow!" he fumed. "I asked you if you have any whiskey!"

Deciding he wouldn't be reprimanded, Pat admitted reluctantly, "I think I might have just a little."

"Get it!" he ordered.

Returning quickly with a flask of whiskey, Pat handed it to the captain. Elevating Amelia's head, Anderson tilted the flask to her lips, pouring a small swallow into her mouth. Coughing, Amelia came to. Sitting beside her, Anderson supported her against his chest.

As Amelia's eyes fluttered open, she saw Pat and Gary kneeling at her feet, their faces showing genuine concern. Slowly she turned her head, observing the man who was holding her. Confronting Anderson without flinching, she said, "The informer isn't dead, is he?"

"No," he admitted.

"Does James Henry know?" Surely James Henry isn't aware of the truth, she thought desperately. Please God, don't let him be a part of this conspiracy to kill me!

"No, he doesn't know. The colonel lied to James Henry."

"But why?" she asked.

"Don't you know why?" he questioned gently.

"Do you?"

"Colonel Garson thinks a lot of James Henry, and he was afraid he would have tried to stop your execution, which would've led to James Henry's own death."

He raised her carefully, untying her hands. "But captain," she began, "you stopped my execution. What will happen to you?"

Removing the rope, he answered, "If the Confederacy learns of my disobedience, I will be killed."

Sitting up straight, Amelia promised, "I'll never tell anyone about this! I give you my word!"

He smiled tenderly. "Before you swear yourself to secrecy, first you had better stop to think about it."

"Why?" she asked.

"Your husband and others are going to want to know why you were held prisoner for so long. What are you planning to tell them? Are you going to confess the truth? Will you tell them that Colonel Garson believed you knew the informer's identity? If you do, then the Union will know there is a spy in their midst, and they will start a search for him. Eventually, the Confederacy will learn of this search and the source it came from. The Confederacy will learn that you were not executed."

"And they will come after you," she sighed despondently.

"Exactly," he answered.

"When I am asked why I was kept a prisoner, what should I tell them?"

Anderson shrugged. "I suppose the only safe explanation is to tell them you don't know why."

"But if I'm evasive, they will suspect I am covering my shame, because your men were . . . were using me!" she exclaimed.

"Some people might believe that, but a few others will more than likely believe you were forced to become my lover. But the less charitable of these people will eventually spread the rumor that you came to me willingly."

"Oh no!" Amelia gasped. "I'll be branded Bill Anderson's whore!"

"There's a chance that you will be, if you swear yourself to secrecy. Also, you will be a traitor if you don't tell the truth to the Union."

"But if I tell the truth, you'll be executed!" she declared.

"It's not an easy choice to make, is it?" he responded compassionately.

She studied him thoughtfully. He had spared her life at the cost of his own. She knew beyond a doubt that he would set her free, even if she told him she was going to tell the Union everything. "Choice?" she questioned. "Captain Anderson, there is no choice! My conscience and reputation are not as important as your life!"

"What will your husband think?" he asked.

"Jason!" she stated with disgust. "He never thinks

349

about anyone but himself!''

"This time, he might be very interested in what you have been doing for the past two months."

"Don't worry, Captain Anderson. I'll handle Jason." But she didn't feel as confident as she sounded.

Standing, Anderson helped Amelia to her feet. Smiling encouragingly, he said, "Maybe we are wrong and your reputation will not be slandered."

Amelia nodded, agreeing. "I am the wife of Captain Bishop, and my husband's name will protect me from malicious gossip."

They looked into each other's eyes, silently communicating their mutual respect for one another. But they both knew Amelia's reputation would not remain totally untarnished.

Amelia looked at Pat and Gary, who were standing at her side, then she brought her attention back to Anderson. "I swear I will never tell my husband, the Union, or anyone else what happened here today, or why I was held captive!"

Gary spoke up first, "I also swear to remain silent."

Somberly, Pat pledged, "I'd give my life to protect the captain, and I'll never tell a livin' soul that he didn't carry out the execution."

Honored, Captain Anderson held out his hand. "Shall we shake on it?"

Amelia enclosed her small hand in his, then Gary and Pat covered Anderson's and Amelia's hands with theirs.

Regarding each of them gravely, Anderson replied, "I hope and pray that none of you are destroyed by this conspiracy." Stepping back, he became military.

"You men ride a little farther with Mrs. Bishop. Escort her about twenty miles from the border. She should be able to make it the rest of the way alone." He spoke to Amelia, "Ma'am, will you walk with me to my horse?"

Complying, she fell into stride beside Anderson. When they reached his horse, he paused to talk to her. "Colonel Garson plans to tell James Henry the truth when they are in Mineral Springs. I am supposed to send a messenger to the colonel to inform him that his order was successfully carried out. James Henry will believe that you were executed."

"Oh no!" Amelia moaned. "Isn't there some way you can get word to James Henry and let him know it isn't true?"

He shook his head. "I'm sorry, Amelia. James Henry believing you are dead is only another cross you must bear if you intend to guard our conspiracy."

Disheartened, she sighed, "It makes no difference. He has no plans to try and find me after the war. I had hoped that he would promise to come for me, but he never did."

"If by some miracle, I'm still alive when this war is over, and I should see James Henry, I'll tell him you were not executed."

"Captain Anderson," she began curiously, "why did James Henry and Buford go to Mineral Springs?"

"The Missouri guerrillas' headquarters are in Mineral Springs," he answered. He knew Amelia still thought James Henry and Buford were Pro-Confederates, and, deciding it would be best if she didn't know they were actually in the Confederate Army, he abruptly halted their conversation by saying briskly, "I must return to camp.''

Suddenly remembering the brush and comb, she said hastily, "Wait! I have the brush and comb you loaned me, and I want to return them.''

"Keep them," he answered quietly.

Surprised, she exclaimed, "But Gary said they belonged to your sister Josephine! They must mean very much to you!''

"They do, and that's why I want you to have them.''

"But why?" she asked.

"I doubt that I will live to see the end of this war, and if the Federals should rummage through my personal belongings, what will happen to Josephine's brush and comb?" He frowned bitterly. "Good Lord! They could end up in some prostitute's possession!'' Lightly, he ran his fingers down Amelia's extremely long hair. "If I give them to you, I will know they are being used to groom a lady.''

"Thank you, Captain Anderson. And I promise you, I will treasure your gift.''

Taking her hand, he squeezed it gently. "Goodbye, Amelia Bishop.''

Grateful, she exclaimed, "Thank you for sparing my life! You are a wonderful man, and I consider it an honor to have known you!''

"No, Amelia," he replied graciously. "Don't make me into an idol. That, my dear, would be a big mistake. I know your loyalties are with the Union, and that makes you my enemy. If you had been a man, I would've ordered your execution without giving it a second thought. I hate Federals and Jayhawkers, and I kill them at every opportunity. I do not spare their lives.''

Amelia moved her hand to Anderson's horse, and absent-mindedly she stroked the silk cord he had tied to his saddle. Glancing at her hand, she suddenly gasped sharply. Clutching the cord, she examined the knots, each one representing a soldier that Anderson himself had killed. Appalled, she suddenly recalled all the horrible rumors she had heard concerning Bill Anderson. Perhaps some were exaggerated, but the story about his silk cord was certainly true!

Horrified, she quickly released her hold on the cord as if it had suddenly been struck by lightning. Facing the Jayhawkers' most hated enemy, tears of compassion for Bill Anderson filled Amelia's eyes. Her voice quivering, she murmured, ''God help you, Captain Anderson!''

Solemnly, he replied, ''God help mankind, Amelia, for we have all surely gone totally mad.'' Reaching over, he touched one of her tears. ''But so long as there are unselfish tears, such as this one, there is still hope for mankind.''

He leaned over to kiss her cheek, but, impulsively, Amelia offered him her lips. His kiss was firm but chaste. Swiftly he mounted his horse, then, looking down at her, he said somberly, ''Goodbye, Amelia.''

''Goodbye, captain,'' she responded softly. With mixed feelings, she watched him until he rode out of sight.

After coming so close to death, Amelia became acutely aware of how precious life could be, and she was thankful to God and Captain Anderson for each breath she took. As she and her companions rode steadily closer to the Kansas border, Amelia grew anxious to see her baby. Her joy at being alive, and her thoughts of her son, made Amelia lighthearted. Indulging in her cheerful mood, she laughed and teased with Gary and Pat as they leisurely traveled through Missouri territory.

Enjoying Amelia's charming company, Gary and Pat temporarily forgot their guerrilla training as they rode dangerously closer to the Kansas border.

It was Pat who finally became aware that they had traveled farther than Captain Anderson had ordered. Realizing he and Gary had foolishly placed themselves in a perilous location, he quickly reined his horse. Stopping, Amelia and Gary looked at him questioningly, wondering why he had halted so abruptly.

All at once, detecting the sounds of horses, Pat cautioned, "Be quiet!" He listened again, trying to determine from which direction the sounds were coming.

Hearing the approaching danger, Gary cursed under his breath, "Damn!"

Before Gary and Pat had the chance to flee, they were suddenly surrounded by blue uniforms. Afraid for her companions, Amelia's heart accelerated with fear as she watched the Union soldiers steadily advancing. They had their weapons drawn, and she knew if Gary and Pat tried to run, the troopers would shoot them down.

Her gaze darted to her friends. She thought they would be frightened, but if they were, she couldn't tell by their manner. Their expressions were calm, and they sat on their horses as if they were totally relaxed. Remembering how, earlier, she had begged for her

354

life, Amelia wished she had the same fearlessness as these two young guerrillas. She was unaware that she had, at the end, faced death courageously.

Encircling them, the soldiers reined their horses. Four men dismounted, and, moving to Gary and Pat, they confiscated their weapons. Suddenly two mounted officers broke through the thicket to join their men.

Gasping, Amelia moaned, "Jason!"

Seeing his wife, Jason rode past his troopers. Halting his horse beside Amelia's, he distastefully examined her attire. He frowned disgustedly when his eyes traveled over her guerrilla shirt.

When Amelia had first seen her husband, her reaction had been one of dread, but now, hoping she could convince him to spare Pat and Gary's lives, she smiled happily. "Jason!" she cried joyfully.

Pleased by her response, Jason decided to overlook her offensive apparel. So she was happy to see him, was she? He smiled smugly. Naturally, she would be overjoyed! Studying her critically, he wished he could tell simply by looking at her if she had been violated, for, if she had, he would never touch her again!

"Amelia, my sweet," he purred. "I have been so worried about you. Are you well?"

"Yes, Jason. I'm fine," she answered.

Lowering his voice so his troopers couldn't overhear, he asked, "Then you weren't mistreated?"

"No," she replied innocently.

Gritting his teeth, he whispered testily, "Damn it, Amelia! You know what I mean! Are you contaminated?"

Her brow furrowing with puzzlement, she repeated

355

vaguely, "Contaminated?"

"Were you raped?" he asked harshly, and much louder than he had intended.

Embarrassed, she stammered, "No . . . no, I wasn't . . . I wasn't."

"Good!" Jason remarked with blatant relief. Deciding he would question his wife later, and in privacy, he turned his attention to Gary and Pat. Smirking, he asked them. "Do you two pieces of filth kiss Quantrill's butt or Anderson's?"

"We don't kiss nobody's butt," Gary answered lazily. "But, then, bein' an ass yourself, I reckon that's just about where your brain is located."

Laughing hatefully, Jason replied, "Oh yeah? Well, your brain is going to be splattered all over the ground!"

"Jason!" Amelia cried.

Swerving sharply, Jason glared at his wife. "Shut up, Amelia!"

"Jason, please!" she pleaded. "I must talk to you!"

"Later!" he spat. Facing his second-in-command, he ordered, "Lieutenant, I want these bastards shot through the head!"

"No!" Amelia yelled desperately. "Jason, for God's sake, you must listen to me!"

Looking at her irritably, he tried to keep his tone on an even keel, "My sweet, I know you must hate them as much as I do, but you are a lady, and I realize violence upsets you. Don't worry, my precious, you won't have to witness their deaths. We shall leave immediately." To the lieutenant, he commanded, "When you and your men have carried out my order, return to Lawrence.''

"Yes, sir!'' he answered.

Looking at his troopers, Jason ordered, "Prepare to ride out!''

"Jason! Wait!'' Amelia shrieked.

Losing his patience, Jason snapped, "Wait for what?''

"I want to talk to you!'' she explained.

"Mrs. Bishop,'' Pat warned, "why don't you just get the hell out of here?''

Riding to Pat's side, Jason slapped him across the face. "You dirty low-down scum! Talk to my wife again, and I'll have you whipped before you're killed!''

Alarmed, Amelia stared increduously at Gary and Pat. Dear God, she had to find a way to save them! She had to! She knew there was only one way. She must tell Jason how Pat and Gary had helped Anderson spare her life, then Jason would retaliate accordingly.

"Jason,'' she began, "I want to tell you what happened today!''

Loudly, Gary cleared his throat, getting Amelia's attention. She looked deeply into his eyes, and, understanding his silent plea, Amelia's heart broke with grief. She couldn't tell Jason! She was sworn to secrecy! If she told Jason about her life being spared, he'd demand to know why she was to be killed. Then she could be compelled to reveal to him that there was an informer in the Union Army. And it would all inevitably lead to the Confederacy's executing Captain Anderson.

Holding back her tears, Amelia lovingly studied Gary and Pat. Suddenly the last two months flashed fleetingly across her mind as she thought about Gary and Pat's mischievous but admirable charms.

Meeting her steady gaze, they smiled very faintly, letting her know they appreciated her silence.

Amelia glanced at Jason, but he wasn't looking at her. Free of her husband's scrutiny, she returned her vision to Gary and Pat. Without uttering a sound, she moved her lips, mouthing the words, "Goodbye, and I love you both."

"Well?" Jason barked brusquely.

Startled, Amelia stuttered, "Wh . . . what?"

"What do you want to tell me?" he asked ill-temperedly.

Bowing her head, she mumbled, "Nothing."

Riding to her, he demanded, "Let's go!"

Reluctantly, Amelia turned her horse. As her roan mare fell into stride beside Jason's chestnut gelding, Amelia was tempted to look back at Gary and Pat. But she was afraid she would dishonor their conspiracy and tell Jason and the whole Union about the informer, if it would save Gary and Pat's lives.

In military fashion, Jason's troops fell into place behind Amelia and their captain. Encouraging their horses into a gallop, the riders quickly placed ground between themselves and the troopers left to execute the Missouri guerrillas.

Minutes later, when the riders heard two shots, they were faint. But to Amelia they echoed like a thunderous cannon, tearing into her heart with excruciating pain. Her whole body jerked awkwardly, but quickly she regained her composure. Her posture was straight, and she held her head high. Jason, involved only in himself, paid no attention to Amelia, but the soldiers, observing her poise, believed her to be unaffected by the gun shots. Riding behind Amelia, the troopers couldn't see her face, so they were unaware of her trembling chin and the tears rolling down her cheeks.

TWENTY-FIVE

Anxious to see her baby, Amelia didn't wait for Jason to help her dismount. The moment they stopped in front of Lillian's store, Amelia swung from the saddle, making a straight beeline for the door. Flinging it open, she rushed inside.

Cynthia was rearranging jars on the shelves behind the counter, so her back was turned to the front door. Thinking Amelia was a customer, she called out, "I'll be right with you."

Happy to see her friend, Amelia exclaimed, "Cynthia!"

Hearing Amelia's voice, Cynthia swerved swiftly. Gasping, she praised, "Thank God!" With a mixture of laughter and tears, she hastened to Amelia. Opening her arms, she welcomed Cynthia into her embrace.

They were hugging each other when Jason stepped into the store. His intrusion caused Cynthia abruptly to release Amelia. She hadn't been comfortable in Jason's presence since he had indiscreetly revealed that he knew she had been in Sam Tyler's bedroom. Since that night, he had always treated her as though she were cheap, smiling smugly as his eyes brazenly ogled her large breasts.

"Where is Aunt Lillian?" Amelia asked.

Trying not to feel intimidated by Jason's rude scrutiny, Cynthia answered, "She's upstairs."

"My baby?" Amelia questioned.

"Addie took him outside in his carriage for some fresh air."

"Oh no!" Amelia cried. Depressed, tears came to her eyes.

To cheer her up, Cynthia quickly informed her, "They should be back at any moment."

Touching his wife's arm, Jason suggested, "Why don't you go upstairs and see your aunt, and I'll ride to the house and get you a change of clothes." Examining her shirt and trousers with loathing, he continued, "And stay upstairs, my sweet. We wouldn't want anyone to see you in that offensive outfit, would we?"

Wishing to avoid an unpleasant scene, Amelia nodded as though she agreed.

Leaning over, Jason kissed her on the cheek. At the touch of his cold lips, Amelia cringed inwardly. "I'll return very shortly, my precious," he promised her.

Cynthia waited until Jason had left before asking, "Amelia, where have you been all this time?"

"I was held captive," she answered.

"By whom?" Cynthia demanded.

"Bill Anderson," Amelia replied faintly.

"Oh, you poor darling!" Cynthia sympathized. "To be kept a prisoner by that terrible man!"

Without stopping first to think, Amelia replied, "He isn't terrible."

"Captain Anderson?" Cynthia spat, cringing. "He's

362

a sadistic maniac! How can you defend a man like him?''

"He was nice to me," Amelia murmured.

Surprised, Cynthia said, "Well, apparently, he treated you like a lady."

"Yes, he did. And so did his men. Cynthia, not all the Missouri guerrillas are like William Quantrill and the men who raided Lawrence." Sighing sadly, she added, "The only thing that sets Confederates apart from Federals is the color of their uniform. Both sides have men who are good as well as men who aren't."

Recalling Buford's compassion, Cynthia replied vaguely, "Yes, I know."

"Well," Amelia began, "I'll go up and see Lillian."

Smiling, Cynthia said, "She'll be so happy to see you!"

"How has she been?"

"Losing Calvin was very hard on your aunt. But she's a strong woman, and she has managed very well."

Amelia moved swiftly to the back stairs, but, suddenly, Cynthia stopped her by asking, "Amelia, why did Captain Anderson hold you a prisoner for two months?"

Wondering how many times she would be asked that question, Amelia turned slowly to face Cynthia. She knew there was only one safe answer, and, looking Cynthia in the eyes, she replied, "I don't know why."

Lillian decided to tend the store, so she could tell the wonderful news of Amelia's return to every customer, so when Jason reappeared it was Cynthia who was up-stairs in the parlor with Amelia.

Entering the room, Jason stepped to the sofa where Amelia was sitting beside Cynthia. Indifferently, Amelia looked at the clothes he had brought. A little puzzled, she noticed there was an object beneath the dress he carried, but she was unable to make it out.

Speaking to Amelia, Jason informed her, "I saw Addie. She was on her way back to the store, but I told her to take the child to our home."

Leaping to her feet, Amelia fumed, "How could you? You knew how anxious I was to see Hank!"

Frowning, he complained, "Must you call our son by that common name?"

Outraged, she pushed by him to leave the parlor and go to her child, but firmly Jason grabbed her shoulder. Shoving the garments into her arms, he demanded, "Change clothes before you take one step outside! I will not have my wife seen in a damned guerrilla shirt! When you finish dressing, give me those dirty rags, and I'll burn them!"

It was then that Amelia recognized the object that had been hidden beneath her dress. "What are you doing with my saddle bags?"

His brown eyes became ice-cold as he remarked, "Everything you have that belonged to those filthy guerrillas will be burned or destroyed!" Opening the saddle bags, he took out the brush and comb. "Including these!" he added.

"Give them to me!" Amelia shrieked.

"Why?" he demanded. "They are probably filled with Missouri lice!"

"Damn you, Jason Bishop! You have no right to destroy something that belongs to me!"

Amelia's cursing surprised Jason. "Obviously, your association with trash has rubbed off on you! Curse again, Amelia, and I will wash your mouth out with soap!"

Amelia stared at him incredulously. What kind of arrogant monster had she married? Throwing the garments into a nearby chair, she made a quick grab for the comb and brush.

Evading her, Jason stepped back. Consumed with jealous suspicion, he snarled, "Why do these mean so much to you?"

"Th . . . they are a gift," she stammered.

"From whom?" he raged.

Knowing she could never tell him they had been given to her by Bill Anderson, she lied, "One of Anderson's men gave them to me. But I don't know who he was."

Catching Amelia off guard, he slapped her across the face. "You lying bitch!"

Rushing over to them, Cynthia placed herself between Amelia and Jason. Cynthia positioned Amelia behind her, and, guarding her friend with her own body, she glared at Jason. "Don't you dare strike her again!" she said furiously.

"Stay out of this!" Jason warned.

Stepping out from behind Cynthia, Amelia screamed, "Give me that comb and brush!"

"Who gave them to you?" he bellowed.

"I don't know!" she yelled.

"I'm going to burn them! Do you understand, Amelia?" he taunted sadistically.

Hurrying into the parlor, Lillian exclaimed breathlessly, "Oh, my goodness! I can hear you two quarreling all the way downstairs! You must stop this foolish bickering!" Moving quickly to Amelia and Jason, she reasoned, "You two should be thankful that you are reunited. Children, you must not spend your first day together arguing."

Ignoring Lillian's presence, Jason ordered, "Amelia, go to the guest room and take off those disgusting clothes!"

"Oh, yes!" Lillian agreed. "Darling, do hurry and get rid of that horrible shirt. The mere sight of it sends cold chills up my spine."

"I won't change my clothes until Jason gives me my comb and brush!" Amelia said stubbornly.

"We'll see about that!" Jason responded. Placing the brush and comb on a chair, he grabbed Amelia. Lifting her up in his arms, he carried her to the guest room.

Futilely, she fought against him. Entering the bedroom, he kicked the door closed. Taking her to the bed, he dropped her onto the mattress.

Amelia continued to struggle, but his strength easily overpowered hers, and within minutes he had her completely undressed.

Taking in her tempting nudity, he suddenly removed his holster. As he began unbuckling his belt, Amelia realized his intentions.

"No," she cried weakly.

"Oh yes, my sweet," he purred. Slipping off his trousers, he continued menacingly, "Don't you want to make love to me? Or do you prefer guerrillas to your husband?"

He removed his underwear, then he reached down

366

and grabbed her hand. Roughly, he jerked her to her feet. Grasping her shoulders, he asked her tensely, "Did Anderson and his men use you?"

"No!" she cried.

"Then why did Anderson hold you captive for two months?"

"I don't know! Believe me, Jason, I don't know why!"

"No man violated you?" he asked harshly.

"Jason, I wasn't raped!" she answered firmly. It was the truth. She hadn't been raped. But recalling the wonderful ecstasy she had shared with James Henry, tears filled her eyes.

Observing her tears, Jason mistook them as a sign of her innocence. "I believe you," he told her. "Don't cry, my sweet. I believe you are still pure, and I promise you I won't cast you aside."

"Cast me aside!" she cried, astounded. "Jason, you are intolerable!"

Responding with anger, he shoved her to the bed. Cruelly, he parted her legs, placing himself over her. Her dryness caused his entry to be painful, and, holding back a sob, Amelia bit into her bottom lip.

Vigorously he pounded into her, causing the buttons of his shirt to make red welts on her breasts. Climaxing prematurely, he pulled her thighs tightly against his as he shuddered with sexual relief.

Rising, he slipped back into his clothes. Strapping on his holster, he told her, "I'll bring you your garments, and, when you're dressed I'll take you home. And, my sweet, make no mistake, I will then destroy everything you brought from Anderson's camp. Including the mare!"

Bolting straight up, she pleaded, "No! Oh, Jason, don't kill the horse!"

Disgusted, he stomped to the door. Opening it, he replied irritably, "Amelia, I can't believe you are actually pleading for a horse's life. It must be your Methodist background that makes you the way you are. My God, it's only an animal, and a dumb one at that!"

"Jason, please don't have the little mare destroyed!" But Jason slammed the door on her plea.

Falling back across the bed, Amelia's body was racked with deep sobs. Her grief over the mare and Anderson's gift filled her heart with resentment for her husband. "I hate you, Jason!" she cried. "I hate you! I hate you!"

Turning to lie on her side, she buried her face into the pillow. Knowing how dearly Bill Anderson had treasured his sister's comb and brush, she murmured sorrowfully, "I'm sorry! Oh, Captain Anderson, I'm so sorry!"

Returning to the parlor, Jason found Lillian alone. "Where is Cynthia?" he asked.

"She went home," Lillian answered.

Fetching Amelia's clothes, he noticed that the brush and comb were missing. Glaring at Lillian, he demanded, "Where are they?"

Surprised by his anger, she replied hesitantly, "Cynthia . . . asked if she could have them. I . . . I didn't think you would mind, so I told her she could take them."

Gathering Amelia's garments, he headed back to the guest room. Realizing Cynthia had taken the articles for Amelia's sake, he cursed Cynthia under his breath. "You goddamned whore!"

He considered barging into Cynthia's house, demanding that she return them, but he knew she would refuse; and by now she would have them safely hidden.

The following day, Cynthia went to Amelia's home, and, finding Jason gone, she told Amelia that she had the brush and comb. It had been apparent to Cynthia that they meant a great deal to Amelia, but she had no idea of their importance until she witnessed her friend's reaction. Clinging to Cynthia, Amelia had cried hysterically while thanking her over and over again. Cynthia had hoped that Amelia would tell her why the brush and comb meant so much, but she offered no explanation, and Cynthia was too polite to ask. When Cynthia asked Amelia if she wanted her to bring her the comb and brush, Amelia panicked, begging Cynthia to keep them hidden where Jason could never find them. Calming her, Cynthia agreed, promising Amelia the articles were in a safe place and would remain there.

Returning home, Cynthia went to the cellar. She set the lit lantern on a shelf where canned goods and jars were stored. Reaching behind the stacked cans, she removed a large jar. Opening it, she took out the brush and comb. Putting the jar back on the shelf, she held the articles close to the lantern. Examining them closely, she admired the fine workmanship. They were elegant and apparently quite expensive. But she was sure it wasn't their original cost that made them so valuable to Amelia. Suddenly, she held them closer to the light. On the base of the comb and underneath the handle of the brush were identical miniature inscriptions. "To J.A. from B.A." Puzzled, Cynthia mumbled, "J.A. and B. A.?" Inhaling sharply, she gasped, "B.A.! Bill Anderson! Oh Amelia, why? Why would you treasure a gift from that brutal man?"

Hastily she returned the comb and brush to the jar, and, hiding it behind the stacked cans, she sighed desperately, "Oh Amelia, surely you aren't in love with Captain Anderson!" She was tempted to go to Amelia and question her, but quickly she decided against it. For a fleeting moment, she felt such a strong resentment of Amelia that her animosity shocked her. But her love for Amelia was more powerful than her anger, and she knew she would continue to protect Amelia's gift.

Cynthia bowed her head, and with tears pouring down her face, she cried over her friend's betrayal. "Oh Amelia!" she sobbed. "It was Captain Anderson and his men who killed David!"

Amelia was visited by Union officials, and asked question after question. Feigning ignorance, she gave them no vital information concerning Anderson and his Pro-Confederates. Believing James Henry to be one of Anderson's men, she knew she would rather die than give the Union one piece of information that could in any way lead to James Henry's death.

The officials were aware that she was being evasive, but they sympathetically believed it was because she was covering up her shame. They were sure Anderson or his men had violated her, and, respecting her feelings, they ceased their interrogation.

Amelia and her stay at the guerrilla camp became the favorite topic of conversation among the gossipers in Lawrence. Some of them believed she had been molested, and they pretended sympathy for Captain Bishop's poor wife. Others, less hypocritical, announced openly that Amelia had been Bill Anderson's lover. Why else would he have kept her a prisoner for two months? She certainly didn't look or act like a woman who had been ruthlessly raped over and over again; which could mean only one thing, she had willingly participated in an illicit affair with Captain Bill Anderson. She was an adulteress and a traitor!

The gossipers in Lawrence were the minority of the population, and the rest of the citizens refrained from judging Amelia Bishop.

Jason's associates were worried that he would learn of these malicious rumors, so they went out of their way to put a stop to the stories about Mrs. Bishop and Captain Anderson. His friends had a lot of influence, and they successfully stopped the spreading rumors before they could reach Jason.

Amelia seldom left the privacy of her home, but she didn't need to mingle in the town to be aware of the rumors. When she had refused to give the Union officials a logical explanation for her captivity, she had been fully conscious of the consequences. It was partly her guilt that kept her home. The stories the gossipers were circulating were partially true. She had had an affair; they simply had her linked to the wrong man.

Adulteress and traitor! Adulteress? Yes, technically the accusation was true. But in her heart she belonged more to James Henry than she had ever belonged to her husband. James Henry was the man she loved and the father of her child.

Traitor? Yes, she supposed she was a traitor as well as an adulteress. The information she had was vital to the Union. But she wasn't a soldier! She had taken no oath to the Union! But she had given her word to Captain Anderson, and she would not betray the man who had so gallantly spared her life.

Living with Jason again was heartbreaking for Amelia. His arrogance and selfishness were overbearing, and she had only her son to bring joy into her life.

She knew James Henry believed her dead, and if he should return to Lawrence, it would be for only one reason—to even his score with Jason. Amelia didn't want James Henry to kill Jason. She still believed his act of vengeance would somehow lead to his own destruction. But realizing James Henry's hate for Jason was the only compulsion that could lead him back to Lawrence, she hoped he would seek his revenge. But she was determined that she would convince him not to kill Jason, and then, if necessary, she would fall to her knees and beg James Henry not to leave Lawrence without taking her and Hank with him.

TWENTY-SIX

Wearing their Confederate uniforms, Buford and James Henry walked toward Colonel Garson's tent. Both men were dashingly handsome, and they would have turned the head of many a southern belle. But Buford and James Henry were not comfortable in their confining uniforms and would rather have been dressed in their usual casual style. They also missed the feel of a holster strapped low on their hips and a pistol fit snugly against their legs.

Complaining, Buford grumbled, "What I don't like about being an officer is when we have to wear that damned scabbard and sword. It's not only awkward, but a downright nuisance."

Chuckling, James Henry replied, "You'll get used to the feel of it, Pappy!"

Scowling, Buford remarked, "You're goin' to be feeling my sword, if you don't stop calling me Pappy!"

Nearing the tent Colonel Garson was temporarily using at the guerrilla camp in Mineral Springs, James Henry commented, "I hope the colonel sent for us to tell us we're pulling out.''

"I'd be willing to bet we'll be leaving in the morning."

"Why do you think that?" James Henry asked.

"Yesterday, the colonel said he was waiting for a message from Captain Anderson, and a short while ago I saw one of Anderson's men. So I imagine he brought the message.''

Puzzled, James Henry's brow furrowed. "I wonder why he'd be waiting to hear from Anderson."

Buford shrugged. "Beats me."

They reached the tent, and the sentry announced their arrival. Receiving permission to enter, James Henry and Buford stepped inside.

The colonel was alone, sitting at a long, narrow table. Returning their salute, he said, "At ease, men!" Picking up an envelope, he fiddled with it as he instructed, "We'll be leaving tomorrow morning. James Henry, you'll be under my command, and Buford, when we rendezvous in Virginia with Colonel Robinson, you are to be assigned to his company. You men will be honored to learn that you will be serving General Lee in the Northern Virginia Army.''

Keeping the envelope in his hand, Colonel Garson leaned back in his chair. Showing it to Buford and James Henry, he informed them, "This is a message from Captain Anderson.''

He fell silent, and Buford and James Henry looked at each other in confusion. If they were supposed to make some kind of comment, they sure as hell didn't know what he was expecting them to say.

Clearing his throat, Colonel Garson broke the

quietness by explaining, "Captain Anderson had a vital order to carry out, and I've been waiting here to make sure it was enforced."

Once again, the colonel ceased speaking. To cover up the awkward silence, Buford asked, "Was it enforced?"

Dropping the envelope on the table, Colonel Garson said somberly, "Yes, God help us!" Standing, he regarded James Henry. "The informer is not dead. I lied to you because at the time it seemed to be the best way to handle the situation."

James Henry's whole body stiffened. His voice strained, he demanded, "What does that message say?"

Dreading James Henry's reaction to his words, the colonel replied reluctantly, "Mrs. Bishop was executed."

Grasping the envelope, James Henry ripped at it as he removed the paper inside. Unfolding it, he read Captain Anderson's report informing the colonel that the execution had been successfully carried out.

For a moment he went limp, letting the envelope and paper fall to the ground. Then, suddenly, moving with fantastic speed, he grabbed the colonel by the front of his jacket. "Damn you!" he raved. "You killed her!"

Forcefully, Buford pulled him back from the colonel. Seizing James Henry's arms, Buford needed all his strength to restrain him.

"Let him go!" Colonel Garson ordered briskly. Cautiously, Buford released his hold. Continuing, the colonel said commandingly, "James Henry, you are a captain in the Confederate Army, and I expect you to act like an officer! Mrs. Bishop's death was tragic, but necessary! And, surely to God, you don't think the order to have her executed was exclusively mine!''

''You lied to me, damn it!'' James Henry shouted.

''Yes, and if I had it to do all over again, I would still lie to you! If you had known the truth, do you think you could have stopped her execution?'' When he wasn't answered immediately, the colonel demanded severely, ''Do you?''

''No!'' James Henry admitted angrily. ''But, at least, she wouldn't have been alone!''

''What did you plan to do?'' Colonel Garson bellowed. ''Die with her? Would your gallant deed have made her any less dead?''

''My God!'' James Henry groaned. ''Haven't you ever loved a woman?''

Dropping into his chair, the colonel replied evenly, ''Yes, I have a wife, and I love her very much.'' He studied James Henry closely, before saying, ''But I don't think you knew, until this moment, that you loved Mrs. Bishop.'' Looking at Buford, he ordered, ''You are both dismissed. Make sure he's ready to ride out in the morning!''

''Yes, sir!'' Buford answered. He reached over, touching James Henry's arm, but he didn't budge.

Standing rigidly, James Henry remained frozen by the colonel's words. ''You loved Mrs. Bishop.'' The statement tore at him painfully.

''Let's go!'' Buford urged, clutching James Henry's arm.

Jerking free, James Henry swerved stiffly, and,

leaving Buford behind, he quickly left the tent.

"Will he be all right?" the colonel asked Buford.

Shaking his head, Buford answered, "He lost his parents, sisters, a brother, and now the woman he loves." He paused, then bitterly he continued, "You ask me if he's going to be all right? Good God, colonel, what do you think?"

Placing his elbows on the table, the colonel leaned over, resting his head on his hands. His gaze lowered, he sighed, "War is pure hell!"

Buford smirked sarcastically, refusing to comment.

Looking up at him, Colonel Garson pleaded, "The Confederacy had no other choice! We had to take her life!"

Buford nodded brusquely. "As you said, colonel, war is hell. And with war as an excuse, we can even justify murder." He started to leave, but, hesitating, he asked, "Knowing how James Henry is going to resent you, why are you keeping him under your command?"

"If I transfer him to another company, it would be the same as admitting the decision the others and I made to execute Mrs. Bishop was wrong. James Henry will have to learn to accept our judgment, or else, face a court-martial."

Quickly Buford saluted the colonel. Leaving, he hurried to the tent he was sharing with James Henry. Drawing a deep breath, he stepped inside. There was an afternoon storm brewing, and the interior was dismal. James Henry was sitting on the edge of his cot. He was staring down at the ground, his arms resting across his legs. Going to his own cot, Buford reached under the pillow, removing a half-empty bottle of whiskey. Joining James Henry, he sat beside him. Opening the bottle, Buford helped himself to a generous drink.

Offering it to James Henry, he encouraged, "Have a drink. In fact, why don't you have a lot of 'em."

Accepting the bottle, James Henry commented, "Drink myself into oblivion, right?"

"It's not a bad idea," Buford remarked calmly.

James Henry took a large swallow, before replying, "It might help me get through today, but what about all the tomorrows?"

"Take it one step at a time, James Henry," his uncle advised.

James Henry nodded, then downed three quick gulps. When he remained silent, Buford asked, "What are you thinking about?"

"The morning I told Amelia goodbye," James Henry began, his voice strained, "I knew she was wanting me to tell her I loved her. She never spoke a word. She just kept looking, her eyes pleading with me." Growing angry with himself, he scowled, "Damn, Buford! Why didn't I tell her what she wanted to hear?"

"Maybe you didn't know you loved her," Buford replied softly.

Shouting, James Henry raged, "How could I help but know?"

"When a man loves a woman, it makes him vulnerable. You're a Stewart, and a Stewart doesn't like to let his guard down.''

Rising, James Henry stared at Buford, his eyes glaring wildly. ''I keep seeing Amelia standing before Anderson and his men waiting to be shot down!'' His voice breaking, he moaned, ''Oh God! Thinking about Amelia facing a firing squad is enough to drive me crazy! Amelia!'' Quickly he finished the whiskey, throwing the bottle across the tent. Violently, he yelled, ''Damn you, Anderson! How in the hell could you kill her? You cold-blooded sonofabitch!''

Getting to his feet, Buford went to his pack, and, finding another bottle of whiskey, returned to James Henry. ''You can't blame Anderson or the colonel. Besides, placing the blame on someone isn't going to make it any easier to accept her death.'' Uncapping the bottle, he commented lazily, ''I sure am glad I decided to buy an extra bottle.'' He took a drink before continuing, ''After giving it serious thought, I've decided to get drunk with you.'' Gesturing to the cot, he said, ''Let's sit down. I don't like to get drunk standing up.''

Calmed by Buford's pacifying presence, James Henry sank to the cot. Bowing his head, he murmured sorrowfully, ''I loved her, Buford.''

Handing him the bottle, Buford replied sympathetically, ''Yeah, I know.''

James Henry took two large swigs, then handed the bottle to Buford. Tilting the bottle, he started to take a swallow, but suddenly he remembered Colonel Garson's ordering him to make sure James Henry was ready to move out in the morning. Lowering the bottle, he gave it back to James Henry.

Rising, he walked to the entrance. There was one thing about the army, if you didn't want to personally carry out an order, you simply transferred it to a lower rank. Stepping outside, he spotted Colonel Garson's lieutenant.

"Lieutenant Benson!" he called.

Hastily the young lieutenant walked over to Buford. Saluting, he said crisply, "Yes, sir?"

Reciprocating, Buford replied, "Lieutenant, at daybreak I want you to come to my quarters, and if I'm still asleep, wake me up."

"Yes, sir!" Lieutenant Benson answered.

"I might be sleeping a little soundly, so make doubly sure that I'm wide awake."

"I sure will, sir!" the lieutenant replied quickly.

Dismissing the lieutenant, Buford reentered the tent. Going to James Henry, he sat down beside him, and, seeing his tears, Buford placed an arm over his nephew's shoulders.

"Buford," he groaned, "I should never have left her. If I had only stopped to think, I'd have realized Colonel Garson was lying. But I was so happy that I didn't think rationally."

"There's nothing you can do about it now. Besides, you couldn't have saved her." Taking the bottle, Buford took a drink, then continued. "That first night you went to her hotel room, I had a gut feeling that something tragic was going to happen because of your relationship with Mrs. Bishop. But I thought it would be your death; not hers."

Accepting the whiskey, James Henry replied, "I wish it had been my death instead of hers." Putting the bottle to his mouth he helped himself to an enormous amount. Taking another drink, and then another, James Henry proceeded to get drunk.

TWENTY-SEVEN

The War between the States and the Border War between Missouri and Kansas continued to rage, and every night before going to bed Amelia would pray that the fighting would soon be over, and peace would once again be restored among Americans.

But as time slowly passed, Amelia began to believe that her prayers and the prayers of countless others, were in vain. Would this cruel war ever be over? It seemed to be endless!

Living only for her son, and the hope that someday she would be reunited with James Henry, Amelia merely existed. She was miserable being married to Jason, and she looked forward to his military excursions, relishing his absence from her daily life.

The four yearly seasons came and left, and Amelia continued to live through each day longing for James Henry's return. As her son grew older, his resemblance to his natural father was uncanny. His steel-blue eyes were identical to James Henry's. Often, gazing into Hank's eyes, Amelia would suddenly pull him into her arms, thanking God that she had James

Henry's son.

In October of 1864, Jason was transferred temporarily to Richmond, Missouri, which was a Union stronghold. He insisted that his family and Addie accompany him. Amelia didn't want to leave Lillian and Cynthia. They were her allies, and now she would be living in a strange town with no one to cling to. Adding to her sorrow was the knowledge that in Richmond Jason would not be riding out on skirmishes, but would be home with her every night.

Jason rented quarters for them in a boardinghouse at the edge of town. There were two bedrooms and a sitting room. They ate their meals downstairs with the other boarders in the large dining room.

Amelia had been living in Richmond for two weeks, and although she missed her aunt and Cynthia, the move hadn't been as unpleasant as she had thought it would be. She detested sharing a bed with Jason every night, but she had met other wives at the boardinghouse, and becoming friends with them had brightened her gloomy days.

Amelia was in the bedroom, sitting in front of her dresser brushing her hair, when, faintly, she detected boisterous laughter coming from the direction of the town. Unconcerned, she shrugged. Apparently the soldiers were overindulging in drinks, which would cause them to become more rowdy than usual.

Placing the brush on the dresser, she gazed at it dreamily, her thoughts turning to another brush. She knew Cynthia still had her gift from Captain Anderson safely hidden. Sighing deeply, she brought Bill Anderson's image to mind, remembering their final parting.

As the vociferous hubbub in town grew even

rowdier, the noise broke into Amelia's reverie. Rising, she hurried toward the window. She was wearing a sheer white dressing gown, and it flowed gracefully with her light steps. Standing at the window, she pulled back the lace curtains and looked outside, but the boardinghouse was situated too far from the center of town for her to see the cause of all the uproar.

Losing interest, she moved slowly to the bed. Sitting on the edge, she glanced around the room. It was furnished adequately and comfortably. It was heated by a fireplace, and on the mantel she had placed a few pieces of her own bric-a-brac, making the room seem more like home.

Suddenly, she heard horses bounding up the street, their riders expelling roisterous yells. Springing from the bed, she darted to the window, once again drawing back the curtains. Glancing down to the street, she saw three soldiers riding speedily past the boardinghouse. Whooping loudly, they were waving their arms, exclaiming, "He's dead! The sonofabitch is dead!"

She watched them until their horses turned from the street, heading toward the center of town.

Releasing the curtains, she moved away from the window. Pausing, she stood in the middle of the room and said aloud, "I wonder who is dead?"

But Amelia didn't have time to ponder the question for very long, because, swinging open the door, Jason entered the room.

She knew he had returned from town, and his clumsy gait made it apparent that he had been drinking heavily.

Seeing Amelia, he instantly smiled. He has such a handsome smile, she admitted to herself, but then

added the bitter thought: It's a shame it usually origi-
nates from one of his sadistic ideas.

"Amelia, my sweet," he said smoothly, "have you
heard the celebrating?"

She nodded. "Yes. Jason, what has happened?"

Moving to her, he swept her into his arms, hugging
her tightly. Then releasing her, he announced heartily,
"Bill Anderson is dead!"

He turned away from Amelia to walk over to the
window, so he missed seeing her look of shock and
grief.

"Were any of his men killed?" she asked, her
thoughts exclusively on James Henry.

"No!" Sourly, he added, "As usual, Anderson was
riding in front of his men."

Returning to her side, he explained what had happened, "He was killed a half a mile north of Orrick.
I'm sure you've heard of the town, Amelia. It's close
to Richmond. Well, Anderson, the arrogant sonofabitch, was riding ahead of his column. He saw both
sides of the trail were lined with Union soldiers. He
was far out in front of his men, but he didn't ride back
to join forces with them. Instead, he stood alone,
drawing his guns. His men were too far back to help
him, and the stupid bastard was riddled with bullets
from the Union's crossfire. His men retreated into the
woods with their tails between their legs." Jason's
eyes gleamed wildly, as he continued, "I wish I could
have been there to see him fall from his horse, dead,
his body drenched with blood from all the bullet
wounds. Oh, it would have done my heart good to
have seen that sonofabitch lying in his own blood!"

"Are you saying that Anderson saved his men by

forcing the Union to fire on him?''

"Well, that's how Southerners will see it, but if you ask me, the bastard probably believed himself immortal. If he'd ridden back to his column, they might have been able to help him escape.''

"He gave his life for his men!'' she stated firmly.

"Well, if he did, a helluva lot of good it'll do them. They can't survive without Anderson's leadership. By God, we'll run 'em all out of the brush, unless they turn tail and head for Texas.''

Grabbing her arm, he pulled her so close to him that his face was only inches from hers. Once again, he smiled, but his smile was so cold that Amelia was frightened by it. "But you haven't heard the best part!'' he chuckled hoarsely.

Amelia didn't want to hear any more. She wanted Jason to go away, so she could fall across the bed and cry. The news of Anderson's death hadn't brought her joy but grief. She had hoped he would survive to see the end of the war, and learn to bury his bitterness and hate, so that he could live out the rest of his days in peace.

"The soldiers brought Anderson's body to Richmond!'' Jason exclaimed, his smile expanding.

Shocked, Amelia gasped, "But why?''

Releasing her arm, Jason was so aroused that he practically danced with uncontrolled exultation. "So we can have a little fun with it.''

Stepping back, Amelia covered her mouth with her hand, holding back the scream she knew was lurking barely under the surface. "W . . . what kind . . . of fun?'' she asked faintly.

"They decapitated the rotten bastard!'' Jason replied bluntly, before doubling over with hysterical laughter. •

Growing pale, Amelia sobbed, "Dear God!"

Unmindful of his wife's reaction, Jason stopped his laughter to continue, "His body is being dragged through town, and his head has been spiked to the top of a telegraph pole. And it will remain there as a warning to all other guerrillas!"

Amelia fought back the sickening bile that was rising in her throat. Her eyes widened with disbelief as she stared at her husband.

"You should see it, Amelia!" Jason said enthusiastically, still unaware of his wife's consternation.

Interrupting, Amelia shrieked, "Shut up, Jason! Oh dear God, will you please shut up!"

Struck suddenly with Amelia's distress, he eyed her suspiciously. Sneering, he asked, "Don't you want to see his head?" Clutching her arm, he ordered, "Get dressed, my sweet, and I'll take you to see the man who held you prisoner for two months."

Recoiling, she cried piercingly, "No!"

Seeing tears in her eyes, tears he knew were for Bill Anderson, Jason verbally tortured her, "After you see his head, I'll take you to view his mangled body. The handsome Captain Anderson is not so handsome anymore!"

Amelia's knees weakened, and she had to clutch at the back of a chair to stay on her feet. Jason's verbal abuse continued, but she had blocked out his words. Feeling faint, she closed her eyes, her body swaying precariously. Jason is mad! she thought. The soldiers and the whole country have gone completely insane!

She tried not to think about the Bill Anderson she

had known, but, against her control, her mind conjured up his image vividly. Once again she could see him as he had been the day they had said their goodbyes. His demeanor had been imposing as he looked deep into her eyes, saying, "God help mankind, Amelia, for we have all surely gone totally mad."

Hanging her head, Amelia remembered how he had touched one of her tears, telling her gently, "So long as there are unselfish tears, such as this one, there is still hope for mankind."

Dear God, he had been a man who had known compassion, and he deserved to die with dignity! Not like this! His body mutilated and put on display as if he had been an animal!

Amelia's grief came to her effusively, and, throwing back her head, she screamed to the man who had been her friend, "You were wrong, Bill Anderson! There is no hope for mankind! They have ravaged your body like a pack of wild dogs!" Losing control, she ranted crazily, "The whole country is mad! God help us!"

His anger smoldering dangerously, Jason grabbed her arm, roughly swinging her around so that she faced him. "The goddamn bastard held you prisoner for two months! You should hate him!" Clutching her shoulders, he shook her powerfully. "Why don't you hate him, Amelia?" he demanded.

Letting her go brusquely, he drew back his arm, slapping her across the face. "Answer me! Why don't you hate him?"

"He was kind to me," she sobbed, holding her hand against her burning cheek.

"You lying little tramp!" he snarled. "He was your lover, wasn't he?"

"No!" she cried.

Jason's eyes glared insanely as he raged, "You slept with him! You let that filthy piece of scum put his hands all over your body!"

"No, Jason!" she pleaded. "You must believe me!"

Trying to keep his temper under control, he told her, "I'm going to give you one more chance to tell me the truth. What was Bill Anderson to you? And don't insult my intelligence by telling me again that he was kind to you. A woman doesn't scream out to a dead man who was merely kind to her!"

Her heart pounding with fear, Amelia met her husband's unwavering stare. She no longer had to remain silent about the informer to protect Anderson's life. But, now, it had become necessary to stay silent to guard her own life. If Jason were to learn that she had known there was a spy in the Union Army and hadn't revealed that vital information, he would kill her. Amelia didn't doubt for one moment that he would wrap his hands around her neck and not let up until he had strangled her!

Anderson's death had not set her free from their conspiracy. It still had her trapped in its vise.

Lowering her gaze, Amelia murmured, "He befriended me."

Placing his hand beneath her chin, Jason jerked her face up to his. His voice dripped with heavy sarcasm. "He befriended you, Amelia? How did he do that, my sweet? By spreading your legs and ramming you full of friendship?"

Gaping, her mouth fell open as she took a step backwards. "Jason!" she cried. "No!"

"You loved him, didn't you?" he demanded.

"What I felt for Captain Anderson wasn't love but compassion!" Squinting angrily, she spat, "Compassion! An emotion you are incapable of feeling!"

Swerving quickly, he stomped to the door that led into the adjoining sitting room, which separated their bedroom from Addie and Hank's. Hastily he locked it, then, moving to the front door, he pushed in the small bolt.

Without looking at Amelia, he went to the bureau, pulling out a drawer. Removing one of her petticoats, he tugged at it, until the flimsy material gave way and ripped. Violently, he tore it into long strips. Keeping two shredded lengths from the petticoat, he began walking slowly to Amelia.

Becoming terrified, she asked shakily, "What are you going to do?"

Reaching her, he moved with incredible speed, and before Amelia had a chance to defend herself, he had her back turned to him and a piece of the petticoat rammed into her mouth. Tying it securely, he explained menacingly, "I wouldn't want you to cry out and disturb the other boarders or our son."

Dear God, what did he intend to do to her? Alarmed, Amelia's knees buckled, and she would have fallen, but Jason lifted her in his arms.

Carrying her to the bed, he dropped her onto the mattress. Placing the remaining strip beside him, he removed her dressing gown by ripping it free. His eyes radiating with madness, he flung the torn gown to the floor. Kneeling over her, he examined her breasts and the golden triangle between her legs.

Driven by her instinct for self-preservation, Amelia spontaneously struck out at him, but he seized her wrists. Using one hand to restrain her, he pinned her arms over her head.

Thickly, he asked, "How did Anderson arouse your passion?" Moving his hand to one of her breasts, he painfully pinched the nipple. "Did he caress your lovely bosom?" he asked sadistically.

Flinching, Amelia groaned deeply. Gazing into her frightened eyes, he purred, "Did he make you groan with desire?"

Suddenly, he had his fingers between her thighs, probing them into her roughly. "Did he do this to you, my precious? Did he stick his dirty fingers in you to release your love juices?"

Moaning in pain, Amelia tossed her head back and forth. She knew Jason could be vicious, but she had never imagined he could go to such lengths to inflict his cruelty.

Swiftly he grabbed the cloth strip, and, leaning over Amelia, he wrapped it around her wrists. She was so tiny that he easily turned her over on her stomach. Straddling her, he tied her wrists to one of the bedposts.

Amelia couldn't see him, but she heard him removing his belt. She tried to scream, but the gag muffled her cries.

"And, now, my precious," he whispered hoarsely, "I am going to punish you. And you can be thankful to me that I have decided to be lenient and not administer the same fate to you that your lover received."

Snapping the leather belt, he moved to her side. Remaining on his knees, he lifted the belt, then brought it down sharply across her buttocks.

The pain was excruciating, and the scream that rose to her throat choked Amelia.

Once again he inflicted his punishment, and the belt struck against her bare skin, leaving an ugly red welt.

Amelia's body jerked violently. Relishing her suffering, Jason delivered blow after blow against her buttocks. Writhing and moaning, tears streamed from Amelia's eyes. The pain was becoming unbearable, and she was on the brink of passing out when, all at once, Jason became sexually aroused. His sudden erection throbbed uncontrollably, and, dropping the belt, he undid his trousers. Sliding them past his hips, he once again straddled his wife.

Believing he had finished with her, Amelia sighed with thankfulness. When his hands roughly grabbed her waist, jerking her to her knees, she understood his intentions. No! her mind screamed. No! No!

Positioning her red and swollen buttocks against him, he shoved his pulsating penis into her female warmness. Jason's climax came to him instantaneously, causing him to shudder convulsively. Shoving her thighs to the mattress, he pulled up his trousers. Taking his belt, he left the bed. Putting it back on, he walked around to the other side and knelt by Amelia.

Untying her hands, he warned, "If you are planning to take my son and leave me, make no mistake, I will find you. And then I will publicly announce that you are a traitor and an adulteress. I will take my son away from you, and you will never see him again."

He removed the gag, and it was on her lips to tell him that Hank was not his son. But, cautiously, she suppressed the impulse. If Jason were to learn that he wasn't the child's father, he might very well take out his anger on Hank.

"You will be my wife in name only," he continued. "I will never again touch your contaminated body." Rising, he glared down at her. Smirking, he growled, "You are filth, Amelia! Do you understand! Filth!"

Swerving swiftly, he walked to the front door. Before leaving, he told her, "I am letting you remain in this marriage for only one reason. I do not wish to be shamed by my wife! But, Amelia, if you push me too far, I will let the whole country know what you are! And I promise you, you will never again lay eyes on your child!" To keep from arousing the other boarders, he opened and closed the door quietly.

Jason didn't return home until the following morning. Amelia was in bed, but she wasn't sleeping. Turning painfully to her side, she watched him as he walked over to the bureau, removing a clean shirt.

Feeling her eyes on him, he turned to look at her. Scowling, he ordered, "From now on, Amelia, you will sleep on the sofa in the sitting room. I will not have Anderson's disgusting leftovers in my bed!"

Amelia kept her face impassive, but she wanted to shout with joy! She would prefer to sleep in a gutter than share a bed with Jason!

Going to the door to the sitting room, he unlocked it. Opening it, he paused, looking back at her. Smiling coldly, he remarked, "I have good news for you, my sweet. It seems the sensitive citizens of Richmond found the soldiers' bloody trophy too sickening for their delicate stomachs. You will be happy to learn that your guerrilla lover has been decently buried.''

Turning her face into the pillow, Amelia sighed inaudibly, ''Thank God!''

''What did you say?'' he questioned sharply.

Although the movement caused her pain, Amelia sat up on the bed. Without flinching, she met his angry stare. Her courage aggravated Jason. He thought the beating he had given her would have broken her spirit and cured her insolence.

Unintimidated, she replied, ''I said, thank God! I thank God that the man is decently buried!''

What Jason hated the most about the Missouri guerrillas was their refusal to be cowed by him. And, now, his wife was confronting him with the same bravery and stamina! Storming into the sitting room, he slammed the door shut, raging, ''You goddamned treacherous whore!''

TWENTY-EIGHT

The Confederate Army was outnumbered by Union soldiers, and the North had more than six times the number of factories and more than twice the railroad mileage of the South. The Confederacy had begun with no regular army, no navy, and only a small number of merchant ships. The South's advantages were its intangible character and superior military leadership, exemplified by such men as Robert E. Lee, Thomas (Stonewall) Jackson, Nathan B. Forrest, Joseph E. Johnston, and James E.B. Stuart. Furthermore, the men in the ranks seemed to have more endurance than their Northern counterparts, and, feeling that they were defending their homes from invasion, they fought accordingly.

But the year 1864 found the Union stronger and the Confederacy weaker than ever before. After their crushing victories of 1863, many Northerners thought the end of the war was in sight. But they underestimated the South's will to endure, and the war was to drag on for another seventeen months.

In March, 1864, Grant was promoted to lieutenant

general and given command of all the Union armies. He planned two major offensives: an invasion of Georgia by Sherman, and an advance on Richmond by the Army of the Potomac, which Grant chose to direct himself. To oppose Grant's 118,000 men, Lee had 60,000, James Henry and Buford Stewart among them.

On May 4, Grant crossed the Rapidan and entered the Wilderness (a wooded area in northeast Virginia), where he was engaged by Lee on May 5–6. Although Lee got the better of the fighting, Grant didn't retreat; instead, he moved off to the southeast in an attempt to get around Lee's flank. This set a pattern that was to be followed for the next month.

After the battle of the Wilderness, the armies next met at Spotsylvania Courthouse, then at the North Anna River, and finally at Cold Harbor. These fierce encounters were characterized by costly frontal assaults on Lee's field fortifications. Grant abandoned his direct approach to Richmond and moved down the peninsula beyond the range of Confederate reconnaissance, then crossed to the south of the James River. His plan was to capture Petersburg, sever Richmond's rail connections with the lower South, and thus force its evacuation. The attack on Petersburg almost succeeded, but was thwarted by the timely arrival of reinforcements from Lee. Grant then decided to beseige Richmond and Petersburg, a seige that lasted over nine months. So far the campaign had cost Grant 64,000 casualties; during the same period (May 5–June 18) the Confederates lost 25,000 to 30,000.

The winter of 1864–65 saw the almost complete collapse of the Southern railroads. Lee's army began to suffer from slow starvation. Because of the lack of forage for draft animals, the army was almost immobilized. Crippled in transport, and without hope of victory, Lee's men were faced with Grant's ever increasing and superbly equipped regiments.

Lee's last offensive battle was fought on March 25, 1865. He assaulted Grant's lines at Fort Stedman near Petersburg, hoping to force Grant to shorten his lines and so allow the dispatch of Confederate troops to oppose Sherman. The attack was halted by the Union with serious Southern losses. Grant began to prepare the last of his flanking movements. Lee sent 10,000 men to defend the railroads only to have them overwhelmed at the battle of Five Forks (April 1). Grant ordered a general assault and breached Lee's lines in several places. Lee gave up the two cities and retreated to the southeast. Grant's fast-moving columns overtook and surrounded the feeble remnants of the Confederate Army of Northern Virginia at Appomattox Courthouse on April 9. Encircled, without food, and outnumbered four to one, Lee had no choice but to surrender. Operations in Virginia came to an end.

Sitting beside the campfire, James Henry reached into his jacket pocket for a cigar. Picking up a stick, he put it into the flames, then used it to light the cigar.

It was early evening, but the captured Confederate camp was unusually quiet, although the majority of the soldiers weren't asleep. It was over! Their cause was dead! General Lee, their commander, had surrendered to Grant! Now, it was only a matter of time before the tattered remains of the Confederacy would also surrender. Soon, the War between the States would cease to exist.

Joining James Henry, Buford sat beside him. The April night was fairly warm and there was no need to find shelter. Deciding to sleep by the campfire, Buford placed his bedroll at his side.

For a long time, both men remained silent, deep in their own thoughts. It was Buford who spoke first. "It seems strange to look on all sides of the camp and see blue uniforms and know, come sunrise, we aren't going to be killing each other."

James Henry nodded, offering no comment.

"Three years ago," Buford began, "I once told your pa and brothers that when this war was over, and the country found itself minus more than half its young men, the people would turn to one another and ask, why?" A gruff groan came from his throat. Looking at James Henry, he continued, "And, now, I find myself asking the same question I predicted others would ask. Why?"

"Militant Southern leaders, that's why," James Henry answered resentfully. He took a long drag from his cigar, then, placing his arm across his raised knees, he explained, "The South's leaders knew that in the new political and economic world they would be a minority. They engineered the split of the Democratic Party at the Charleston convention. Once the seven states seceded, the question of secession became academic. Secession itself was a declaration of war. The South's aggression caused this war, Buford. The Southern delegates and politicians insisted that slavery be extended into the territories. Lincoln was willing to leave it alone where it already existed."

Smiling with fondness, Buford replied, "Well, being that you're so smart, as well as long-winded, maybe you can also explain why in the hell you and I got into this war. We didn't favor secession, and we sure as hell weren't concerned about slavery in the territories. We didn't own slaves and didn't plan to own any."

"General Lee himself regarded secession as 'nothing but revolution,' but he resigned from the U.S. Army to offer his services to the Confederacy. Virginia has his first claim to loyalty. Well, I suppose we're a lot like Lee, our loyalties lie with our homeland. Southern blood runs through our veins." Grinning, he added, "As the saying goes, blood is thicker than water."

Seriously, Buford muttered, "Well, I just thank God the war is over." But he proceeded humorously, "The only cause you and I were fighting for was 'cause we're dumb sonofabitches!"

Laughing, James Henry replied, "Damn, Pappy! Just a few minutes ago you told me I was smart!"

They smiled, but their good humor was short-lived. The tribulations of war were still too immediate, and, once again, they retreated solemnly into their own thoughts.

Finally, Buford mumbled, "I wonder how things are going in Missouri."

"I hope to God that Luther is still alive," James Henry replied.

"Well, it won't be long until the Union can set us free, and then we can head out for your Pa's farm." When James Henry made no reply, he asked, "What do you plan to do about Bishop?"

Flipping the ashes from his cigar, James Henry answered coldly, "If the bastard isn't dead, I'm going to kill him!"

Studying James Henry, Buford could see a bitterness in him that hadn't been there before the war. But, then, the war had hardened a lot of men, including himself.

"James Henry, why don't we just forget Bishop? After we find out about Luther, let's just go back to Texas. Damn, aren't you tired of killing?"

Angered, James Henry spat, "Of course, I'm sick of killing! But I'm going to even the score with Bishop, if it's the last thing I do!"

"It's because of your pa, isn't it?" Buford asked.

"What do you mean?"

"You're going after Bishop because you know it's what Paul would want you to do. You know he was disappointed in you because you wouldn't join up with the Missouri guerrillas. And, now, you're bound and determined to carry out this act of revenge to live up to your pa's expectations."

"Pa isn't my only reason. There's also Anne and Becky, not to mention Luther."

"What has Luther got to do with it?"

"If Luther and Bishop are still alive, and I don't go after Bishop, Luther will."

"And being that you're the oldest, it's your place to go, right?"

"Right!" James Henry agreed, smashing his cigar into the ground.

"Well, you're wrong," Buford muttered.

Surprised, James Henry asked, "Why am I wrong?"

"If you're determined that Bishop die, then I'll kill

the sonofabitch, because I'm the oldest."

"It's my fight! Stay out of it!" James Henry snapped.

Buford spread out his blanket, remarking as he lay down, "James Henry, you aren't ever going to get big enough to tell me what I can and can't do!"

"We'll see about that!" James Henry retorted.

Turning his back to him, Buford ignored James Henry's comment. "Knowing I don't have to get up in the morning and fight Yankees is sure goin' to make me sleep good tonight."

Grinning, James Henry replied, "You aren't by yourself. There's going to be a lot of men on both sides sleeping soundly."

Buford became quiet, and James Henry gazed dreamily into the campfire, watching the flickering flames. Talking about Bishop brought Amelia to mind. It was over a year since she had been executed. He had seen her last in October of 1863, but he could still recall her vividly, her turquoise-blue eyes that had been so innocent and trusting, her long golden hair that had cascaded past her waist. He recalled how, when she was dressed in her borrowed guerrilla clothes, she had appeared to be no more than a child, until he removed them, and then she had become all woman.

He sighed deeply. Countless times he had been plagued by the same regrets that had troubled him since the colonel had first told him that Amelia had been executed. Why hadn't he broken his word to Colonel Garson and helped her escape? Why hadn't he realized that the colonel had been lying about the informer's death? And, God, how he wished he had told Amelia that he loved her!

403

He felt a sudden urge to talk to Buford about Amelia, but Buford was so quiet that James Henry believed him to be asleep. Losing the urge, he continued to stare into the glowing fire, his thoughts remaining on Amelia.

But Buford wasn't sleeping, he was wide awake, thinking about Amelia and James Henry's son. If Bishop was dead, then the little fellow was an orphan. He hoped he had been placed in Lillian's care, so they'd have no problem finding him. The boy was a Stewart, and he belonged with his real father. Well, they'd take the child with them to Texas, if they had to kidnap him. He was sure no one knew that James Henry was the boy's father, except for himself and Amelia. Now that left only him knowing the truth. What if something were to happen to him? James Henry would never learn about his son. Should he tell him, or wait first and see what took place when they reached Lawrence? If Bishop wasn't already dead, he soon would be. Buford didn't doubt for a moment that one of them would kill him; it was only a question of who got to him first. Sighing resolutely, he decided to wait before telling James Henry he had a son. He had stayed silent this long, he might as well keep quiet a little longer.

Rolling onto his back, Buford crossed his arms under his head, looking up at the stars glittering brightly against the dark Virginia sky. He wondered if Cynthia would still be in Lawrence. If she were, he planned to ask her to marry him. He seriously doubted that she would accept his proposal. Cynthia had loved her husband, her alliances were with the Union. Could she possibly love him enough to break that alliance? It was a slim hope, but, nonetheless, he would hold on to it.

"I thought you were asleep," James Henry said, breaking into Buford's thoughts.

"Naw," Buford drawled. "I can't seem to put my mind to rest."

Lying back on his blanket, James Henry suggested, "It's still early, but we might as well try to go to sleep." He added restlessly, "There's nothing else to do."

The same restlessness gnawing at James Henry was being felt by soldiers throughout the camp. For the first time since Grant crossed over into Virginia, there was nothing to do.

TWENTY-NINE

"The Bishops make such a handsome couple!" Mrs. Kelley praised.

As Cynthia was gathering her order, Mrs. Kelley was standing at the store window, gazing outside. Watching Jason and Amelia strolling down the sidewalk, she noticed how Jason protectively kept his hand on Amelia's arm. "It's so obvious that Captain Bishop idolizes his wife," she continued.

Adding up Mrs. Kelley's purchases, Cynthia asked flatly, "Why should you think that?"

Strutting to the counter, Mrs. Kelley replied, "Why, one can tell simply by watching him. His eyes absolutely glow with love when he looks at her." Admiringly, she exclaimed, "Oh, he's such a splendid man! Amelia is so fortunate to have him for a husband!"

Cynthia and Mrs. Kelley were alone, and there was no reason for Mrs. Kelley to lower her voice, but to put emphasis on her statement she commented secretively, "It's so gallant of Captain Bishop to love his wife . . . considering."

"Considering what?" Cynthia asked impatiently.

Leadingly, Mrs. Kelley whispered, "Well, you know."

Placing the articles into Mrs. Kelley's shopping bag, Cynthia replied testily, "No, I don't know!"

"Considering Amelia's captivity," Mrs. Kelley explained.

"Mrs. Kelley, that was almost two years ago. Must you find it necessary to still talk about it?"

"My dear, ugly rumors never die," Mrs. Kelley replied sweetly.

"They would die, if people like you ceased discussing them!" Cynthia fumed.

Defending herself, Mrs. Kelley answered, "I didn't mean to sound as though I was gossiping. Heaven knows, I never spread ugly gossip! You misunderstood me, my dear. I was merely admiring Captain Bishop and feeling sorry for poor Amelia."

"Why do you feel sorry for Amelia?" Cynthia asked.

"Well, after all, she was kept a prisoner for two months. Now, I don't believe for one minute that Amelia willingly became Bill Anderson's lover." As she grew excited, Mrs. Kelley's words raced. "But I'm sure that brutal man forced himself on her time and time again!" Her eyes gleaming with curious maliciousness, she continued, "Oh, how degrading it must have been for Amelia to have that man attacking her night after night! I understand, though, that Bill Anderson was quite young and very handsome. But, all the same, I'm sure she found him appalling, and my heart goes out to poor Amelia!"

Handing Mrs. Kelley her shopping bag, Cynthia

snapped, "Mrs. Kelley, that is impossible, because you don't have a heart!"

Offended, Mrs. Kelley huffed, "Well!" Taking the shopping bag, she stomped to the door replying frigidly, "You can put this order on my bill!" Determined to get in the last word, she added smugly, "Cynthia, ever since you became involved with that uncouth Sam Tyler, you have become very ill-mannered!" Before darting outside, she turned to look at Cynthia, adding venomously, "A lot of good it did you to throw yourself at him! Sam Tyler used you, and then ran out on you!"

As Mrs. Kelley slammed the door behind her, Cynthia made a desperate effort to hold back her tears. Failing, she hurried to the back of the store, letting the tears flow.

Slowly she made her way to the room that Buford had temporarily occupied. Opening the door, she stepped inside. The bed was stripped and the bureau was bare, making the small room feel as empty as Cynthia's heart.

The war was over! Would Buford abide by his promise and return to Lawrence?

Going to the bed, she sat down. Did she want him to come back? She didn't know! One part of her longed for his return, but the other part balked at the thought of any relationship developing between herself and a man who hadn't fought for the Union. Oh, how could she possibly choose between Buford and honor?

But, then, she might never be confronted with the choice. He might not come back to her. His promise had been made on the spur of the moment, and now he more than likely didn't even think about her. Or, if he did, he probably considered her a woman with no moral values, because she had shamelessly allowed him to bed her.

The fear that Cynthia had kept suppressed forced its way into her thoughts. Had he been killed? Dear God, would it be his death that would keep him away from Lawrence? No! She'd rather he had callously abandoned her than that he be dead!

Falling across the bed, she pillowed her head in her arms. "Oh, Buford!" she cried. "I can't bear the thought of you being dead!" Doubling her hands into fists, she prayed, "Please God, let him be alive! Please!"

It was two weeks since Amelia and Jason had moved from Richmond back to Lawrence. Amelia had been happy to come home. She had desperately missed Lillian and Cynthia.

Her marriage to Jason was becoming unbearable to Amelia. Although he had never again physically violated her, he tortured her emotionally. True to his word, he had not demanded his husbandly rights, and his refusal to make love to Amelia was her salvation.

To protect his reputation, Jason insisted that publicly they project the role of the perfectly married couple. When they weren't in the seclusion of home, Jason pretended to worship his wife, as well as their son. But, privately, he abused Amelia verbally and simply ignored the child.

When Mrs. Kelley spotted them in town, they had been on their way home from a lunch date with Colonel Rhodes and his wife. The colonel had been transferred to Lawrence to oversee the surrender of the Pro-Confederates in that area. Jason resented the army's sending Colonel Rhodes. The colonel hadn't fought against the Missouri guerrillas, and he had no animosity toward them. Jason knew the man would accept them as surrendering soldiers and treat them accordingly. Jason believed the dirty pieces of scum should be arrested and shot down in cold blood. He was fully aware that, even if he were in charge, he could never order the slaughter of the Missouri guerrillas. But he could have made their surrender humiliating, which, of course, would have angered many of them. And when a guerrilla got his dander up, he usually became violent, and then he could justifiably have ordered the ones rioting to be shot down.

Feeling as if he had been cheated, Jason jerked the front door open, stepping into the house ahead of Amelia.

Wondering why he was so upset, Amelia followed him inside, asking, "Is something bothering you, Jason?"

Going straight to the liquor cabinet, he removed a decanter. Taking one of the glasses, he filled it with brandy. He helped himself to a generous drink before turning to face Amelia.

"You're damned right, something is bothering me! Colonel Rhodes!" he fumed.

"Colonel Rhodes?" she questioned. "He seemed very nice to me. Why should you find him upsetting?"

"Do you know why the army sent him here?" he shouted angrily.

Understanding the reason for his resentment, she smiled spitefully. "The Army sent him here to take

411

charge over the surrender being negotiated with the Pro-Confederates.''

Observing her smile, he sneered, ''You treacherous little bitch! You'd like to see them treated as soldiers, wouldn't you?''

''Decently!'' she remarked undaunted. ''I want to see them treated decently!''

''Did Quantrill treat the men and boys of Lawrence decently?'' he challenged.

''No,'' she replied, unruffled. ''But, then, Quantrill is dead, so he won't be surrendering.''

''But some of his men will be!'' he pointed out. ''And they were the ones who actually carried out the bloody massacre!''

''Not all of them,'' she answered evenly. ''And the ones who refused to murder innocent people should not be punished. But during surrender, the guiltless cannot very well be separated from the guilty.''

Setting down his glass, he hurried to her side. Clutching her arm, he raged, ''Weren't you satisfied loving Anderson? Did you have to find it necessary to love every Missouri guerrilla? What did you do, Amelia? Did you spread your legs for the entire column of Missouri filth?''

Pulling away from him, she said firmly, ''Jason, I have told you over and over again, that I felt compassion for Bill Anderson!'' She decided to ignore the last part of his accusation.

''And I have told you over and over again that I don't believe you!''

Going to the sofa, she sat down. Dispassionately, she replied, ''I don't give a damn what you believe.'' Looking up at him, she added icily, ''Because I don't

412

give a damn about you!''

Enraged, Jason bellowed, ''Amelia, your insolence is going to be your ultimate downfall. One of these days, you will push me too far!''

''What will you do?'' she taunted. ''Beat me with your belt, and then force yourself on me?''

Grinning vindictively, he warned, ''No! I will divorce you on grounds of adultery, and then make sure you are forbidden to see your son!''

Amelia wanted to retaliate and lash out at him, but she couldn't. Jason was in complete control! She didn't doubt for a moment that he would live up to his threat and take Hank away from her.

Reading her thoughts, Jason said smugly, ''Now, my precious, you will apologize for your insolence.''

Resentfully, Amelia swallowed her pride, and quietly murmured, ''I'm sorry.''

''I didn't hear you!'' he snapped. ''Speak up, my sweet!''

Glaring, she spat, ''I'm sorry!''

Returning to his glass of brandy, he replied triumphantly, ''That's better! You need to learn your place and how to keep it! I must leave, but I'll be back in time to dine with you. While I'm gone, I suggest you practice on how to be humble.'' Finishing the brandy, he set the glass down sharply.

He moved across the room. Pausing in front of the sofa, he added obnoxiously, ''Tonight I will be watching you closely to see if you are behaving humbly. So practice well, my sweet!''

He walked from the room, and, laughing loudly, he left the house.

Limply, Amelia leaned back on the sofa. How much

413

longer could she endure Jason's arrogance without reaching her final breaking point?

"Oh, James Henry," she sighed desperately, "please, please come back to Lawrence!"

Suddenly, Amelia stiffened. Why hadn't she thought of it before now? James Henry might be one of the guerrillas who would lay down their arms to Colonel Rhodes! Oh, she must be present at the surrender! James Henry might very well be riding into town right now with the other Missouri guerrillas to concede to Colonel Rhodes. If James Henry was among them, she would somehow find a way to speak privately with him. She'd tell him that Hank was his son. He might not be in love with her, but surely he would care about his son! Hating Jason, he wouldn't want him raising his child! But, she must convince him that killing Jason was unnecessary, and that he must first consider his son's welfare. She would beg him, plead with him, to help her and Hank escape from Jason!

Restless, Amelia rose from the couch. Pacing the floor, her thoughts continued to race. James Henry was her only hope! If he didn't return to Lawrence, her life would fall apart! All these months and months, her only inspiration had been the hope that someday she would be reunited with the man she loved.

Her steps halted abruptly. What if he had been fatally wounded? She had no guarantee that James Henry was still alive! But, surely, she would know some of the guerrillas who would be surrendering! If James Henry wasn't present, maybe one of them would know what had happened to him. If it became necessary, she would ask every man she recognized about James Henry, until she found one who knew of his fate. Oh

God, what if she were to learn that he had been killed!

Returning to the sofa and dropping down to the cushions, she sobbed, "Oh my darling, without you, my life is nothing!" She knew that if it weren't for her child, if she were to find out that James Henry was dead she would seriously contemplate taking her own life. But, as long as she had Hank, she had a reason to go on living.

THIRTY

The citizens of Lawrence turned out in droves to view the surrender of the Pro-Confederates. As the Missouri guerrillas rode through the streets of the town, a few of the people were able to restrain their hostility, but most of them shouted insults and obscenities.

Colonel Rhodes, riding at the head of the column, was worried that the citizens' harassments would arouse the guerrillas, causing violence to erupt. As a precautionary measure, he ordered his troops to guard the Pro-Confederates by encircling them and covering their flank.

The act was being performed in a strictly military manner. Colonel Rhodes had ridden out with his troops, and, a mile from town, he had rendezvoused with the guerrillas. Now, he was escorting them into Lawrence and down the streets to the provost marshal's office.

Trying to remain inconspicuous so Jason wouldn't see her, Amelia stood in the center of the large crowd gathered at the office building. The jammed spectators kept nudging forward, forcing the Union soldiers to continually push them back.

Hearing the people becoming excited, Amelia rose on her tiptoes, trying to see over their heads. If she had been taller, she could have gotten a clearer view, but instead, she barely made out the horsemen who were entering the street.

Jason had informed her that sixty-five guerrillas were expected to surrender. Sixty-five! Oh, how was she to spot James Henry among that many men?

Colonel Rhodes guided his horse away from the others, and, dismounting, he handed the reins to a soldier. A long table had been placed in front of the office building, and, walking over to stand behind it, the colonel took his place beside the provost marshal.

Remaining encircled by the Union soldiers, the Pro-Confederates crowded their horses into the street. The guerrilla acting as their leader raised his hand and the riders came to a halt.

For the first time, the ragged partisans were being treated as enemy soldiers. Now they tried to act accordingly. At their leader's command, they dismounted as a company and stood to horse. The leader rasped out another order, and his men stepped two paces forward.

Colonel Rhodes spoke firmly. "You men are to step up to this table, and, one by one, you will lay down your weapons!"

Hastily Amelia shoved her way through the spectators, maneuvering her way closer to the colonel. If the guerrillas had to walk to the table, then, if James Henry was among them, she would see him! She knew it was risky to be so close to the action; it increased the chance that Jason would see her. Well, it was a chance she would have to take!

Amelia tried not to feel sorry for the guerrillas as she watched them laying down their arms. She had already betrayed the Union by not telling them about the informer and by loving a man who had been their enemy. She didn't want to be guilty again of being disloyal to the Union. But, against her will, her heart ached for the beaten guerrillas as they gave up their weapons. She noticed how proudly they moved. They kept their heads held high, and their gazes never once dropped sheepishly. Turning her attention to the Union soldiers, she observed in them the same pride and intrepidity. American men are so brave! she cried silently. Our country was built on their kind of bravery! Oh, why? Why did they fight against each other? If our American men join together, no country can ever be as strong as this one! Suddenly, she sighed deeply. But that had been the real cause of the war. The Union had fought to keep the country united.

Wiping at her tears, Amelia watched as the guerrillas stepped to the table and laid down their rifles. Next, heavy pistols and belts were unstrapped and placed on top of the carbines.

She recognized a few men who had been at Anderson's camp, but she didn't see anyone she knew well, until the last man stepped up to the table. Placing her hand over her mouth, she gasped, "Bulldog!" Neither James Henry nor Buford were present, but surely Bulldog would know what had happened to them. Oh, somehow, she must find a way to talk to him!

The Missouri leader told his men to file before the provost marshal. Standing calmly, each man raised his hand, and, as the provost marshal read the oath of allegiance to the U.S., they repeated his words. Next, parole certificates were issued to each man.

Their leader ordered them to return to their horses. After mounting, the ex-guerrillas looked to Colonel Rhodes, waiting for him to give his permission for them to leave.

Colonel Rhodes was a stately soldier, in his early fifties. Basically, he was a compassionate man, and he had hated the war. Now, he was thankful that it had ended. Moving out from behind the table filled with confiscated weapons, he stepped into the street. Standing tall, his eyes regarded the defeated Missourians.

Colonel Rhodes spoke in a deep, clear voice, "The war is over! Return to your homes and live in peace!"

Amelia panicked! The ex-guerrillas were leaving! Reacting irrationally, she pushed her way through the throng of people. Moving out into the street, she fled to Bulldog. Running beside his horse, she clutched frantically at his leg.

"Bulldog!" she cried. "Where is James Henry?"

Captain Bishop's wife running after a guerrilla shocked the spectators, the soldiers, and the Pro-Confederates. All motion seemed to become suspended, as everyone stared incredulously at Amelia and Bulldog.

Halting his horse, Bulldog sneered, "Mrs. Bishop, do you wanna get me killed?"

She looked at him with confusion. What was he talking about? He wouldn't be killed because she was speaking to him!

"Where is James Henry?" she asked again.

"I don't know," he grumbled.

Jason was slow coming out of his shock, but, recovering, he hurried to Colonel Rhodes. Forcefully, he demanded, "Colonel, I want that man arrested!"

Irritably, the colonel replied, "I can't have him arrested for talking to your wife! Good God, the man was just given a parole certificate!"

"But, sir, you don't understand!" Jason said hastily. "A couple of years ago, he tried to rape my wife, and I want to bring charges against him!"

The colonel started to ask him why his wife would run to a man who had tried to rape her, but there wasn't time for questions. Later, he would investigate this case thoroughly. "Very well, captain! Have your men place him under arrest!"

Oblivious of Jason or the others, Amelia pleaded with Bulldog, "What do you mean, you don't know where he is?"

"James Henry and Buford haven't been seen since the morning they rode out of Anderson's camp with Colonel Garson. It is believed among the guerrillas that James Henry and Buford are dead."

"No!" she cried piercingly. "No!"

Amelia wasn't aware of whose hands had suddenly clutched her shoulders from behind, until she heard his lowered voice, "Damn you, Amelia! You goddamned flaunting little whore!"

Frantically, she fought against Jason's tenacious grip. "Let me go!" she yelled.

Three mounted troopers rode over to them, and, still holding on to Amelia, Jason ordered, "Place that man under arrest, and take him to the guardhouse!"

Openly defying his order, Amelia shouted, "No! You can't arrest him! He hasn't done anything!"

Knowing there was no longer a reason to be concerned with what people would say, Jason grabbed hold of Amelia's arm, dragging her away. He was tempted to kill her for bringing down this shame on him! But, somehow, he would find a way to cover up this scandalizing incident. He would claim that the sight of the guerrillas who had kidnapped her had caused Amelia to go temporarily insane. She had been beside herself and was too irrational to know what she had been saying or doing. Yes, it would work. Oh, a few people might be a little skeptical, but in time the rumors would die. Besides, his station in Lawrence was only temporary. Soon he would be receiving his transfer to the West. But Amelia would pay dearly for her act of defiance!

Resigned, Amelia had ceased fighting Jason, and submissively she allowed him to pull her down the sidewalk to their house.

Keeping his hand on her arm, Jason opened the front door. Jerking Amelia through the doorway, he stepped in behind her. Seeing Addie and Hank in the parlor, he bellowed gruffly, "Take the child to Lillian's, and stay there until I come for you!"

Frightened by Captain Bishop's apparent anger, Addie quickly gathered Hank into her arms. Hurrying, she left the house with the child.

Roughly, Jason dragged Amelia down the hallway to his bedroom. Flinging the door open, he shoved her inside. Losing her balance, Amelia fell to the floor. Slamming the door closed, Jason ordered harshly, "Remove your clothes!"

Amelia wanted to be brave, but her fear overcame her courage, and she hated the way her voice trembled as she pleaded, "What are you going to do to me?"

Smiling icily, he answered calmly, "I'm going to beat you, my sweet."

"No!" she begged. "Jason, please don't hurt me!"

Stepping to her, he jerked her to her feet. Forcefully, he ripped and tore at her clothes until he had them removed and she was left standing naked before him.

His eyes bored into her flesh, raking the parts of her body that he hadn't seen in months. Thinking about the red welts that would soon be inflicted on her flawless skin, Jason could feel himself becoming sexually aroused. Chuckling menacingly, he slowly removed his belt.

"Oh, Jason, please!" Amelia pleaded. "Please don't beat me!"

Her begging delighted him, and, throwing back his head, Jason laughed victoriously, causing him to miss detecting the changed expression that suddenly covered Amelia's face.

Although her knees were shaking, Amelia straightened her frame to its full height. Never again would she beg and give him a reason to laugh at her! He could torture her! He could kill her! And still, she wouldn't beg him!

Seeing no trace of fear left on her face angered Jason. "Lie across the bed!" he commanded.

Turning sharply, she moved to the bed, her steps never faltering. Placing herself on her stomach, she lay across the mattress.

Aggravated by her courage, Jason stood motionless. Glaring at him, she taunted, "Well, what are you waiting for? Go ahead and get it over with!"

Crossing the room in long, demanding strides, he

went to the bed. He snapped the belt loudly, and the sharp threatening crackle sent cold chills up Amelia's spine. The first blow landed across her back, and the intense pain caused her to bite into her bottom lip. She was determined not to cry out, but as the lashes kept striking against her back and buttocks, Amelia couldn't control the groans that escaped deep in her throat.

Seeing Amelia's lovely flesh marred by the ugly, swelling welts excited Jason. His hard erection began throbbing uncomfortably against its confinement. Dropping the belt, he unbuttoned his pants.

Understanding his intentions, Amelia raised her head to look back at him. The movement pained her considerably, but, concealing her discomfort, she said unemotionally, "Jason, if I have a choice between you or more lashes, I much prefer the lashes."

Her sarcastic remark shattered his desire, and his hard penis instantly shriveled. Goddamn, how he despised her insolence! "You whoring bitch!" he spat, fastening his trousers.

Putting on his belt, he stomped across the floor and to the door. Jerking it open, he raged, "That piece of Missouri trash you were talking to will pay for your insolence, Amelia!"

"Jason, no!" she yelled.

Smirking, he replied, "Before I am through with him, he will be begging me to kill him and get him out of his misery!" Quickly he shut the door behind him.

"Bulldog!" Amelia moaned. "Oh, I'm so sorry!" Losing control, she pounded her small fists against the mattress, raving, "I wish you were dead, Jason! You're a heartless, cruel monster, and I wish you were dead!"

The word "dead" screamed through her heart, bringing back Bulldog's words. "It's believed among the guerrillas that James Henry and Buford are dead. . . ."

Crying convulsively, Amelia shrieked over and over again, "No, James Henry isn't dead! He isn't! . . . He isn't! . . . He isn't!"

Mrs. Kelley had been the first customer to enter Lillian's store, exclaiming breathlessly that Amelia had actually fled after one of those disgusting guerrillas. Oh, poor Captain Bishop had been so upset, and her heart had just ached for the poor man! To be publicly shamed by his wife in such an insulting manner! Oh, poor, poor Captain Bishop!

Learning of Amelia's irrational behavior worried Cynthia, and she was tempted to go to the Bishops' home. She didn't trust Jason. She had witnessed him slapping Amelia, and she knew he was capable of physically abusing his wife. When Addie and Hank arrived at the store, and Addie revealed that Captain Bishop had seemed to be extremely angry, Cynthia's mind was made up. Telling Lillian she was taking off the rest of the day, she rushed to Amelia's home.

Cynthia banged repeatedly on the front door, but received no answer. She checked to see if it was unlocked. The doorknob turned in her hand, and the door swung open. Hesitantly, she entered the house.

"Amelia?" she called. "Are you home?" She was answered by silence. Cautiously she made her way down the narrow hallway, and, hearing soft sobs coming from Jason's bedroom, she paused at the door.

"Amelia?" she called quietly. She knocked lightly on the door. "Amelia, are you in there?"

Once again, she received no answer. Slowly, Cynthia inched the door open. Peeking inside, she saw Amelia lying nude across Jason's bed. Gasping, she stepped inside. Nearing Amelia, she caught sight of the welts on her back and buttocks. "Oh, dear Lord!" she exclaimed, her steps halting abruptly.

Hearing Cynthia's voice, Amelia forced herself to sit up. With tears streaming from her eyes, she cried pathetically, "Oh Cynthia, please help me!"

Instantly Cynthia fled to the bed. Sitting beside Amelia, she longed to take her into her arms, but, realizing Amelia would find the embrace painful, she tried to console her by patting her hand.

"Amelia," she pleaded, "you must go to Colonel Rhodes and tell him what Jason has done to you! He's a kind and just man, and he will see that Jason is severely reprimanded."

Amelia shook her head, replying, "I can't."

"Why not?" Cynthia asked.

"Will you go to my room and get my dressing gown? Then, I'll explain everything to you."

Standing, Cynthia nodded. "But first, I'm going to put some antiseptic on those cuts." The lashes Jason had delivered had cut Amelia's skin.

After Amelia's injuries were tended to and she had slipped into her dressing gown, she sat on the bed beside Cynthia. "I don't know where to begin," Amelia sighed.

Smiling encouragingly, Cynthia coaxed, "Try starting at the beginning."

A tiny smile touched the corners of Amelia's mouth.

"I suppose that would be the logical place to start."
Grasping Cynthia's hand, she cried earnestly, "I'm so
afraid that when you learn the truth, you'll hate me!"

Tenderly, Cynthia assured her, "I could never hate
you, Amelia. Besides, I already know the truth."

Surprised, Amelia stammered, "Wh . . . what?"

"You were in love with Bill Anderson, weren't
you?"

"No!" Amelia exclaimed. "Oh, Cynthia, why do
you think I loved Captain Anderson?"

"The brush and comb set," Cynthia explained.
"Weren't they a gift from Anderson?"

"But how did you know?" Amelia questioned.

"I'll explain that later," Cynthia replied hastily.
"But, darling, if you didn't love him, why did his gift
mean so much to you?"

Amelia smiled. "To explain why I treasure his gift,
it will be necessary to start at the very beginning. And
the beginning of my story goes all the way back to the
time Sam and Jamie Tyler came to Lawrence."

"Sam Tyler?" Cynthia breathed.

"Please, Cynthia, don't interrupt. Just let me explain everything."

"Very well," Cynthia agreed.

Remaining perfectly quiet, Cynthia listened to
Amelia's entire explanation. She told Cynthia everything. Unashamed of her love for James Henry, she
admitted that she felt no guilt in her heart where James
Henry was concerned. Without hesitating, she revealed that James Henry had fathered her child. She
elaborated on her stay at the guerrilla camp and about
the warm friendship that had developed between herself and Captain Anderson. When she explained how

Bill Anderson had spared her life at the risk of his own, tears came to her eyes.

Cynthia permitted Amelia to talk uninterrupted, until her story reached the present and she repeated the words Bulldog had spoken.

Leaping from the bed, Cynthia's hand flew over her heart. "Buford dead!" she gasped. "No! Oh Amelia, no!"

Dumbfounded, Amelia could only stare at her friend, wondering why she should be so upset over Buford.

Sinking back to the bed, Cynthia said softly, "Amelia, I also have a story to tell." Turning to Amelia, she took her hand into hers, and as she spoke of her relationship with Buford, she unintentionally dug her fingers into Amelia's flesh.

When she had finished, Amelia exclaimed, "But, Cynthia, why haven't you told me this before now?"

"Why didn't you tell me about James Henry?"

"Because I was afraid you wouldn't understand and would think badly of me."

Smiling, Cynthia replied, "I kept silent for the same reason."

Suddenly, grasping Cynthia's hand, Amelia announced heartily, "We are both in love with Stewarts!"

"Stewart?" Cynthia questioned.

"Yes! Their last name is Stewart. Buford is James Henry's uncle."

Her eyes becoming misty, Cynthia pleaded desperately, "Amelia, do you think they are dead?"

"No!" Amelia cried quickly.

"Neither do I," Cynthia said. Rising, she sauntered

428

to the window. Pulling back the curtain, she gazed outside. Speaking softly, she predicted, "Someday, Amelia, when we least expect it, an old rickety wagon is going to make its reappearance in Lawrence."

"Rickety wagon?" Amelia questioned.

Turning from the window, Cynthia's eyes gleamed into Amelia's. "Sam and Jamie Tyler!" she explained. "They will have no choice but to resume the roles they used during the war." Swiftly she returned to the bed, sitting beside Amelia. Tenderly, she said, "James Henry will take you and Hank away from here. Oh darling, I just know he will return and save you two from Jason!"

Amelia smiled hopefully. "He and Buford own land in northern Texas. Maybe James Henry will take Hank and me to his ranch." All at once, Amelia cried happily, "Maybe someday you and I will be neighbors living on ranches in Texas!"

"No," Cynthia sighed despondently.

Surprised, Amelia questioned, "Don't you believe Buford will ask you to marry him?"

"It doesn't matter," Cynthia replied. "I can't marry Buford."

"Why?" Amelia cried.

"You forget that I was married to David, and I loved him dearly. How can I possibly marry a man who served under Bill Anderson? It was Anderson and his men who killed David! The bullet that killed my husband could have come from Buford's own gun!"

Desperately, Amelia pleaded, "But the war is over!"

"But my love for David isn't over!" Cynthia said firmly. "Oh Amelia, I can't be disloyal to David's memory! If I were to marry a man who had been his enemy, my guilt would eventually destroy me and my marriage. A marriage between myself and Buford Stewart would be doomed to failure.''

Amelia wanted to plead with Cynthia to change her mind, but she didn't. Cynthia had truly loved David, and although she was disappointed in her decision, she understood how she felt.

Squeezing Amelia's hand, Cynthia replied, ''But I want only the best for Buford. And I hope and pray that he and James Henry are alive and well.''

Suddenly remembering Bulldog, Amelia whispered raspingly, ''While you are praying, don't forget to pray for Bulldog. I shudder to think of what Jason will do to him!'' Knowing Bulldog's fate was in Jason's cruel hands, Amelia moaned, ''It's all my fault! Oh Bulldog, I'm so sorry!''

After inflicting his brutality on Amelia, Jason had gone straight to Colonel Rhodes. Pretending to be slightly embarrassed, he told the colonel that he had been mistaken, and the man he had arrested was not the man who had tried to rape his wife. But to make amends, he and three of his soldiers would personally escort the man safely from Lawrence.

Captain Bishop's claim of mistaken identity irritated the colonel, but apparently the captain was willing to try and make up for the inconvenience he had caused the ex-guerrilla. Admiring Captain Bishop's sense of fairness, he gave him permission to take the prisoner from the guardhouse and accompany him out of Lawrence.

The three soldiers Jason chose to ride with him were Jayhawkers, and they hated Missouri guerrillas as much as he did. When Jason and his men went to the guardhouse, demanding the prisoner's release, Bulldog knew what was going to happen to him. Realizing it would be futile to complain to the soldiers at the guardhouse, he asked for permission to see Colonel Rhodes. But quickly Jason saw to it that his request was denied.

Bulldog remained silent as Jason and his men led him out of Lawrence and into a wooded area. Captain Bishop's reputation for mercilessness was well known among Pro-Confederates, and Bulldog was perfectly aware that he would soon be facing a fate worse than the depths of hell!

When they came upon a secluded area, Jason told two of his men to dismount, but ordered the other man to ride a distance and keep a lookout for guerrillas who might not have returned to Missouri. He knew guerrillas had a way of sticking together, and some of the man's comrades might have found their friend's arrest highly suspicious, and they could still be in the area.

Getting down from his mount, Jason told his men to drag the Missouri piece of filth from his horse and throw him to the ground.

Bulldog was extraordinarily strong, and the two men doubted if they could even pull him from his horse, let alone throw him to the ground.

Understanding his men's hesitancy, Jason drew his pistol. Grinning sardonically, he mocked, "I'll make it easier for you two weaklings to drag him from his horse." Stepping over to Bulldog's horse, Jason placed the barrel of his pistol against the animal's head and pulled the trigger.

The horse dropped at a deadfall, and Bulldog had to leap from the saddle to prevent his legs' being trapped beneath the animal's body.

The horse had been a healthy, sleek animal, and Bulldog had ridden him through the entire war. Sickened by a good horse's being wasted, he raged, "You goddamned sonofabitch!"

The two men were still uncertain about forcing the huge man to the ground, and, laughing sadistically, Jason replied, "I'll also make it easy for you two to keep this pile of shit on the ground!" His aim perfect, Jason shot Bulldog in one leg and then in the other leg.

Groaning with pain, Bulldog fell to his knees, and, moving speedily, Jason's boot struck him under the chin, sending him to the ground.

"Now," Jason smirked to his men, "do you think you can restrain him, or must I also make his arms inoperative?"

Quickly the men knelt beside Bulldog, each one grabbing hold of one of Bulldog's arms.

Keeping his pistol in his hand, Jason stepped closer to Bulldog, staring down at him. It was on his lips to question him about Amelia, but cautiously he decided against it. He didn't want his men to witness the interrogation. Amelia's treacherous infidelity with Anderson must never be known. Quickly, he ordered one of the troopers to get a rope and tie Bulldog's arms.

Obeying, the soldier hurried to his horse to fetch the rope. Returning, he pulled Bulldog to a sitting position, and, jerking his arms behind him, he tied the rope around his wrists.

Gruffly, Jason ordered his men to join the third

trooper and keep an eye out for guerrillas.

The moment they left, Jason knelt beside Bulldog. Putting the barrel of his pistol beneath Bulldog's swollen chin, he turned his face to his. "Why was my wife talking to you?" he asked hoarsely.

"She wanted to know if I had the time of day," Bulldog answered sarcastically.

Jason was outraged. The man was totally at his mercy, and still he showed no fear! What was wrong with these stinking guerrillas? Were they too goddamned dumb to be scared?

His face blood-red with anger, Jason warned, "My next shot will castrate you, if you don't answer me with respect! Now, you ugly sonofabitch, you tell me the truth. Was my wife Bill Anderson's whore?"

He was answered by Bulldog's sudden spit, the spittle landing between Jason's eyes.

Jason's roar sounded more like an inhuman howl, as, losing rationality, he struck the barrel of his pistol across Bulldog's jaw.

If Jason's men hadn't shown up, he would have beaten Bulldog to within an inch of his life, before finishing him off by sending a bullet into the man's scrotum.

"Captain!" one of the soldiers yelled. "There's a bunch of Missouri guerrillas headed this way! I don't know how they came by weapons, but those sonofabitches are armed! They spotted us, so we better get the hell out of here!"

Standing, Jason wiped the spittle from his face, replying gruffly, "They probably have a complete artillery hidden in the woods. A damned guerrilla can't be trusted to give up his guns! He'd give up his mother first!''

For a moment, Jason considered killing Bulldog, but, afraid the arriving guerrillas would deliver the man's body to Colonel Rhodes, he decided to let him live. The colonel was a righteous bastard, and Jason didn't doubt for a moment that he would have him busted and facing a court-martial. If the sonofabitch was left alive, his friends would simply let the matter rest, and take him to a doctor in Missouri.

Jason returned his pistol to its holster, then drawing back his leg, he kicked Bulldog upside the head, causing him to fall back on the ground. Unable to control his cruelty, Jason didn't stop until he had viciously kicked the man three times between the legs.

Minutes later, when the ex-guerrillas reached their beaten comrade, Jason and his men were already heading speedily for Lawrence.

THIRTY-ONE

To the two men riding up to the house, the Stewarts' home looked the same as it had in the past. The darkness of night concealed the barren fields, where crops had once flourished. The quietness in the house caused the younger of the two men to visualize the Stewart children in bed, and the single lamp burning in the front window being used to cast light on the mending Sarah Stewart had always done before bedtime. The man could picture Paul Stewart sitting in his favorite chair, dozing in front of the fireplace.

Dismounting, the man remembered the sounds of hushed voices coming from the loft. The voices of Paul Stewart's three sons, who weren't sleeping as their father believed, but making plans for the next day. The mischievous kind of plans that only boys can make.

But the man getting down from his tired horse was fully aware that the fields were barren. He didn't have to wait for sunrise to be conscious of the desolation. He also knew that the lamp shining in the window was not being used by Sarah Stewart, and that Paul Stewart wouldn't be dozing in his chair. There were no children sleeping in the house, not downstairs or upstairs, and no young boys were in the loft making plans for the next day.

James Henry knew the house would never again shelter the Stewart family, unless it was the next generation.

Dismounting, Buford remarked, "Luther must be here."

Stepping up to the porch beside Buford, James Henry knocked on the door saying, "God, how I hope he's all right!"

"Who's there?" they heard Luther ask.

Smiling, James Henry answered, "Open the door, and you'll find out!"

"James Henry!" Luther cried, flinging the door wide open. He threw himself into his brother's arms, and, seeing Buford, he began hugging both men at the same time. Unashamed, Luther allowed his tears to stream down his face as he exclaimed, "I thought you were both dead! Where have you been? My God, you two just disappeared off the face of the earth!"

James Henry didn't answer. He couldn't! He was too choked up. He had been so afraid that his youngest brother had been killed.

It was Buford who broke the embraces, as he said gruffly, trying to conceal the emotion in his voice, "Let's go inside, and then we'll tell you where we've been."

Luther stepped back, permitting them to enter first. The inside of the house shocked them both. What little furniture was left had been broken into pieces. The Federals had ransacked the cupboards, and the fine china and crystal that Sarah Henry had brought to her marriage were gone. The living room curtains that Anne and her mother had worked on so diligently were ripped into shreds.

"It doesn't look so bad now," Luther began. "You should've seen the house when I first got here. But the table is still intact. Sit down, and I'll fix a pot of coffee."

Going to the table, the two men sat down. James Henry watched Luther closely as he began preparing the coffee. He was nineteen, but he looked ten years older. He had lost a lot of weight, and his shoulders were slumped. His movements were slow, much too slow for a young man.

Putting the coffee pot on the stove, Luther went to the table and sat down beside his brother.

"Before we discuss the war and where Buford and I have been," James Henry began, "I want you to tell me your plans."

"Plans?" Luther questioned, as if he had no conception of the word.

"What do you want to do?" James Henry asked patiently.

Luther shrugged. "I don't know. I used to think I'd like to stay here on the farm. But damn, James Henry, there's no crops, no grain, the house is bare, and I don't have any money."

Placing his arm over Luther's lean shoulders, he replied, "If you want to stay here, Buford and I can give you the money you need to rebuild the farm. But, if you'd rather, you can come to Texas with us."

"Texas!" Luther exclaimed. "Hell, I don't want to live in Texas. This is my home! But where in the hell did you two get any money?''

"We've had it all along. We brought some money with us from Texas.''

"Where is it?'' Luther asked.

"That first night we got here, Buford and I buried it out back behind the well.''

"Well, I'll be damned!'' Luther declared.

"In the morning, we'll take what we need to get us back to Texas and give you the rest.''

"But I don't feel right about taking all your extra money!'' Luther objected.

"That's all right. We have some more buried on our land,'' James Henry explained.

Wiping at the tears springing to his eyes, Luther sobbed, "I can't believe Pa's farm is going to survive the war!''

It took only a gentle coax from James Henry to get Luther to come into his embrace. Holding him close, he said, "Find yourself a good woman, get married, and fill this house with children. When I come back to visit, I want to hear the voices of Stewart children filling these rooms.''

Stiffening, Luther sat straight up. "There's something I have to do before I can think about the future!''

"What's that?''

"Kill Bishop!'' Luther answered coldly.

"Where is Bishop?'' James Henry asked.

"The bastard is living in Lawrence. Two weeks ago, he almost killed a friend of yours.''

"Who?'' James Henry asked urgently.

"A man called Bulldog,'' Luther answered.

"Why in the hell did Bishop try to kill Bulldog?''

"He didn't exactly try to kill him. He just beat him

438

up real bad. But Bulldog might as well be dead.''

"Why?" James Henry asked.

"That goddamned Bishop shot him in both legs. The bullet shattered the bone in his right leg, and Bulldog will never walk on it again. But that's not the worst of it. Bishop kicked the poor bastard between the legs three times. The doctor said Bulldog is ruined. Hell, Bulldog's not even a man anymore. A crippled eunuch, that's what he is!''

"Good God!" James Henry groaned. "But why in the hell did Bishop attack him?''

"I don't know," Luther answered. "Norman Jarrette told me what had happened, but he didn't know the reason behind it.''

"Luther," James Henry began firmly, "I want you to forget about killing Bishop!''

His face red with sudden rage, Luther blurted, "Damn it, James Henry! The war didn't change you at all! You didn't want Ben and me to avenge Ma, and now you don't want me going after Bishop!''

Getting to his feet, Buford grumbled, "Don't get all riled up, Luther.'' Going to the stove, he asked, "Are there any cups?''

"In the cupboard to the right. They only took Ma's good dishes.''

Getting the cups, Buford placed them on the table. Propping his foot on the bench that ran alongside the table, he rested his elbow on his knee, and, looking at Luther, he explained calmly, "James Henry doesn't want you running after Bishop, because he wants to kill the bastard himself.''

Facing James Henry, Luther asked eagerly, "Are you really planning to kill him?''

"Yeah, and the sooner the better. Buford and I will be leaving in a couple of days. Is Pa's old wagon still in the barn?"

Luther nodded. "Hell, James Henry, what do you want with that old thing? It's so damned rickety, the Feds didn't even take it."

James Henry grinned humorously. "I have my reasons."

"I'm going with you!" Luther decided.

"No, you aren't," James Henry replied. "You can't ride into town with us. Do you think ex-guerrillas are welcomed in Lawrence?"

"But you and Buford were guerrillas, and you two are going to Lawrence! Hell, James Henry, the citizens will probably have you both tarred and feathered, if the Feds don't kill you first!"

Buford went to the stove, and, returning with the coffee pot, he filled the cups. "The citizens and the soldiers aren't goin' to pay us any mind," Buford explained. " 'Cause they're goin' to know us as two simple farmers from Illinois." He took the pot back to the stove. Returning, he sat down. He picked up his cup, took a drink, and mumbled, "The people in Lawrence and the soldiers know James Henry and me as Sam and Jamie Tyler."

Puzzled, Luther questioned, "Sam and Jamie Tyler?"

Buford looked at James Henry. "Do you want to tell him, or do you want me to explain everything?"

Grinning, James Henry answered, "You tell him, Pappy."

* * *

The night was late, but James Henry and Buford were still awake. Luther was sleeping on a pallet on the living room floor. James Henry and Buford had bedded down their horses, and had their bedrolls in the house. Now they were sitting at the kitchen table, drinking their second pot of coffee.

"First thing in the morning," James Henry began, "we need to get some food in this house. The only supplies in the pantry are flour, a couple of potatoes, and a bag of oats."

Buford nodded. "Luther's way too skinny. I wonder when the boy last had a decent meal." He sighed, continuing, "But, then, we haven't been eating too good ourselves."

"Tomorrow," James Henry stated, "We're all going to enjoy a feast."

Buford eyed him questioningly. "Are you cooking?"

He chuckled. "I'm no chef, as you very well know, but I'll give it a try."

"Hell, even burnt food would taste good," Buford muttered.

"Are you insinuating I'm going to burn our dinner?"

"No, I'm just stating a fact," Buford grumbled, smiling. Toying with his cup, Buford began hesitantly, "James Henry, before we head out for Lawrence, there's something I have to tell you."

"What's that?"

"Well," Buford replied, "do you remember Cynthia Coffman?"

James Henry thought for a moment before replying, "Amelia's friend?"

"Yeah," Buford answered.

"Sure, I remember her. She was a nice-looking woman."

"When I was working at the Adams' store, Cynthia and I saw a lot of each other. Her husband was killed, and she was working part time for Mrs. Adams. Well, to make a long story short, Cynthia and I . . ."

When his explanation faded, James Henry asked good-humoredly, "Are you trying to tell me that you and Cynthia became intimate friends?"

Buford grinned, answering, "Well, we were intimate, but I don't know about being friends. The last time I saw her, she had a derringer pointed at me."

"This is getting intriguing," James Henry commented. "But why don't you start at the beginning, instead of the end, so I won't become more confused than I already am?"

"Well, that's what I was intending to do!" Buford fussed. "But you had to butt in about intimate friends!"

"I'm all ears, Pappy! So tell me about yourself and the widow Coffman."

As quickly as possible, Buford explained everything to James Henry. He finished by saying, "So if Cynthia is still in Lawrence, she might give us away. She knows we aren't Sam and Jamie Tyler."

"Do you think she will?" he asked.

Buford shrugged. "I don't know. But I don't think she would without warning us first."

"Well, it's a chance we'll have to take," James Henry decided.

Both men remained silent for a long time, before James Henry asked, "If she's in Lawrence, are you planning to ask her to marry you?''

Buford nodded. ''Even though I was once married, Comanche style, I've never asked a woman to marry me. But I'm gonna give it a try.'' Firmly, he added, ''I'll ask her, but I'll only ask one time.''

Smiling, James Henry replied, ''Some women like to be persuaded.''

''Well, I'm not the persuading type. I say what I mean and take what I want. As Cynthia Coffman very well knows.''

Standing, James Henry replied, ''I wish you luck, Pappy. Maybe there'll be three of us traveling to Texas.''

James Henry thought he had kept his feelings hidden, but Buford detected his sadness. ''Cynthia makes you think of Amelia, doesn't she?''

Nodding, James Henry admitted, ''Yes, she does. They were close friends. When we were working at the Eldridge House, I used to see them together a lot. But, Buford, don't let it worry you. If you and Cynthia are married, I'm sure, in time, she won't have that effect on me.'' Heading to his bedroll, he continued casually, ''Well, I think I'll turn in for the night. I'm so tired, I'll probably fall asleep as soon as I lie down.''

Buford knew James Henry wasn't telling the truth. He was fully aware that his nephew would stay awake for a long time, remembering Amelia Bishop.

THIRTY-TWO

Holding Hank's hand, Jason led him out of Lillian's store, with Amelia and Addie following closely behind.

It was a sunny day, and as Amelia stepped outside, she quickly placed her bonnet on her head. She already had too many freckles, without the sun's making more.

The Bishops made an attractive family. Jason was dashingly handsome in his uniform. The two-year-old Hank was a beautiful child. He was dressed in blue knee pants and matching shirt. He still had his baby fat, and his chubby knees were dimpled. Peeking out from beneath his blue cap were black curls that fell to collar length. His eyes were strikingly blue, framed by dark eyebrows and long black lashes. His mother was looking extremely lovely. She was wearing a white dress, patterned with miniature yellow flowers surrounded by dainty green leaves. Her bonnet was white, trimmed with green ribbon. Her golden tresses were pulled back from her face and caught into a cluster of long curls cascading down her back.

Knowing he was in the public eye, Jason fawned over his child and wife. He had some business to take care of, and Amelia, Hank, and Addie were returning to the house. Jason was leaning over to kiss Amelia's cheek when the Rhodes' carriage pulled up in front of the store.

Mrs. Rhodes was holding their six-month-old grandchild, and the colonel carefully assisted her from the carriage. Their son had been killed during the war, and his wife had died in childbirth. The Rhodes had taken the baby to raise in their own home.

Amelia liked the colonel and his wife, and the smile she gave them was sincere.

Mrs. Rhodes hurried to Amelia to proudly show her the baby's first tooth. Exclaiming over the momentous occasion, Amelia took the infant into her arms.

The Bishops and the Rhodeses were too busy discussing babies and their ages for cutting teeth to notice the rickety old wagon entering the end of the street.

As the wagon slowly made its way closer to Adams' Mercantile, Buford was the first to notice Amelia. Brusquely, he pulled up the horses, causing the wagon to jolt to a stop.

"What the hell!" James Henry grumbled, repositioning himself on the seat. He faced Buford with puzzlement, but, noting his shocked expression, he followed Buford's gaze.

Seeing that Amelia was alive, James Henry's first reaction was one of great exultation, and, smiling joyfully, he exclaimed, "He couldn't do it, Buford! Anderson couldn't kill her!" His voice dropped to a thankful whisper, as he moaned, "Anderson! I should have known all along that you wouldn't kill her!"

Blinking back tears of joy, James Henry continued to gaze at the woman he loved. God, she was beautiful! His smile didn't fade all at once, it died slowly, agonizingly slowly, taking his jubilation with it. Not only was she beautiful, but she was also apparently very happy. And, now, the mother of two children.

Moving stiffly, James Henry stepped down from the wagon. The street was busy, and, making his way across it, he mingled with the people walking down the sidewalk. No one paid any attention to the man wearing farmer's overalls, as he paused in the shadow of the barber shop to watch the two families gathered in front of the Adams' store.

Amelia's sudden laughter ringing out with merriment tormented James Henry. If he had known she was alive, he would never have believed that she could have been happy living with Jason Bishop. His jaws clenched tightly, and, fuming, he swore under his breath, "Damn you, Amelia! How can you be happy living with that bastard?"

Amelia was still holding the Rhodes' grandchild, and when she placed a kiss on the baby's cheek, James Henry took it for granted that she was kissing her and Bishop's child. He could tell the baby was too young to have been conceived at Anderson's camp.

Hank's hand was still enclosed in Jason's, but in his other hand the child held a red ball. It was too large for him to continue grasping it, and it slipped loose. It took one solid bounce before rolling down the sidewalk.

Jerking free from Jason's grip, Hank began running after his ball. His short legs were slow in maneuvering, and the ball easily left its owner far behind.

By the time the ball neared James Henry, it had slowed down considerably, and it came to rest at his feet. Kneeling, James Henry picked it up. Perusing the child toddling toward him, he was quite taken with the boy. He started to smile at the child, but the smile never materialized. Instead, it was replaced by a sharp gasp. As Hank drew steadily closer to him, James Henry's eyes became fixed on the child, recognizing his own black hair and blue eyes. Amelia had lied to him! This child didn't belong to Bishop! My God, the boy was his! My son! James Henry realized, the knowledge tearing painfully into his heart . . . My son! He's mine!

Pausing in front of the man, Hank smiled, the smile placing a dimple in each chubby cheek. Holding out his hand for the ball, he said politely, "Tank you, sir."

James Henry was still kneeling, his face eye level with Hank's. Restraining the urge to take the child into his arms, he handed him the ball saying, "You're welcome . . . son."

Turning swiftly, Hank began hurrying back toward the others. Before he was halfway, he was met by Addie, scolding him for running away. Fussing, she took his hand to lead him the rest of the way. Suddenly, Hank turned back around to look at the man who had given him his ball.

James Henry could see an expression of bewilderment on the child's face, before Addie tugged gently at his hand, forcing him to continue moving down the sidewalk.

Standing up, James Henry watched his son's departing back. Remembering that Amelia had named the child Hank, he whispered, "For an instant, Hank, you knew. In some mysterious way, you sensed that we are of the same blood. But you're too innocent to understand what you felt."

Joining him, Buford placed his hand on his nephew's shoulder. Looking at Hank hurrying his short steps to keep pace with Addie's fast strides, Buford remarked calmly, "I knew if you ever saw him, you'd know the truth. He's the spitting image of you."

Brushing Buford's hand from his shoulder, James Henry raged, "Damn you! You knew he was mine, and you didn't tell me!"

"I was going to," Buford replied quickly.

Disgusted with his uncle, Amelia, and his life in general, James Henry's voice was edged with fury as he ordered, "Just get the hell away from me!"

Being short-tempered himself, Buford said angrily, "I was planning to tell you about the boy, James Henry! But if I had told you before, and you had known that Bishop was in charge of your son, would the knowledge have brought you any peace of mind? Hell, knowin' you, you'd probably have deserted the army to come back here and take your son from Bishop."

His rage cooling, James Henry answered, "I'm sorry. I shouldn't have flown off the handle." Grabbing Buford's arm, he clenched it tightly as he continued desperately, "But just how much am I supposed to take without reaching a breaking point? Everyone in my family, except for you and Luther, is dead! The woman I loved is a damned fake! She pretended all those weeks that I actually meant something to her, when all along she was perfectly contented being married to Bishop! Well, apparently she enjoys pretending with her husband, too! Pretending my son is his!''

"Now, damn it," Buford warned gruffly. "You're jumping the gun! You don't know that she's happy with Bishop!''

At that moment, Amelia, enjoying Mrs. Rhodes' company, laughed merrily. As James Henry and Buford looked on, Jason, projecting the role of the blissfully married husband, placed his arm over Amelia's shoulder to draw her close to his side. Playing his role to perfection, Jason kissed his wife's cheek. Jason's chaste kiss sickened Amelia, but, knowing she would suffer Jason's cruelty if she didn't respond properly, she smiled as if his show of affection had meant the world to her.

James Henry's steel-blue eyes gleamed resentfully, as he swore, "I lost most of my family, I lost the woman I loved, but I'll be damned if I'll lose my son!''

Buford shook his head in disbelief. He had sure misjudged Amelia. She knew what kind of man her husband was, and yet she was happy with him. But, all the same, she was Hank's mother. Urgently, Buford replied, "I hope you aren't planning on taking that boy away from his mother.''

"She can keep Bishop's child, but by God, she isn't keeping mine!" Swerving swiftly, James Henry headed for the saloon across the street.

Following him, Buford cursed, "Damn that Stewart temper that flows through our veins!''

An hour later, when James Henry stepped out of the saloon with Buford, his steps were straight. He had indulged in quite a few drinks, but he could carry his liquor well. Looking straight ahead, he didn't see Jason and his three soldiers getting ready to enter the saloon from the side. Jason was fully aware of James Henry's presence, and, knowing him as Jamie Tyler, he purposely bumped into him.

Shoving James Henry aside, he shouted, "Get out of my way, you dirt farmer!"

James Henry didn't say anything, but his inner rage was beginning to boil. Knowing his nephew wouldn't be able to keep a lid on his temper, Buford said gruffly, "Come on, Jamie. Let's go to the hotel."

Reminding himself that the day was coming when he could meet Bishop on equal terms, James Henry decided to take Buford's advice. He took a step to leave, but quickly Jason stuck out his foot, tripping him.

Losing his balance, James Henry tottered precariously, until Jason suddenly shoved him, causing him to fall to the street. He landed face down, and Bishop and his friends were not aware of the uncontrolled anger flickering dangerously in James Henry's eyes.

Grinning shrewdly, Buford turned to the men, listening to their laughter. He didn't need to see his nephew's face to know that Jamie Tyler had temporarily ceased to exist and James Henry Stewart was reborn.

"Bishop!" Buford called dryly, getting his attention. "You're gonna get the hell beat out of you."

Unaware of James Henry getting to his feet, Jason smirked, "Oh yeah? By whom?"

Nodding toward the man leaping at Bishop, Buford replied casually, "By him."

James Henry's body slammed into Jason, sending them both crashing through the saloon doors and onto the floor. The customers jumped from their chairs, as Jason's men and Buford rushed inside.

Springing to his feet, James Henry doubled his strong hands into fists. His handsome face distorted with hate, he bellowed, "Get up, you sonofabitch!"

Temporarily shocked, Jason stared at the man he believed to be Jamie Tyler. Then suddenly, he sneered. Hell, that farmer couldn't whip him. He'd beat the dumb ass to a pulp, and then kick in his face for good measure!

Lithely, Jason leaped to his feet. Jason's swing was fast and strong, but, moving defensively, James Henry blocked the right hook with his left arm. Countering, James Henry jabbed with his right, catching Jason flush on the jaw.

The solid blow knocked Jason stumbling backwards. Believing the man's punch had to be one of pure luck, Jason came back at James Henry, intending to strike him across the jaw before delivering a blow to his stomach.

But James Henry was ready for Jason, and, taking him off guard, his fist plowed into Bishop's face, landing across his nose.

Knocked to his knees, Jason's hand flew to his injured nose. Seeing blood dripping through his fingers and down onto his uniform, Jason panicked. Goddamn, the man could actually fight! Well, he'd be damned if he'd put up with his disrespect to his superiors! He'd teach the dirt farmer a thing or two!

Standing, Jason lunged for a whiskey bottle. Grabbing it, he smashed it against a table, turning it into a jagged and dangerous weapon.

Sneering sardonically, he inched his way closer to

James Henry. "You bastard!" Jason threatened. "I'm going to cut you to pieces!"

Bouncing lightly on the balls of his feet, James Henry grinned. "Come on, captain! I'm ready for you!"

Thrusting smoothly, Jason swung the broken bottle, but, avoiding it, James Henry backed away. Once again, Jason swung at him, but this, too, James Henry easily dodged.

Frustrated, Jason swung the bottle wildly, and, ducking it as it went over his head, James Henry lunged at Jason, shoving him across the floor and to the end of the room. As Jason's back hit against the wall, James Henry clutched the man's wrist, his grip tightening painfully. Forcefully, he pounded Jason's hand against the solid wall until he dropped the broken bottle. Then, grabbing Jason by the lapels on his jacket, he swung him around. Drawing back his arm, he hit him over the left eye, sending Jason sprawling to the floor.

Realizing he couldn't win the fight, Jason reached for his pistol, jerking it out of its holster. But, moving quickly, Buford kicked the gun from his hand.

"Come on, captain." Jason's men encouraged. "Get up and fight!"

Leaning over Jason, Buford grabbed him by the shoulders, assisting him. "I'll help you to your feet, captain."

Jason didn't want to get back up to fight. He wanted to run out of the saloon. But if he did, he knew he could never live down the shame. He had no choice but to take a beating, but, by God, Jamie Tyler would rue the day he had publicly humiliated him! He would kill the bastard, if he had to wait until Jamie entered a dark alley to shoot him in the back.

The moment Jason was standing, James Henry came at him. His fists seemed to be everywhere, delivering a sharp blow to Jason's chin, a powerful jab to his stomach, and sending him back to the floor with a sudden right hook to the side of Jason's head.

Dropping to the floor, James Henry straddled Jason, and, his hate driving him mad, he continued striking his fists across Jason's face.

Knowing James Henry was perfectly capable of killing, Buford lunged for him, forcefully pulling him off Bishop. Restraining him, Buford warned quietly, "Damn it! If you kill Bishop here in front of witnesses, the law will lock you away for a lifetime, if they don't decide to hang you instead."

Buford's warning got through to James Henry, and, relaxing, he answered, "I'm all right."

Before releasing him, Buford asked cautiously, "Are you sure?"

James Henry nodded. "Yeah. You can turn me loose, Pappy."

Respectfully, the soldiers and the customers stepped aside for the two men to leave. It had been a fair match and one helluva good fight!

As they walked outside, Buford nearly bumped into the woman strolling past the saloon. "Excuse me, ma'am," he mumbled, before looking at her.

Coming face to face with Buford, Cynthia gasped sharply, "Buford!" she cried.

Smiling, he replied, "Cynthia!"

But quickly, before he could say anything to her, she gathered her long skirts in her hands and fled down the sidewalk.

Turning to James Henry, Buford said hastily, "Go to the hotel and get our rooms. I'll meet you there later."

As Buford hurried after Cynthia, James Henry called, "Good luck, Pappy!"

Reaching Cynthia's home, Buford leaped the short flight of steps leading up to the porch, and, crossing it in two long strides, he knocked on the door. When he received no answer, he struck his large fist against it, banging the door so powerfully that it vibrated.

"Cynthia!" he yelled. "Open this door, or I'll break it down!"

Slowly, the door opened a few inches, leaving a narrow slit for Cynthia to see through. "Please, Buford, go away!" she pleaded.

Buford shoved the door aside, and as he stomped through the doorway Cynthia backed away from him. Grabbing the door, he slammed it closed.

Standing in the small foyer, Buford's eyes raked over Cynthia. She was even lovelier than he had remembered. She had retired her widow's weeds and was wearing a dress patterned with bright colors. It was cut low in front, revealing the soft swell of her ample breasts. Her chestnut-brown hair was piled on top of her head, with long ringlets framing her face. Looking into her large gray eyes, he murmured, "I told you I'd come back."

"I wish you hadn't!" she gasped, breathing rapidly.

"Why did you run away from me?" he demanded. Wringing her hands nervously, she stammered,

"What happened between us before must never happen again."

"Why?" he asked gruffly.

Pleadingly, she cried, "Surely you must know why! You were my husband's enemy! I loved and respected David, and I won't dishonor his memory!"

"I wasn't responsible for your husband's death!" he replied.

Upset, she shouted furiously, "You rode under Bill Anderson, and it was Anderson and his men who killed David!"

For a moment, her accusation confused him, but then, understanding, he explained quickly, "I didn't serve under Anderson."

Enraged, she fumed, "Oh, don't you dare lie to me! How can you stand there and tell me you never rode with Captain Anderson!"

Unruffled, he replied, "All right. I did ride with him a few times, but I never killed any Federals. When the shooting began, I was surrounded by Anderson's men. They protected me with their own bodies as they got me away from the fighting as quickly as possible."

"Why were you protected?" she asked.

"Because I wasn't a Missouri guerrilla. I was a Confederate spy."

Taken aback, she cried, "A Confederate!"

"I was in the Confederate Army. The man you know as Jamie is my nephew James Henry. Before we joined the Confederate troops in Virginia, we were spies. But we never spied for Missouri. So I was not even remotely responsible for your husband's death."

Cynthia was relieved to learn that the man she loved hadn't been a guerrilla. But, all the same, her loyalties to the Union held steadfast. Flustered, she stuttered, "But . . . but you're a Southerner and . . . and I'm a Northerner." Her voice gaining conviction, she stated firmly, "We could never bridge such a distance!"

Buford grinned, and, observing his smile, she recalled how it could so easily tear down her defenses. Slowly he began approaching her, and she wanted desperately to flee, but her knees were growing so weak that she couldn't move.

Still grinning, Buford effortlessly swept her into his strong arms. "Where's your bedroom?" he asked.

"No!" she protested. "Put me down!"

"It's a small house," he remarked calmly. "I'm sure I can find it."

As Cynthia fought against him, he quickly carried her down the narrow hallway and into the bedroom, where he laid her down on the soft mattress.

Immediately she attempted to get up, but before she could succeed, he was beside her. Placing one leg over hers, he grabbed her wrists, pinning her to the bed.

She was helpless against his superior strength, and, surrendering, she ceased her fighting.

Keeping her arms restrained with one hand, he used his other hand to caress her breasts. Leaning over her, he sent fleeting kisses down her neck, before he moved his lips upwards, finding her mouth with his.

His tongue darted between her teeth, exploring the inside of her mouth. Continuing to kiss her, he moved his hand down to her full skirts. Tugging at them, he slipped his hand beneath her petticoats, his fingers touching her bare skin.

Gently he parted her legs, so he could run his palm along the inside of her leg as it traveled upwards.

When he touched the softness between her thighs, Cynthia groaned beneath Buford's lips. He broke their kiss long enough to whisper, "I love you, Cynthia." Then immediately his mouth was back on hers, the intensity in his kiss stimulating her passion.

He freed her wrists, and, placing her arms about his neck, she pressed her lips closer to his.

Feeling her respond, Buford's own passion soared, and nimbly he moved his hand to the inside of her lace pants, his fingers finding and entering her warmth.

He lowered his head to the swell of her breasts, and, as he kissed her soft flesh, his fingers worked magic, driving Cynthia to heights of ecstasy. Excited beyond reason, she parted her legs wider, relishing his possession of her. Suddenly his lips were once again on hers, and, matching his passion, she kissed him intimately and boldly. His fingers quickly probing in and out of her, Buford brought Cynthia to such an electrifying satisfaction that she trembled uncontrollably.

Kneeling on the bed, Buford began to remove her clothes. Impatient to have him take her completely, she hurriedly assisted him.

Stepping to the floor, he hastily discarded his own clothes. Returning to the bed, he knelt between her spread legs. His eyes never leaving hers, he ran his hands across her shoulders, over her breasts, down to her waist, and finally, to the brown triangle between her thighs.

"Buford!" she sighed passionately. "I want you!"

Still kneeling, he grasped her, easing her farther down the bed. Then, placing his hands on her legs, he wrapped them around his waist. Positioning her, he began sliding his throbbing phallus into her, and, feeling her heat enclose him, he groaned fervently.

"Oh Buford!" Cynthia purred, loving his male hardness entering her deeper and deeper.

Clutching her waist, he pulled her closer as he began thrusting against her. He pounded into her strongly, sending stimulating chills through Cynthia's entire being. Knowing his need for Cynthia had gone beyond his control, Buford lunged forward for his deepest penetration. Grabbing her legs, he placed them over his shoulders, causing her to cry out with an ecstasy she had never before experienced.

His hips moving back and forth, Buford took her powerfully, bringing them both to an exciting and fulfilling climax.

Exhausted, Buford dropped to the bed beside her. "Damn!" he moaned. "You're one helluva woman!"

Flustered, Cynthia made no reply. Why did she respond so wantonly to this man? She and David had never made love like this! Why, my goodness, Buford made her act like a shameless hussy! But . . . but he also made her feel like a complete woman!

Lying on his side, Buford raised up on his elbow, and, leaning his head on his palm, he smiled down into Cynthia's flushed face. Understanding her dilemma, he teased, "Beneath all that ladylike primness, you're a hot little woman."

Offended, she spat, "How dare you!"

Chuckling, he took her into his arms, hugging her tightly. "All my life," he began, "I've been looking for a real woman, and now, at last, I've found one." Looking into her eyes, he asked, "Cynthia, will you marry me?"

"No!" she cried quickly.

Her refusal didn't surprise Buford, but it did anger him. Brusquely, he released her, and stood. He began putting on his clothes. "You're a fool, Cynthia! Because you believe you owe your dead husband and the Union your unselfish and undying loyalties, you're going to throw away the good life we could have together."

"Oh, Buford, I could never make you understand!" she replied desperately.

Slipping on his trousers, he answered, "I told you I'd come back and ask you to marry me. Well, I did what I said I was goin' to do. But I won't beg or plead with you to change your mind." Rising, he put on his shirt and buttoned it. He continued, "James Henry and I will be in Lawrence for a few days. I hope I can trust you not to give our true identities away. I'll be staying at the Eldridge House, so if you should have second thoughts about my marriage proposal, you know where to find me."

"Buford," she began pleadingly, "I didn't refuse your proposal because I don't love you. I do love you! But as I said before, we could never bridge that endless distance between us!"

The sudden anger on his face startled Cynthia. Stepping to the bed, he grabbed her legs, jerking them to the edge. Quickly he undid his trousers, and, releasing the buttons, he freed himself. Seeing his unexpected erection, Cynthia gasped. Parting her legs, he placed himself over her, entering her swiftly. Instantly her passion was aroused, and, wrapping her legs around him, she met his demanding thrusts, time and time again.

Buford's second climax came to him suddenly, and,

clutching her buttocks, he held her tight against him.

Releasing her abruptly, he stood beside the bed. Impatiently, he grumbled, "That, you little fool, is how we can bridge the distance!"

Before Cynthia had time to think of a reply, he had his trousers buttoned, his boots on, and had stormed out of her room.

THIRTY-THREE

Barging into the house, Jason closed the door by slamming it. Amelia was in the parlor dusting bric-a-brac, and the sudden noise caused her almost to drop one of her most treasured pieces. Returning it to the mantel above the fireplace, she whirled quickly, observing Jason as he stomped into the room.

Catching sight of his bruised face, Amelia gasped, "My goodness, Jason! What happened to you?"

Going to the liquor cabinet, he poured himself a glass of brandy. Before taking a big drink, he answered impatiently, "What in the hell do you think happened? I was in a fight!"

Holding back the urge to smile, Amelia went to his side. Examining him, she saw that his left eye was cut badly, his nose was swollen, and his cheeks and chin were full of abrasions. Lowering her gaze, she studied his hands, but not one knuckle had been bruised or cut.

Raising her eyebrows, she said cunningly, "Apparently, you never got in so much as one punch."

Frowning, he snapped, "You'd like to see me beaten to a pulp, wouldn't you?"

In public, Amelia knew she had no other choice but to behave the way Jason wanted her to, but in private she made no bones about the way she felt. She would say whatever came to her mind, which was usually a flippant remark. For a short time, Jason would tolerate her disrespect. But his patience would quickly give out, and he'd threaten her with Hank. Submissively, Amelia would return to being docile; until the next time.

Smugly, she replied, "Any beating you received, Jason, would be one you richly deserved."

Jason's anger was still boiling. He had never been so publicly humiliated! Taking out his anger on Amelia, he drew back his hand, slapping her across the face.

Her cheek was stinging, but she refused to let him see that his brutality had any effect. Holding her head haughtily, she asked, "Who did you fight with? I want to go to the man and personally thank him."

Amelia's insolence cost her another slap to the face, but still she refused to be browbeaten. Calmly, she walked away from him and returned to her dusting. Picking up one of the pieces of bric-a-brac, she asked again, "Who did you fight with, Jason? Who is my hero of the hour?"

Finishing his brandy, he set the glass down heavily. Furiously, he grumbled, "Jamie Tyler!"

The porcelain figurine Amelia was holding slipped from her hand, and, hitting the floor, it shattered into little pieces.

Disgusted, Jason complained, "Must you be so clumsy?"

Her heart pounding rapidly, she cried, "Did you say

Jamie Tyler?''

Unmindful of his wife's excitement, he mumbled, ''That goddamned farmer who used to work at the hotel!''

''When did he come back to town?'' she asked urgently.

''I don't know!'' he answered testily. ''I suppose they got in sometime today.''

''They?'' she questioned.

Impatient with her questions, he snapped, ''That uncouth Sam Tyler is with him!''

Buford! Amelia exclaimed to herself. Oh, Cynthia! They came back! Just as you predicted they would! James Henry! James Henry! Amelia's heart cried over and over.

''Where are they staying?'' she asked suddenly.

''How in the hell would I know?'' Jason shouted. Crossing the room, he told her, ''I'm going to wash up. In a few minutes, bring the medical kit to my room. I want you to doctor my cuts.''

The moment he left, Amelia removed her apron, throwing it on the sofa. Hurrying to the mirror hanging above the hat rack, she made a quick examination of her hair. It was a little mussed, but it would do.

Fleeing, she headed for the front door. Opening it, she glanced down the hallway toward Jason's bedroom. All the resentment she had for her husband gleamed in her eyes as she cursed under her breath, ''Doctor your cuts yourself, you bastard!''

Flinging the door closed, Amelia darted across the porch and down the walkway. Where would she find James Henry? Where? The Eldridge House, of course! James Henry and Buford would need to stay at a hotel, and naturally they would choose that one.

Amelia never had a calm thought as she rushed down the sidewalk into town and toward the Eldridge House. Her hopes and dreams had come true! James Henry had come back to Lawrence!

Darting into the hotel, Amelia raced to the front desk. Breathless, she asked Mr. Cramer, "Is Jamie Tyler staying here?"

Wondering why Mrs. Bishop would want to visit Jamie Tyler, he answered hesitantly, "Well . . . yes, ma'am, he is."

"Which room?" she snapped, her eyes glittering with excitement.

Concerned, he inquired, "Mrs. Bishop, are you well?"

"Of course, I'm well!" she blurted testily. But, suddenly, she smiled radiantly. "In fact, I have never felt better!" When Mr. Cramer made no reply, her temperament changed rapidly. Frowning, she spat, "Well?"

"Well, what?" he questioned, confused.

"Which room is Jamie Tyler in?" she demanded crossly.

"Room 215," he answered. She turned to leave, but Mr. Cramer said hastily, "Mrs. Bishop, wouldn't you rather I sent someone for him, and then you can talk to him in the lobby?"

"Why would I want to talk to him in the lobby?" she exclaimed.

A trifle embarrassed, Mr. Cramer explained, "Well, you are a lady, and it isn't proper for you to be alone with a gentleman in his room."

Laughing, Amelia rushed to the stairs. "It's perfectly all right, Mr. Cramer. Don't worry!'' Before climbing the steps, she looked back at him. Distinctly, she ordered, ''And, Mr. Cramer, see to it that Jamie and I are not disturbed!''

Leaving Mr. Cramer dumbfounded, she fled up the stairs. Entering the hallway, she hurried to room 215. Pausing in front of the door, she doubled her hand into a fist to knock, but instead she moved her hand to her mouth, nervously nibbling at her knuckles. James Henry believed her to be dead! My goodness, seeing her again, so unexpectedly, would be very traumatic for him. Should she first call out to him and soften the shock? Amelia smiled happily. No! she decided. She wanted to see his face when he saw her. She knocked lightly on his door, waiting enthusiastically for him to open it. Oh, his handsome face would be so full of wonder and joy!

The door swung open, and James Henry, standing in the doorway, looked at Amelia with cold resentment. ''What do you want?'' he asked irritably.

Astounded, Amelia cried, ''James Henry! Dear Lord, what's wrong with you? Don't you even care that I'm alive?''

Shrugging, he replied unemotionally, ''I'm thankful that you're alive.'' Moving away from the doorway, he ambled over to the window. Gazing outside, he asked ill-temperedly, ''Why are you here?''

Hesitantly, Amelia entered the room, closing the door behind her. She wanted to run to him and throw herself into his arms, but his attitude held her at bay. What was wrong? Didn't she mean anything to him?

Holding back her tears, she stood quietly, studying him intently. In the privacy of his room, James Henry

467

had exchanged the loose overalls for tan trousers and a brown shirt. Her eyes examined every inch of him, loving his tall, slim frame. His black hair had grown longer and was touching his collar. His sideburns were thick, tapering down to his short, trimmed beard. His shirt was unbuttoned, revealing the dark mass of hair that covered his chest. She lowered her gaze. His pants clung skin-tight across his hard thighs and long, muscular legs. Her eyes came to rest on the male bulge at his crotch. Her breathing deepened, and her knees grew weak as the passion he could so easily awaken in her began racing through her pulse.

Slowly, he turned his gaze from the window. Looking at her, he noticed how the sun's rays filtering into the bedroom fell across her golden tresses, making them shine radiantly. She was wearing her hair pulled away from her face, caught up into a cluster of curls at the back of her neck. Remembering how he loved to see it free, falling gracefully to her hips, James Henry said impulsively, "Let down your hair."

Surprised by his unexpected request, she stammered, "Wh . . . what?"

"You heard me!" he snapped.

Hurt and confused by his unjust anger, her hands trembled as she released her long tresses. Watching the golden strands cascading over her shoulders and down past her waist, he caught his breath. Raspingly, he moaned, "You're so damned beautiful!"

Amelia waited with anticipation for him to say more but he fell silent. She tried to read his expression, but it was emotionless. Feeling ill at ease, she attempted to make conversation. Stammering, she questioned, "Why . . . why were you . . . fighting with Jason?"

Amelia didn't care about the reason behind their fight. She asked the question because she was at a loss for words. But, misunderstanding her purpose, he asked angrily, "Is that why you're here? Are you worried about your husband's welfare? Did you come here to plead for his worthless life?"

Taken aback, she cried softly, "No, of course not!"

Unable to control his temper, James Henry became unreasonable. "Well, if you aren't here for Bishop's benefit, then you must be here for your own! What is it that you want from me?" He smirked bitterly, "Does your husband still leave you cold in bed, so you came here to reclaim your virile stud?" Unexpectedly, his rage cooled, and, grinning, he continued, "Well, I haven't enjoyed a woman since you and I stayed at Anderson's camp. Let's see, that was . . . twenty months ago. So, Mrs. Bishop, I should have no problem getting it up for you." Gruffly, he ordered, "Take off your clothes and get in bed!"

Speechless, Amelia could only stand motionless as she watched him close the drapes, then go to the door and lock it.

Glaring at her, he snapped, "Well? What are you waiting for? Take off your clothes, so your stud can service you!"

All the pain and heartache Amelia had suffered for the past twenty months turned into uncontrolled rage. She was holding her hairpins, and, her temper flaring, she threw them at him. As they bounced off his chest, she yelled resentfully, "How dare you come back into my life and treat me so heartlessly! For nearly two years, I have dreamed and prayed for the day you and I would be together again! The hope that you would re-

469

turn to Lawrence was all that saved my sanity! And, now, you act as if you couldn't care less about me! You aren't even happy that I'm alive!''

"Happy?" he repeated, sneering. "When I first saw you a couple of hours ago, I was more than happy to see you alive. I was ecstatic!''

"A couple of hours ago?" she asked, puzzled.

"When Buford and I came into town, I saw you in front of your aunt's store. You, a colonel, and a woman I presume was his wife, Bishop, and your two children.''

"Two children?" she questioned. Then, understanding, she explained quickly, "The baby isn't my child. He's the colonel's grandson.''

Her reply startled James Henry. He had never thought the child might not be hers. But the knowledge did nothing to lighten his bitterness, and irritably he continued expressing his anger. "I stood at the barber shop, watching the domestic gathering. I listened to your laughter, and I wondered how in the hell you could be so giddy and lighthearted with that sonofa-bitch who is your husband standing at your side. Buford told me not to be so fast to pass judgment, but when Bishop kissed you, and I saw you look at him as if he were the most wonderful man in the world, I knew you as the fake you are!'' Stepping forward, he grabbed her wrist, clutching it painfully. His eyes glaring madly, he snarled, "You know him for the heartless bastard he is! How in God's name can you love him?''

Outraged, Amelia jerked free of his grip. Her eyes rolling hysterically, she shrieked, "Love him? I hate him! I despise him!''

470

Retorting angrily, he raged, "Is that why you look at him with open worship?"

For a moment Amelia was so distressed that she lost her voice and could only gasp convulsively. Finally, controlling herself, she explained weakly, "When Jason and I are in public, if I don't play the role of the loving wife, I suffer his cruelty."

"Cruelty?" he scoffed.

Amelia moved her hands to the back of her dress, but they were shaking so badly that she could barely get the tiny buttons loose. Clutching the top of her dress, she pulled it down to her waist. Then, tugging at the straps to her petticoat, she jerked it downwards, baring herself from the waist up.

Staring into James Henry's confused face, she spat, "Yes, his cruelty, which he inflicts like this!" Whirling, she turned her back to him.

James Henry's gasp was so strong that it sounded throughout the room. The lashes Jason had delivered across Amelia's back were two weeks old, but they hadn't faded. The worst ones were still bright red.

All the fight drained from Amelia, and, bowing her head, she began crying pathetically.

James Henry took a step toward her, but his rage toward Bishop and himself caused him to swerve to the door, hitting it powerfully with his fist.

Startled, Amelia whirled about. Her heart breaking for the man she loved, she watched him as he pounded his fist against the solid door until, finally, his rage mellowed. Then, placing his arm across the door, he leaned his head on his arm, moaning, "Oh God, Amelia, how can you ever forgive me?"

Pulling up her petticoat, she hurried to him. Gently,

she touched his shoulder, and as he turned to look at her, she whispered, "I love you, James Henry."

She could see a trace of tears in his eyes, as he confessed hoarsely, "I love you! I've always loved you!"

He drew her into his arms, and for a long time he simply held her close. Then, tenderly, he moved her so that he could bring his mouth to hers.

Wrapping her arms about his neck, Amelia pressed her body to his. Relishing his kiss, she parted her lips beneath his. James Henry's passion began to simmer, and, enclosing her tiny waist within his arms, he held her thighs tightly to his. Feeling him growing hard, she moaned with longing as her tongue entered his mouth, driving him wild with desire.

Removing his lips from hers, James Henry gasped, "I can't wait any longer! I must have you now!"

Her own need was burning out of control, and, breathing rapidly, she murmured, "Oh yes! Yes, my darling!"

Quickly he helped her to undress. Then, leading her to the bed, he drew back the covers. He watched her as she lay on the bed, waiting for the man she loved to claim her. Lying at her side, he kissed her mouth, then moved his lips to her breasts, her stomach, and then to the most intimate part of her body. His warm tongue flickered against her, and Amelia groaned passionately, as tingling chills ran up and down her spine. She parted her legs, and he moved between them. Fervently, she cried, "Oh, James Henry, I have never belonged to any man but you! Oh darling, love me! Love me!"

Knowing how to please the woman he loved, James Henry's hands, mouth, and tongue took Amelia to such heights of arousal that she trembled, writhed, and moaned with ecstasy.

Stepping to the floor, he hastily removed his clothes, letting them drop in a disorderly heap. Returning to the bed, and lying again at her side, he placed her leg over his hip. She was ready for his entry, and he pulled her toward him, his hard organ easily penetrating her.

Loving the feel of him, she shoved her thighs to his, taking him all the way inside her. "Oh, James Henry!" she whispered shakily.

"I know . . . I know, little one. It feels so wonderful!" he groaned.

His mouth came crushing down on hers, and, excited beyond reason, she moved her hips back and forth, riding him uncontrollably.

Enjoying her domination, he remained inside her as he sat up on the bed, taking her with him. Sitting on the edge of the bed, he held her in his lap. She bent her legs beside him, and, placing his hands on her waist, he guided her up and down, causing his erection to slip in and out of her. Her yearning carrying her to its glorious peak, Amelia wrapped her legs around his waist, and, putting his hands beneath her buttocks, James Henry groaned aloud as she thrust against him, time after time.

His passion reaching its highest point, he held Amelia to him tightly, releasing his seed deep inside her.

Gently he eased Amelia to the bed, and, lying beside her, he took her into his arms. For a long time, they remained silent. They were too contented being close to each other to find words necessary.

Amelia snuggled her head on his shoulder, and, sighing deeply, she realized the time had come to tell James Henry about Hank. Recalling how relieved he had been when he believed he hadn't fathered her child, she became hesitant. But he had to be told! She couldn't keep it a secret any longer!

"James Henry," she whispered.

Pulling her closer, he murmured, "What, little one?"

"I have something I must tell you. It has to do with my son."

"Your son?" he questioned. "Don't you mean our son?"

Surprised, she sat up, looking down at him. "How did you know?" she cried.

"This afternoon when you and the others were in front of the store, do you remember when Hank's ball rolled down the sidewalk?"

"Yes, I remember. Hank chased after it, and I sent Addie to get him."

"Well, the ball rolled to where I was standing. I knelt and picked it up for him. I took one look at the boy and knew he was my son." He paused, then asked, "Why didn't you tell me he was mine?"

"The day you, Buford, and Colonel Garson found me in the woods, I would rather have died than admit to you that you had fathered my child. But, later, there were times when I wanted to tell you."

"Why didn't you?"

"I kept remembering how relieved you had been when I told you you weren't his father."

Gently, he drew her back into his arms. "I was relieved, but not for the reasons you probably believed. I couldn't have borne the thought of Bishop claiming a child that belonged to me.''

Smiling, Amelia asked, ''When you saw Hank, what did you think of him?''

Enthused, he answered, ''He made me so proud, I felt ten feet tall! By the way, why did you name him Hank?''

''You don't like his name?'' she asked, feeling disappointed.

''I was just wondering how you came to give him the name. But don't misunderstand me. I like the name just fine.''

Relieved that he approved, she answered, ''It's a nickname for Henry. You see,'' she added happily, ''his Christian name is James Henry.''

''What!'' he exclaimed.

Quickly she explained that Hank was named after her father and Jason's.

Laughing, he replied, ''Well, I'll be damned!'' He hugged her tightly for a moment, then, loosening his grip, he said seriously, ''Amelia, I want you to begin with the day I left you at Anderson's camp, and tell me everything that has happened to you.''

The minutes ticked by as Amelia brought James Henry up to date on her life. When she had told Cynthia about the conspiracy she shared with Captain Anderson, she had known that Cynthia had sympathized with her. But, all the same, Amelia knew that Cynthia couldn't possibly understand how she could have remained loyal to a man who was the Union's enemy. But as she explained it all to James Henry, she could tell he understood completely, and she read in his eyes how much he admired her for holding steadfast to her promise, even at the cost of being labled a traitor and an adulteress. Amelia found it very painful to discuss Gary and Pat's deaths, as well as Bill Anderson's. When she told James Henry about the circumstances that instigated the two beatings she had received from Jason, he made no comment, but she knew his hate for Jason had grown stronger.

When she finished telling him everything, he in turn told her about his life. She learned that he had never been a Missouri guerrilla, but a Confederate spy, and had finally been transferred to the Northern Virginia Army.

"Whatever happened to Colonel Garson?" she asked curiously.

"He's alive and well," he answered. Sitting up, James Henry continued, "I want you to get dressed, then go home and get Hank. If Bishop isn't there, pack both of you some clothes. But if he's home, forget the clothes. Take Hank with you to your aunt's store and wait there for me."

"What are you going to do?" she asked.

Slipping into his clothes, he answered, "Buford should be here soon. He and I have plans to discuss."

"What kind of plans?"

"I'm going to ask Buford to take you and Hank out of Lawrence and head for Texas."

Bolting straight up, she objected, "No! Not without you!"

"I'll catch up to you later," he answered firmly.

"You're staying here to kill Jason, aren't you?" she accused angrily.

"You're damned right!" he shouted.

Desperately, she pleaded, "James Henry, forget revenge! Let's just run away to Texas and be happy!"

"Happy?" he smirked. "I could never be happy as long as that sonofabitch is walking the face of this earth! He killed Anne, caused my father and Becky's deaths, beat you, and tried to cripple Bulldog! And, if what Luther heard is true, Bulldog may now be only half a man!"

"What do you mean?" she cried.

"Bishop shot Bulldog in both legs, and the bullet shattered the bone in his right leg. Then the sorry bastard kicked Bulldog in the groin three times!" Sympathizing with his friend as one man to another, James Henry continued harshly, "Bulldog might never again know the pleasure of a woman!"

Finding her husband's treatment of Bulldog too horrible to think about, Amelia blocked it from her mind, unaware that her refusal to accept it was being controlled by her guilt. If she had never talked to Bulldog that day, nothing would have happened to him.

Leaping from the bed, she pleaded, "James Henry, please don't go after Jason! I'm so afraid he'll kill you!"

"There's no power on this earth that could keep me from Bishop!" he answered flatly.

"Not even my love?" she asked intensely.

He shook his head. "I'm sorry, Amelia."

Slowly she began putting on her clothes. As a thought suddenly struck her, she said hastily, "What about Cynthia? She might want to marry Buford."

"Then she'll have to leave on the spur of the moment, just like the rest of you."

She slipped into her dress, and, turning around so that he could fasten the buttons, she asked carefully,

477

"What should Buford and I do if you don't join us?" They both knew only his death could prevent him from catching up to them.

He placed his hands on her shoulders, and, pulling her against him, he answered, "You'll go to Texas. My home will belong to you and my son. With Buford to take care of you both, you'll be all right. Even if he marries Cynthia, he'll always be there to help you and Hank."

Turning, she flung herself into his arms. Holding him close, she cried, "Oh James Henry, please forget Jason! Killing him won't bring you any pleasure! The Bible preaches, vengeance is mine, sayeth the Lord! Oh James Henry, I beg you to let God deal with Jason!"

"If God was going to deal with Bishop, He would have sent him to the Devil long before now!"

Grasping on to her last shred of hope, Amelia held him tightly, whispering, "But the Lord works in mysterious ways."

Mysteriously, at that moment, there was a huge bulk of a man slipping up to the Bishops' door. Finding it unlocked, he pulled out his Colt revolver and crept silently into the house.

THIRTY-FOUR

The man closed the door, then quietly secured the lock. His right leg was stiff, making it difficult for him to walk soundlessly. Limping, he investigated the parlor, but, finding no one there, he moved down the hallway. When he reached Jason's bedroom, the door was ajar. Pausing, he looked inside, and seeing Jason asleep, he entered the room. His strides were awkward, but silent, and, going to the bed, he pulled up a hard-backed chair. Easing his huge frame onto it, he stretched out his lame leg. Frowning, he massaged it. Damn, the leg pained him! Resting, his discomfort was relieved. Toying with his Colt revolver, he turned his attention to Bishop, who was sleeping soundly. He was fully dressed, lying on top of the covers. The man started to wake him, but changed his mind. His body wasn't healed yet, and the ride to Lawrence had tired him. He would rest for a few minutes, before he killed the sonofabitch.

Darting out of the hotel, Amelia rushed down the sidewalk. She must hurry! She had to return home, get

479

Hank, and then go to Lillian's store to wait for James Henry. She hoped desperately that Jason would be gone, so she could pack clothes for Hank and herself. She was tempted to ask Buford to take only Hank and leave her here with James Henry, but she knew he would never agree. She had no choice but to leave the man she loved and pray that he would soon be joining her.

To reach her house, she had to pass the Adams' Mercantile, and as she approached the store, she caught sight of Addie walking out the door.

Hurrying to her, she asked, "Addie, where is Hank?"

"He's visiting with Mrs. Adams. I hope you don't mind. But I have a little shopping I need to do, and Hank so enjoys being with your aunt."

"No, of course not," Amelia replied quickly.

"Well, ma'am, I think I'll get on with my shopping."

"Please, don't let me keep you," Amelia answered vaguely, her thoughts racing fluidly.

As Addie walked away, Amelia tried to decide what to do. Should she take the chance that Jason would be gone, and go home and pack clothes, or should she stay here?

Before Amelia could make a decision, the door to the store was opened again. Stepping outside, Colonel Rhodes exclaimed, "Mrs. Bishop! I'm so glad I ran into you! I was just on my way to your home to see you and Captain Bishop. I have some very good news to tell you both!"

"News?" she repeated vacantly.

"Yes! It has to do with your husband's transfer," he

480

replied brightly.

"Oh," she mumbled, not in the least interested.

Moving to her side, he touched her arm saying, "I have my horse, but I'll walk you to your house."

She couldn't take Colonel Rhodes home with her! If Jason was there, and they had a guest to entertain, it could be an hour or longer before she could get away from the house. And if Jason wasn't home, the colonel might decide to wait for him.

"B . . . but I wasn't going home," she stammered.

"Nonsense!" he objected. "You must be there when I tell Captain Bishop the news. You see, Mrs. Bishop, not only has he been granted the transfer he wanted, but he has also received a promotion!"

Not knowing what else to say, she once again mumbled, "Oh."

The colonel was disappointed at her lack of enthusiasm. But never one to pass judgment harshly, he decided it was because she was a woman, and how was a woman to understand the honor and prestige that went with a promotion. He was sure the captain would want his wife at his side when he heard the wonderful news, and he insisted, "Come, my dear, I'll walk home with you."

Hesitantly, she began walking beside him. Somehow, she would find a way to leave the house and sneak back to the store!

They had only taken a few steps, when Mrs. Kelley, strolling in the opposite direction from Amelia and the colonel, met them head on. At once, Mrs. Kelley halted them to begin one of her lengthly conversations, and, plastering a smile on her face, Amelia pretended to be listening. She could feel time literally slipping

481

away. She wondered how long Mrs. Kelley would talk.

Sitting up straight, the man positioned his stiff leg, trying to make himself more comfortable. The time had come to rouse the sonofabitch. Leaning over, he grabbed the side of the bed, shaking it.

Being awakened so abruptly, Jason's eyes flew open, and, bolting straight up, he grumbled, "What the hell!" Suddenly, seeing the man sitting beside his bed, Jason paled. "Bulldog!" he gasped.

Smiling, Bulldog replied, "So you remember me, huh?"

"What are you doing here?" Jason exclaimed, his voice tinged with fright.

Evenly, Bulldog answered, "Now, just what in the hell do you think I'm doin' here?"

"Good God, man!" Jason bellowed desperately. "If you kill me, you'll never get away with it! The army will catch you! Do you want to be hanged?"

"Don't make much difference to me one way or another," Bulldog answered dryly. Gesturing with his pistol, Bulldog ordered, "Get up and walk over there by the bureau. I ain't never shot a man while he's in bed, and I don't aim to start now. But I understand *you* like killin' a man when he's bedridden."

"I have no idea what incident you are referring to!" Jason snapped.

"Nope, don't reckon you do. A heartless bastard like you wouldn't remember killin' Wade Jarrette, or Anne Stewart." His patience wearing thin, Bulldog ordered harshly, "Get out of that goddamned bed and stand by the bureau!''

Jason obeyed, but his legs were shaking so badly that he barely made it.

Shifting in his chair so that he faced Bishop, Bulldog remained seated. ''I would show you a little respect, and get up, but I got this problem with my right leg. One day, 'bout two weeks ago, this bastard shot me in both my legs. Well, the left one wasn't damaged very bad, but the right one is in a helluva mess.''

''Bulldog!'' Jason pleaded. ''I could've killed you, but I didn't! I spared your life, the least you can do is spare mine!''

Bulldog laughed sardonically. ''Why in the hell should a weasel like you be allowed to live?''

''I have a family!'' he pointed out.

''And I reckon the next thing you're gonna tell me is that they need you.''

''Of course they do!'' Jason cried.

Bulldog shook his head. ''No, I don't think they do. I've been watchin' your house, waitin' to catch you alone. I saw your wife leave, and a little later, the boy and his nurse.'' Bulldog paused, and, grinning, he continued, ''The boy looks just like his daddy.''

''The child doesn't resemble me!'' Jason huffed.

''I didn't say he did. I said he looks like his daddy. Yep, he's the spittin' image of James Henry.''

''Who?'' Jason yelled.

''James Henry Stewart,'' Bulldog replied. ''You probably know him as Jamie Tyler.''

Shocked, Jason clutched the edge of the bureau to keep his balance. ''What did you say?'' he demanded.

In a drawling voice, Bulldog began, ''Yesterday, I stopped at the Stewarts' farm and had a long talk with

James Henry's brother, Luther. It seems James Henry weren't no guerrilla, like the others and I thought he was. No siree! He was a genuine Confederate spy. He was sent here to Lawrence as Jamie Tyler. He pretended to be convalescin' from a chest wound so the Union wouldn't question why he wasn't in the army. Well, I already knew 'bout him posin' as Jamie Tyler, 'cause your wife told me all about it at Anderson's camp. But she and I both thought he was spyin' for Missouri. While he was workin' at the hotel, and you were off killin' Pro-Confederates, he and your wife were enjoyin' a love affair.''

"That's preposterous! I don't believe a word of it!"

"You better believe it, 'cause it's the truth. Miss Amelia didn't tell me 'bout the boy bein' James Henry's, but after seein' him, there ain't no doubt in my mind who he belongs to. So don't stand there and hide behind the kid, by tellin' me he needs you. He's got James Henry to take care of him. And your wife sure as hell don't need you. She's in love with James Henry.''

"This James Henry," Jason began, "was he at Anderson's camp when my wife was there?"

"Yep, he sure was. They had them a real cozy little cave to snuggle up in.''

"That's a lie!" Jason raged. "She was Bill Anderson's whore!''

Calmly, Bulldog explained, "Miss Amelia and Captain Anderson were good friends. And that's all it was, just friendship.''

Comparing Hank to Jamie Tyler, Jason knew Bulldog had told the truth about the child. The resemblance between the two was uncanny. Despising Amelia, he

484

yelled, "How dare that bitch pass off her little bastard as my son!"

"Well," Bulldog drawled, "the kid won't be a bastard much longer. After I kill you, James Henry can marry Miss Amelia and claim the boy as his own."

His eyes bulging with panic, Jason rasped, "Isn't there something I can say or do to make you change your mind? Do you want money? I'm not a rich man, but I'll give you what I have."

"I ain't here for money," Bulldog replied lazily. "I'm just here to even the score."

"But I didn't kill you! I let you live!" Jason shouted frantically. "And, apparently, you have recovered from your injuries!"

"If what the doctor says is true, then I ain't ever goin' to heal completely. But doctors have been known to be wrong. The doc said I'd never walk on my right leg, but I'm already a-hobblin' around on it. He also told me the blows you delivered to my nuts ruined me. But I'm goin' to prove him wrong 'bout that, too. Just yesterday, I seen this good-lookin' woman, and I could swear I felt a little dab of life a-stirrin' in me."

Terrified, Jason rambled, "If you're going to make a full recovery, why do you find it necessary to kill me? Why don't you simply beat the hell out of me?"

Smiling lazily, Bulldog studied Jason's bruised face. "Looks like somebody did it for me." Chuckling, he added, "I'd be willin' to bet my last dollar you tangled with James Henry."

Wringing his hands, Jason begged pathetically, "Please don't kill me!"

Using his good leg, Bulldog leaned his chair back so that it rested on its back legs. Unemotionally, he grumbled, "I reckon, I gotta kill you."

"Why?" Jason pleaded, fear making his voice rise to a womanish pitch.

Flatly, Bulldog answered, "You shot my horse."

"Good God, man!" Jason exclaimed. "Surely you don't intend to kill me over a damned horse!"

"Well, if the law can hang a man for stealin' a horse, I reckon I can shoot a man for killin' one."

The thought of dying was driving Jason to the brink of madness, and, dropping to his knees, he cried, "I'm begging you not to kill me! I don't want to die! Dear God, I don't want to die! He hung his head, and deep sobs shook his shoulders. My God, he was going to die! This filthy guerrilla was going to end his life! But he was still young, and had everything to live for! This wasn't really happening! It was some kind of crazy nightmare!

Smirking, Bulldog mumbled, "I ain't never shot a Yankee while he was on his knees. Any Yankee I ever killed died like a man. Now, don't no one hate Yankees any more than I do, but out of respect to them Yankees who died like men, I want you to stand up and take off that uniform. You ain't fittin' to die in it." When Jason didn't obey, Bulldog bellowed, "Take it off, or I'll get the lamp over yonder, drench you full of kerosene, strike a match, and burn it off!"

Trembling, Jason got to his feet. Jason had never had true dignity or courage, they had only been a pretense. Now, his true character surfaced, and while he undressed, he pleaded pathetically for his life.

When he was left wearing only his underwear, Bulldog let his chair drop back to its four legs. Using his pistol to point at his intended targets, Bulldog explained coldly, "My first shot is gonna send a bullet into your left leg, then my second shot is gonna send a bullet into your right leg." Grinning vindictively, he aimed the gun at Jason's crotch. Jason gasped so convulsively that, for a moment, Bulldog thought the man would pass out. Laughing, he raised the pistol to Jason's face, continuing, "My third and last shot is gonna send a bullet between your eyes." Getting to his feet, Bulldog asked, "Where's your gun?"

"My gun?" Jason choked.

"Yeah," Bulldog smirked. "That weapon you been usin' for the past four years to kill unarmed men. Where in the hell is it?"

Feebly, Jason nodded toward the dresser. "It's in the top drawer."

Keeping a close watch on Jason, Bulldog inched his way to the dresser. Reaching into the drawer, he took out the pistol and holster. Moving back to the chair, he pitched them onto the bed.

"Real easy-like," Bulldog began, "you pick up that gun and holster. Then strap it on."

My God, Jason thought. The man is a fool! He's going to give me a chance to draw against him! Taking the holster from the bed, he grinned slyly. He had a fast draw, and he knew it. He'd blow the dirty, ugly Missouri ape to hell. And, then, he'd find a way to kill Amelia, her Confederate lover, and the little bastard they were passing off as his son!

Bulldog understood Jason's cocky grin, causing him to grin himself. During the war, the greatest advantage the Missouri guerrillas had had over the Federals had been their expertise with the Colt revolver. And Anderson's men had been exceptionally fast and accurate.

487

Smiling shrewdly, Bulldog eased his Colt revolver into its holster.

When Jason finished strapping on his gun, Bulldog drawled, "I'm bettin' my life against yours, that I can shoot you in both legs and between the eyes, 'fore you can even get your gun out of the holster."

"You stupid bastard!" Jason sneered. "I'm gonna send you to hell!"

"Oh yeah?" Bulldog scoffed. "Well, don't just stand there a-yappin' 'bout it. Draw!"

Colonel Rhodes would have preferred to walk at a leisurely pace, but for some odd reason, Mrs. Bishop seemed to be in a great hurry. The Bishops' house was secluded, at the very edge of town, and the colonel found the brisk walk quite tiring. Hiding his exhaustion, he kept his strides even with Amelia's as they entered the walkway leading up to her home.

When the first shot rang out from inside the house, Amelia and Colonel Rhodes stopped in their tracks. The second shot followed immediately, and, momentarily shocked, they could only stare at each other.

Suddenly, reacting, the colonel reached for his pistol, but before he had time to draw it, the third and final shot sounded.

Freeing his gun from its holster, he told Amelia, "Run and get help!"

But Amelia wasn't about to run for help. She was sure that while she and the colonel were being held up by Mrs. Kelley, James Henry had somehow slipped by her; and, now, he had killed Jason!

As the front door slowly opened, Amelia's first instinct was to lurch for the colonel's pistol and knock it from his hand. But she was too frightened to move.

When she saw it was Bulldog stepping out to the porch, and not James Henry, Amelia was so relieved that her knees almost gave way.

Holding his gun on Bulldog, Colonel Rhodes warned, "Halt, or I'll shoot!"

Bulldog was still holding his revolver, but his hand was resting at his side.

"Drop your weapon!" the colonel ordered.

In a split second, Amelia's mind told her that Bulldog would never surrender, and her decision to try and save him was instantaneous.

Pretending hysteria, Amelia began screaming irrationally as she grabbed the colonel's arm, shoving it downwards, causing the barrel of the pistol to point to the ground. Shrieking wildly, she pulled and tugged at his arm, as she raved, "Jason! Oh please check on Jason! Oh colonel, please! You must help him!"

As Colonel Rhodes attempted to free himself from the hysterical woman, Bulldog hurried to his horse, but his lame leg slowed him down considerably. It would have been easy for him to simply stop and shoot the colonel, but he knew Amelia wasn't trying to save his life at the cost of the colonel's. So, out of respect to her, he kept hurrying to his horse.

Although Amelia was acting her role to perfection, she could see that Bulldog's injury was going to prevent his escape. There was no possible way for her to continue restraining the colonel.

Colonel Rhodes raised his other arm to shove her aside, but, as he did, his hand relaxed on the pistol. Amelia lunged for the weapon, grabbing it from his hand.

By now, Bulldog had reached his horse, and, pointing the pistol at him, she shrieked, ''I'm going to kill you!'' Moving the barrel of the gun way off target, she fired.

Clutching her arm, the colonel roared, ''Give me that gun! You crazy fool! He's getting away!''

Her hysteria appeared to be completely out of control, as she wrestled determinedly with Colonel Rhodes to keep possession of the pistol.

Swinging into the saddle, Bulldog turned his horse, sending him into a breakneck run.

Taking the pistol from Amelia, the colonel looked down the street. He got off one missed shot, and then Bulldog was out of range.

Swerving to Amelia, he shouted, ''You silly fool!'' Putting the gun into its holster, he raved ''You damned crazy woman!''

Amelia had pretended hysteria, but she didn't need to fake the tears that were now streaming from her eyes. She knew without entering the house that Jason was dead. Her tears were a mixture of compassion for Jason and relief for herself, because, at last, she was free!

THIRTY-FIVE

Following Jason's funeral, Amelia's home was filled with guests, including Sam and Jamie Tyler. Minutes after Jason was killed, the news of his death spread through town, and James Henry and Buford learned about it from Mr. Cramer. During the past two days, Amelia and James Henry had found opportunities to talk privately, but their times together had been short.

Slowly the guests began departing, and Amelia was relieved to see them leaving. She hated playing the role of the grieving widow, and often she had been tempted to tell them all that she had despised Jason. But, out of respect to Lillian, who would remain living in Lawrence after she and Hank were gone, Amelia pretended to be solemn.

When Mrs. Kelley finally departed, only Addie, Lillian, Cynthia, and Buford were left in the parlor. James Henry had disappeared over an hour ago, and, believing he had returned to the hotel, Amelia didn't ask Buford about him. Instead, she asked Addie, "Did you put Hank to bed?"

"No, ma'am," Addie replied. "He's on the front porch with Jamie Tyler."

"Jamie!" Amelia exclaimed.

Springing from her chair, Addie replied apologetically, "Mrs. Bishop, I didn't think you would mind! But I've never seen Hank take to anyone the way he has taken to Jamie. And . . . and Jamie is so good with him. Oh, dear me, I'm sorry! I'll go fetch the child."

"No!" Amelia objected. "Addie, I'm not upset. Please, sit back down and finish your coffee. I'll check on Hank."

Anxious to be with James Henry, Amelia rushed out to the porch. Seeing him sitting on the swing with Hank snuggled in his lap sleeping soundly, Amelia smiled. Stepping quietly, she crossed the porch. Sitting beside them, she murmured, "This is the first time Hank has ever fallen asleep in a man's arms."

Lightly, he brushed his lips across the child's forehead. "It may be the first time, but it won't be the last." He paused for a moment, before asking, "Do you think Hank will miss Bishop?"

"No," Amelia replied softly. "Jason never paid any attention to Hank, unless we were in public. Hank is a loving child, but he didn't love Jason. The man he thought was his father never gave him a reason to love him.

"He's very young. He'll soon forget Bishop."

"Yes," she agreed. "You'll become his father."

"I want his name changed to Stewart. He's my son, and I want him to know who he really is."

Amelia nodded. Relaxing for the first time in two days, she sighed deeply. "Sitting here beside you and

Hank, in the quietness of night, I feel so peaceful."

"I know what you mean. All the hate and bitterness of the war and Bishop are now behind us."

Smiling, she said passionately, "James Henry, I love you!"

Shifting Hank so that he could free one arm, he reached over and took her hand into his. "I love you, Amelia." Glancing down at the child, he added, "I also love this little guy."

Amelia's smile faded, and he could tell something was bothering her. "What's wrong, little one?" he asked tenderly.

Speaking what had been on her conscience for the past two days, she exclaimed desperately, "Oh, James Henry, was it wrong of me to protect Bulldog?"

"What do you think?" he questioned quietly.

"I don't know," she sighed. "I not only protected Bulldog, but I also protected Bill Anderson."

"Are you feeling guilty?"

"I'm not sure," she mumbled. Looking at him, her brow furrowed with confusion. "Lillian believes Bill Anderson was a cruel and brutal demon. Do you think he was the cold-blooded murderer that Lillian and others believe?"

James Henry shrugged, answering evenly, "It was wartime. But, yeah, in a way, I suppose he was a murderer."

"So is Bulldog!" she cried. "And, yet, I protected them both! Why? Oh why?"

"Why not?" James Henry responded. "They were your friends."

"Friends?" she repeated.

"Bill Anderson was more a friend to you than the

Union. He spared your life at the risk of his own. You owed him your loyalty. And as far as Bulldog goes, it was your fault that he had to suffer Bishop's brutality. The day the Pro-Confederates surrendered, you had to know how Bishop would react when you ran after Bulldog. I'm sure you blocked it from your mind, but you knew your husband for the bastard he was, and you had to realize what would inevitably happen. So, Amelia, you owed it to Bulldog to help him." Squeezing her hand, he asked intensely, "If you had it to do all over again, would you be disloyal to Anderson?"

"No," she replied honestly.

"Would you help Bulldog escape?"

Sighing deeply, she answered truthfully, "Yes, I'd help him."

Bringing her hand up to his lips, he kissed it. "You have no reason to feel guilty, little one."

As the door opened, he released her hand. Stepping out to the porch, Addie asked, "Mrs. Bishop, do you want me to put Hank to bed?"

"Yes, please," Amelia answered.

Standing, James Henry took the child to Addie, placing him in her arms. Holding the door open, he assisted her into the house. Closing it behind them, he returned to the swing. Taking Amelia's hands, he drew her to her feet.

Going into his arms, she asked, "When are we leaving?"

"The end of this week," he answered. "I've been giving our departure a lot of thought, and I have a plan that will make it easy for us to leave, and also save your aunt any embarrassment."

Moving out of his embrace so she could see into his

494

face, she asked, "What is your plan?"

"The people of Lawrence will believe you are returning to your home in Massachusetts, and you hired Sam and Jamie Tyler to drive you."

Amelia smiled. "Of course, how simple! We can leave this town together, and no one will think anything of it."

"Buford and I are buying two wagons and another pair of horses."

"Two wagons?" she questioned.

"One for him, and one for us," he explained. "On their honeymoon, a man and his wife need their privacy."

"Honeymoon?" she exclaimed.

"We'll stop at the farm and tell Luther goodbye. The Reverend Howard lives only a couple of miles from there, and I'll ask him to come to the house and marry us." Amelia smiled pertly, and he asked, "What are you thinking about?"

"You said a man and his wife need their privacy on their honeymoon. Aren't you forgetting our son?"

Grinning, he replied, "Well, I was kinda hoping he's a sound sleeper."

Wrapping her arms about his neck, she answered happily, "Hank sleeps so soundly that a cannon exploding wouldn't wake him."

Before pressing his lips to hers, he replied, "I had a feeling Hank would cooperate with his old man."

Buford was sitting on the sofa beside Lillian, and Cynthia was seated on a chair across from them. As Lillian rattled on about how Jason had been a trifle arrogant, but a loving husband and father, Cynthia only pretended to be listening. Her thoughts, as well as her eyes, remained on Buford. Except to exchange polite hellos, he hadn't spoken to Cynthia since the day he had followed her home.

Rising, Buford remarked in Sam Tyler's voice, "Well, I reckon I'll mosey on back to the hotel." Without bothering to look at Cynthia, he mumbled, "Goodnight, ladies."

Cynthia suppressed the urge to leap to her feet and flee after him. Oh, how wonderful it would feel to be in his strong arms!

As Buford reached the front door, James Henry and Amelia entered. "Are you leaving, Pappy?" James Henry asked.

Abruptly, Buford answered, "Yep." Moving past them, he stepped outside. Understanding his brusque departure, James Henry glanced at Cynthia, shaking his head. In his opinion, Cynthia Coffman was a fool.

Fidgeting nervously, Cynthia stammered, "Well . . . well, I suppose I'll go home. It's getting pretty late."

As she got to her feet, James Henry offered, "I'll walk you home, ma'am."

"Mr. Tyler," Lillian began, "if you are walking Cynthia home, would you mind also escorting me to the store? I don't relish walking alone at night."

"No!" Amelia objected strongly.

Surprised, Lillian questioned, "Darling, what's wrong?"

"Aunt Lillian, I want you to stay here. I must talk to you. James . . . I mean Jamie, won't mind coming back and then walking you home."

496

Puzzled, Lillian replied, "Very well, dear."

Going to the door, James Henry opened it. "Are you ready, Mrs. Coffman?"

Cynthia nodded hesitantly. Moving to Amelia, she kissed her on the cheek. "I'll see you tomorrow."

Smiling, Amelia answered, "Goodnight, Cynthia."

As soon as they were left alone, Amelia went to the sofa, and, sitting beside Lillian, she sighed, "My goodness, I don't know how to begin." Taking her aunt's hand into hers, she continued, "Aunt Lillian, what I'm going to tell you will come as a big shock to you."

"What is it, darling?" Lillian asked, greatly concerned.

Taking a deep breath, Amelia replied, "I love James Henry."

"Well, of course you do!" Lillian replied. "He's your son."

"I don't mean my son. I mean Jamie."

Lillian paled as she exclaimed, "Jamie Tyler?"

Smiling, Amelia squeezed Lillian's hand. "Let's go into the kitchen, and while I make us a cup of tea, I'll explain everything."

Walking Cynthia home, James Henry told her about his and Amelia's plans. Although Cynthia would miss her dearest friend, she was happy for her. As they were stepping up to her front door, Cynthia told James Henry how she felt.

"It's not necessary that you miss her, you know. There's no reason why you can't leave with us," James Henry said.

Unlocking the door, Cynthia replied, "All the way to my house you refrained from mentioning Buford, and I appreciate your consideration. Why must you now find it imperative to bring him into our conversation?"

Amused, James Henry answered, "I didn't say one word about Buford. You're the one who is bringing him into the conversation."

Stammering, she replied, "When you invited me to leave with you and Amelia, it was really Buford you had in mind."

"He's on your mind too, isn't he?"

Opening the door, Cynthia entered the house followed by James Henry. "Of course, he's in my thoughts," she answered.

"He loves you," James Henry stated calmly.

Turning sharply to face him, she questioned crisply, "Did he ask you to come to me and plead his case?"

James Henry laughed loudly. "Now, I know why you're afraid to marry Buford. You don't even know him!" He clutched her wrist, and, seriously, he demanded, "You've never tried to know him, have you? You don't want to see beyond the color of the uniform he wore during the war! Why? What are you afraid of seeing?"

"Nothing!" she cried.

"You're lying, Cynthia! You're lying to yourself as well as to me. You don't want to know Buford, because you're afraid you'll realize he means more to you than your husband's memory!"

"No!" she protested feebly.

Realizing he had hit on the truth, he continued excitedly, "That's it, isn't it? Buford makes you feel guilty because you love him more than you loved Lieutenant Coffman. All this talk about loyalty to the Union is only an excuse you're using to hide the truth from yourself!''

Sobbing, she moaned, ''Oh, how can I be so unfaithful to David?''

''Unfaithful!'' James Henry yelled. ''Good God, woman! Your husband is dead! While he was alive you were a faithful and loving wife! What in the hell does your marriage to him have to do with the present?''

Breaking down, she covered her face with her hands. Until this moment, she had never even admitted the truth to herself. ''David was always afraid that he would be killed. And one night, he made me promise that I would never love a man more than I loved him.''

''Did you make that promise?'' he asked gently.

''Yes!'' she cried. ''Because at the time, I didn't believe it was possible for me to ever love a man more than I loved David!''

''At the time, it probably wasn't possible. But that was the past. Now, you're living in the present, and you're very foolish to feel guilty over a promise that never should have been made in the first place.'' James Henry opened the door to leave, and, looking back at Cynthia, he said, ''To answer the question you asked a few minutes ago, no, Buford didn't ask me to plead with you. In fact, except to tell me you had refused his proposal, he hasn't mentioned one damned word about you. Buford asked you to marry him, and you turned him down. As far as he's concerned, that's the end of it! If you think he will come here and plead with you to marry him, then madam, you are badly mistaken! You'll have to come to terms with your guilt without Buford's help. So, if you have any doubts about your refusal of his proposal, you have until Saturday to make up your mind. I know Buford, and once he leaves this town, that'll be it! You could write to him and beg him to come back for you, but he wouldn't come.''

''Why wouldn't he?'' she pleaded.

Before leaving, James Henry replied bitterly, ''Why in the hell should he?''

When James Henry returned to Amelia's house to walk Lillian home, no one noticed him slip the extra key from its place on the wall and into his pocket.

Later, when Amelia was in bed drifting into sleep, a hand suddenly covered her mouth. Frightened, her eyes opened wildly, but the moonlight filtering through the window silhouetted the man sitting on the edge of her bed. Her eyes softened with love.

''If you promise not to scream,'' he began hoarsely, ''I'll remove my hand.''

She nodded, letting him know she wouldn't cry out.

Taking his hand from her mouth, he proceeded gruffly, ''I didn't come here to rape you. I only want to seduce you. If, after five minutes I have failed to arouse your passion, I will leave. And I promise you, little one, you won't be molested.''

''You mean I won't be violated or . . . or hurt?''

''I don't want to hurt you. I only want to love you.''

Boldly, she invited, ''Well, in that case, why don't you take off your clothes and hop into bed!''

Complying, he hastily removed his clothes, and, drawing back the covers, he got into bed beside her.

Going into his arms, she asked, "James Henry, how did you get into the house? I remember locking the door before I came to bed."

"As I once told you that night at the Eldridge House, where there's a will, there's a way."

"Yes, and I responded by asking you if you were only a figment of my imagination."

Taking her hand and moving it down to his erection, he replied, "And I asked you if that felt like a figment of your imagination."

Running light kisses over his neck, across his chest, and down to his stomach, she said seductively, "I must investigate it before I decide if it's real or imaginary."

Smiling with anticipation, he answered, "You will investigate it thoroughly, I hope."

"It will be my pleasure, Mr. Stewart," she murmured, running fluttering kisses across his chest and down to his stomach. As her fingers encircled his manhood, James Henry moaned with pleasure. Feeling him grow even more erect with desire, Amelia lowered her mouth, loving him as intimately as he had always loved her. Just as James Henry felt he couldn't take the wonderful torture any longer without turning her onto her back and taking her powerfully, Amelia brought her mouth up to his, kissing him passionately.

Locking his arm around her waist, he rolled her over, and mounted her anxiously. "I want you, little one," he whispered fervently.

"Yes! Oh, yes!" Amelia gasped, passion heavy in her voice.

His entry was swift and deep, causing Amelia to groan with longing. Wrapping her arms about his neck, she locked her ankles behind his back. At first, James Henry took her tenderly and tantalizingly, letting their desire build slowly. But as their passions began to soar, his thrusting became demanding. Holding on to him tightly, Amelia allowed him to take her with him to love's wonderful ecstasy.

Remaining inside her, James Henry whispered, "Amelia, I love you."

Brushing her fingers through his dark hair, she confessed from the bottom of her heart, "James Henry, no woman could ever love you more than I do."

"I know, little one," he replied softly. "I waited my whole life for someone like you. And now that I've found you, I'm never going to let you go."

Smiling, she murmured, "James Henry, I'm so happy. So very, very happy."

Their last night in Lawrence, Amelia and Hank spent the night at Lillian's. Amelia had closed up the house and the belongings she was taking with her to Texas had been packed in the wagon.

The next morning, James Henry and Buford arrived early. After breakfast, Buford offered to go out back to the stable and hitch up the wagons.

As he strolled out the back door, he saw Cynthia placing a small package in the rear of one of the wagons. Cynthia's unexpected presence startled him, and, for a moment, his steps hesitated. He didn't want to see Cynthia. He would have preferred to leave town without coming into contact with her. Every time she came into sight it was a renewed and painful reminder to him of how much he loved her.

Thinking she had brought the package for Amelia, he called out, "You're putting that in the wrong wagon. Amelia's things are in the other one."

She hadn't heard Buford leaving the house, and, surprised, she turned swiftly. Watching his approach, she smiled as she answered, "Yes, I know Amelia's using the other one."

"Then why are you putting the package in my wagon?"

She had her purse with her, and, placing it on the wagon wheel, she waited until he reached her before replying, "It's a dress I made for myself last month. But I have never worn it." Her eyes pleading with his, she continued, "I thought perhaps it could be my wedding dress."

Astounded, he could only stare at her with wonder. When he made no response, she asked hopefully, "Buford, will it be my wedding dress?"

His smile started faintly at the corners of his mouth before expanding into glorious laughter. Pulling her into his arms, he lifted her off her feet, swinging her around. "Cynthia!" he exclaimed. "I don't believe it! You've decided to marry me!"

"Yes!" she answered, crying and laughing at the same time. "I love you, and I want to marry you!"

Placing her back on her feet, he took her into his embrace, and, flinging her arms about his neck, she confessed, "Oh Buford, I love you more than I have ever loved any man!" Admitting the truth brought Cynthia no guilt, only a feeling of ecstatic happiness.

Looking at her tenderly, he replied, "But I'm so much older than you. How can you love an old man like me more than you loved young Coffman?"

Smiling warmly, she answered, "I loved David from the time we were children, but I realize now that it was a love that grew sedately with the passing years." Her gray eyes flashing brightly, she remarked pertly, "And, Buford Stewart, you are not an old man! But, regardless of your age, there is nothing sedate in the way I feel about you!"

Grinning, he replied, "When it comes to makin' love, the word sedate isn't even in my vocabulary."

Blushing attractively, Cynthia confessed, "I love you when you're being aggressive."

"Do you?" he questioned, his expression cocky. "Well, just stick around little darlin', there's a helluva lot more aggression to come!"

Cynthia had already packed a few boxes to take with her, and James Henry left with Buford to go to Cynthia's house to put them in the wagon.

Lillian, Amelia, and Cynthia were sitting at the table in Lillian's kitchen, waiting for the men to return. Addie was in the parlor taking care of Hank. So far as Addie knew, Amelia was moving back to Massachusetts, and her good friend Cynthia had decided to travel with her. She supposed Mrs. Coffman would eventually replace her as Hank's nurse. But Addie felt no resentment. She had no desire to move to Massachusetts. Lawrence was her home, and Mrs. Adams had offered her a job at the store. She was sure Mrs. Coffman's landlord would rent her the small house Cynthia had been living in. Mrs. Bishop had given her quite a few household goods, and with everything Mrs. Coffman was leaving her she would have no problem making herself a comfortable home. So Addie was perfectly content with the way things had worked out.

Pouring herself a second cup of tea, Lillian exclaimed breathlessly for at least the tenth time, "I can't get over how you two girls have shocked me! All this time, you two were in love with Jamie and Sam Tyler, and I was never once the least suspicious."

Patiently, Amelia corrected, "James Henry and Buford Stewart. Not Jamie and Sam Tyler."

Frowning, Lillian replied, "Well, whatever their names are." But, all at once, she smiled as she continued sincerely, "I hope and pray that you will be happy. Both of you. And, thank goodness, you two have no more shocks in store for me. I don't think I could take another one without swooning!"

Suddenly remembering her purse, Cynthia opened it, taking out the brush and comb Bill Anderson had given Amelia. Handing them to Amelia, she said, "Here darling. I almost forgot to give these to you."

Seeing her treasured gift, tears filled Amelia's eyes. Noticing her niece's distress, Lillian asked urgently, "What's wrong, dear?"

Caressing the brush and comb, Amelia was reminded of the day Bill Anderson had told her to keep them. Her voice breaking with emotion, she explained, "They are a gift from a man who was a very, very dear friend."

Picking up her teacup, Lillian asked casually, "Oh? Who was your friend?"

"Captain Bill Anderson," Amelia replied.

Shocked, Lillian choked, "That terrible Bill Anderson? Oh, Amelia, how could you!" She dropped the cup, then fell back in her chair.

Leaping to her feet, Amelia cried, "Cynthia, get a glass of water! I think she's going to swoon!"

The moment the two wagons reached the outskirts of Lawrence, James Henry pulled up the horses. As he jumped down to the ground, Buford halted his wagon behind James Henry's.

"What in the hell are you doing?" Buford bellowed.

"I'm getting rid of Jamie Tyler! Permanently!" James Henry replied, pulling off his overalls.

Cynthia was sitting beside Buford, and she put her head against his shoulder, hiding her eyes.

Laughing, Buford told her, "It's all right, darlin'. He's got his pants on beneath the overalls."

Looking up at Amelia and his son, who were sitting on the wagon seat watching him, James Henry grinned joyously as he threw the overalls into the surrounding bushes, exclaiming, "To hell with the Tylers and the damned war!"

Leaping into the wagon, he took hold of the reins. Glancing back at Buford and Cynthia, he shouted, "Are you two ready to go to Texas?"

"You're damned right, we're ready!" Buford answered heartily, before leaning over and giving Cynthia a kiss so filled with aggression that she felt as if her heart would burst with love and happiness.

Turning to Amelia, James Henry asked tenderly, "How about you, little one? Are you ready to go to Texas?"

"Oh James Henry!" she gleamed. "I've been ready

for a long time!''

Brushing his fingers through Hank's black curls, he questioned, ''Are you ready to head for Texas, son?''

Nodding, the child answered excitedly, ''Giddy-up horses! Giddy-up!''

Giving Amelia a wink, James Henry flapped the reins against the horses, and as the wagon lurched forward Hank clapped his hands with excitement, shouting, ''We're goin' to Tekas! We're goin' to Tekas!''

BESTSELLING ROMANCES BY JANELLE TAYLOR

SAVAGE ECSTASY (824, $3.50)

It was like lightning striking, the first time the Indian brave Gray Eagle looked into the eyes of the beautiful young settler Alisha. And from the moment he saw her, he knew that he must possess her—and make her his slave!

DEFIANT ECSTASY (931, $3.50)

When Gray Eagle returned to Fort Pierre's gates with his hundred warriors behind him, Alisha's heart skipped a beat: would Gray Eagle destroy her—or make his destiny her own?

FORBIDDEN ECSTASY (1014, $3.50)

Gray Eagle had promised Alisha his heart forever—nothing could keep him from her. But when Alisha woke to find her red-skinned lover gone, she felt abandoned and alone. Lost between two worlds, desperate and fearful of betrayal, Alisha hungered for the return of her FORBIDDEN ECSTASY.

BRAZEN ECSTASY (1133, $3.50)

When Alisha is swept down a raging river and out of her savage brave's life, Gray Eagle must rescue his love again. But Alisha has no memory of him at all. And as she fights to recall a past love, another white slave woman in their camp is fighting for Gray Eagle!

TENDER ECSTASY (1212, $3.75)

Bright Arrow is committed to kill every white he sees—until he sets his eyes on ravishing Rebecca. And fate demands that he capture her, torment her . . . and soar with her to the dizzying heights of TENDER ECSTASY!

Available wherever paperbacks are sold, or order direct from the Publisher. Send cover price plus 50¢ per copy for mailing and handling to Zebra Books, 475 Park Avenue South, New York, N.Y. 10016. DO NOT SEND CASH.

SENSATIONAL SAGAS!

WHITE NIGHTS, RED DAWN   (1277, $3.95)
by Frederick Nolan
Just as Tatiana was blossoming into womanhood, the Russian Revolution was overtaking the land. How could the stunning aristocrat sacrifice her life, her heart and her love for a cause she had not chosen? Somehow, she would prevail over the red dawn —and carve a destiny all her own!

IMPERIAL WINDS   (1324, $3.95)
by Priscilla Napier
From the icebound Moscow river to the misty towers of the Kremlin, from the Bolshevick uprising to the fall of the Romanovs, Daisy grew into a captivating woman who would courageously fight to escape the turmoil of the raging IMPERIAL WINDS.

KEEPING SECRETS   (1291, $3.75)
by Suzanne Morris
It was 1914, the winds of war were sweeping the globe, and Electra was in the eye of the hurricane—rushing headlong into a marriage with the wealthy Emory Cabot. Her days became a carousel of European dignitaries, rich investors, and worldly politicians. And her nights were filled with mystery and passion . . . .

Available wherever paperbacks are sold, or order direct from the Publisher. Send cover price plus 50¢ per copy for mailing and handling to Zebra Books, 475 Park Avenue South, New York, N.Y. 10016. DO NOT SEND CASH.

THE BEST IN HISTORICAL ROMANCE
by Sylvie F. Sommerfield

CHERISH ME, EMBRACE ME   (1199, $3.75)

Lovely, raven-haired Abby vowed she'd never let a Yankee run her plantation or her life. But once she felt the exquisite ecstasy of Alexander's demanding lips, she desired only him!

SAVAGE RAPTURE   (1085, $3.50)

Beautiful Snow Blossom waited years for the return of Cade, the handsome halfbreed who had made her a prisoner of his passion. And when Cade finally rides back into the Cheyenne camp, she vows to make him a captive of her heart!

REBEL PRIDE   (1084, $3.25)

The Jemmisons and the Forresters were happy to wed their children —and by doing so, unite their plantations. But Holly Jemmison's heart cries out for the roguish Adam Gilcrest. She dare not defy her family; does she dare defy her heart?

TAMARA'S ECSTASY   (998, $3.50)

Tamara knew it was foolish to give her heart to a sailor. But she was a victim of her own desire. Lost in a sea of passion, she ached for his magic touch—and would do anything for it!

DEANNA'S DESIRE   (906, $3.50)

Amidst the storm of the American Revolution, Matt and Deanna meet—and fall in love. And bound by passion, they risk everything to keep that love alive!

Available wherever paperbacks are sold, or order direct from the Publisher. Send cover price plus 50¢ per copy for mailing and handling to Zebra Books, 475 Park Avenue South, New York, N.Y. 10016. DO NOT SEND CASH.